VITAL SIGNS

Also published in Large Print
by Robin Cook:

Outbreak
Mindbend
Godplayer

VITAL SIGNS

Robin Cook

G.K. HALL &CO.
Boston, Massachusetts
1991

Published in Large Print by arrangement with
G.P. Putnam's Sons.

G.K. Hall Large Print Book Series.

Set in 16 pt. Plantin.

Library of Congress Cataloging-in-Publication Data

Cook, Robin, 1940–
    Vital signs / Robin Cook.
      p.   cm.—(G.K. Hall large print book series)
    ISBN 0-8161-5303-5 (lg. print).—ISBN 0-8161-5304-3 (pbk. : lg.
print)
    1. Large type books.   I. Title.
[PS3553.O5545V58   1991b]
813'.54—dc20
                                                               91-23237

This book is dedicated to the countless couples who have suffered the emotional and physical trials and tribulations of infertility and its modern treatments.

ACKNOWLEDGMENTS

Vital Signs could not have been written without the assistance of Jean Reeds, whose professional and personal knowledge of the human heart is matched only by her own.

Prologue

FEBRUARY 16, 1988

The infecting bacteria came in a swift gush as if flushed from a sewer. In an instant, several million slender, rod-shaped microorganisms filled the lumen of the fallopian tubes. Most were grouped in small, tight clumps. They settled against the velvety convolutions of the mucosa, nestling in the warm, fertile valleys, absorbing the abundant nutrients and expelling their own foul excretions.

The delicate cells lining the interior of the oviducts were helpless in the face of the sudden invading horde. The putrid waste of the bacteria—caustic proteins and greasy fats—burned like acid, resulting in instant destruction of the fine cilia whose normal function was to move an egg toward the uterus.

The tubular cells released their defensive and messenger chemicals, signaling the body for help. Unfortunately, the defensive secretions had no effect on the bacteria, whose membranes were protected by a brownish waxy envelope of lipid.

Medical students fresh from their microbiological labs would have recognized the bacteria—or so they would have thought. The fatty bacterial cell walls were "acid fast," capable of absorbing certain stains and resisting decolorizing with acid alcohol. The medical students would have cried in unison, "Tuberculosis," with a self-congratulatory sense of satisfaction.

Tubercular or not, as far as the tubal cells were concerned, any kind of invading bacteria meant trouble. The messenger chemicals that the cells had released initiated the complex immunological defense against foreign invaders which had evolved over the entire billion-year evolution of earthly life.

The chemicals released initiated a change in the local blood vessels. The blood flow increased and opened up tiny fenestrations, releasing plasma into the tissue. Specialized, first-line-of-defense cells called granulocytes migrated from the bloodstream directly into the bacterial horde. These cells released more chemicals, including potent enzymes. They also combatted the bacteria directly. But for them it was a kamikaze exercise—after releasing their granules, nearly all the granulocytes perished.

Soon, larger cells called macrophages answered the chemical call, mobilizing themselves from lymph nodes and the bone marrow. They too passed through the pores of the capillaries to join the melee. They were more successful than the granulocytes in engulfing some of the bacteria. They also released chemicals into the developing pus, which was now taking on a greenish cast.

Within seven hours lymphocytes began to accumulate, marking the beginning of another level of immunological defense. Since this particular type of bacteria had not been encountered before, there were no specific antibodies circulating. But the process to *make them had begun. T-lymphocytes massed and underwent chemical-induced alterations. They also stimulated the arrival of more macrophages which in turn stimulated more T-cell aggregation in an ever-increasing spiral of cellular activity.*

After twenty-four hours, the balance of the struggle had already tipped away from the bacteria. The tubular cells were winning but the victory was Pyrrhic. Vast areas of the delicate mucosal lining of the fallopian tubes had been destroyed by the immunological reaction. Extensive scarring was inevitable. Interference with the blood flow added to the injury. And on top of that, the remaining bacteria and their waste continued to stimulate the immune system's response. The body persisted in amassing more cellular troops, unaware that the battle had been won. Macrophages continued to arrive, and their activity caused more destruction. In their frenzy, some of the cells underwent nuclear division without subsequent cellular division, resulting in giant cells with multiple nuclei.

Again, the medical students would have smiled knowingly if they'd had a chance to view this sequence through the lens of a microscope. They would have nodded with appreciation at the distorted architecture of the developing granuloma.

This cellular drama continued to play out over several weeks within the dark recesses of thirty-year-old Rebecca Ziegler's womb. Rebecca herself had no idea of frantic chemical battles being waged within her body, nor of the resultant cellular destruction. There had been a few hints: subtle changes in her vital signs in the form of a low-grade fever and a mildly elevated pulse. She had even experienced some cramps, lower abdominal tenderness, and a mild vaginal discharge, but none of these signs and symptoms seemed cause for concern. Even a mildly abnormal Pap smear which had caused her momentary worry had been proven to have been perfectly normal after all.

Rebecca ignored these petty maladies. After all, everything else in her life was wonderful. Six months earlier she'd married, to her mother's relief, and her life had taken on new meaning. She'd even accepted a new job as one of the youngest litigators for a prestigious Boston law firm. Everything was perfect, and she was not about to let some mild physical complaints mar her mood.

Yet there was more to this episode than Rebecca could have known. The bacteria had started a chain of events that went beyond the immunological. The consequences were destined to come back to haunt her, to rob her of her happiness, and eventually, indirectly, to kill her.

FEBRUARY 21, 1988

An agonizing screech of metal scraping against metal jangled Marissa Blumenthal's already frayed nerves as the aging MBTA subway train strained to navigate the sharp turn into the Harvard Square station in Cambridge, Massachusetts. Marissa closed her eyes for a moment in a vain attempt to shield herself from the grating racket as she clutched an upright pole. She wanted to get out of the train. Besides peace and quiet, she needed fresh air. Wedged among a crowd of six-foot-plus giants, five-foot Marissa felt more claustrophobic than usual. The air in the subway car felt oppressively warm. It was a rainy February day and the damp smell of moist wool added to her discomfort.

Like everyone else in the train, Marissa tried to avoid eye contact with the people pressed up against her. It was a mixed crowd. Harvard Square attracted both ends of the spectrum. To Marissa's right was an Ivy League lawyer-type with a black ostriche briefcase, his nose buried in a crisply folded copy of *The Wall Street Journal*. Directly in front of her was a fetid-breathed skinhead, outfitted in a denim jacket from which the sleeves had been cut. He had clumsily tattooed swastikas on each knuckle of his hands. To her left was a massive black man with a ponytail of dreadlocks, wearing gray sweats. His sunglasses were so dark that Marissa could not see his eyes as she furtively glanced in his direction.

With a final lurch that all but sent Marissa to the floor, the train stopped and the doors slid open. Breathing a sigh of relief, Marissa stepped out onto the platform. Normaly she would have driven her car from her office and left it under the Charles Hotel, but she wasn't sure how she would be feeling after her minor surgical procedure, so she'd decided it was more prudent to take the T. There had been talk of her having some kind of sedative or intravenous painkiller, an idea that Marissa was not averse to. She freely admitted that she was not good with pain. If she was groggy after the anesthesia, she thought it best not to drive.

Marissa hurried past a trio of street musicians playing for commuters' donations and quickly went up the stairs to the street. It was still raining so she paused briefly to raise her folded umbrella.

Marissa buttoned her trench coat and held her umbrella tight as she traversed the square and headed up Mount Auburn Street. Sudden gusts of wind foiled her attempt to stay dry; by the time she reached the Women's Clinic at the end of Nutting Street, a plethora of raindrops were sprinkled across her forehead like beads of perspiration. Beneath the glass-enclosed walkway that spanned the street and connected the main building of the clinic to its overnight ward and emergency facilities, Marissa shook her umbrella and folded it closed.

The clinic building was a postmodern structure, built of red brick and mirrored glass, which faced a bricked courtyard. The main entrance was off the courtyard and was reached by a wide run of granite steps.

Taking a deep breath, Marissa climbed the front steps. Although as a physician she was accustomed to entering medical facilities, this was the first time she was doing so as a patient, coming in not just for an examination but for surgery. The fact that it was minor surgery had less of a mitigating effect than she'd imagined. For the first time Marissa realized that from a patient's point of view, there was no such thing as "minor" surgery.

Only two and a half weeks earlier Marissa had climbed the same steps for a routine annual Pap smear only to learn a few days later that the results were abnormal, bearing the grade CIN #1. She'd been genuinely surprised, having always enjoyed perfect health. Vaguely she'd wondered if the abnormality had anything to do with her recent marriage to Robert Buchanan. Since their wedding, they had certainly been enjoying the physical side of their relationship a great deal.

Marissa grasped the brass handle of the massive front door and stepped into the lobby. The decor was rather stark although it reflected good taste and certainly money. The floor was surfaced in dark green marble. Ficus trees in large brick planters lined the windows. In the middle of the room was a circular information booth. Marissa had to wait her turn. She unbuttoned her coat and shook the moisture from her long brown hair.

Two weeks previously, having received the surprising result of the Pap smear, Marissa had had a long phone conversation with her gynecologist, Ronald Carpenter. He had strongly recommended the culdoscopy-biopsy procedure.

"Nothing to it," he'd said with conviction. "Piece of cake, and then we know for sure what's going on in there. It's probably nothing. We could wait for a while and do another smear, but if it were my wife, I'd say do the culdoscopy. All that means is looking at the cervix with a microscope."

"I know what a culdoscopy is," Marissa had told him.

"Well, then, you know how easy it is," Dr. Carpenter had added. "I'll give the old cervix a good look, snip out a tiny piece of anything suspicious, and that will be it. You could be outta here in an hour. And we'll give you something in case there's any pain. In most centers they don't give any analgesia for biopsies, but we're more civilized. It's really easy. I could do it in my sleep."

Marissa had always liked Dr. Carpenter. She appreciated his offhand, easygoing manner. Yet his attitude about a biopsy made her appreciate the fact that surgeons viewed surgery in a fundamentally different way than patients did. She wasn't concerned about how easy the procedure was for him. She was concerned about its effect on her. After all, above and beyond the pain, there was always the possibility of a complication.

Yet she was reluctant to procrastinate. As a physician, she was well aware of the consequences of putting off a biopsy. For the first time, Marissa felt medically vulnerable. There was a remote but real possibility that the biopsy might prove to be positive for cancer. In that case, the sooner she knew the answer, the better off she'd be.

"Day surgery is on the third floor," the receptionist said cheerfully in response to Marissa's question. "Just follow the red line on the floor."

Marissa looked down at her feet. A red, a yellow, and a blue line ran around the information booth. The red line led her to the elevators.

On the third floor, Marissa followed the red line to a window with a sliding glass panel. A nurse dressed in a standard white uniform opened the panel as Marissa approached.

"I'm Marissa Blumenthal," Marissa managed. She had to clear her throat to get it out.

The nurse found her folder, glanced at it briefly to see if it was complete, then extracted a plastic ID bracelet. Reaching across the countertop, the nurse helped Marissa secure the bracelet.

Marissa found the procedure unexpectedly humiliating. From about the third year in medical school, she'd always felt in control in a hospital setting. Suddenly the tables were turned. A shiver of dread passed through her.

"It will be a few minutes," the nurse intoned. Then she pointed to some double doors. "There's a comfortable waiting room just through there. Someone will call you when they are ready." The glass panel slid shut.

Dutifully Marissa went through the doors into a large, square room, furnished in a nondescript modern style. About thirty people were waiting. Marissa felt the stare of silent eyes as she self-consciously hurried to an empty seat at the end of a couch.

There was a view of the Charles River across a small green park. Silhouetted against the gray water were the leafless skeletons of the sycamore trees that lined the embankment.

By reflex, Marissa picked up one of the glossy-covered magazines from the side table and absently flipped through the pages. Surreptitiously she glanced over the top of the magazine and was relieved to see that the eyes of the other people in the room had gone back to their own magazines. The only sound was of pages being turned.

Marissa stole quick glances at some of the other women, wondering what they were there for. They all seemed so calm. Surely she couldn't be the only one who was nervous.

Marissa tried to read an article on upcoming summer fashion trends, but she couldn't concentrate. Her abnormal Pap smear seemed like a hint of internal betrayal: a warning of what was to come. At thirty-three years old, she had been having the barest exterior reminders of getting older, like the fine lines appearing at the outer corners of her eyes.

Focusing for the moment on the many ads that filled the women's magazine in her hands, Marissa gazed at the faces of the sixteen- and seventeen-year-olds who populated them. Their youthful, blemish-free faces seemed to mock her and make her feel old beyond her years.

What if the biopsy was positive? What if she had cancer of the cervix? It was rare but not unknown in women her age. Suddenly the possibility bore down on Marissa with a crushing intensity. My God! she thought. If it was cancer, she might have to have a hysterectomy, and a hysterectomy would mean no children!

A dizzy feeling spread through Marissa, and the magazine in her hands momentarily blurred. At the same time her pulse began to race. The thought of not having children was anathema to her. She'd married only six months previously, and although she hadn't planned on starting a family immediately, she had always known that children would eventually be a big part of her life. If it turned out that she could not have children, she hated to consider the consequences, both for herself and for her husband. And until that very moment, waiting for the biopsy that Dr. Carpenter said would be "a piece of cake," she'd never given the possibility serious thought.

All at once Marissa felt hurt that Robert had not been more concerned and that he had taken her at her word when she'd said she'd be perfectly fine going to the clinic by herself. Looking around the room again, Marissa saw that most of the other patients were accompanied by their spouses or boyfriends.

"You're being ridiculous," Marissa silently chided herself as she tried to keep her emotions in check. She was surprised and a little embarrassed. It was not like her to be so hysterical. She liked to think she wasn't easily upset. Besides, she knew that Robert couldn't have come with her even if he'd wanted to. That morning he had an important meeting of the executive staff of his health care management, investment, and research company. It was a critical meeting that had been planned months in advance.

"Marissa Blumenthal!" a nurse called.

Marissa jumped up, placed the magazine on the side table, and followed the nurse down a long, blank white corridor. She was shown into a changing room with an inner door opening into one of the procedure rooms. From her vantage point in the changing area, Marissa could see the table with its gleaming, stainless steel stirrups.

"Just to be on the safe side," the nurse said as she twisted Marissa's wrist to check her ID. Satisfied she had the right patient, she patted some clothes on a bench and added: "Slip into this johnny, slippers, and robe and hang your clothes in the closet. Any valuables can be locked in the drawer. When you're done, go in and sit on the examining table." She smiled. The woman was professional, but not without warmth. She closed the door to the hall behind her.

Marissa stepped out of her clothes. The floor was cold on her bare feet. As she struggled to tie the straps of the johnny behind her, she acknowledged how much she liked the staff at the Women's Clinic, from the receptionists to her doctor. But the main reason she patronized the clinic was because of its private status and the consequent confidentiality it had to offer. Now that she was having a biopsy, she was even more thankful for her choice. Had she gone to any one of the major Boston hospitals, especially her own hospital, the Boston Memorial, she would have undoubtedly come in contact with people she knew.

Marissa had always been careful to keep her private life private. She never wanted personal matters like birth control, annual pelvic exams, a couple of episodes of cystitis and the like to be topics of gossip with her colleagues. And even if people didn't talk, she did not want to worry about passing her GYN man in the hospital corridor or in the hospital cafeteria.

The flimsy robe, the open-backed hospital johnny, and the paper slip-on slippers completed Marissa's transition from doctor to patient. With her ill-fitting slippers flopping, she padded into the procedure room and sat on the edge of the examining table as instructed by the nurse.

Glancing around at the usual accoutrements which included an anesthesia machine and cabinets of instruments, her panic swelled anew. Beyond her fear of the procedure, and the possible need for a hysterectomy she kept reminding herself was remote, Marissa now felt a strong intuition of disaster. She realized how much she had come to prize her life, particularly in the last few years. Between her new husband, Robert, and her recent acceptance into a fine pediatric group, her life seemed to be going almost too well. She had so much to lose, it made her terrified.

"Hello there, I'm Dr. Arthur," a burly man said as he entered the room with a powerful flourish, clutching a handful of cellophane-covered packages and an IV bottle. "I'm from anesthesia, and I'll be giving you something for your upcoming procedure. Allergic to anything?"

"Nothing," Marissa assured the man. She was glad for the company, relieved to have someone take her away from her own thoughts.

"We'll probably not need this," Dr. Arthur said as he deftly started an IV in Marissa's right wrist.

"But it's good to have it just in case. If Dr. Carpenter needs more anesthesia, it can be given easily."

"Why would he need more anesthesia?" Marissa asked nervously. She watched the droplets of fluid fall in the micropore filter. She'd never had an IV before.

"What if he decides to do a cone biopsy rather than a punch?" Dr. Arthur replied as he slowed the IV to a mere trickle. "Or if he decides to do any more extensive procedure? Obviously we'd have to give you something in addition. After all, we want this to be as pleasant as possible."

Marissa shuddered at the term "more extensive procedure." Before she could stop herself she blurted out, "I want to make it absolutely clear that I only signed a consent for a biopsy and not anything more extensive like a hysterectomy."

Dr. Arthur laughed, then apologized for finding her reminder humorous. "No need to worry on that score," he said. "We certainly don't do hysterectomies in the minor procedure room."

"What will you be giving me?' Marissa asked sheepishly.

"You want to know the specific drugs I'll be using?" Dr. Arthur asked.

Marissa nodded. No one at the clinic knew she was a doctor, and Marissa preferred it that way. When she'd first signed for the clinic's services, she'd filled out a form which only asked for her employer. She'd listed the Boston Memorial since at the time she was taking a year of fellowship in pediatric endocrinology. The fact that she was a physician wasn't a secret and if they asked her, she'd certainly have told them. But no one had asked, a fact she took as further confirmation of the kind of confidentiality she had come to expect of the clinic.

Dr. Arthur looked puzzled for a moment, shrugged, then replied. "I'll be using a mixture of a small amount of Valium and a drug called ketamine." He then cleaned up the remains of the IV paraphernalia. "It's a good little cocktail. It's great for pain, and it has the added appeal of occasionally providing a touch of amnesia."

Marissa was aware of ketamine. It was used frequently at the Boston Memorial for dressing changes with burned children. But she wasn't aware of its use in outpatient settings. When she mentioned this to Dr. Arthur, he smiled paternalistically.

"Been doing a little reading, huh?" he teased. Then he warned: "Remember, a little knowledge is a dangerous thing. Actually, the outpatient environment is the most common use for the drug." He stared at Marissa. "My, you do seem a little tense."

"I've been trying to fight it," Marissa admitted.

"I'll give you a hand," Dr. Arthur offered. "Let's give you a little taste of Valium and ketamine right now." He went to fetch a syringe from the cabinet. "This biopsy stuff is a piece of cake," he called over his shoulder.

Marissa nodded without enthusiasm. She had already tired of the pastry metaphor. The fact was that she was nervous, and despite having felt a bit better when Dr. Arthur first appeared, now she felt decidedly worse. His offhand manner of referring to more extensive procedures had not left her feeling reassured. Again, her intuition began sending out alarms of imminent disaster. Marissa had to fight against the irrational urge to flee. "I'm a doctor," she silently repeated to herself over and over again. "I shouldn't be feeling like this."

The door to the hall burst open. In swept Dr. Ronald Carpenter dressed in surgical scrubs which included a hat and a mask. With him was a woman also in scrub clothes although her mask was draped down over her chest.

Marissa recognized Dr. Carpenter immediately despite the mask. His bright, crystal-blue eyes and tanned skin were unmistakable. "This is only a biopsy?" Marissa questioned nervously. Dr. Carpenter was dressed for major surgery.

"Miss Blumenthal is nervous about having a hysterectomy," Dr. Arthur explained, snapping the side of a needle to release the air bubbles. He returned to Marissa's side.

"Hysterectomy?" Dr. Carpenter asked with obvious confusion. "What are you talking about?"

Dr. Arthur raised his eyebrows. "I think our patient here has been doing a little reading." He picked up the IV tubing and injected the contents of the syringe. Then opened the IV to flow rapidly for a moment.

Dr. Carpenter stepped over to Marissa and put his hand on her shoulder. He looked into her dark brown eyes. "We're only doing a simple biopsy. There's been no talk of a hysterectomy. If you are wondering about my clothes, I've just come from surgery. The mask is because I have a cold and don't want to spread it to any of my patients."

Marissa looked up into Dr. Carpenter's bright blue eyes. She was about to reply when the blue brought back a memory that she'd been long suppressing: the terror of being attacked in a hotel room in San Francisco a few years earlier and the horror of having to stab a man repeatedly to save her own life. At that moment the episode came back to her with such startling clarity, she could actually feel the man's hands around her throat. Marissa started to choke. The room began to spin and she heard a buzzing noise that gradually got louder.

Marissa felt hands grabbing at her, forcing her down on her back. She tried to fight since she felt she could breathe easier if she were upright, but it was to no avail. Her head touched the examination table, and as soon as it did, the room stopped spinning and her breathing became easier. Suddenly she realized her eyes were closed. When she opened them, she was looking up into the faces of Dr. Arthur, the woman, and the masked face of Dr. Carpenter.

"Are you okay?" Dr. Carpenter asked.

Marissa tried to speak but her voice wouldn't cooperate.

"Wow!" Dr. Arthur said. "Is she ever sensitive to the anesthetic!" He quickly took her blood pressure. "At least that's okay. I'm glad I didn't give her the whole dose."

Marissa closed her eyes. At last she was calm. She heard more conversation, but it sounded as if it were someplace in the distance and didn't involve her. At the same time she felt as if an invisible lead blanket were settling over her. She felt her legs being lifted, but she didn't care. Then the voices in the room receded further. She heard laughter and then a radio. She felt instruments and heard the sound of metal hitting metal.

She relaxed until she felt a cramp like a menstrual cramp. It was pain but not normal pain in that it was more alarming than uncomfortable. She tried to open her eyes but her lids felt heavy. Again she tried to open her eyes but quickly gave up. It was like a nightmare from which she could not awaken. Then there was yet another cramp, sharp enough to bring her head off the examining table.

The room was a drug-induced blur. She could just make out the top of Dr. Carpenter's head as he worked between her draped knees. The culdoscope was pushed to the side on his right.

The sounds of the room still came to her as if from a great distance, although now they had a peculiar, echoing quality. People in the room were moving in slow motion. Dr. Carpenter raised his head as if he could sense her eyes on him.

A hand grasped Marissa's shoulder and eased her back. But as she lay down, her numbed mind replayed the blurred image of Dr. Carpenter's masked face and, despite her drugged state, a shiver of terror coursed through her veins. It was as if her doctor had metamorphosed into a demon. Instead of his eyes being crystal blue, they had become distorted. They appeared to be made of black onyx as dense as stone.

Marissa started to scream but she held herself in check. Some part of her brain was rational enough to remind her that all her perceptions were being altered by the medication. She tried to sit up again to take another look for reassurance, but hands restrained her. She fought against the hands, and once again her mind took her back to the hotel room in San Francisco when she'd had to fight with the killer. She remembered hitting the man with the telephone receiver. She remembered all the blood.

Unable to contain herself any longer, Marissa screamed. But no sound came out. She was on the edge of a precipice and slipping. She tried to hold on but she slowly lost her grip, falling into blackness. . . .

FEBRUARY 27, 1988

"Damn!" Marissa said as her eyes rapidly roamed her office. She could not imagine where she could have put her keys. For the tenth time she pulled open her central desk drawer, the place where she always put them. They weren't there. Irritated, she shuffled through the contents of the drawer, then slammed it.

"Holy Toledo!" she said as she looked at her watch. She had less than thirty minutes to get from her office over to the Sheraton Hotel where she was scheduled to receive an award. Nothing seemed to be cooperating. First she had an emergency: six-year-old Cindy Markham with a severe asthma attack. Now she could not find her keys.

Marissa pursed her lips with frustration and tried to retrace her steps. Suddenly she remembered. She'd taken home a bunch of charts the night before. Stepping over to the file cabinet, she saw the keys immediately. She snatched them up and headed for the door.

She got as far as her hand on the doorknob when the phone rang. At first she was tempted to ignore it, but her conscience quickly intervened. There was always a chance it involved Cindy Markham.

With a sigh, Marissa went to her desk and leaned over to pick up the receiver. "What is it?" she asked with uncharacteristic curtness.

"Is this Dr. Blumenthal?" the caller queried.

"This is she," Marissa said. She didn't recognize the voice. She had expected her secretary, who was aware of her time constraint.

"This is Dr. Carpenter," said the caller. "Do you have a minute?"

"Yes," Marissa lied. She felt a rush of anxiety, having expected his call over the last few days. She held her breath.

"First I'd like to congratulate you on your award today," Dr. Carpenter said. "I didn't even know you were a physician, much less an award-winning researcher. It's kind of embarrassing to find out about your patients in the morning paper."

"Sorry," said Marissa. "I guess I could have said." She looked at her watch.

"How on earth did a pediatrician get involved doing research on Ebola Hemorrhagic Fever?" Dr. Carpenter asked. "It sounds pretty esoteric. Let me see, I have the newspaper right here. 'The Peabody Research Award goes to Dr. Marissa Blumenthal for the elucidation of the variables associated with the transmission of Ebola virus from primary to secondary contacts.' Wow!"

"I spent a couple of years at the CDC in Atlanta," Marissa explained. "I got assigned to a case where Ebola virus was being intentionally spread in HMOs."

"Of course!" Dr. Carpenter said. "I remember reading about that. My God, was that you?"

"Afraid so," Marissa said.

"As I recall, you almost got killed!" Dr. Carpenter said with obvious admiration.

"I was lucky," Marissa said. "Very lucky." She wondered what Dr. Carpenter would have said if she told him that during her biopsy his blue eyes had reminded her of the man who had tried to kill her.

"I'm impressed," Dr. Carpenter admitted. "And I'm glad to have some good news for you. Usually my secretary makes these calls, but after reading about you this morning, I wanted to call myself. The biopsy specimens were all fine. It was merely a mild dysplasia. As I told you that day, the culdoscopy suggested as much, but it is nice to be a hundred percent certain. Why don't you schedule a follow-up Pap smear in four to six months? After that, we can let you go for a year at least."

"Great," said Marissa. "I will. And thanks for the good news."

"My pleasure," Dr. Carpenter said.

Marissa shifted her feet. She was still embarrassed by her behavior at the biopsy. Gathering her courage, she apologized again.

"Hey, don't give it another thought," Dr. Carpenter said. "But after your experience I've decided I don't like that ketamine stuff. I told anesthesia not to use it on any more of my cases. I know the drug has some good points, but I've had a couple of other patients with bad trips like yours. So please don't apologize. But tell me, have you had any other problems since the biopsy?"

"Not really," Marissa said. "The worst part of the whole experience was the drug-induced nightmare. I've even had the same dream a couple more times since the biopsy."

"I'm the one who should be apologizing," Dr. Carpenter said. "Anyway, next time we won't give you ketamine. How's that for a promise?"

"I think I'll be steering clear of doctors for a while," Marissa said.

"That's a healthy attitude," Dr. Carpenter said with a laugh. "But as I said before, let's see you back in four months or so."

Hanging up the phone, Marissa rushed from her office. She waved hastily to her secretary, Mindy Valdanus, then repeatedly hit the Down elevator button. She had fifteen minutes to get to the Sheraton, an impossible feat given Boston traffic. Yet she was pleased with her conversation with Dr. Carpenter. She had a good feeling about the man. She had to chuckle when she thought about the sinister creature he had been transformed into in her nightmare. It amazed her what drugs could do.

At last the elevator arrived. Of course the best thing about the phone conversation was learning that the cervical biopsy was normal. But then a stray thought cropped up as the elevator descended to the garage. What would she do if the next Pap smear proved to be abnormal?

"Damn!" she said aloud, dismissing the gloomy thought. There was always something!

VITAL SIGNS

1

MARCH 19, 1990
7:41 A.M.

MARISSA STOPPED in her tracks in the middle of the elegant Oriental carpet that dominated the master bedroom. She was on her way to her walk-in closet to retrieve the dress that she had chosen the night before. The TV was on in the massive French armoire set against the wall opposite the king-sized bed; its doors were propped open by books. The television was tuned to *Good Morning America*. Charlie Gibson was joking about baseball spring training with Spencer Christian. Weak winter sunlight spilled into the room through half-open curtains. Taffy Two, Marissa and Robert's cocker spaniel, was whining to be let out.

"What did you say?" Marissa called to her husband, who was out of sight in the master bath. She could hear the shower running.

"I said I don't want to go to that damn Women's Clinic this morning," he shouted. His face appeared at the partially opened doorway, half covered with shaving cream. Then he lowered his voice, keeping it loud enough to compete with the television: "I'm not up to providing a sperm

1

sample this morning. I'm just not. Not today." He shrugged, then disappeared back into the bathroom.

For a minute, Marissa didn't move. Then she ran her fingers through her hair, trying to control herself. Blood pounded in her ears as she replayed Robert's casual refusal to go to the clinic. How could he back out at the last minute like this?

Spotting the clock radio which had awakened them half an hour ago, she felt an almost irresistible desire to step over to the night table, yank its plug from its socket, and dash the whole thing against the fireplace; she was that furious. But she held herself in check.

Inside the bathroom she heard the shower door open and then close. The sound of the water changed; Robert had gotten into the shower.

"I don't believe this," Marissa muttered. She marched to the bathroom and pounded the door fully open with a bang. The dog followed her to the threshold. Steam was already billowing out over the top of the shower stall. Robert liked his showers piping hot. Marissa could see her husband's athletic nude body through the stall's smoked glass.

"Run that by me once more," Marissa called to him. "I don't think I heard you correctly."

"It's simple," he said. "I'm not going to the clinic this morning. I'm not up to it today. I'm not some kind of sperm dispenser."

Of all the ups and downs of the infertility treatments, this was something Marissa had not antici-

2

pated. It was all she could do to keep from kicking in the shower door while Robert finished. The dog, sensing her state of mind, ducked under the bed.

Finally Robert turned off the water and stepped from the stall. Drops of water cascaded down his muscular frame. Despite his heavy work schedule, he still managed to exercise three or four times a week. Even his trimness irritated Marissa at the moment. She was unpleasantly cognizant of the extra ten pounds she'd put on through the course of her treatment.

When he saw her standing there, Robert seemed surprised.

"You're telling me that you won't come with me this morning to give a sperm sample?" she asked, once she knew she had his attention.

"That's right," Robert said. "I was going to tell you last night, but you had a headache. No surprise, lately you always have a headache or a stomachache or some other kind of ache. So I thought I'd spare you. But I'm telling you now. They can unfreeze some sperm from the last time. They told me they froze part of it. Let them use that."

"After all I've gone through, you won't even come in to the clinic and give up five minutes of your precious time?"

"Come on, Marissa," Robert said as he toweled off, "you and I both know we're talking about more than five minutes."

Marissa was beginning to feel more frustrated

by Robert than she was by her infertility. "I'm the one who's had to put in all the serious time," she said, exploding. "And I'm the one who has been pumped full of all these hormones. Sure I've had headaches. I've been in a constant state of PMS to produce eggs. And look at all these needle marks on my arms and legs." Marissa pointed to the multiple bruises she had covering her extremities.

"I've seen them," Robert said without looking.

"I'm the one who has had to have general anesthesia and laparoscopy and biopsy of my fallopian tubes," Marissa shouted. "I'm the one who has had to endure all the physical and mental traumas, all the indignities."

"Most of the indignities," Robert reminded her, "but not all."

"I've had to take my temperature every morning for months on end and plot it on that graph before I even get out of bed to pee."

Robert was in his closet, selecting a suit and an appropriate tie. He turned his head toward Marissa, who was blocking the light from the bedroom. "You were also the one who doctored the graph with the extra Xs," he said flippantly.

Marissa fumed. "I had to cheat a little so that the doctors at the clinic wouldn't think we weren't trying by not making love often enough. But I never cheated around ovulation time."

"Making love! Ha!" Robert laughed. "We haven't made love since this whole thing started. We don't make love. We don't even have sex. What we do is rut."

4

Marissa tried to respond but Robert interrupted her.

"I can't even remember what lovemaking is like!" he shouted. "What used to be pleasurable has been reduced to sex on cue, rutting by rote."

"Well you haven't been 'rutting' very often," Marissa lashed back. "As a performer you've been less than the greatest."

"Careful," Robert warned, feeling Marissa was getting nasty. "Just keep in mind that this rutting is easy for you. All you have to do is play dead while I do all the work."

"Work? My God," Marissa questioned with disgust.

Marissa tried to speak again but all she could do was stifle a sob. Robert was right, in a way. With all the fertility therapy, it was hard to feel spontaneous about anything that went on in the bedroom lately. In spite of herself, her eyes welled with tears.

Seeing that he had hurt her, Robert suddenly softened. "I'm sorry," he said, "this hasn't been easy on either of us. Especially you. But I've got to say, it's not been easy on me either. As for today, I really can't make it to the clinic. I have an important meeting with a team of people from Europe. I'm sorry, but my business cannot always be ruled by the whim of the doctors at the Women's Clinic or the vagaries of your menstrual cycle. You didn't tell me until Saturday about this egg retrieval today. I didn't know you were going to

5

give yourself that releasing injection or whatever you call it."

"We've followed the same schedule as we have on three previous in-vitro fertilization cycles," said Marissa. "I didn't think I had to spell it out for you every time."

"What can I say? When this meeting was scheduled we weren't involved with infertility treatments. I haven't reviewed my entire calendar with your fertilization cycles in mind."

Marissa suddenly felt angry again. Robert went to the armoire to get a freshly laundered shirt. Above his head Joan Lunden was interviewing a celebrity on the TV screen.

"All you think about is business," she muttered. "You have meetings all the time. Can't you postpone this one for half an hour?"

"That would be difficult," Robert said.

"The trouble with you is that business is more important than anything else. I think you have a mixed-up set of values."

"You are entitled to your opinion," Robert said calmly, trying to avoid another round of mutual recriminations. He pulled on his shirt and started buttoning it. He knew he should remain silent, but Marissa had hit a sore spot. "There is nothing inherently wrong with business. It puts food on the table and a roof over our heads. Besides, you knew how I felt about business before we were married. I enjoy it and it's rewarding on many levels."

"Before we were married you said children were

6

important," Marissa retorted. "Now it seems that business comes first."

Robert stepped over to the mirror and started to put on his tie. "That was how I felt before we learned that you couldn't have a child, at least not the normal way." Robert paused. He realized he'd made a mistake. He turned his head to look at his wife. He could tell by her face that the careless comment had not gone unnoticed. He tried to take it back. "I mean, before we learned that *we* couldn't have a child the normal way."

But his restatement didn't mitigate the blow. In a flash, Marissa's anger dissolved to despair. Tears welled anew and Marissa began to sob.

Robert tried to put his hand on her shoulder, but she pulled away from him and ran into the bathroom. She tried to shut the door behind her, but Robert pushed his way in and enveloped her in a hug, pressing his face into the crook of her neck.

Marissa's whole body shook as she wept. It took her a full ten minutes to begin to recover. She knew that she wasn't acting like herself. No doubt the hormones that she'd been taking contributed to her fragile emotional state. But that knowledge didn't help her pull herself together any faster.

Robert released her long enough to get her a tissue. Choking back new tears, she blew her nose. Now she felt embarrassed on top of her anger and her grief. In a shaky voice she admitted to Robert that she knew she was to blame for their infertility.

"I don't care if we don't have children," Robert

said, hoping to soothe her. "It's not the end of the world."

Marissa eyed him warily. "I don't believe you," she said. "You've always wanted children. You told me so. And since I know all this is my fault, why don't you be honest about your feelings. I could deal with honesty better than your lying to me. Tell me that you're angry."

"I'm disappointed but I'm not angry," Robert said. He looked at Marissa. Marissa stared back at him. "Well, maybe there have been a few moments," he confessed.

"Look what I've done to your clean shirt," Marissa said.

Robert glanced down at his chest. There were patches of dampness from Marissa's tears both on his shirt and on his half-tied tie. Robert took a deep breath. "It doesn't matter. I'll put on another." He quickly pulled off the shirt and tie and threw them into the laundry basket.

Gazing at her red and swollen eyes in the mirror, Marissa had a hopeless feeling about the task of making herself presentable. She slipped into the shower.

Fifteen minutes later Marissa felt significantly calmer, as if the hot water and suds had cleansed her mind as well as her body. As she dried her hair, she returned to the bedroom to find Robert just about ready.

"I'm sorry I got so hysterical," she said. "I just can't help it. Lately all I ever seem to do is overreact. I shouldn't have gone off the deep end just because you don't feel like going to the clinic for the umpteenth time."

"I'm the one who should be apologizing," said Robert. "I'm sorry for picking such an idiotic way of expressing my frustrations about this whole experience. While you were showering, I changed my mind. I'll come with you to the clinic after all. I already called the office to arrange it."

For what seemed like the first time in weeks, Marissa felt her spirits rise. "Thank you," she said. She was tempted to take Robert in her arms, but something held her back. She wondered if she was afraid he might somehow reject her. She was hardly looking her best. She knew that their relationship had been changing through the course of their infertility therapy. And like her figure, the changes hadn't been for the better. Marissa sighed. "Sometimes I think this infertility treatment is just too much to bear. Don't get me wrong; I have no fonder wish than to have our baby. But I've been feeling the stress of it every waking moment of every day. And I know it hasn't been much easier for you."

With panties and a bra in hand, Marissa went into her closet. While she dressed, she called out to Robert. Sometimes recently it seemed easier to talk to him without meeting his eyes. "I've only told a few people about our problem, and only in very general terms. I've just said we're trying to get me pregnant. Everyone I tell feels compelled to give me unsolicited advice. 'Relax,' they say. 'Take a vacation.' The next person who tells me that, I'm going to tell the truth. No amount of relaxing will help me because I've got fallopian tubes that are sealed shut like hopelessly clogged drains."

Robert didn't say anything in response, so Marissa went to the door of her closet and looked into the bedroom. He was sitting on the edge of the bed putting on his shoes.

"The other person who is bugging me is your mother," Marissa said.

Robert looked up. "What does my mother have to do with this?"

"Simply that she feels obligated every time we get together to tell me it's time for us to have children. If she says that to me once more, I'm going to tell her the truth as well. In fact, why don't you tell her yourself so that she and I can avoid a confrontation?"

Ever since she and Robert had begun dating she had been trying to please his mother, but with only marginal success.

"I don't want to tell my mother," Robert said. "I've already told you that."

"Why not?" asked Marissa.

"Because I don't want to hear a lecture. And I don't want to hear her tell me it serves me right for marrying a Jewish girl."

"Oh, please!" Marissa exclaimed with a new burst of anger.

"I'm not responsible for my mother's prejudices," Robert said. "And I can't control her. Nor should I."

Angry again, Marissa turned back to her dressing, roughly buttoning buttons and yanking her zipper.

But soon Marissa's fury at Robert's mother reverted back to self-loathing for her own infertility. For the first time in her life, Marissa felt truly cursed by fate. It seemed unreasonably ironic how much effort and money she'd spent on birth control in college and medical school so that she wouldn't have a child at the wrong time. Now, when it was the right time, she had to learn that she couldn't have a child at any time except through the help of modern medical science.

"It's not fair," Marissa said aloud. Fresh tears streamed down her face. She knew she was at the edge of her endurance with the monthly emotional roller coaster of hope to despair each time she failed to conceive, and now with Robert's increasing impatience with the process. She could hardly blame him.

"I think you've become obsessed with this fertility stuff," Robert said softly. "Marissa, I'm really beginning to worry about you. I'm worried about us."

Marissa turned. Robert was standing in the closet doorway, his hands gripping the jambs. At first Marissa couldn't see the expression on his face; he stood in shadows with his sandy hair backlit from the bedroom light. But as he moved toward her she could see that he looked concerned but determined; his angular jaw was set so that his thin lips formed a straight line.

11

"When you wanted to go this infertility treatment route I was willing to give it a try. But I feel it's gotten way out of hand. I'm coming to the conclusion that we should think about stopping before we lose what we do have for the sake of what we don't."

"You think I'm obsessed? Of course I'm obsessed! Wouldn't you have to be obsessed to endure the kind of procedures I've been going through? I've been willing to put up with it all because I want to have a child, so that we can have a family. I want to be a mother and I want you to be a father. I want to have a family." Without meaning to, Marissa steadily raised her voice. By the time she finished her last sentence, she was practically shouting.

"Hearing you yell like this only makes me more convinced we have to stop," Robert said. "Look at the two of us. You're strung out; I'm at the end of my rope. There are other options, you know. Maybe we should consider them. We could just reconcile ourselves to being childless. Or we could look into the idea of adopting."

"I just cannot believe that you would pick this time to say these things," Marissa snapped. "Here it is the morning of my fourth egg retrieval, I'm prepared to face the pain and the risk, and, yes, I'm an emotional wreck. And this is the time you pick to talk about changing strategy?"

"There is never a good time to discuss these issues with this in-vitro fertilization schedule," said Robert, no longer able to control his anger.

12

"You don't like my timing, okay. When would be better, when you're crazy with anxiety, wondering if you are pregnant? Or how about when you're depressed after your period starts again? Or how about when you are finally coming out of your grief and starting a new cycle? You tell me; I'll come talk to you then."

Robert studied his wife. She was getting to be a stranger. She'd become impossibly emotional and had gained considerable weight, especially in her face, which appeared swollen. Her glare was so cool, it chilled him to the bone. Her eyes seemed as dark as her mood, and her skin was flushed as if she might be running a fever. She was like a stranger, all right. Or worse: just then she seemed like some irrational hysteric. Robert wouldn't have been surprised if she suddenly sprang at him like an angry cat. He decided it was time to back down.

Robert edged a few steps away from her. "Okay," he said, "you're right. It's a bad time to discuss this. I'm sorry. We'll do it another day. Why don't you finish getting dressed and we'll head down to the clinic." He shook his head. "I just hope I can produce a sperm sample. The way I've been feeling lately, I'm hardly up to it. It's not purely mechanical. Not anymore. I'm not sixteen."

Without saying anything, Marissa turned back to her dressing, exhausted. She wondered what they would do if he failed to produce the sperm sample. She had no idea how much using thawed sperm would lower the chances of a successful fertilization. She assumed it would, which was part of the reason she was so angry when he had initially refused to go to the clinic, especially since the last in-vitro cycle had failed because fertilization had not occurred. Catching a glimpse of herself in the mirror, and seeing the high color of her cheeks, Marissa realized just how obsessed she was becoming. Even her eyes looked like those of a stranger in their unblinking intensity.

Marissa adjusted her dress. She warned herself about getting her hopes up too high after so many disappointments. There were so many stages where things could go wrong. First she had to produce the eggs, and they had to be retrieved before she ovulated spontaneously. Then fertilization had to occur. Then the embryos had to be transferred into her uterus and become implanted. Then, if all that happened as it was supposed to, she'd be pregnant. And then she'd have to start worrying about a miscarriage. There were so many chances for failure. Yet in her mind's eye she could see the sign on the waiting room wall in the in-vitro unit: YOU ONLY FAIL WHEN YOU GIVE UP TRYING. She had to go through with it.

As pessimistic as she was, Marissa could still close her eyes and envision a tiny baby in her arms. "Be patient, little one," she whispered. In her heart she knew that if the child ever arrived, it would make all this effort worthwhile. She knew she shouldn't be thinking this way, but Marissa was beginning to feel it would be the only way to save her marriage.

2

MARCH 19, 1990
9:15 A.M.

WALKING BENEATH the glass-enclosed walkway that separated the main clinic building from the overnight ward and emergency area, Robert and Marissa entered the brick courtyard and started up the front steps of the Women's Clinic. The particular color and pattern of the granite made Marissa think about all the times that she'd climbed the steps, facing innumerable "minor procedures." Involuntarily her footsteps slowed, no doubt a response conditioned by the collective pain of a thousand needle pricks.

"Come on," Robert urged. He was gripping Marissa's hand and had sensed her momentary resistance. He glanced briefly at his watch. They were already late.

Marissa tried to hurry. Today's egg retrieval was to be her fourth. She well knew the degree of discomfort she could expect. But for Marissa the fear of the pain was less of a concern than the possibility of complications. Part of the problem of being both a doctor and a patient was knowing all the terrible things that could go wrong. She

15

shuddered as her mind ticked off a list of potentially lethal possibilities.

Once Robert and Marissa were inside the clinic, they skirted the main information booth and headed directly to the In-Vitro Fertilization Unit on the second floor. They had traveled this route on several occasions, or at least Marissa had.

Stepping into the usually quiet waiting room with its plush carpet and tapestry-upholstered chairs, they were treated to a spectacle neither had been prepared to see.

"I am not going to be put off!" shouted a well-dressed, slim woman. Marissa guessed she was about thirty years old. It was rare in any of the clinic's waiting rooms to hear anyone speak above a whisper, much less shout. It was as surprising as hearing someone yelling aloud in a church.

"Mrs. Ziegler," said the startled receptionist. "Please!" The receptionist was cowering behind her desk chair.

"Don't Mrs. Ziegler me," the woman shouted. "This is the third time I've come in here for my records. I want them now!"

Mrs. Ziegler's hand shot out and swept the top of the receptionist's desk clean. There was the jolting shatter of glass and pottery as pens, papers, picture frames, and coffee mugs crashed to the floor.

The dozen or so patients waiting in the room froze in their chairs, stunned by the outburst. Most trained their eyes on the magazines before

16

them, afraid to acknowledge the scene being acted out before their eyes.

Marissa winced at the sound of the breaking glass. She remembered the clock radio she had so wanted to smash not half an hour earlier. It was frightening to recognize in Mrs. Ziegler such a kindred spirit. There had been several times Marissa had felt equally pushed to the edge.

Robert's initial response to the situation was to step directly in front of Marissa and put himself between her and the hysterical patient. When he saw Mrs. Ziegler make a move around the desk, he feared she was about to attack the poor receptionist. In a flash, he shot forward and caught Mrs. Ziegler from behind, gripping her at the waist. "Calm down," he told her, hoping to sound commanding as well as soothing.

As if expecting such interference, Mrs. Ziegler twisted around and swung her sizable Gucci purse in a wide arc. It hit Robert on the side of his face, splitting his lip. Since the blow did not dislodge Robert's grip, Mrs. Ziegler cocked her arm for yet another swing of the purse.

Seeing the second blow in the making, Robert let go of her waist and smothered her arms in a bear hug. But before he could get a good grip, she hit him again, this time with a clenched fist.

"Ahhhh!" Robert cried, surprised by the blow. He pushed Mrs. Ziegler away. The women who had been sitting in the area fled to the other side of the waiting room.

Massaging his shoulder, which had received the punch, Robert eyed Mrs. Ziegler cautiously.

"Get out of my way," she snarled. "This doesn't involve you."

"It does now," Robert snapped.

The door to the hall burst open as Dr. Carpenter and Dr. Wingate dashed in. Behind them was a uniformed guard with a Women's Clinic patch on his sleeve. All three went directly to Mrs. Ziegler.

Dr. Wingate, director of the clinic as well as head of the in-vitro unit, took immediate control. He was a huge man with a full beard and a slight but distinctive English accent. "Rebecca, what on earth has gotten into you?" he asked in a soothing voice. "No matter how upset you might be feeling, this is no way to behave."

"I want my records," Mrs. Ziegler said. "Every time I come in here I get the runaround. There is something wrong in this place, something rotten. I want my records. They are mine."

"No, they are not," Dr. Wingate corrected calmly. "They are the Women's Clinic records. We know that infertility treatment can be stressful, and we even know that on occasion patients displace their frustration on the doctors and the technicians who are trying to help them. We can understand if you are unhappy. We've even told you that if you want to go elsewhere, we will be happy to forward your records to your new physician. That's our policy. If your new physician wants to give you the records, that's his decision.

18

The sanctity of our records has always been one of our prized attributes."

"I'm a lawyer and I know my rights," Mrs. Ziegler said, but her confidence seemed to falter.

"Even lawyers can occasionally be mistaken," Dr. Wingate said with a smile. Dr. Carpenter nodded in agreement. "You are welcome to view your records. Why don't you come with me and we'll let you read over the whole thing. Maybe that will make you feel better."

"Why wasn't that opportunity offered to me originally?" Mrs. Ziegler said as tears began to stream down her face. "The first time I came here about my records, I told the receptionist I had serious questions about my condition. There was never any suggestion I would be allowed to read my records."

"It was an oversight," Dr. Wingate said. "I apologize for my staff if such an alternative wasn't discussed. We'll send around a memo to avoid future problems. Meanwhile, Dr. Carpenter will take you upstairs and let you read everything. Please." He held out his hand.

Covering her eyes, Mrs. Ziegler allowed herself to be led from the room by Dr. Carpenter and the guard. Dr. Wingate turned to the people in the room. "The clinic would like to apologize for this little incident," he said as he straightened his long white coat. A stethoscope was tucked into a pocket, several glass petri dishes in another. Turning to the receptionist, he asked her to please call housekeeping to clean up the mess on the floor.

Dr. Wingate walked over to Robert, who'd taken the handkerchief from the breast pocket of his suit to dab at his split lip.

"I'm terribly sorry," Dr. Wingate said as he eyed Robert's wound. It was still bleeding, although it had slowed considerably. "I think you'd better come over to our emergency facility," Dr. Wingate said.

"I'm okay," Robert said. He rubbed his shoulder. "It's not too bad."

Marissa stepped over for a closer look at his lip. "I think you'd better have it looked at," she said.

"You might even need a stitch. A butterfly, maybe," Dr. Wingate said as he tipped Robert's head back to get a better view of his lip. "Come on, I'll take you."

"I don't believe this," Robert said with disgust, looking at the bloodstains on his handkerchief.

"It won't take long," Marissa urged. "I'll sign in and wait here."

After a moment's hesitation, Robert allowed himself to be led from the room.

Marissa watched the door close behind him. She could hardly blame Robert if this morning's episode added to his reluctance to proceed with the infertility treatment.

Marissa was suddenly overwhelmed by a wave of doubt about her fourth attempt at in-vitro fertilization. Why should she dare hope to do any better this time around? A feeling of utter futility was beginning to bear down on her.

Sighing heavily, Marissa fought back new tears.

20

Looking around the waiting room, she saw that the other patients had calmly retreated to the pages of their magazines. For some reason, Marissa just couldn't force herself back in step. Instead of approaching the receptionist to check in, she went over to an empty seat and practically fell into it. What was the use of undergoing the egg retrieval yet again if the failure was so certain?

Marissa let her head sink into her hands. She couldn't remember ever feeling such overwhelming despair except when she'd been depressed at the end of her pediatric residency. That was when Roger Shulman had broken off their long-term relationship, an event that ultimately led her to the Centers for Disease Control.

Marissa's mood sank lower as she remembered Roger. In late spring their relationship had still been going strong, but then out of the blue he had informed her he was going to UCLA for a fellowship in neurosurgery. He wanted to go alone. At the time she'd been shocked. Now she knew he was better off without her, barren as she was. She tried to shake the thought. This was crazy thinking, she told herself.

Marissa's thoughts drifted back a year and a half, back to the time she and Robert decided to start their family. She could remember it well because they had celebrated their decision with a special weekend trip to Nantucket Island and a giddy toast with a good Cabernet Sauvignon.

Back then they both thought conceiving would take a matter of weeks, at the most a couple of

21

months. Having always guarded so carefully against the possibility of becoming pregnant, it never occurred to her that conceiving might be a problem for her. But after about seven months, Marissa had begun to become concerned. The approach of her period became a time of building anxiety, followed by depression upon its arrival. By ten months she and Robert realized that something was wrong. By a year they'd made the difficult decision to do something about it. That's when they'd gone to the Women's Clinic to be seen and evaluated in the infertility department.

Robert's sperm analysis had been the first hurdle, but he passed with flying colors. Marissa's first tests were more complicated, involving X-ray study of her uterus and fallopian tubes.

As a physician Marissa knew a little about the test. She'd even seen some pictures of the X-rays in textbooks. But photographs in books had been no preparation for the actual experience. She could remember the test as if it had been yesterday.

"Scoot down a little farther," Dr. Tolentino, the radiologist, had said. He was adjusting the huge X-ray fluoroscopy unit over Marissa's lower abdomen. There was a light in the machine, projecting a grid onto her body.

Marissa wriggled farther down on the rock-hard X-ray table.

An IV was hooked into her right arm. She'd been given a bit of Valium and was feeling lightheaded. In spite of herself she was mildly apprehensive that she might suffer a second drug-induced nightmare.

"Okay!" Dr. Tolentino said. "Perfect." The grid was centered just south of her umbilicus. Dr. Tolentino threw a few electrical switches and the cathode tube monitor of the fluoroscopy unit gave off a light-gray glow. Going to the door, Dr. Tolentino called for Dr. Carpenter.

Dr. Carpenter entered along with a nurse. The two of them were wearing the same sort of heavy lead apron Dr. Tolentino had on to shield his body from ambient radiation. Seeing such heavy protective gear made Marissa feel all the more exposed and vulnerable.

Marissa could feel her legs being lifted and parted to be placed in stirrups. Then the end of the table dropped away so that her backside was perched on the very edge.

"You'll feel the speculum now," Dr. Carpenter warned.

Marissa clenched her teeth as she felt the instrument slip inside of her and spread.

"Now you are going to feel a prick," Dr. Carpenter said. "I'm going to put in the local anesthetic."

Marissa bit her lip in anticipation. True to Dr. Carpenter's warning, she felt a sharp stab localized somewhere in her lower back.

"And again," Dr. Carpenter said.

He injected her in several locations, explaining to her that he was giving her a paracervical block to anesthetize the cervix.

Marissa breathed out. She hadn't realized she'd been holding her breath. All she wanted at that moment was for the study to be over.

"Just a few minutes more," Dr. Carpenter said as if reading her mind.

In her mind's eye Marissa could see the long, scissor-shaped instrument with its jaws shaped like two opposing fangs. She knew those fangs were about to bite through the delicate tissue of her cervix.

But Marissa felt no pain when she heard the sharp metallic sound of the instrument handles lock, just a sensation of pressure and a pulling. She could hear Dr. Carpenter talk to both the nurse and Dr. Tolentino. She heard the X-ray machine go on and could just barely see part of an image that had appeared on the fluoroscopy screen.

"Okay! Marissa," Dr. Carpenter said, "as I explained earlier, the Jarcho cannula is now in place and I'm about to inject the dye. You'll probably feel this a bit."

Marissa held her breath again, and this time the pain came. It was like a severe cramp that built to the point that she could not keep from moving.

"Hold still!" Dr. Carpenter commanded.

"I can't," Marissa moaned. Just when she thought she couldn't bear the pain for a moment longer, it abated. She let her breath out with relief.

"The dye didn't go anyplace," Dr. Carpenter said with surprise.

"Let me take a spot film," Dr. Tolentino said.

"I think I can just make out the dead ends of the tubes here and here." He was pointing at the screen with a pencil.

"Okay," Dr. Carpenter said. He then told Marissa they were going to take an X-ray and for her to stay still.

"What's wrong?" Marissa asked with concern. But Dr. Carpenter ignored her or didn't hear. All three people disappeared behind the screen. Marissa looked up at the huge machine suspended over her.

"Don't move," Dr. Tolentino called out.

Marissa heard a click and a slight buzz. She knew that her body had just been bombarded by millions of tiny X-rays.

"We are going to try again," Dr. Carpenter said as he returned. "This might hurt a little more."

Marissa gripped the sides of the X-ray table.

The pain that followed was the worst she'd ever experienced. It was like a knife thrust into her lower back and twisted. When it was over she looked at the three people grouped around the fluoroscopy screen.

"What did you find?" Marissa questioned. She could tell from Dr. Carpenter's face that something was abnormal.

"At least we know now why you haven't been making babies," he said solemnly. "I couldn't get dye into either of your tubes. And I really pushed—as you probably felt. Both of them seem to be sealed as tight as a drum."

25

"How could that be?" Marissa asked with alarm.

Dr. Carpenter shrugged. "We'll have to look into that. Probably you had some infection. You don't remember anything, do you?"

"No!" Marissa said. "I don't think so."

"Sometimes we can find the cause of blocked tubes and sometimes we can't," Dr. Carpenter said. "Sometimes even a high fever as a child can damage them." He shrugged and patted her on the arm. "We'll look into it."

"What's the next step?" Marissa asked anxiously. She already felt guilty enough about being infertile. This puzzling discovery about her tubes made her wonder if she could have picked up anything from one of her former lovers. She had never been loose, not by any stretch of the imagination, but she'd had sex, especially with Roger. Could Roger have given her something? Marissa's stomach was in knots.

"I'm not sure this is the time to talk about strategy," Dr. Carpenter said. "But we'll probably recommend a laparoscopy and perhaps even a biopsy. There's always the chance that the problem is amenable to microsurgery. If that doesn't work or isn't feasible, there's always in-vitro fertilization . . ."

"Marissa!" Robert called harshly, abruptly bringing Marissa back to the present.

She lifted her face. Robert was standing in front of her.

"What are you doing?" Robert asked, his frustration all too apparent. "I asked after you and the receptionist said you hadn't even checked in."

Marissa got to her feet. Robert was looking at his watch. "Come on!" he said as he turned and headed over to the receptionist's desk. Marissa followed. She gazed at the sign behind the desk. That was the one that said: YOU ONLY FAIL WHEN YOU GIVE UP TRYING.

"I'm sorry," the receptionist said, "with all the excitement, I've been in a dither. It didn't dawn on me that Mrs. Buchanan hadn't checked in."

"Please!" Robert said. "Just let the doctors know she is here."

"Certainly!" the receptionist said. She stood up. "But first I want to thank you for your help earlier, Mr. Buchanan. I think that woman was about to attack me. I hope you weren't hurt badly."

"Only two stitches," Robert said, mellowing to a degree. "I'm fine." Robert then lowered his voice and, after a furtive glance around the waiting room, asked: "Could you give me one of those, errrr . . . plastic containers?"

"Of course," the receptionist said. She bent down and opened a file drawer. She produced a small, graduated, red-topped plastic container and handed it over. Robert palmed it.

"Ah . . . this will make it all worthwhile," Robert whispered sarcastically to Marissa. Without a second glance at his wife, he strode off toward one of the doors leading into a series of cubicle-like dressing rooms.

Marissa watched him go, lamenting the widening gulf separating them. Their ability to communicate, especially where their feelings were concerned, was reaching a new low.

"I'll let Dr. Wingate know you're here," the receptionist said.

Marissa nodded. Slowly she walked back to her seat and sat down heavily. Nothing was working out. She wasn't getting pregnant and her marriage was disintegrating before her eyes. She thought about all the business trips Robert had been taking of late. For the first time since she'd been married, Marissa wondered if he could be having an affair. Maybe that was the reason behind this sudden talk of not providing a sperm sample. Maybe he'd been giving samples out elsewhere.

"Mrs. Buchanan!" a nurse called from an open doorway, beckoning for Marissa to follow her.

Marissa got to her feet. She recognized the nurse, Mrs. Hargrave.

"Are you ready to harvest those eggs?" the woman asked brightly as she got a robe, a johnny, and slippers for Marissa. She had an English accent similar to Dr. Wingate's. Marissa had asked her about it once. She'd been surprised to learn that Mrs. Hargrave was Australian, not English.

"An egg retrieval is just about the last thing in the world I want to do just now," Marissa admitted with dejection. "I really don't know why I'm putting myself through this."

"Feeling a little depressed, are we?" Mrs. Hargrave asked as gently as she could.

Marissa didn't answer. She merely sighed as she

took the clothes from Mrs. Hargrave and started into the changing room. Mrs. Hargrave reached out and touched her shoulder.

"Anything you'd like to talk about?"

Marissa gazed up into the woman's face. There was warmth and sympathy in those gray-green eyes.

At first Marissa could only shake her head as she fought back tears.

"It's common for emotional problems to burden people involved with in-vitro," Mrs. Hargrave said. "But it usually helps to talk about it. It's been our experience that part of the problem is the isolation the couples feel."

Marissa nodded in agreement. She and Robert had been isolated. As the pressures mounted, they started avoiding friends, especially those with children.

"Has there been a problem between you and your husband?" Mrs. Hargrave asked. "I don't mean to pry, but we truly have found it best for people to be open."

Marissa nodded again. She looked at Mrs. Hargrave's understanding face. She did want to talk, and with a few tears that she wiped away with the back of her hand, she told her about Robert's initial refusal to cooperate that morning, and their consequent quarrel. She told Mrs. Hargrave she was beginning to think they would have to stop the infertility treatments.

"It's been pure hell for me," Marissa admitted. "And for Robert."

"I think it is safe to say that something would be wrong with you both if it weren't," Mrs. Hargrave said. "It's stressful for everyone, even the staff. But you've really got to learn to be more open. Talk to other couples. That will help you learn to talk to each other and to be aware of each other's limitations."

"We are ready for Mrs. Buchanan," another nurse called through the door to the ultrasound room.

Mrs. Hargrave gave Marissa a comforting squeeze on her shoulder. "You'd better get on with this," she said. "But afterwards I'll come back and we'll talk some more. How about it?"

"Okay," Marissa said, trying to muster some enthusiasm.

Fifteen minutes later, Marissa again found herself on her back in the ultrasound room, facing yet another painful and potentially risky procedure. She was lying supine with her legs straight out. In a few minutes her legs would be put up in the all-too-familiar stirrups. Then there would be the disinfectant, followed by the local anesthetic. She cringed at the thought.

The room itself seemed scary. It was a cold, forbidding, futuristic environment filled with electronic instruments, some of which Marissa recognized and some she didn't. Multiple cathode-ray screens were set into the instrumentation. Mercifully, the foot-long egg-retrieval needle was kept out of sight.

The nurse-technician who had brought Marissa

into the room was busy with preparations for the procedure. Dr. Wingate, who performed most of the clinic's infertility procedures including the in-vitro fertilization, had not yet arrived.

A knock on the door got the attention of the nurse-technician, who stepped over and opened it. Marissa turned her head to see Robert standing in the threshold.

Although the procedure room made him feel even more uncomfortable than it made Marissa feel, he forced himself to step into the high-tech room. He pointed over his shoulder for the nurse-technician's benefit. "Mrs. Hargrave said I could come in for a moment," he explained.

The nurse-technician nodded, motioned toward Marissa, then went back to her preparations.

Robert gingerly walked over to the ultrasound unit and looked down at his wife. He was careful not to touch any of the delicate instrumentation, or Marissa herself, for that matter.

"Well, I did it," he said as if he had accomplished some major task. "And now that my part's over, I'll be heading to the office. Unfortunately, because of the stitches, I'm later than I planned. So I've got to run. But I'll come back after the meeting and pick you up. If it looks like the meeting is going to run over, I'll call and leave word with Mrs. Hargrave. Okay?"

"Okay," Marissa said. "Thanks for providing a sample. I appreciate it."

Robert wondered if Marissa was being sarcastic. He couldn't detect any irony in her tone. "You're welcome," he said finally. "Good luck with the egg retrieval. Hope you get a full dozen." With a tentative pat on her shoulder, he turned and left the room.

Marissa felt tears welling up again, but she didn't know if they were from sadness or anger. She felt so terribly alone. Lately Robert had been so businesslike, even when it came to her. She was hurt that he could leave her to face such an ordeal alone.

The Robert of today seemed so different from the man she had married so blissfully only a few years ago. In so many ways he was telling her that business came first; it was his identity and his escape. A single tear ran down into her ear. She closed her eyes tightly, hoping to block out the whole world. It seemed that her life was falling apart and there was nothing she could do to stop it.

"Excuse me, Dr. Wingate," Mrs. Hargrave said, stopping the doctor on his way into the ultrasound room. "Could I have a brief word with you?"

"Is it important?" Dr. Wingate asked. "I'm late for Mrs. Buchanan."

"It's Mrs. Buchanan I want to discuss," Mrs. Hargrave said. She held her head back. She was a tall woman herself, almost six feet. Even so, she looked slight next to Dr. Wingate's impressive bulk.

"Is it confidential?" Dr. Wingate asked.

"Isn't everything confidential?" Mrs. Hargrave said with a sly smile.

"True enough," Dr. Wingate said. He briskly walked down the hallway to his office. They entered a back door directly from the corridor, bypassing his secretary. Wingate closed the door behind them.

"I'll be brief," Mrs. Hargrave said. "It's come to my attention that Mrs. Buchanan . . . actually, I should say Dr. Buchanan. You do remember that she is a doctor, don't you?"

"Yes, of course," Dr. Wingate said. "Dr. Carpenter told me that two years ago. It was a surprise, I recall. Dr. Carpenter only knew through reading it in the *Globe*."

"I think the fact that she is a physician herself should be kept in mind," Mrs. Hargrave said. "As you know, doctors can be difficult patients at times."

Dr. Wingate nodded.

"At any rate," Mrs. Hargrave continued, "I believe she is suffering from a certain amount of depression."

"That's not unexpected," Dr. Wingate said. "Almost all of our in-vitro patients experience depression at one time or another."

"There is a suggestion of marital discord as well," Mrs. Hargrave said. "Even some talk about stopping after this cycle."

"Now that would be unfortunate," Dr. Wingate agreed, interested at last.

"Depression, marital problems, and the fact

that she is a physician make me think we should perhaps alter the treatment protocol."

Dr. Wingate leaned against his desk, hooking a thumb under his chin and resting his nose on an index finger while he pondered Mrs. Hargrave's suggestion. She definitely had a point, and flexibility had always been an approach he'd advocated.

"She also witnessed the scene with Rebecca Ziegler," Mrs. Hargrave added. "That can only have contributed to her emotional distress. I'm very concerned about her."

"But she has been stable up until now," Dr. Wingate said.

"That's true," Mrs. Hargrave replied, "I suppose it is the problem of her being a physician that makes me feel uneasy."

"I appreciate your concern," Dr. Wingate said. "It's attention to detail that makes the Women's Clinic so successful. But I think it will be safe to continue as usual with Dr. Blumenthal-Buchanan. She'll tolerate another couple of cycles, but perhaps it would be wise to recommend some in-house counseling for both her and her husband."

"Very well," Mrs. Hargrave said. "I'll suggest it to her. But as a physician, she might be resistant to such an idea."

With the matter decided, Dr. Wingate moved to the door and opened it for Mrs. Hargrave.

"Speaking of Rebecca Ziegler," said Mrs. Hargrave, "I trust she's being well taken care of?"

"She's reading her records as we speak," Dr. Wingate said, following Mrs. Hargrave into the hallway. "Unfortunately, it will be upsetting for her."

"I can well imagine," Mrs. Hargrave said.

3

MARCH 19, 1990
11:37 A.M.

DOROTHY FINKLESTEIN hurried under the overhead walkway and entered the brick courtyard of the Women's Clinic. As usual, she was late. She was always late. Her appointment for her annual exam had been scheduled for eleven-fifteen.

A sudden gust of wind caught the edge of her hat and lifted the brim. She reached up just in time to prevent the hat from sailing off her head. At the same time, something above caught her eye. A high-heeled shoe was plummeting toward her. It landed near her, falling into a planter filled with rhododendrons.

Despite her haste, Dorothy stopped as her eye traveled upward, tracing the shoe's trajectory. At the very top story of the Women's Clinic, six floors up, her gaze became transfixed by what looked like a woman sitting on a window ledge, her legs dangling over, her head tilted down as if she were studying the pavement below. Dorothy blinked, hoping her eyes were deceiving her, but the image remained: it wasn't her imagination, it was a woman on the ledge—a young woman!

Dorothy's blood ran cold as she watched as the woman seemed to inch forward, then pitch head-first in a slow somersault. The woman fell like a life-sized doll, picking up speed as she passed each successive floor. She landed in the same planter as her shoe, hitting with a dull thump like a heavy book dropped flat on a thick rug.

Dorothy winced empathetically, as if her own body had suffered the fall. Then she screamed as the reality sank in. Pulling herself together, she ran toward the planter without any idea of what she would do. As a buyer for a large Boston department store, she had scant training in emergency first aid, although she had attended a CPR course in college.

A few passersby responded to Dorothy's scream. After recovering from their initial shock, several followed her to the planter. Someone else ducked back into the clinic to sound an alarm.

Arriving at the edge of the planter, Dorothy stared down in horror. The woman was on her back. Her eyes were open and they stared sky-ward, focused on nothing. Not knowing what else to do, Dorothy bent down in the bushes and started to give mouth-to-mouth resuscitation. It was apparent to her that the woman was not breathing. She blew into the woman's mouth several times, but she had to stop. Turning her head, she vomited her coffee-break blueberry muffin. By then, a doctor in a crisp white jacket had arrived.

36

"Of course I remember you," Dr. Arthur said. "You were the woman who was so sensitive to ketamine. How could I forget?"

"I just wanted to be sure you wouldn't use it again," Marissa said. She hadn't recognized Dr. Arthur at first since he'd not treated her since the biopsy. But after he'd started her IV, something jogged her memory.

"All we need today is a little Valium," Dr. Arthur reassured her. "And I'm going to give you a little right now. This should make you pretty sleepy."

Marissa watched him inject the drug into the side port of her IV. Then she rolled her head straight. Now that the egg retrieval was about to begin, her attitude about the procedure had changed from fifteen minutes earlier. She was no longer ambivalent.

As the Valium hit her system, Marissa's mind calmed, but she didn't sleep. She dwelt on the thought of her blocked tubes and what might have caused the blockage. Then she began to consider the different procedures she had undergone. She remembered how she felt waking up from the general anesthesia after her laparoscopy.

As soon as she was lucid, Dr. Carpenter had told her that her tubes appeared so scarred that microsurgery was totally out of the question. He said that all he'd been able to do was take a biopsy. He let her know then that her only chance for a baby was in-vitro fertilization.

"Are we ready?" a booming voice called.

Marissa lifted her head, raised heavy eyelids, and looked up at the bearded face of Dr. Wingate. Lying back, she tried to dissociate herself from her body to cope with her anxiety. Her mind wandered back to her visit to Dr. Ken Mueller in the department of pathology at the Memorial after her laparoscopy. The Women's Clinic frequently sent some of their specimens to the Memorial to confirm their diagnoses. Marissa had been told that her fallopian tube biopsy had been forwarded there.

Hoping to maintain her anonymity, Marissa had searched for her slides herself. She knew that the Women's Clinic used her social security number as her case number.

Once Marissa had the slides, she sought out Ken. They'd been friends since medical school. She asked him to look at the microscopic sections for her, but didn't say they were hers.

"Very interesting," Ken said after a brief scan of the first slide. He sat back from the microscope. "What can you tell me about the case?"

"Nothing," Marissa said. "I don't want to influence you. Tell me what you see."

"Sort of a quiz, huh?" Ken said with a smile.

"In a way," Marissa said.

Ken went back to the microscope. "My first guess is that it's a section of fallopian tube. It looks as if it's been totally destroyed by an infectious process."

"Right on," Marissa said with admiration. "What can you say about the infection?"

For a few minutes Ken silently scanned the specimen. When he finally spoke, Marissa was stunned. "TB!" he announced, folding his arms.

"Tuberculosis?" Marissa almost fell off her chair. She'd expected nonspecific inflammation, never TB. "What makes you say that?" she asked.

"Look in the field," Ken told her.

Marissa gazed into the scope.

"What you are looking at is a granuloma," Ken said. "It's got giant cells and epithelioid cells, the sine qua non of a granuloma. Not a lot of things cause granulomas. So you have to think of TB, sarcoid, and a handful of funguses. But you'd have to put TB at the head of the list for statistical reasons."

Marissa felt weak. The idea that she had any of those diseases terrified her.

"Can you do any other stains to make a definitive diagnosis?" Marissa asked.

"Sure," Ken said. "But it would help to have some history on the patient."

"Okay," Marissa said. "She's a healthy Caucasian woman, mid-thirties, with a completely normal medical history. She presented with asymptomatically blocked fallopian tubes."

"Reliable historian?" Ken questioned as he chewed the inside of his lip.

"Completely," Marissa said.

"Negative chest X-ray?"

"Completely normal."

39

"Eye problems?"

"None."

"Lymph nodes?"

"Negative," Marissa said with emphasis. "Except for the blocked tubes, the patient is completely normal and healthy."

"GYN history normal?" Ken asked.

"Yup!" Marissa said.

"Well, that's weird," Ken admitted. "TB gets to a fallopian tube via the bloodstream or the lymphatics. If it's TB, then there has to be a nidus somewhere. And it doesn't look like fungus without some hyphae or something. I'd still say TB is the leading contender. Anyway, I'll do some additional stains . . ."

"Marissa!" called a voice, bringing Marissa back to the present. She opened her eyes. It was Dr. Arthur. "Dr. Wingate is about to inject the local anesthesia. We don't want you to suddenly jump."

Marissa nodded. Almost immediately she felt a number of points of stinging pain, but they faded quickly and she went back to her musing, remembering her panicked visit to an internist the same day that she'd seen Ken. But a complete work-up had failed to find anything wrong except for a positive PPD test, suggesting that she indeed had had TB.

Although Ken tried numerous other tests on Marissa's slide, he found no organisms, TB or otherwise. But he stuck by his original diagnosis of a tuberculous infection of the fallopian tube despite Marissa's inability to explain how she could have picked up such a rare illness.

"Dr. Wingate!" a harried voice called. Marissa's attention was again brought back to the present. She turned her head. Mrs. Hargrave was at the ultrasound-room door.

"Can't you see I'm busy, for chrissake?" Dr. Wingate snapped.

"I'm afraid there has been an emergency."

"I'm doing a bloody egg retrieval!" Dr. Wingate shouted, venting some of his frustration on Mrs. Hargrave.

"Very well," Mrs. Hargrave said as she backed out of the door.

"Ah, there we go!" Dr. Wingate said with satisfaction. His eyes were glued to the cathode-ray-tube screen.

"Want me to see what the emergency is?" Dr. Arthur asked.

"It can wait," Dr. Wingate said. "Let's get some eggs."

For the next half hour, time seemed to crawl. Marissa was sleepy but unable to sleep under the torturous probing.

"All right," Dr. Wingate said at last. "That's the last of the visible follicles. Let me take a look at what we've gotten."

Laying the probe aside and stripping off his gloves, Dr. Wingate disappeared with the nurse-technician into the other room to examine the aspirate under a microscope.

"Are you okay?" Dr. Arthur asked Marissa.

Marissa nodded.

Within a few minutes, Dr. Wingate came back into the room. He had a broad smile. "You were a very good girl," he said. "You produced eight fine-looking eggs."

Marissa breathed out audibly and closed her eyes. Although she was happy about getting eight eggs, it hadn't been a good morning. She felt drugged and exhausted and, with the stress of the procedure gone, Marissa soon lapsed into a troubled, drugged sleep. She was only vaguely aware of being moved to a gurney and being transported across the glass-enclosed walkway to the clinic's overnight ward. She woke up briefly to help switch herself from the gurney to a bed where she at last sank into a deeper, Valium-induced sleep.

Of all the sundry responsibilities and duties of running the Women's Clinic, Dr. Norman Wingate's heart rested firmly with his work associated directly with the biological part of the in-vitro fertilization unit. As an MD, PhD, cellular biology held the strongest intellectual appeal. And as he gazed at Marissa's ova through the lenses of his dissecting microscope, he was filled with pleasure and utter awe. There, within his field of vision, was the unbelievable potential of a new human life.

Marissa's eggs were indeed fine specimens, attesting to the expert administering of the hormones she'd been given during the ovarian hyperstimulation period. Dr. Wingate carefully inspected each of the eight eggs. They were all quite mature. Reverently, he placed them in a previously prepared, slightly pink culture medium within Falcon organ culture dishes. The dishes were then placed in an incubator that controlled the temperature and the gaseous concentrations.

Turning his attention to Robert's sperm, which had been allowed to liquefy, Dr. Wingate started the process of capitation. A perfectionist, he preferred to do all the cellular biology himself. The efficacy of in-vitro fertilization was as much an art of the individual investigator as it was a science.

"Dr. Wingate!" Mrs. Hargrave called, coming into the lab. "I'm sorry to bother you, but there's been another development with the Rebecca Ziegler case that needs your attention."

Dr. Wingate looked up from his work. "Can't you handle it?" he asked.

"It's the press, Dr. Wingate," Mrs. Hargrave said. "There's even a mobile TV news crew. You'd better come."

Reluctantly, Dr. Wingate looked at the flask containing Robert's sperm. He hated it when his bureaucratic responsibilities interrupted his biological work. But as the director of the clinic, he had little choice. He glanced up at the nurse-technician. "This is your chance," he said to her. "Go ahead and finish the capitation, the concentration, and the 'swim up.' You've seen me do it often enough, so go to it. I'll be back as soon as

43

I can." Then he turned and left the room with Mrs. Hargrave.

"Mrs. Buchanan! Hello! Mrs. Buchanan! Are you with us?" a friendly voice called.

From the depths of a disturbing dream, Marissa became aware of the voice calling to her. She had been dreaming that she was stranded in the middle of a barren landscape. At first she tried to incorporate the voice into the dream, but the nurse was determined to rouse her.

"Mrs. Buchanan, your husband is here!"

Marissa opened her eyes. She was staring directly into the broadly smiling face of a nurse. The nurse's name tag read "Judith Holiday." Marissa blinked to bring the rest of the room into focus. It was then she saw Robert standing behind the nurse, his Burberry coat over his arm.

"What time is it?" Marissa asked as she pushed herself up on an elbow. It felt as if she had only just gone to sleep. Surely Robert couldn't have had time to have his meeting and get back.

"It's four-fifteen in the afternoon," Judith said as she wrapped a blood pressure cuff around Marissa's arm and blew it up.

"How do you feel?" Robert asked.

"Okay, I guess," Marissa said. She wasn't entirely sure. The Valium was still in her system. Her mouth felt as dry as the desert landscape in her dream. She was amazed that the day had passed so quickly.

"Vital signs are okay," Judith said as she re-

44

moved the cuff. "If you're up to it, you're free to go on home."

Marissa swung her legs over the side of the bed. She felt a momentary dizzy sensation. It reoccurred when she slid off the bed and her feet touched the cold floor.

"How do you feel?" Judith asked her.

Marissa said she was all right, just feeling a little weak. She took a drink from a glass on the side table. She felt better.

"Your clothes are in the closet," Judith said. "Will you need any help?"

"I don't think so," Marissa said. She smiled weakly at the friendly and helpful nurse.

"Just yell if you do," Judith said as she backed out the door. She closed it, but not all the way. It stood ajar by about three inches.

"Let me," Robert said as he saw Marissa start toward the closet.

Twenty minutes later, Marissa found herself walking unsteadily down the front steps of the clinic. She got into the passenger side of Robert's car. Her body felt heavy and all she could think about was getting home and climbing into bed. She looked out at the rush-hour Harvard Square traffic with a sense of detachment. It was beginning to get dark. Most of the cars already had their lights on.

"Dr. Wingate told me your egg retrieval went very well," Robert said.

Marissa nodded and looked across at him. His

sharp profile was silhouetted against the evening lights. He didn't look at her.

"We got eight eggs," she said, emphasizing the "we." She studied him to assay his response. She was hoping he'd pick up on her meaning. Instead, he changed the subject.

"Did you hear about the tragedy at the clinic?"

"No!" Marissa said. "What tragedy?"

"Remember that woman who hit me?" Robert asked, as if Marissa could have forgotten. "The one carrying on in the waiting room when we arrived? She apparently committed suicide. Took a swan dive from the sixth floor into one of the flower beds. It was on the noon news."

"My God!" Marissa said. She remembered too well her own vivid identification with the woman. She had understood the woman's frustration, feeling it so frequently herself.

"Did she die?" Marissa asked, half hoping there was a chance that the woman had not succeeded.

"Instantly," Robert said. "Some poor patient on her way into the clinic saw the whole thing. Said the lady was sitting on a window ledge, then just dove headfirst."

"That poor woman," Marissa said.

"Which one?" Robert asked.

"Both," Marissa said, although she had been referring to Rebecca Ziegler.

"I'm sure you'll tell me this also isn't the right time to talk about this in-vitro protocol," Robert said. "But having that lady go berserk like she did underlines what I was feeling this morning.

Clearly we're not the only ones to feel the pressure. I really think we should stop this infertility stuff after this cycle. Think about what it's doing to your practice."

The last thing Marissa cared to think about was her pediatric practice. "I've spoken candidly with the director of my group and he understands," Marissa explained, not for the first time. "He's sympathetic to what I am going through, even if other people aren't."

"That's fine for the director to say," Robert said. "But what about your patients? They must be feeling abandoned."

"My patients are all being taken care of," Marissa snapped. In truth, she had been concerned about them.

"Besides," Robert added, "I've had it with this 'performing' stuff. Going into that clinic and getting that plastic cup is demeaning."

"Demeaning?" Marissa echoed, as if she'd not heard correctly. Despite the Valium, she found herself once again strongly provoked. After she had suffered that very day through a painful and risky procedure, she could hardly believe that Robert was making an issue of his brief, painless contribution to the process. She tried to restrain herself, but she couldn't help speaking her mind. "Demeaning? You find it demeaning? And how would you find spending a day flat on your back with your legs spread before an array of your colleagues while they poke and probe?"

"My point exactly," said Robert. "I didn't

mean to suggest this has been easy for you. It's been tough on us both. Too tough. Too tough for me, anyway. I want to call it quits. Now."

Marissa stared ahead. She was angry and she knew Robert was. They seemed to be quarreling constantly. She watched the road ahead as it sped toward her. They stopped at the toll booth on the entrance to the Mass. Pike. Robert slammed the coins into the hopper with an angry gesture.

After ten minutes of driving in silence, Marissa had significantly calmed down. She turned to Robert and told him that Mrs. Hargrave had come to visit her that afternoon. "She was very sympathetic," Marissa said. "And she had a recommendation."

"I'm listening," Robert said.

"She suggested that we avail ourselves of the counseling services that the clinic offers," Marissa said. "I think it might be a good idea. As you said, others in our circumstances have been feeling the pressures. Mrs. Hargrave told me many people have found counseling to be a great help." Although she'd not been excited about the suggestion initially, the more Marissa thought about it, especially seeing how she and Robert were getting along, the better it sounded. They needed help; that much was obvious.

"I don't want to see a counselor," Robert said, leaving no room for discussion. "I'm not interested in investing more time and money for someone to tell me why I'm fed up with a process that's guaranteed to make us unhappy and put us at each other's throats. We've spent enough time, effort, and money already. I hope you are aware that we've already spent over fifty thousand dollars."

They lapsed back into silence again. After a few miles, Robert broke it. "You did hear me, didn't you? Fifty thousand dollars."

Marissa turned to him, her cheeks flushed. "I heard you!" she snapped. "Fifty thousand, a hundred thousand. What does it matter if it is our only chance to have our child? Sometimes I don't believe you, Robert. It's not as if we are hurting. You had enough to buy this silly expensive car this year. I really wonder about your priorities."

Marissa faced around front again, angrily folding her arms across her chest and sinking into her own thoughts. Robert's business mentality was so contrary to her own, she wondered how they had ever become attracted to each other in the first place.

"Contrary to you," Robert said as they neared the house, "fifty thousand seems like a lot of money to me. And we have nothing to show for it save for some ill feelings and a disintegrating marriage. Seems a heavy price to pay, at both ends. I'm getting to hate that Women's Clinic. I've never felt comfortable there. And being attacked by a distraught patient didn't help. And did you see that guard?"

"What guard?" Marissa asked.

"The guard who came in with the doctors when the lady was carrying on. The Asian guy in the uniform. Did you notice he was armed?"

"No, I didn't notice he was armed!" Robert had an infuriating way of changing the subject with insignificant details. Here they were struggling with their relationship and their future, and he was thinking about a guard.

"He had a .357 Colt Python," Robert said. "Who does he think he is, some kind of Asian Dirty Harry?"

Switching on the light, Dr. Wingate entered his beloved lab. It was after eleven P.M. and the clinic was deserted. Across the street in the overnight ward and in the emergency room there was staff, but not in the main clinic building.

Taking off his coat, Dr. Wingate slipped on a clean white lab coat, then washed his hands carefully. He could have waited for morning, but after getting the eight superb mature eggs from Marissa that day, he was eager to check on their progress.

That afternoon, after having dealt with the unfortunate Rebecca Ziegler affair as best he could, he'd returned to the lab to find that the nurse-technician had done a fine job preparing the sperm. By two P.M. all eight eggs had been placed in a meticulously prepared insemination medium contained in separate organ culture dishes. To each dish Dr. Wingate had carefully added roughly 150,000 capitated, mobile sperm. The eggs and the sperm had then been co-incubated in 5% CO_2 with 98% humidity at 37 degrees Centigrade.

Turning on the light for his dissecting microscope, Dr. Wingate opened the incubator and removed the first dish. Placing it under the scope, he looked in.

There, in the middle of the microscopic field, was the beautiful egg, still surrounded by its corona cells. Looking more closely as he deftly handled a micropipette, Dr. Wingate experienced the thrill of creation as he observed two pronuclei within the ooplasm of the egg. The egg had fertilized and looked entirely normal.

Repeating the procedure with the other dishes, Dr. Wingate was extremely pleased to see that all the eggs had fertilized normally. There had been no polyspermic fertilization, in which more than one sperm penetrates the egg.

Working deliberately, Dr. Wingate transferred the fertilized oocytes to fresh growth medium containing a higher concentration of serum. Then all the fertilized eggs went back into the incubator.

When he was finished, Dr. Wingate went to the phone. Despite the hour, he called the Buchanan residence. He reasoned it was never too late to relay good news. After the fifth ring, he wondered if he'd made a mistake. By the sixth ring, he was about to hang up when Robert answered.

"Sorry to be calling so late," Dr. Wingate said.

"No problem," Robert said. "I was in my study. This is my wife's line."

"I have some good news for you folks," Dr. Wingate said.

"We can use a bit of that," Robert said. "Hold on, I'll wake Marissa."

"Maybe you shouldn't wake her," Dr. Wingate said. "You can tell her in the morning or I'll call back then. After what she's been through today, perhaps we should let her sleep."

"She'll want to hear," Robert assured him. "Besides, she can go right back to sleep. That's never been one of her problems. Hang on."

A few moments later, Marissa's tired voice came over the line as she picked up an extension.

"Sorry to wake you up," Dr. Wingate said, "but your husband assured me you wouldn't mind."

"He said you had some good news?"

"Indeed," Dr. Wingate said. "All eight eggs fertilized already. It was very quick, and I'm optimistic. Usually only eighty percent or so fertilize at best. So you got a particularly healthy crop."

"Wonderful," Marissa said. "Does this suggest the transfer is more likely to be successful?"

"I'll have to be honest," Dr. Wingate said. "I don't know if there is any association. But it can't hurt."

"What made it different this time?" Marissa asked. In the last cycle none of the eggs had fertilized.

"I wish I knew," Dr. Wingate confided. "In some respects, fertilization remains a mystifying process. We don't know all the variables."

"When will we do the transfer?" Marissa asked.

"In forty-eight hours or so," Dr. Wingate said. "I'll check the embryos tomorrow and see how they are progressing. As you know, we like to see some divisions."

"And you'll be transferring four embryos?"

"Exactly," Dr. Wingate said. "As we've already discussed, experience has shown that more than four has a higher risk of resulting in a multiple pregnancy without significantly raising the efficacy of the transfer. The other four embryos we'll freeze. With this many good eggs, you can have two transfers without having to undergo another hyperstimulation."

"Let's hope this transfer is successful," Marissa said.

"We'll all be hoping for the best."

"I was sorry to hear about the woman who killed herself," Marissa said. The tragedy had been on her mind all evening. She wondered how many cycles the poor Ziegler woman had endured. Having identified with the woman, she was already anticipating the psychological effect of yet another failure. Since there had been so many in the past, she had trouble being optimistic. Would another failure push her beyond her limits?

"It was a terrible tragedy," Dr. Wingate said. His previously enthusiastic tone became somber. "We were all crushed. The staff is usually adept at picking up such symptoms of depression. Until her outburst yesterday, we had no indication Rebecca Ziegler was so distraught. Apparently she and her husband had separated. We'd tried to get them into counseling, but they wouldn't go."

"How old was she?" Marissa asked.

"Thirty-three, I believe," Dr. Wingate said. "A tragic loss of a young life. And I'm concerned about its effect on other patients. Infertility is an emotional struggle for everyone involved. I'm sure it didn't help your state of mind seeing Mrs. Ziegler's outburst in the waiting room."

"I identified with her," Marissa admitted. Especially now, Marissa thought, hearing about the woman's marital problems. She and Rebecca were even close in age.

"Please don't say that," Dr. Wingate said. "On a happier note, let's look forward to a successful embryo transfer. It's important to stay positive."

"I'll try," Marissa said.

After hanging up the phone, Marissa was glad for having brought up the topic of the suicide. Merely having talked about it eased the impact to a degree.

Getting out of bed, Marissa pulled on her robe, and went down the hall to Robert's study. She found him seated at his computer console. He glanced up as Marissa came into the room.

"They all fertilized," Marissa said as she sat on a love seat below a wall of built-in bookshelves.

"That's encouraging," Robert said. He was looking at her over the top of his half-glasses.

"That's the first hurdle," she said. "Now all they have to do is to get one of the embryos to stick in my uterus."

"Easier said than done," Robert said. He was already looking back at his computer screen.

"Can't you be just a tiny bit supportive?" Marissa asked.

Robert looked back at her. "I'm starting to think that my being supportive and not telling you what I'm thinking has just encouraged you to keep beating your head against a wall. I've still got serious questions about this whole process. If it works this time, fine; but I don't want to see you setting yourself up for another disappointment." He turned back to his screen.

For a moment Marissa didn't say anything. As much as she hated to admit it at the moment, Robert was making sense. She was afraid of getting too hopeful herself.

"Have you thought any more about the idea of counseling?" Marissa asked.

Robert turned to Marissa a third time. "No," he said. "I told you, I'm not interested in going to a counselor. There has already been too much interference in our lives. Part of the problem for me is that we have lost our private life. I feel like a fish in a fishbowl."

"Dr. Wingate told me that one of the reasons the woman who killed herself today did so was because she and her husband did not seek counseling."

"Is this some kind of not-so-veiled threat?" Robert asked. "Are you telling me you're thinking of diving off the roof of the Women's Clinic if I don't agree to see one of their counselors?"

"No!" Marissa said heatedly. "I'm just telling you what he told me. The woman and her husband were having difficulties. Counseling was recommended. They didn't go. Apparently they broke up, which is one of the things that made the woman so upset."

"And counseling would have solved everything?" Robert asked sarcastically.

"Not necessarily," Marissa said. "But I doubt it would have hurt. I'm beginning to think that we should seek counseling whether we continue with the IVF or not."

"What do I have to say to you?" Robert asked. "I'm not interested in spending time and money on a counselor. I know why I'm upset and unhappy. I don't need someone else to tell me."

"And you don't want to try to work on it?" asked Marissa. She hesitated to say "together."

"I don't think a counselor is the way to work on it," Robert said. "You don't have to be a rocket scientist to know what is wrong. Anyone would feel stressed out by what we've been through in the past few months. Some things in life you have to deal with. Others you don't. And we don't have to deal with this infertility therapy anymore, if we so choose. At this point, I'd prefer to put it out of our lives."

"Oh, for goodness' sake!" Marissa said with disgust. She got up from the love seat and left Robert to his beloved computer and spreadsheets. She wasn't up to having another argument.

Marissa stomped down the hall and into the

bedroom, slamming the door behind her. It seemed that instead of getting better, everything was getting a whole lot worse.

4

MARCH 20, 1990
8:45 A.M.

Highly reactive ions called hydronium ions, which were nothing but hydrated protons, knifed through the delicate cell membranes of four of Marissa's developing embryos. The hydronium ions came in a sudden wave, catching the dividing cells off-guard. Buffer systems were mobilized to neutralize some of the initial reactive particles, but there were too many to combat. Slowly at first, then more rapidly, the pH of the cells began to fall. They were becoming acidic. Hydronium ions inevitably resulted wherever acid was added to an aqueous medium.

Within the very depths of the embryos, molecules of DNA were in the process of replicating themselves in preparation for another division. As weak acids themselves, they were terribly susceptible to the hydronium ions that swarmed in their midst. Their replication process continued, but with some difficulty: the enzymes responsible for the chemical reactions were also sensitive to acid. Soon replication mistakes started to occur. At first there were only a few errors, none that would have mattered in the long run given the

57

redundance of genes. But as more and more of the acid particles intervened, entire gene pools found themselves replicating sheer gibberish. The cells were still dividing, but it was only a matter of time. The mistakes had become lethal.

"It's beautiful!" Marissa cried. It was hard for her to comprehend that she was looking at the barest beginning of one of her children. The embryo, now at a two-cell stage, appeared transparent in the crystal-clear culture medium. Unfortunately, Marissa could not see the chaos that was occurring on a molecular level at the very moment she was admiring the cell's microscopic appearance. She thought she was seeing the beginnings of a new human life. What she was witnessing was the first steps of its death.

"Amazing, isn't it?" Dr. Wingate said. He was standing next to Marissa. She had come in unexpectedly that morning, asking if she could see one of her embryos. At first he had questioned the wisdom of granting such a request, but, remembering she was a doctor, he realized that it would be difficult to refuse, even though at this stage he didn't like anyone handling the embryos.

"I just cannot believe that little speck could become an entire person," Marissa said. She'd never seen a live two-celled embryo before, much less her own.

"I think we'd better get the little devil back into the incubator," Dr. Wingate said. He carefully carried the organ-culture dish to the incubator and

58

slid it onto the appropriate shelf. Marissa followed him, still awed. She saw that the dish had joined three others.

"Where are the other four?" she questioned.

"Over there," Dr. Wingate pointed. "In the liquid-nitrogen storage facility."

"They've already been frozen?" Marissa asked.

"I did it this morning," Dr. Wingate said. "Our experience has been that two-celled embryos do better than larger ones. I selected the four that I thought would tolerate the freezing and thawing the best. We'll keep them in reserve, just in case."

Marissa walked over to the liquid-nitrogen storage unit and touched its lid. The idea that four potential children were inside, frozen in a kind of suspended animation, gave her an eerie feeling. Such high-tech intrusion reminded her a little too much of *Brave New World.*

"Want to see inside?" Dr. Wingate asked.

Marissa shook her head. "I've taken too much of your time already," she said. "Thank you."

"My pleasure," Dr. Wingate said.

Marissa hurried from the lab. She went to the elevators and pushed the Up button. What had brought her to the clinic that morning was an appointment to see Linda Moore, a psychologist.

Between the final talk with Robert the night before and his decision to sleep in the guest room, Marissa had decided to call about counseling first thing in the morning. Whether Robert went or not, Marissa decided she needed to talk to a professional about the emotional stresses of IVF.

When she'd made the call, she thought she'd have to wait for an appointment, but Mrs. Hargrave had warned the staff psychologist that if Marissa called, she should be seen quickly.

Linda Moore's office was on the sixth floor, the very floor from which Rebecca Ziegler had jumped. The coincidence made Marissa a bit uncomfortable. As she walked down the hall, she morbidly tried to guess which window Rebecca had leaped from. She wondered if the woman's last straw had been something she'd gleaned from her clinic record. Marissa remembered that Rebecca had left the downstairs waiting room with the express purpose of reading her record.

"Go right in," the secretary said when Marissa identified herself.

As she moved toward the door, Marissa questioned if she truly wanted to go through with the appointment. It hardly took a professional to tell her IVF was stressful. Besides, she was embarrassed to have to make excuses why Robert wouldn't come with her.

"Go right in!" the secretary repeated, seeing Marissa pause at the door.

Realizing she no longer had a choice, Marissa entered the office.

The room was soothingly decorated with comfortably upholstered furniture and muted tones of green and gray. The window, however, looked out on the stark brick courtyard six floors below. Marissa wondered what Linda Moore had been doing when Rebecca made her leap into infinity.

"Why don't you close the door?" Linda suggested, gesturing with her free hand. She was young; Marissa guessed, in her late twenties. She also had an accent, just like Mrs. Hargrave.

"Have a seat and I'll be with you in a moment," Linda said. She was on the phone.

Marissa sat down on a dark green chair facing Linda's desk. The woman was rather petite, with short reddish hair and a sprinkling of freckles across the bridge of her nose. Her phone conversation was obviously with a patient, and it made Marissa uncomfortable. She tried not to listen. But it was soon over, and Linda turned her full attention to Marissa.

"I'm glad you called," she said with a smile.

Almost immediately, Marissa felt glad too. Linda Moore struck her as being both competent and warm. Encouraged by Linda, Marissa soon began to open up. Although Linda saw patients with a wide variety of problems at the Women's Clinic, Marissa learned that a good portion of her practice involved IVF. She understood exactly what Marissa had been going through, perhaps better than Marissa did herself.

"Basically, the problem is a Sophie's choice," Linda said halfway into the hour. "You have two equally unsatisfactory possibilities: you can accept your infertility without further treatment as your husband is suggesting and thereby live a life that is contrary to your expectations, or you can continue with the IVF, which will lead to continued stress on yourself and on your relationship, continued cost as your husband has pointed out, and continued stress for you both with no guarantee of success."

"I've never heard it put so succinctly," Marissa said.

"I think it is important to be clear," Linda said. "And honest. And being honest starts with yourself. You have to understand what your choices are so you can make rational decisions."

Gradually, Marissa began to feel more comfortable about revealing her feelings, and the surprising part was that by doing so, she became more self-aware. "One of the worst problems I have is that I can't fix things myself."

"That's true," Linda said. "With infertility it doesn't make any difference how hard you try."

"Robert used the term 'obsessed,'" Marissa admitted.

"He's probably right," Linda agreed. "And it's only made worse by the emotional ups and downs of IVF: the recurrent flipflop from hope to despair, grief to rage, and envy to self-reproach."

"What do you mean by envy?" Marissa asked.

"The envy you feel toward women who have children," Linda said. "The pain you might experience seeing mothers with kids in the grocery store. That kind of stuff."

"Like the anger I have at the mothers in my practice," Marissa said. "Especially those who I think are neglecting their kids in some way."

"Exactly," Linda said. "I can't think of a worse practice for an infertile woman than pediatrics.

Why couldn't you have specialized in something else?" Linda laughed and Marissa laughed with her. Pediatrics was a particularly cruel field for someone in her circumstances. It probably was one of the reasons she'd been avoiding going to work as much as possible.

"Anger and envy are okay," Linda said. "Let yourself feel them. Don't try to bottle them up just because you feel they are inappropriate."

Easier said than done, Marissa thought to herself.

"Before we break," Linda continued, "there are a couple of important points I want to make. We'll be going over all of this in more detail in future sessions, and I hope we can get Robert in here for one or two of them. But I want to warn you against letting this longed-for child become the embodiment of all your hope. Don't persuade yourself everything will be different if only you have this baby, because it doesn't work that way. What I want to suggest is that you set a realistic time frame for IVF attempts. As I understand it, you are on your fourth. Is that correct?"

"That's right," Marissa said. "Tomorrow I'll have the embryo transfer."

"Statistically, four is probably not enough," Linda said. "Perhaps you should think of setting eight tries as a cutoff. Here at the Women's Clinic we have a very high success rate around the eighth attempt. If after eight you haven't achieved pregnancy, then you should stop and consider other options."

"Robert is talking about other options now," Marissa countered.

"He will be more willing to be cooperative if he knows you've established a cutoff point—that this ordeal won't go on forever," Linda said. "That's been our experience. In every couple there is one who is more committed to the process than the other. Give him a little time. Respect his limitations as well as your own."

"I'll see what I can do," Marissa said. Considering Robert's latest words on the subject, she wasn't optimistic.

"Are there any other issues you'd like us to concentrate on?" Linda asked.

Marissa hesitated. "Yes," she said at last. "We mentioned guilt briefly. That's a big problem for me. Perhaps because I'm a doctor, it has bothered me that I haven't been able to find out how I got the infection that blocked my fallopian tubes."

"I can understand," Linda said. "It's natural to think that way. But we'll have to try to change your thinking. The chance that any past behavior was the cause is infinitesimally small. It's not as if it were VD or anything."

"How do I know?" Marissa asked. "I feel as if I have to find out. It's become an increasingly important issue for me."

"All right, we'll be sure to talk more about it." Opening up the scheduling book on her desk, Linda made a second appointment for Marissa. Then she stood up. Marissa did the same.

"I'd like to make one more suggestion," Linda

said. "I've got the distinct impression that you've been experiencing a good deal of isolation as a result of your infertility."

Marissa nodded, this time in genuine agreement.

"I'd like to encourage you to give Resolve a call," Linda continued. She handed a card with a telephone number to Marissa. "You might have heard of the organization. It's a self-help support group for people with infertility problems. I think you would benefit from the contact. They talk about the same issues you and I have been discussing. It will be reassuring to realize that you are not alone in all this."

Leaving the psychologist's office, Marissa felt pleased that she'd made the effort. She felt a hundred times better about the session than she'd imagined she would. She looked at the card with the Resolve phone number on it. She even felt positive about calling the organization. She'd heard about it before, but had never seriously thought of calling, in part because she was a physician. She had always assumed that the main purpose of the group was to explain the scientific aspects of infertility to lay people. That Resolve dealt with emotional aspects of infertility was news.

Riding down in the elevator, Marissa realized she'd forgotten to ask Linda about Rebecca Ziegler. She made a mental note to do it at their next session.

From the Women's Clinic, Marissa went to her

pediatric group. Robert had been right. Her practice was in disarray. Given her frequent absences, her secretary, Mindy Valdanus, was being used as a "float" to cover for other secretaries who were on vacation. Marissa wasn't surprised to find Mindy's desk empty when she passed by on her way to her office.

On her own desk, Marissa found a pile of unopened mail as well as a fine layer of dust. Hanging up her coat, Marissa called Dr. Frederick Houser, the senior partner of the group. He could see her, so she went directly up to his office.

"I have an embryo transfer scheduled for tomorrow," Marissa told her mentor once they were seated in the conference room. "It might be the last cycle if my husband has his way."

Dr. Houser was an old-school physician. He was a large, portly man, mostly bald save for a ring of silver hair that ran around the back of his head. He wore wire-rimmed glasses and an ever-present bow tie. He had a warm, generous air about him that made everyone feel comfortable in his presence, from patients to colleagues.

"But if it is not successful," Marissa continued, "and if I can smooth things out with Robert, we'll try a few more. But no more than eight. So one way or another, I'll be back to normal within half a year at most."

"We wish you the best," Dr. Houser said. "But we will have to lower your salary again. Of course that will change as soon as you start contributing significantly to the group's income."

"I understand," Marissa said. "I appreciate your patience with me."

Back in her office, Marissa took out the card Linda had given her and called the number. A friendly female voice answered.

"Is this Resolve?" Marissa asked.

"Sure is," the woman answered. "I'm Susan Walker. What can I do for you?"

"It was suggested I give you people a call," Marissa said. "I'm involved with the in-vitro fertilization unit at the Women's Clinic."

"Staff or patient?" Susan asked.

"A patient," Marissa said. "I'm on my fourth cycle."

"Would you and your husband like to come to our next meeting?" Susan asked.

"My husband probably will refuse to come," Marissa said, a bit embarrassed.

"Sounds familiar," Susan said. "It happens with most couples. Husbands are reluctant until they come for one session. After that, most of them love it. That's what happened with my own husband. He'll be happy to call your husband to talk to him. He's fairly persuasive."

"I don't think that would be a good idea," Marissa said quickly. She could just imagine Robert's response if a stranger called up about a self-help infertility group. "I'll speak with him myself. But if he doesn't come, would it be awkward if I came by myself?"

"Heavens, no!" Susan said. "We'd love to have you. You'll have plenty of company. There are a number of women currently going through IVF. Several of them will be solo as well." She then gave Marissa the date and the directions.

Hanging up the phone, Marissa hoped the experience would be as rewarding as the session with Linda Moore. Although she had her doubts, she was willing to give it a try, mainly because of Linda's recommendation. Donning a short white coat, Marissa went down to the main walk-in clinic area to try to earn some of the small salary she was still receiving.

After seeing a handful of children with runny noses, middle ear infections, and sore throats, Marissa found herself in an examination cubicle with an eight-month-old infant and a disinterested teenage mother.

"What's the problem?" Marissa asked, even though she could see well enough herself. The child had a number of suppurating sores on his back and arms. In addition, he was filthy dirty.

"I dunno," the mother said as she cracked her gum and stared around the room. "The kid cries all day long. He never shuts up."

"When was the last time you bathed this infant?" Marissa demanded as she looked at the pustules. She guessed it was staph.

"Yesterday," the mother said.

"Don't give me that," Marissa snapped. "This child hasn't been bathed in a week, if then."

"Maybe it was a few days ago," the mother admitted.

Marissa was livid. She was tempted to tell the

girl she wasn't fit to be a mother. Resisting the impulse, she buzzed one of the nurses and asked her to come to the examination room.

"What's up?" Amy Perkins asked.

Marissa could not bring herself to look at the mother. She only gestured in her direction. "This child needs to be bathed," she told Amy. "Also, these open sores need to be cultured. I'll be back."

Stepping from the examination room, Marissa went into the deserted supplies closet. She put her face in her hands, fighting back tears. She was disgusted with her lack of control. It was scary to be this close to the edge. She could have hit that girl. It made the discussion she'd just had with Linda Moore seem a lot less academic.

For the first time she wondered if she should continue seeing patients in this hyperemotional state.

"Why don't we go out for dinner?" Robert suggested after coming home late as usual from his office. "Let's go to that Chinese restaurant. We haven't been there for months."

Marissa thought it was a fine idea to get out of the house. She wanted to talk to Robert, particularly after he'd slept in the guest room the night before. That had been a disturbing first. Besides, she was starved and Chinese food sounded particularly appetizing to her.

After he'd taken a quick shower, they climbed into Robert's car and headed into town. Robert seemed in good spirits, which Marissa thought was a good sign. He was pleased about a deal that he'd struck that day with European investors concerning building and managing retirement-nursing homes in Florida. Marissa listened with half an ear.

"I went to see the counselor at the Women's Clinic today," Marissa said when Robert's story came to an end. "She was even more helpful than I'd anticipated."

Robert didn't respond. Nor did he look at her. Marissa could sense immediate resistance to her turning the subject of their conversation to their infertility problems.

"Her name is Linda Moore," Marissa persisted, "and she's very good. She's hopeful that you will come in for at least one session."

Robert glanced at Marissa, then back at the road. "I told you yesterday, I'm not interested," he said.

"It might be helpful for us," Marissa added. "One thing that she suggested was deciding in advance how many cycles we are willing to try before giving up. She says it is less stressful knowing that the process is not open-ended."

"How many did she suggest?" Robert asked.

"Eight," Marissa answered. "Four isn't enough to take advantage of the statistics."

"That's eighty thousand dollars," Robert said.

Marissa couldn't answer. Was money always on his mind? How could he reduce a child to a simple dollar value?

They traveled in silence for a while. Marissa's

interest in talking with Robert cooled, yet she still wanted to bring up the issue of his sleeping in the guest room. She had to say something.

Nearing the restaurant, Robert had no trouble finding a parking place. As Marissa opened her door, she found the courage to ask him about it. She discovered Robert wasn't in the mood to discuss it.

"I need a vacation from all this," he said irritably. "I've been telling you that this in-vitro stuff is driving me crazy. If it's not one thing, then it's something else. Now it's this counseling garbage!"

"It is not garbage!" Marissa snapped.

"There you go again," Robert said. "Lately I can't talk to you without you flying off the handle."

They stared at each other over the top of Robert's car. After a moment of silence, Robert changed the subject again by saying, "Let's eat."

Disgusted, Marissa followed him into the restaurant.

The China Pearl was run by a family who had recently moved from Chinatown to Boston's suburbs. The restaurant's decor was typical: simple Formica-topped tables and a couple of ceramic red dragons. By that late hour only four or five of the twenty or so tables were still occupied.

Marissa sat down in a chair facing the street. She felt horrible. All of a sudden she wasn't hungry anymore.

"Good evening," said the waiter as he handed

them menus. Marissa glanced up at the man as she took the long, plastic-coated menu.

Robert asked her if she'd like to split an appetizer. But before she could respond, Marissa felt cold sweat break out all over her body. In a flash, she was back at the Women's Clinic having her cervical biopsy. The vision was starkly vivid, as if she were actually there again.

"Get him away from me," yelled Marissa. She leaped to her feet and tossed the menu aside. "Don't let him touch me. No!" she screamed, as illusion and reality merged.

In her mind's eye, Marissa saw the face of Dr. Carpenter come up between her sheet-draped knees, having been transformed into a demon. His eyes were no longer blue. They were distorted and shiny, like cold, black onyx.

"Marissa!" Robert shouted, feeling a mixture of concern, shock, and embarrassment. Other diners had paused to cast startled looks in Marissa's direction. Robert stood and reached for her.

"Don't touch me!" she shouted again. She knocked Robert's hand away from her. Spinning on her heels, she fled from the restaurant, banging open the door.

Robert chased after her, practically tackling her outside the door. Grabbing her by the shoulders, he shook her hard. "Marissa, what's wrong with you?"

Marissa blinked several times as if waking from a trance.

"Marissa?" Robert yelled. "What's going on? Talk to me!"

"I don't know what happened," Marissa said groggily. "All at once I was back at the clinic having a biopsy. Something keyed off a replay of the bad trip I'd had from ketamine." She glanced back into the restaurant. People were at the window, staring out at her. She felt foolish and embarrassed as well as scared. It had been so real.

Robert put his arms around her. "Come on," he said. "Let's get out of here."

He walked her to the car. Marissa held back, her mind frantically trying to find some answers. She'd never lost control to such a degree. Never. What was happening to her? Was she going crazy?

They climbed into the car. Robert didn't start it immediately. "Are you sure you're all right?" he asked. The episode had unnerved him.

Marissa nodded. "At this point I'm just scared," she said. "I've never experienced anything like that. I don't what set if off. I know I've been overly emotional lately, but that hardly seems like an explanation. I was hungry, but I certainly can't blame it on that. Maybe it was that pungent smell in there. The nerves of smell connect directly with the limbic system in the brain." Marissa was searching for a physiological explanation so she wouldn't have to probe for a psychological one.

"I'll tell you what it says to me," Robert said. "It tells me you've been taking too many drugs. All those hormones can't be good for you. I think it is just one more sign we should stop this in-vitro nonsense. Pronto."

Marissa didn't say anything. She was scared enough to think that perhaps Robert was right.

5

"WANT TO flip to see who does the incision?" Ken Mueller said to Greg Hommel, the junior pathology resident who had been assigned to him for a month's rotation doing postmortems. Ken was particularly pleased with Greg. The kid was eager and smart as a whip. Ken smiled to himself calling Greg a kid; the guy was only five years younger than himself.

"Heads I win, tails you lose," Greg said.

"Flip," Ken said, already engrossed in the chart. The patient was a thirty-three-year-old woman who'd fallen six stories into a rhododendron planter.

"Tails!" Greg called out. "You lose." He laughed happily.

Greg loved doing posts. Whereas some of the other junior residents hated it, he thought it was a gas; a detective story wrapped up in the mystery of a body.

Ken didn't share Greg's enthusiasm for posts,

74

but he accepted his teaching responsibilities with equanimity, especially with a resident like Greg. Yet looking at the patient's chart, he felt a little irritated. It had been well over twenty-four hours since the patient's death, and Ken liked to do posts as soon as possible. He thought he was able to learn more.

The patient in this case had been brought to the Memorial by ambulance for a brief resuscitation attempt but the woman had been declared DOA. Then the body had sat in cold storage. It was supposed to have been sent to the medical examiner's office, but between a rash of shootings and other trauma, the ME had been swamped. Finally, a request had come through for them to do the post at the Memorial and Ken's chief had gladly agreed. It was always politically wise to stay on the ME's good side. You never knew when a return favor would be needed.

With his gloved left hand providing counter-traction, Greg was about to make the typical Y-shaped autopsy incision when Ken told him to hold up.

"Have you gone over the chart?" Ken asked.

"Of course," Greg said, almost hurt by the implication.

"So you know about this infertility stuff?" Ken asked while he was still reading. "The in-vitro attempts and the blocked tubes."

Blocked tubes had rung a bell, and Ken recalled Marissa's visit.

"Yup, and she looks like a pincushion because of it," Greg said.

Ken glanced at the body as Greg pointed to the multiple hormone-injection sites as well as the multiple bruises where blood had been drawn to measure estrogen levels. "Ouch," Ken said, looking down.

"And here's a fresh one," Greg said, pointing to the crook of the left elbow. "See the heme staining under the skin? She had blood drawn within hours of her jumping out the window. Couldn't have been from our ER. She was dead when she arrived."

Slowly, the doctors' eyes met. They were thinking the same thought. The patient certainly wasn't a drug addict. "Maybe we should extend the toxicology screen," Greg said ominously.

"Just what I was about to suggest," Ken said. "Remember, we're being paid to be suspicious."

"*You're* being paid," Greg laughed. "As a resident, my salary is more like alms."

"Oh, come on!" Ken said. "When I was at your stage . . ."

"Spare me," Greg said, holding the knife aloft. He laughed. "I've already heard what medicine was like in medieval times."

"What about the evidence of the trauma from the fall?" Ken asked.

Rapidly, Greg ticked off the external signs of impact. It was apparent that both legs were broken, as was the pelvis. The right wrist was also bent at an abnormal angle. The head, however, was intact.

"All right," Ken said, "cut away."

With a few deft strokes, Greg used the razor-sharp knife to cut through the skin, exposing the omentum-covered intestines. Then, with large clippers, he cut through the ribs.

"Uh-oh!" Greg said, lifting off the manubrium, or breastbone. "We got some blood in the chest cavity."

"What does that suggest?" Ken asked.

"I'd say aortic rupture," Greg said. "Six stories could have generated the two thousand pounds of force necessary."

"My, my," Ken teased, "you must be doing some extracurricular reading."

"Occasionally," Greg admitted.

Carefully, the two men extracted the blood from both lung cavities. "Maybe I'm wrong about the aortic rupture," Greg said, staring at the graduated cylinder when they were done. "Only a few hundred cc's."

"I don't think so," Ken said. He withdrew his hand from inside the chest cavity. "Feel along the aortic arch."

Looking up at the ceiling as he concentrated on feel, Greg palpated along the aorta. His finger slipped inside. It was an aortic rupture, all right.

"You have promise as a pathologist after all," Ken said.

"Thanks, all-seeing, all-knowing Karnak the Magnificent," Greg joked, though he was obviously pleased with the compliment. He turned his attention to the evisceration of the corpse. But as he worked, his forensic mind was beginning to set off alarm bells in his head. There was something wrong with this case; something very wrong.

Having gone through an embryo transfer before, Marissa knew what to expect. There wasn't much pain involved, especially in comparison with the myriad procedures she'd been enduring over the year, but it was still an uncomfortable and humiliating exercise. To keep her uterus in a dependent position, she had to lie prone with her knees raised to her chest and with her rear end sticking up in the air. Although she had a sheet draped over her, Marissa felt completely exposed. The only people present were Dr. Wingate, his nurse-technician, Tara MacLiesh, and Mrs. Hargrave. But then the door opened and Linda Moore came in. The fact that people could come in and out was part of the reason Marissa felt so vulnerable.

"It's important for you to be relaxed," Linda said, positioning herself near Marissa's head. She patted Marissa's shoulder. "I want you to think relaxing thoughts."

Marissa knew the therapist meant well, but telling her to think relaxing thoughts seemed absurd. She hardly saw how it would help. And it was particularly hard to relax knowing Robert was outside waiting. Marissa had been surprised he'd come with her that morning since he'd slept in the guest room again.

"Everything is ready," Dr. Wingate said, keeping Marissa informed, as usual. "And just like we did last time, the first thing we have to do is assure asepsis."

Marissa felt the sheet drawn back. Now she was literally exposed. She closed her eyes as Linda continued to drone on about relaxing. But Marissa couldn't relax. So much was riding on this transfer, maybe even her marriage. Robert had accompanied her to the clinic, but neither of them had said a single word through the entire drive from Weston to Cambridge.

"First the sterile speculum," Dr. Wingate said. A few seconds later, she felt the instrument. "Now I will be rinsing with the culture medium," Wingate continued.

Marissa felt the rush of fluid inside her. Then she felt a hand on her shoulder. Opening her eyes, she saw that Linda Moore's freckled face was inches from her own. "Are you relaxed?" Linda asked her.

Marissa nodded, but it was a lie.

"We're ready for the embryos now," Dr. Wingate told Tara. Tara went back into the lab. Then to Marissa, Dr. Wingate said: "You might feel a tiny bit of cramping with the insertion, but don't worry. It will be just like last time."

Marissa would have preferred he'd not made the comparison: last time the transfer had not worked. She heard Tara come back into the room. Marissa could picture the Teflon catheter, called a Tomcat.

"This is it," Dr. Wingate continued.

"Remember to relax," Linda said.

"Think of a fine, healthy baby," Mrs. Hargrave said.

Marissa felt a strange deep sensation like a pain, but not strong enough to be called a pain.

"We should be within one centimeter of your uterine fundus," Dr. Wingate said. "I'm injecting now."

"Breathe deeply," Mrs. Hargrave said.

"Relax," Linda suggested.

Despite her hopes, Marissa didn't feel optimistic.

"Perfect," Dr. Wingate said. "I'm coming out now."

Marissa held her breath as she experienced an extremely mild cramp.

"Now don't move until we ascertain that the embryos have all been extruded from the catheter," Dr. Wingate said. He and Tara disappeared into the lab.

"You feel okay?" Mrs. Hargrave asked.

"Fine," said Marissa, as self-conscious as ever, always concerned someone else was about to barrel through the door.

"Now that it's over," Linda said, giving Marissa's shoulder another pat, "I'll be going. I think I'll have a word with your husband on my way out."

Good luck, Marissa thought. She didn't think her husband would be approachable that day.

Dr. Wingate returned just as Linda was departing.

"All the embryos were planted," Dr. Wingate said. Marissa felt the speculum being removed. He tapped her gently on the top of her rump. "Now you can lower yourself to your tummy. But don't roll over. Just like the previous transfer: I want you to remain on your stomach for three hours, then you can roll over on your back for an hour. Then you'll be free to go." He pulled the sheet over Marissa's lower half.

Mrs. Hargrave released the brakes on the gurney and started pushing. Tara held open the door to the hallway. Marissa thanked Dr. Wingate.

"You're very welcome, love," he said, his Australian accent suddenly more pronounced. "We'll all be keeping our fingers crossed."

As they came abreast of the waiting room, Marissa heard Mrs. Hargrave call out Robert's name. The conversation with Linda must have been brief, as she was already gone.

Robert fell in beside them as Mrs. Hargrave pushed Marissa across the glassed walkway to the overnight ward.

"I was told everything went smoothly," he said.

"We're very optimistic," Mrs. Hargrave said. "They were fine eggs and fine embryos."

Marissa didn't say anything. She could tell Robert wasn't happy. Linda had no doubt irritated him.

The room that Marissa was placed in for her four-hour wait was pleasant enough. There were yellow curtains over windows that looked out onto the Charles River. The walls were a restful light green color.

Marissa was gingerly transferred from the gurney to the bed. Following orders, she lay quietly on her abdomen, her head to the side. Robert sat in a vinyl chair facing her.

"You feel okay?" he asked.

"As well as can be expected," Marissa said evasively.

"You'll be all right?" he asked.

Marissa could tell he was impatient to go. "All I'm doing is lying here," she told him. "If you have things to do, please, go do them. I'll be fine."

"You're sure?" Robert stood up. "I suppose if you are comfortable, there are some things I ought to attend to."

Marissa could tell he was grateful to be excused. Before he left he gave her a quick peck on the cheek.

The way she'd been feeling lately, Marissa was initially more comfortable left alone. But as the hours crawled by, she started to feel lonely, even abandoned. She began to look forward to the infrequent visits by one of the Women's Clinic staff who dropped by to check on her every now and then.

When four hours had passed, Mrs. Hargrave came back to help her dress. At first, Marissa was reluctant to stand up, fearing she would spoil the transfer, even though the prescribed time had gone by. Mrs. Hargrave was nothing but encouraging.

Before Marissa left the clinic, Mrs. Hargrave advised her to take it easy for the next few days. She also told her to avoid sex for a little while.

No problem there, Marissa thought forlornly, especially if Robert continued to sleep in the guest room. She couldn't remember the last time the two of them had had sex.

Marissa arranged for a cab to come pick her up. The last thing she wanted to do was call Robert for a ride.

She spent the remainder of the day resting. At seven o'clock she watched the news, keeping an ear out for the sound of Robert's car in the driveway. By eight o'clock she began eyeing the phone. At eight-thirty she broke down and called his office.

Marissa let the phone ring twenty-five times, hoping that he was there by himself and would eventually hear it even if it wasn't ringing in his private office. But no one picked up.

Hanging up the receiver, Marissa stared at the clock, wondering where Robert could be. She tried to tell herself he was probably on his way home. Marissa had promised herself she wouldn't cry. She was afraid it might somehow jeopardize the embryos. But as she sat alone in the dark waiting for Robert to come home at last, loneliness overcame her. Despite her best intentions, tears began to slide down her cheeks. Even if she was pregnant, at this point she wasn't sure it would be enough to save her marriage. With deepening despair, she wondered what was going to happen to her life.

Marissa exited from Storrow Drive onto Revere Street at the base of Beacon Hill. As usual, she felt anxious. It had been almost a week since her embryo transfer, and it was difficult for her to think of anything other than the question of whether she was pregnant or not. In just a few days she was scheduled to return to the Women's Clinic to have blood drawn for a test that would indicate whether or not the transfer had been successful.

While waiting for a red light, Marissa looked at the directions she'd written down when she'd spoken to Susan Walker about the Resolve meeting. She was supposed to take a right on Charles, then a left on Mt. Vernon, and another right on Walnut. The directions advised her to take any parking place she could find on Beacon Hill.

When the light turned green, Marissa turned right. But before she got to Mt. Vernon, she found a parking place. She took it.

Susan Walker's house turned out to be a cute little Georgian-style town house nestled among several others on picturesque Acorn Street.

The door was opened by an extremely attractive, dark-haired woman in her mid-thirties. She was exquisitely attired in a silk dress that immediately made Marissa feel underdressed. Marissa had worn wool slacks and a sweater.

"I'm Susan Walker," the woman said, extending her hand and shaking Marissa's firmly. Marissa told her her name.

"We're so glad you could come," Susan said as she gestured for Marissa to step into the living room.

In the living room, between twenty and thirty people were milling about, engaging in conversation. The impression was a normal cocktail party with a slight but obvious preponderance of women.

Playing the good hostess, Susan took Marissa around and introduced her to a number of the people present. But then the door chimed again and Susan excused herself.

To Marissa's surprise and relief, she was immediately put at ease. She had thought she would feel out of place, but she didn't at all. All the women seemed warm and friendly.

"And what do you do?" asked Sonya Breverton. Susan had just introduced her to Marissa before leaving to answer the door. Sonya had told Marissa that she was a stockbroker with Paine Webber.

"I'm a pediatrician," Marissa replied.

"Another doctor!" Sonya remarked. "It's reassuring that you professionals suffer along with the rest of us. There's another doctor here, an ophthalmologist. Wendy Wilson."

"Wendy Wilson!" Marissa exclaimed, her eyes immediately sweeping the room. She felt a surge of excitement. Could it be the Wendy Wilson she'd gone to Columbia Medical School with? Her eyes stopped on a woman across the room who was not much taller than herself, with short, sandy-blonde hair.

Marissa excused herself and began to weave her way through the people to her old friend. As she got closer, the impish, pixie-like features were immediately unmistakable.

"Wendy!" Marissa shouted, interrupting the woman in mid-sentence. Wendy turned her eyes to Marissa.

"Marissa!" Wendy cried, giving her a big hug. Wendy quickly introduced Marissa to the woman with whom she'd been speaking, explaining that Marissa was an old medical school chum she'd not seen since graduation.

After exchanging a few pleasantries, the other woman politely excused herself, suspecting they had a lot of catching up to do.

"When did you get to Boston?" Marissa demanded.

"I've been here for over two years. I finished my residency at UCLA, worked for several years at the hospital, then came east with my husband, who took a surgical position at Harvard. I'm at the Mass. Eye and Ear. What about you? When I first got back, I asked about you and was told you'd moved to Atlanta."

"That was just for a two-year stint at the CDC," Marissa explained. "I've been back for about three years." Quickly she filled Wendy in on her marriage, her practice, where she lived.

"Weston!" Wendy laughed. "We're neighbors.

86

We live in Wellesley. Hey, you're not here as tonight's lecturer, are you?"

"Afraid not," Marissa said. "How about you?"

"I wish," Wendy said. "My husband and I have been trying to have a child for two years now. It's been a disaster."

"Same with me," Marissa admitted. "I can't believe this. It takes being infertile to meet up with you. And here I was worried that I'd meet someone I knew."

"Is this your first Resolve meeting?" Wendy asked. "I've only been to five or so, but I've never heard your name."

"First one," Marissa admitted. "I'd always been reluctant to come, but recently a counselor recommended it."

"I've enjoyed it," Wendy said. "Problem is, I can't get my granite-headed husband here. You know how surgeons are. He hates to admit that somebody might have something to offer in the way of information or expertise."

"What's his name?" Marissa asked.

"Gustave Anderson," Wendy said. "And he's just what he sounds like: one of those white-blond Swedes from Minnesota."

"I can't get my husband, Robert, to get near anything that smacks of therapy," Marissa said. "He's no surgeon, but just as rock-headed."

"Maybe they can talk to each other," Wendy suggested.

"I don't know," Marissa said. "Robert doesn't like to think he's being manipulated. The therapist tried talking with him after my last transfer, but it only made things worse."

"Excuse me, everybody!" Susan Walker called out over the general din. "If everyone could find a seat, we'll get going."

Marissa and Wendy sat down on a nearby couch. Marissa was still full of questions for her old friend and had to force herself to be patient. She and Wendy had been quite close during medical school. The fact that they had lost touch was purely a function of geography and their busy careers. After the long forced isolation of infertility, Marissa was overjoyed to find such a former friend in whom she could confide.

But Marissa's patience paid off, and she soon found herself mesmerized by the meeting. A number of the women stood up and addressed the group, telling their own stories.

It was an emotional experience for Marissa as she heard story after story with which she could identify. When one woman confessed to screaming at a shopper in a grocery store who she thought was neglecting her children, Marissa nodded, remembering the teenage mother with the dirty child.

Even one of the husbands got up to talk, making Marissa particularly sorry that she'd been unable to get Robert to come. He talked about the stress from the male point of view, giving Marissa a slightly better appreciation of what Robert had been trying to tell her about his response to "performing."

One woman lawyer stood up and spoke of the need for couples going through unsuccessful IVF to grieve for their lost potential children. After eloquently outlining such couples' predicaments, she added quietly, "If there were formal supports for the infertiles' grief, maybe my friend and colleague Rebecca Ziegler would be with us tonight."

For a few moments, after the lawyer sat down, the room maintained a respectful silence. Clearly many had been touched by mention of the dead woman. When the next speaker got up, Marissa turned to Wendy.

"Was Rebecca Ziegler a frequent attendee of these meetings?" she asked.

"Yes, poor thing," Wendy said. "I even spoke with her at the last meeting. It was a shock to hear she'd killed herself."

"Had she been very depressed?" Marissa asked.

Wendy shook her head. "I never saw signs of it."

"I saw her the day she died," Marissa said. "In fact, she hit my husband."

Wendy looked at Marissa in surprise.

"It was at the Women's Clinic. She was out of control," Marissa explained. "Robert was trying to restrain her. The curious thing was that she didn't act depressed then either. She was angry, yes, but not depressed. Was she pretty calm in general?"

"Seemed to be every time I saw her," Wendy said.

"Weird," Marissa said.

"Time for a coffee break," Susan Walker announced after the final speaker. "Then we'll have tonight's guest give her talk. We are honored to have with us Dr. Alice Mortland from Columbia Medical Center in New York. She will be talking to us about the newest aspects of GIFT, or Gamete Intra-Fallopian Transfer."

Marissa looked at Wendy. "Are you interested in the lecture?" she asked.

"Not in the slightest," Wendy said. "With both my fallopian tubes stopped up, GIFT can't help."

"Holy Toledo!" Marissa exclaimed. "I've got the same problem: sealed tubes."

"My word," Wendy said with a short laugh of disbelief. "What are we, identicial twins? Let's pretend we're in medical school and skip the lecture. We could sneak down to that bar with the Cheers flag and catch up."

"Will we offend the hostess?" Marissa asked.

"Not Susan," Wendy assured her. "She'll understand."

Ten minutes later, Marissa and Wendy were seated opposite each other in low-slung vinyl chairs. They were at a large mullioned window that looked out on busy Beacon Street with the darkened Boston Garden beyond. In the light of the lamps, the grass was just starting to become green, one of the first signs of spring.

Both women ordered mineral water and laughed at each other. "No alcohol! Well, hope springs eternal," Wendy said.

"I had my fourth embryo transfer about a week ago," Marissa admitted.

"Another coincidence," Wendy said. "So did I. Only mine was my second. What program are you involved with?"

"Women's Clinic in Cambridge," Marissa said.

"I don't believe this," Wendy said. "I'm there as well. Dr. Wingate?"

"Yup!" Marissa said. "Dr. Carpenter is my regular GYN man. I have Dr. Wingate for in-vitro fertilization."

"I go to Megan Carter," Wendy said. "I've always preferred a woman gynecologist. But I had to go to Wingate since he runs the IVF show."

"It's amazing we haven't run into each other," Marissa said. "But then again, they are very good about the confidentiality side of things, which is one of the reasons I started using the clinic in the first place."

"My feelings too," Wendy said. "I could have gone to someone at the General, but I wasn't comfortable with that."

"Was it a shock to you when you discovered your fallopian tubes were sealed?" Marissa asked.

"Completely," Wendy said. "I'd never expected it. It was ironic, I thought, considering all the birth control precautions I took all through college and med school. Now I can't remember what it was like not to want a child."

"I feel the same way," said Marissa. "But I was even more surprised to learn the cause was TB salpingitis."

Wendy slammed her mineral water to the table. "These coincidences are getting spooky," she said. "I had the same diagnosis: granulomatous reaction consistent with tuberculosis. I even had a positive PPD skin test."

For almost a full minute the two women stared at each other over the table. This was too much of a coincidence to be believed.

With her epidemiologic training, Marissa was instantly suspicious. The parallels in their cases were extraordinary. And the only time their lives intersected was during medical school.

"Are you thinking what I'm thinking?" Wendy asked.

"Probably," Marissa said. "I'm wondering about those months we spent on that elective rotation at Bellevue. Remember those TB cases we saw, especially the drug-resistant ones? Remember they were thinking that there was an upswing in TB?"

"How could I forget?"

"Luckily my chest X-ray is perfectly clear," Marissa said.

"So's mine," Wendy said.

"I wonder if we are isolated cases or part of a bigger pattern. TB salpingitis is supposed to be rare, especially in a healthy nation like the United States." She shook her head. It didn't make sense.

"Why don't we go back to the Resolve meeting and ask if there is anybody else with the same diagnosis?" Wendy suggested.

"Are you serious? The chances are so small, they'd be negligible."

"I'm still curious," Wendy said. "Come on, it's close and we have a captive audience."

As they walked back toward Acorn Street, Marissa broached the subject of her marital situation. It was hard for her to talk about it, but she felt the need to discuss it with someone. She told Wendy that she and Robert were having serious problems.

"He's taken to sleeping in the guest room," Marissa confided. "And he refuses to see a therapist. He says he doesn't need someone to tell him why he's unhappy."

"A lot of us infertiles have marriage problems," Wendy said. "Especially those of us in in-vitro. It seems to go with the territory. Of course everybody deals with it differently. My husband, Gustave, has just transferred what little attention he used to give me to his work. He's always at the hospital. I practically never see him."

"Robert's doing that more and more," Marissa said. "Unless one of these embryos implants, I'm not all that optimistic we'll be able to weather the storm."

"You've come back!" Susan cried when she opened the door for Marissa and Wendy. "Just in time for dessert."

Wendy told Susan what they wanted to do. Susan took their coats, then preceded them into the living room, where guests were busily conversing in small groups as they ate chocolate cake.

"Can I have everyone's attention for one last time," Susan called out. She explained that Wendy had some questions for them.

Positioning herself in the middle of the room, Wendy introduced herself in case there was anyone who wasn't aware that she was a doctor. She then asked how many of the women present had blocked fallopian tubes as the cause of their infertility.

Three people raised their hands.

Looking at these three women, Wendy asked: "Have any of you been told that your tubes were sealed by tuberculosis or what looked like TB under the microscope?"

Each made a questioning gesture, raising their eyebrows. They weren't sure.

"Have any of you been advised to take a drug called isoniazid or INH?" Marissa asked. "It would have been suggested that you take it for months."

Two of the women raised their hands. Both said that they had been sent to their internists after their laparoscopies and that a drug was mentioned that they'd have to take for an extended period of time. In both instances, however, the drug was not given, and they'd been told to come back every three months.

Marissa wrote down their names and phone numbers: Marcia Lyons and Catherine Zolk. Both promised to inquire with their family doctors to find out for certain if the drug had been isoniazid.

Utterly astonished, Marissa took Wendy aside.

"This is unbelievable. I think we have four cases. But if these two women had TB, then our medical school rotation at Bellevue is off the hook."

"Four cases doesn't make a series," Wendy cautioned.

"But it is mighty suspicious," Marissa said. "Four cases of a rare disease in one geographical area. Besides, it sounds as if none of us has any signs of infection elsewhere. I think we are on to something. I'm going to follow up on it," Marissa vowed.

"Let's do it together," Wendy suggested.

"Wonderful," Marissa agreed. "The first step will be to take advantage of my contacts at the CDC. We can start that tonight. Where is your car?"

"It's over at the Mass. Eye and Ear Infirmary," Wendy said.

"Mine's closer," Marissa said. "I'll drive you to yours and you can follow me home. You game?"

"I'm game," Wendy said.

Saying their goodbyes and thanking their hostess, Marissa suddenly had an idea. She asked Susan if she knew the cause of Rebecca Ziegler's infertility.

"I think it was blocked tubes," Susan said after thinking for a moment. "I can't be sure, but I believe that's what it was."

"Do you happen to have her phone number?" Marissa asked.

"I believe I do," Susan said.

"Would you mind giving it to me?" Marissa asked.

Susan got the number from her study and gave it to Marissa.

"You aren't going to call Rebecca's husband, are you?" Wendy asked when they got to the street. "The poor man is probably in shock."

"I will if I have the courage," Marissa said. "Besides, I was told they'd separated."

"As if that would make much difference," Wendy said. "If anything, I would think that would make him feel worse, even responsible."

Marissa nodded.

On the drive home, Marissa's excitement rose. Four cases of isolated TB salpingitis took her case out of the realm of anomaly and suggested a possible trend of public health importance.

Marissa pulled directly into the garage, then exited through the garage door to meet Wendy, who'd parked in the driveway. They entered the house through the front door.

"Nice house," Wendy said as she followed Marissa down a corridor into her study.

"Think so?" Marissa said without enthusiasm. "It had been Robert's house before we were married. To tell you the truth, I've never liked it."

Marissa went straight to her Rolodex for Cyril Dubchek's home telephone number. "I'm calling one of the CDC department heads," Marissa explained. "We were involved for a little while during my last year at the CDC. He's quite an attractive man."

Marissa found the number and propped the file open with a letter opener.

"Didn't work out?" Wendy asked.

Marissa shook her head. "It was a stormy relationship from the start. The ironic part is that our major disagreement was over children. He'd had several before his wife died. He wasn't interested in any more. Obviously that was before I knew about my fallopian tubes."

Marissa punched the number on her telephone, then waited for the connection to go through. "It's quite a story," she said. "We were at loggerheads during my first couple of months at the center. Then there was romance. At the end we'd evolved into being good friends. Life is unpredictable."

Wendy started to say something, but Marissa hushed her with a raised hand, indicating Cyrill had answered.

The first part of the call was friendly chitchat. Finally Marissa got around to the reason for her call. "Cyrill," she said, "I have a doctor friend sitting with me and I'm going to put you on the speakerphone." Marissa pushed the appropriate button. "Can you hear me?"

Cyrill's voice filled the room as he responded in the affirmative.

Marissa got to the point. "Have you heard any talk around the center of TB salpingitis, like a relatively recent upswing in cases?"

"Not that I can recall offhand," Cyrill said. "Why do you ask?"

"I have reason to believe that there are four such

cases up here in Boston. All in relatively young women, and all without any apparent nidus of infection elsewhere, particularly nothing in the lungs."

"What do you mean by 'relatively young women'?" Cyrill asked.

"Late twenties, early to mid-thirties," Marissa answered.

"That's a little old for a pediatrician to be treating," Cyrill said. "How have these cases come to your attention?"

Marissa smiled. "I should have known I couldn't be cagey with you, Cyrill," she said. "The fact of the matter is that I'm one of the infected. I've been involved with in-vitro fertilization for almost a year. Tonight I discovered three other women with the same unusual diagnosis."

"I'm sorry to hear about your troubles," Cyrill said. "But I haven't heard anything about TB salpingitis in the usual CDC gossip. What I can do is ask over in bacteriology. If there has been anything at all, they'd be sure to have heard. I'll get back to you as soon as I can."

After appropriate goodbyes, Marissa hung up. Following a slight pause, she asked Wendy what she thought of calling Rebecca Ziegler's number.

Wendy looked at her watch. "I'm not sure I'd have the emotional fortitude," she said. "Besides, it's after ten."

"I think it's worth the risk," Marissa said with determination. She got the number out and dialed. The line rang seven times before someone finally

98

picked up. Loud music could be heard in the background. It sounded like a party.

Marissa asked if she had reached the Ziegler residence.

"Just a minute," the voice at the other end said. Marissa and Wendy could hear the man yell to others to "pipe down a sec." Then he came back on the line.

"Are you Rebecca Ziegler's husband?" Marissa asked.

"I was," the man said. "Who is this?"

"I'm Dr. Blumenthal," Marissa said. "I hope I'm not catching you at a bad time. I got your number from Resolve, the organization for infertile couples. Are you familiar with it?"

"Yeah," the man said. "What's up?"

"If it wouldn't be too much of a bother," Marissa said, "I'd like to ask a personal question about Rebecca's condition."

"Is this some kind of crank call?" the man asked. There was a sudden burst of laughter in the background.

"No," Marissa said. "I can assure you it isn't. I just wanted to ask if Rebecca's problem had anything to do with her fallopian tubes. Those are the tubes that transport the eggs to the uterus."

"I know what fallopian tubes are," the man said. "Just a minute." Then to his guests, the man yelled: "Come on, you guys, shut up! I can't hear!" Coming back on the line he apologized for the commotion. "My friends," he explained. "They're a bunch of animals."

99

"About Rebecca?" Marissa questioned, rolling her eyes for Wendy's benefit.

"Yeah," the man said. "She had blocked tubes."

"Do you happen to know how they became blocked?" Marissa persisted.

"I just know they were blocked. More than that, you'll have to ask her doctor." There was a crash in the background, and the shatter of broken glass. "Jesus!" the man said. "Hey, I gotta go." Then the line went dead.

Marissa pushed the disconnect button.

They stared at each other. Finally Wendy broke the silence. "So much for the grieving widower."

"At least we don't have to feel guilty about calling," Marissa said. "And she had blocked tubes. I think it will be worth looking into the cause. If by any chance her tubes were blocked in the same way as ours, it could put a whole new spin on this affair."

Wendy nodded.

"Wait a second!" Marissa cried.

"What's the matter?" Wendy asked.

"We forgot to ask those other two women where they are being treated. I know Rebecca was at the Women's Clinic."

"You have their numbers," Wendy said. "Give them a call."

Marissa quickly dialed. Both women were available and both gave the same answer: they were being treated at the Women's Clinic.

"This is getting interesting," Wendy said.

100

"That's an understatement," Marissa said. "I think we'd better make a visit to the Women's Clinic, the sooner the better. Like tomorrow morning. Are you with me?"

"I wouldn't miss it for the world," Wendy said.

"Hello," a voice called. Both Marissa's and Wendy's eyes were drawn to the doorway. It was Robert, dressed in a V-necked sweater, tan chinos, and loafers without socks. His reading glasses were in his hand.

Marissa stood up from her desk chair and introduced Wendy to Robert, explaining that they'd met at the Resolve meeting. She told him that Wendy was involved with in-vitro fertilization with Dr. Wingate too. Robert shook Wendy's hand.

"I was on my way to the kitchen to make some tea," Robert said. "Can I interest anyone else?"

"I'd love some," Wendy said.

Robert turned and disappeared toward the kitchen. "Wow," Wendy said. "And I thought Gustave was handsome."

Marissa nodded. "I do love him," she admitted. "We're just going through a particularly rough time." She shrugged. "At least that's what I tell myself."

By the time they got to the kitchen, Robert already had the kettle on the stove and boxes of different teas on the table along with three mugs.

"So how was the meeting?" Robert asked as he got out the sugar and honey.

Marissa described the meeting, emphasizing

101

how pleasant it was and how many husbands were in attendance.

"Was your husband there?" Robert asked Wendy.

"He was in surgery and couldn't make it," Wendy answered evasively. She neglected to say that he probably wouldn't have attended even if he'd been free. But Robert was a good cross-examiner.

"Has he been to any of the others?" he asked. Just then, the kettle began to whistle. Robert went to get it.

Marissa answered for Wendy. "He hasn't been able to make any of the meetings."

"I see," Robert said as he poured boiling water into each of the mugs. He had one of those half-smiles that galled Marissa.

"I'm certain you'd feel differently about the meetings if you had an open enough mind to attend one," Marissa said.

"Maybe I should talk with Wendy's husband," Robert said. "He sounds like a kindred soul." He took the kettle back to the stove.

"Great idea," Wendy agreed.

"All I can say is that the meeting was extremely rewarding for me," Marissa said. "Not only did I meet Wendy, we happened to learn that four of us have the same odd diagnosis."

"Are you talking about the TB stuff?" Robert asked.

"Exactly," Wendy said. "I'm one of the four."

"No kidding?"

Marissa launched into breathless explanation of exactly how unusual the number of cases was. "It's so unexpected, we have to look into it. Tomorrow we'll go to the Women's Clinic to launch our official investigation."

"What do you mean your 'official investigation'?" Robert asked.

"We want to know how many cases like ours have been seen. We want to find out if Rebecca Ziegler had the same problem. We already know she had blocked tubes."

"The Women's Clinic is not going to give you that kind of information."

"Why not? It could be important," Marissa said. "For all we know it might have serious public health consequences. We could really be on to something . . . something along the lines of toxic shock syndrome."

Robert looked at Marissa, then at Wendy. He found their ardor unsettling, especially in view of Marissa's recent outburst at the Chinese restaurant. No doubt Wendy was strung out on the same hormones.

"I think you guys ought to calm down," Robert told them. "Even if you get to the bottom of this, it's not like it's going to reverse your condition. And I seriously doubt you'll get very far with the clinic. It would be highly unethical, even illegal, for them to disclose information about their patients without the patients' consent."

But Marissa would hear none of it. "This TB issue has bothered me from the start. I mean to get to the bottom of it. I don't care what it takes. I just talked to Cyrill Dubchek and he can put the authority of the CDC behind it."

Robert just shook his head. He clearly disapproved. "Well then," he said curtly, "I'll leave you two sleuths to your plotting."

With that, he picked up his mug and walked away.

Wendy broke the uncomfortable silence once his steps were out of earshot. "He is right," she said. "We may have a problem getting access to those medical records."

"We have to give it a try. Maybe we can muster some authority as doctors. You know, take the professional approach. If that doesn't work, we'll just think of something else. You are with me, aren't you?"

"Absolutely," Wendy said. "United we stand."

Marissa smiled. She could hardly wait for morning.

6

MARCH 29, 1990
9:30 A.M.

STRUGGLING WITH their umbrellas in the wind, Marissa and Wendy passed into the courtyard of the Women's Clinic.

Entering the front door, they shook water from

their coats. Their rain-slicked hair was plastered to their foreheads.

"Do you know where the medical records department is?" Marissa asked Wendy.

"I haven't the faintest idea," Wendy said. "I'll ask."

While Marissa fought to close her umbrella, which had turned inside out in the wind, Wendy made her inquiries at the information booth. She motioned for Marissa to follow her to the elevators. "Sixth floor," she said when Marissa joined her.

"I should have guessed," Marissa said. "Rebecca Ziegler jumped from the sixth floor right after reading her records."

"Makes you wonder what she could have read."
Marissa nodded.

Once on the sixth floor, it was easy to find the department. The clatter of typewriters could be heard immediately outside the elevators. Marissa was relieved it was in the opposite direction from Linda Moore's office. For the moment, Marissa did not want to run into someone she knew.

There was no mistaking the medical records department. Dozens of file cabinets lined the room. There were three secretaries with headphones, typing dictation. A woman occupying the desk to the right of the entrance greeted Marissa and Wendy. "Can I help you?" she asked. The woman, who was about fifty, Marissa guessed, had a name tag: Helen Solano, Medical Records

105

Librarian. In front of her was a computer terminal.

"I'm Dr. Blumenthal," Marissa said professionally. "And this is Dr. Wilson."

Wendy nodded. Mrs. Solano smiled.

"We have a question for you," Wendy said. "We're curious if the Women's Clinic record system is such that cases of a specific diagnosis such as fallopian tube blockage can be printed out."

"Absolutely," Mrs. Solano said.

"How about granulomatous blockage?" Marissa asked.

"That specific category I'm not certain of," Mrs. Solano said. "I'd have to look it up in our diagnostic code. Let me see." She swiveled in her chair to face a bookcase filled with looseleaf manuals. She pulled one out and began flipping through.

"We do have a code for granulomatous infections of the fallopian tubes," Mrs. Solano said, glancing up from the manual.

"Wonderful," Marissa said with a smile. "If it wouldn't be too much trouble, we'd like to get a printout with that diagnosis."

"No trouble at all," Mrs. Solano said.

Marissa and Wendy exchanged a satisfied glance.

"Where is your authorization requisition?" Mrs. Solano asked.

"We didn't think we needed one for research purposes," Wendy said.

"You need one for any purpose," Mrs. Solano explained.

"Fine," Marissa said. "Who do we see to get the proper authorization?"

"There is only one person who can issue such a requisition," Mrs. Solano said. "And that is Dr. Wingate, the director of the clinic."

Back at the elevators, Marissa shook her head at Wendy. "Damn," she said. "I thought we were home free when she told us they had the granulomatous diagnostic category."

"Me too," Wendy said. "But now I'm thinking that your husband was right. I don't think we'll be able to persuade Wingate to give us the authorization."

"Let's not get discouraged so soon," Marissa said as they boarded the elevator.

Dr. Wingate's offices were on the second floor. He had one office as the director of the clinic and another as director of the in-vitro fertilization unit. Marissa and Wendy went to the first but were directed to the second. Dr. Wingate, they learned, was busy in the lab.

"I'll tell the doctor that you are here," the receptionist said.

Marissa and Wendy sat down. "It's nice not to be here for another procedure," Wendy whispered. Marissa smiled in agreement.

"Dr. Wingate can see you now," the receptionist called out about a half hour later. She directed them down a long hall to the third door on the right.

Wendy knocked. Dr. Wingate told them to come in.

"Well, well!" he said, standing up from a lab bench and a microscope. Save for a desk and a couple of file cabinets, the room looked more like a lab than an office. "I didn't know you two knew each other."

Wendy explained they had been friends in medical school.

"What can I do for you ladies today?" He motioned for them to be seated, although he remained standing. "I have to tell you, I'm about to do a fertilization, so I don't have a lot of time."

"It won't take long," Marissa assured him. She gave him a quick rundown of how she and Wendy had discovered they had the same basic problem and how they'd found two other possible cases. "Four cases of rare granulomatous fallopian tube infection consistent with TB is extraordinary," she said. "Obviously we want to look into it. We are interested in this as a research project."

"But we need authorization from you," Wendy said. "We want to see if there are additional cases."

"That I cannot do," Dr. Wingate said. "The clinic policy is one of strict confidentiality. I cannot allow access to the patient files. And that directive comes from the central office in San Francisco."

"But this may have public health implications," Marissa said. "These cases might represent a new clinical entity like toxic shock."

"I can see that," Dr. Wingate said. "And thank you for alerting us. We will be sure to look into it. I'm sure you understand my situation."

"We could talk to the women involved and get releases," Wendy said.

"I'm sorry, ladies," Dr. Wingate said with impatience creeping into his voice. "I've told you our rules. You have to respect them. And now I have to get back to work. Aren't both of you due to have your hormone levels checked soon?"

Both Wendy and Marissa nodded. Marissa said: "Can you at least think about it and let us know later?"

"I don't have to think about it," Dr. Wingate said. "It is impossible for me to give you authorization. And that's final. Now if you will excuse me."

At the elevators the women regarded each other. "Don't tell me that Robert was right," Marissa warned. "If you do, I'll scream."

On the first floor near the information booth, they stopped. "Do you know anybody well enough on the staff here to get them to try to access the computer?" Wendy asked.

Marissa shook her head. "Unfortunately no, but I just had another idea that won't help our problem here but might answer some questions about Rebecca Ziegler. As a suicide, she must have gone to the medical examiner. They'd have done a post. Maybe they looked at her fallopian tubes."

"It's worth a try," Wendy said. "Let's go down to the city morgue and see. But first I'd better call my office and make sure things are going okay without me."

"I'll call the medical examiner," Marissa said.

Together they walked over to a bank of public phones. Wendy was finished first and she waited for Marissa to hang up.

"I'm still clear," Wendy told Marissa.

"Good," Marissa said. "It was a lucky thing I called the ME's office. Although Rebecca Ziegler was an ME's case, they authorized the Memorial to do the post. Let's head over there."

After the disappointment and lack of success at the Women's Clinic, Marissa was encouraged to find that her friend Ken Mueller had done the post on Rebecca Ziegler. She was confident there wouldn't be any problem finding out the results.

"Ken is in the autopsy room," a secretary told Marissa. "He just went in a few minutes ago and I don't expect him to be out for an hour or so."

"Which room?" Marissa asked.

"Three," the secretary said.

"Can't we wait?" Wendy asked as they walked through pathology toward the autopsy area. Autopsies had never been a favorite of Wendy's. Some of her medical school recollections were already making her feel queasy.

"I think we'd better talk to him while we can," Marissa said. But then as she was about to back into the autopsy room, she caught sight of Wendy's pale face. "Are you okay?" she asked.

110

Wendy confessed that autopsies had never been her strong suit.

"You wait out here," Marissa said. "I'll be quick. I'm not fond of them either."

Stepping through the door, Marissa was immediately assaulted by the offensive odor of the autopsy room. Her eyes scanned the room, coming to rest on two gowned and gloved men wearing protective goggles. Between the men was a pale nude body of a young male stretched out on a stainless-steel table.

"Ken?" Marissa called timidly. Both men looked up. They were in the process of eviscerating the corpse.

"Marissa, how are you!" Ken answered through his mask. "Come on over here and meet the worst junior resident the Memorial has ever seen."

"Thanks a lot," Greg said.

Marissa advanced to the foot of the autopsy table. Ken formally introduced Greg to Marissa, changing his joking evaluation to one of high praise. Greg waved at Marissa with his scalpel.

"Interesting case?" Marissa asked to make conversation.

"They are all interesting cases," Ken said. "If I didn't feel that way I would have gone into dermatology. Is this a social visit?"

"Hardly," Marissa said. "I was told you did a post on a woman by the name of Rebecca Ziegler."

"Was that the woman who couldn't fly?" Ken asked.

"Spare me the pathology humor," Marissa said.

"But yes, she was the one who jumped from a sixth-story window."

"I did the post," Greg said. "Ken watched."

"It was an interesting case—" Ken said.

"You just said they were all interesting," Greg interrupted.

"All right, wise guy," Ken said to Greg. Then to Marissa he said: "This was a particularly interesting case. The woman ruptured her aorta."

"Did you look at the fallopian tubes?" Marissa asked. She wasn't interested in gross injuries.

"I looked at everything," Greg said. "What do you want to know?"

"Did you look at the slides yet?" Marissa asked.

"Of course," Greg said. "She had granulomatous destruction of both tubes. I sent a bunch more slides off to be processed with various stains, but last time I looked they weren't back yet."

"If you're curious whether they looked like those slides you showed me months ago," Ken said, "they did. Exactly the same. So our tentative diagnosis of her problem in her fallopian tubes was an old, resolved TB lesion. But of course, that was just an incidental finding. It didn't have anything to do with her death."

"You going to tell her about the other stuff?" Greg asked.

"What other stuff?" Marissa asked.

"Something that Greg and I have been mulling over," Ken said. "I'm not sure we should tell you."

"What are you talking about?" Marissa insisted.

112

"Why wouldn't you tell me? Come on, you're making me curious."

"We can't make up our own minds," Greg said. "There are a couple of things that are bugging us."

"Give me a try," Marissa pleaded.

"Well, don't say anything to anybody," Ken said. "I might have to discuss it with the medical examiner, and I don't want him to hear it from anyone else first."

"Out with it," Marissa demanded. "You can trust me."

"Everybody thinks pathology is cut and dry," Ken said evasively. "You know, the last word, the final answer. But it ain't so. Not always. There are times when your intuition is telling you something even though you cannot document it categorically."

"For chrissake, tell her," Greg said.

"All right," Ken said. "We noticed that Rebecca Ziegler had a recent venipuncture in one of her arm veins."

"Oh, for goodness' sake!" Marissa said with exasperation. "The woman was undergoing in-vitro fertilization. She was getting hormones and blood tests all the time. Is that what you've made this big buildup for? Please!"

Ken shrugged his shoulders. "That's part of it," he said. "If it were only that, we wouldn't be concerned. We know she'd been stuck a lot of times over the last months. There were marks all over her body. But this stick gave the appearance of being done just before she died. That makes it suspect. So we decided to expand our toxicology screen to look for drugs other than the usual hormones. As pathologists we're supposed to be suspicious."

"And you found something?" Marissa asked with horror.

"Nope," Ken said. "Toxicology was clean. We're trying a few other tricks, but so far nothing has turned up."

"Is this some kind of joke?" Marissa said.

"No joke," Ken said. "The other part of the puzzle is that she only had a few hundred cc's of blood in her chest."

"Meaning . . ."

"When someone ruptures an aorta there is usually a lot of blood in the chest," Ken said. "A bit more than a few hundred cc's. It's possible to have only that much, but it's not probable. So finding only a few hundred cc's is not something concrete, it's just suggestive."

"Suggestive of what?" Marissa asked.

"Suggestive that she was already dead when she fell," Ken said.

Marissa was stunned. For a moment she couldn't speak. The implications were too horrendous.

"So you can see our problem," Ken said. "If we say something like this officially, we have to have more proof. We have to come up with an explanation of what killed her before she fell. Unfortunately, we haven't found anything on gross or microscopic. We went over her brain extremely carefully and found nothing. The only chance is toxicology and so far we've gotten a big zip."

"What about her dying as she fell?" Marissa suggested. "From fright or something?"

"Come on, Marissa, be serious," Ken said with a wave of his hand. "That only happens in the movies. If she was dead before she hit the ground, then she was dead before she fell. Of course that means she was tossed out of the building."

"Maybe she hadn't paid her bill," Greg suggested jokingly. "But with all due respect, I think we'd better get on with our present case before the body putrefies."

"If you want, I'll call you if we come up with anything," Ken said.

"Please," Marissa answered. She was in a daze as she headed for the door.

Ken stopped her by calling out: "Remember, Marissa, mum's the word. Don't say anything to anybody."

"Don't worry," Marissa called over her shoulder. "Your secret is safe with me." But of course she'd have to tell Wendy.

At the door, Marissa paused again. Turning around, she called out to Ken. "Do you have a chart on her?" she asked.

"Not really," Ken said. "Just the stuff they wrote in the ER, which wasn't much."

"But I suppose the business office got some details for billing," Marissa said.

"I'm sure," Ken said.

"You didn't happen to know if they got her social security number?" Marissa asked.

"You got me there," Ken said. "But if you want to look, the chart is on my desk."

Marissa pulled open the door and left the autopsy room.

"My feeling is that we can't assume it's true," Wendy said, twirling her ice cubes in her mineral water. "Thinking Rebecca Ziegler was killed and then tossed out of a window is too preposterous. It can't be true. The amount of blood in a chest after an aortic rupture has to be defined by a bell-shaped curve. Rebecca Ziegler was just at one end of the curve. That has to be the explanation."

Wendy was sprawled in the corner of the couch in Marissa's study. Taffy Two was sitting on the floor, hoping for another Goldfish cocktail cracker. Marissa was at her desk.

They were waiting for Gustave to arrive. He'd had late-afternoon emergency surgery, but was due any moment. At Wendy's urging, the women had decided to get together with their husbands for a casual dinner of pizza. They were hoping that if the men got to know each other, they might decide to come to one of the Resolve meetings. Wendy thought that would be extremely helpful. Marissa wasn't so sure.

"At least I got her social security number from her chart," Marissa said. "If we can figure out a way to get into the Women's Clinic records, we can see what poor Rebecca read on her last day. That is, if she read anything."

"Here you go again with that wild imagination of yours," Wendy said. "So now you think they took her upstairs, bumped her off, then tossed her out the window. Come on, it's too farfetched even to consider."

"Regardless," Marissa said. "We'll let it go for the time being. At least we did find out that she had the same infectious process in her tubes. That we know for sure."

Suddenly Marissa fumbled through her papers, searching for the phone numbers for Marcia Lyons and Catherine Zolk.

Calling each woman in turn, Marissa learned what she intuitively suspected: both women confirmed that their internists had talked about their taking isoniazid. The internists had been worried about TB.

Hanging up the phone, Marissa said: "Now we have five definite cases. Damn Wingate and his confidentiality. We can't make many statistical inferences from five cases. We have to find out if there are more."

"Let's be fair," Wendy said. "Wingate is following orders from above. Maybe he has already started looking into it."

"I hope so," Marissa said. "Meanwhile, let's check our own hospitals and see if we can come up with more cases. You take the General and I'll take the Memorial."

Taffy Two took off at the sound of the doorbell,

117

barking madly. Wendy swung her feet to the floor. "That must be Gustave," she said as she stood up and stretched. She checked her watch; it was almost nine P.M.

Marissa was struck by Gustave's stature. From her five-foot height, he towered over her like a giant. He was a six-foot-six, squarely built man with very blond, curly hair. His eyes were a soft pastel blue.

"Sorry I'm so late," Gustave apologized after being introduced to Marissa and Robert. Robert had come out of his study at the sound of the bell. "We had to wait for anesthesia before we began our case."

"It makes no difference at all," Marissa assured him. She told Robert to see what Gustave wanted to drink while she and Wendy called for the pizza.

When the pizza arrived, they all gathered around the table in the family room off the kitchen. The men were drinking beers. Marissa was pleased but a little surprised that Robert was enjoying Gustave's company. He usually didn't get along with doctors.

"We haven't heard about your visit to the Women's Clinic today," Robert said when there was a lull in the conversation.

Marissa looked over at Wendy. She wasn't sure if she wanted to get into a discussion about their visit, knowing that she'd have to hear Robert's "I told you so."

"Come on," Robert urged. "What happened?"

Turning to Gustave, Robert explained that the women had tried to access the clinic's computer.

"We asked and they said no," Wendy admitted.

"I'm not surprised," Robert said. "Were they nasty about it?"

"Not at all," Wendy said. "We had to go to the director of the clinic, the same man who runs the in-vitro unit. He said it was a policy made at the home office in San Francisco."

"I think it is shortsighted," Marissa said, finally speaking up. "Although we didn't find anything out at the clinic, we did learn that there are five cases, and five cases of a rare problem in one geographical location deserves to be investigated."

"Five cases?" Gustave questioned. "Five cases of what?"

Wendy quickly filled Gustave in on the situation, explaining it involved her apparent TB of the fallopian tubes.

"So we went back to the clinic to see if there are other cases," Marissa explained. "But they would not let us search their files for reasons of confidentiality."

"If you were running a clinic," Robert asked Gustave, "would you let a couple of people off the street come in and access your records?"

"Absolutely not," Gustave agreed.

"That's what I tried to explain to the ladies last night," Robert said. "The clinic is only operating in a reasonable, ethical, and legal fashion. I would have been shocked if they had given any information at all."

"We are hardly 'people off the street,' " Wendy said heatedly. "We're doctors as well as patients."

"Being two of the five in your own series hardly makes you objective," Gustave pointed out. "Especially with the hormones you women have been taking."

"I'll drink to that," Robert said, raising his beer bottle.

Wendy and Marissa exchanged frustrated glances.

After wiping his mouth with the back of his hand, Robert turned back to Marissa. "Five cases?" he said. "Last night you mentioned four."

"Rebecca Ziegler had the same problem," Marissa answered.

"No kidding," Robert said. Turning to Gustave, he said, "She was the woman who committed suicide over at the Women's Clinic. She went berserk in the waiting room just as Marissa and I arrived, the very day she jumped. I tried to restrain her but she slugged me."

"Wendy told me about her," Gustave said. "You tried to restrain her before she jumped?"

"Nothing so dramatic," Robert said. "She was about to attack a receptionist. Seems the receptionist wouldn't let her see her records. It wasn't until later that she jumped out of the window. And that was from the top floor, not the waiting room."

Gustave nodded. "Tragic case," he said.

"It may be more tragic than you think," Marissa blurted without thinking. "Wendy and I learned something else today. Rebecca Ziegler might not have committed suicide. She might have been murdered. That's how reasonable, ethical, and legal the Women's Clinic is being run."

As soon as Marissa had mentioned this shocking possibility, she regretted it. There were a number of reasons she shouldn't have said anything, her promise to Ken foremost among them. She tried to change the subject to tuberculosis, but Robert wouldn't let it go.

"I think you'd better explain," he insisted.

Realizing her mistake, Marissa decided she had no choice but to tell the whole story. After she'd finished, Robert sat back in his chair and looked at Gustave. "You're a doctor," he said. "What do you think of what you just heard?"

"Circumstantial," Gustave said. "Personally, I think those two pathologists are letting their forensic imaginations run wild. As they said themselves, there is no concrete proof. They have a ruptured aorta. That certainly is lethal. Probably the heart was in diastole at the moment of impact, so that it was filling when it was shocked into stopping. The only bleeding came from backflow, meaning the blood that was in the aorta itself."

"Sounds reasonable to me," Robert said.

"Gustave is probably right," Marissa agreed, glad to get off the subject. She wasn't about to bring up her own question regarding the fact that Rebecca had hardly acted depressed in the waiting room.

"Even so," Marissa continued, "Rebecca's

death makes us even more eager to access the Women's Clinic's computer. I'd love to read what's in her record; what she saw had to contribute to her death."

"Maybe we could find some whiz-kid hacker over at MIT," Wendy said. "It would be classic if we could get at their files from off-site."

"That would be fantastic," Marissa agreed. "But what's more realistic is for you and me to sneak in there at night and just use one of the terminals. Someone could do that at the Memorial with only a little creativity."

"Hold on," Robert said. "You guys are getting way out of hand. Unauthorized access of someone's private computer files is considered grand theft in Massachusetts. If you do something crazy like that, you could find yourselves felons."

Marissa rolled her eyes.

"That's no joke," Robert said. "I don't know what's in your minds."

"Wendy and I happen to think this TB salpingitis is extremely significant," Marissa told him. "We think it ought to be followed up. We seem to be the only ones willing to do it. Sometimes risks have to be taken."

Gustave cleared his throat. "I'm afraid I'm in agreement with Robert on this one," he said. "You can't be serious about breaking into the clinic files. Despite your motivations, it would be a crime nonetheless."

"The problem is truly one of priorities," Marissa said. "You men don't realize how important this issue could be. By following up on it we are being responsible, not the reverse."

"Maybe we should change the subject," Wendy suggested.

"I think it should be settled before you women get into serious trouble," Gustave said.

"Be quiet, Gustave!" Wendy snapped.

"These five cases may be the tip of an iceberg," Marissa said. "As I've already said, it reminds me of the discovery of toxic shock syndrome."

"That's not a fair comparison," Robert said. "It's not like anyone's died."

"Oh yeah?" Marissa challenged. "What about Rebecca Ziegler?"

7

MARCH 30, 1990
8:15 A.M.

ROBERT OPENED the mahogany-paneled door to his private office in the old City Hall building and stepped inside. He tossed his briefcase onto the couch and stepped over to the window. His view out onto School Street was marred by rivulets of water streaming across the outside of the window. He'd never experienced such a rainy March in Boston.

Behind him he heard his private secretary, Donna, come into the room, bringing his usual morning coffee and his usual stack of phone messages.

123

"Some weather!" Donna said. Her strong Boston accent made the word sound like "wethah."

Robert turned. Donna had seated herself to the left of his desk to go over the phone messages, which was their usual routine. Robert looked at her. She was a big girl, almost five-ten. In her heels, she practically looked him in the eye. Her hair was dyed blonde, the dark roots clearly visible. Her features were rounded but not unpleasant, and her body was toned from daily aerobic exercise. She was a great secretary: honest, devoted, and dependable. She also had simple needs, and for a moment Robert wondered why he hadn't married someone like Donna. Life would have been so much more predictable.

"Would you like sugar in your coffee?" she asked pleasantly. Coffee sounded more like "cawfee."

"No, I don't want coffee," Robert said sharply.

Donna looked up from her notes. "Aren't we testy this morning," she said.

Robert rubbed his eyes, then came around and sat down at his desk. "I'm sorry," he said to Donna. "My wife is driving me crazy."

"Is it that infertility stuff?" Donna asked timidly.

Robert nodded. "She began to change just about the time we admitted that we might have a problem," he said. "Now, between this in-vitro fertilization rigmarole and all the hormones she's on, she is truly out of control."

"I'm sorry," Donna said.

124

"To make matters worse, she's met up with an old medical school friend who's in the same situation and who is behaving equally irrationally," Robert said. "They seem to be feeding off each other. Now they are threatening to break into a health care clinic to get into their records. Unfortunately, I have to take her seriously in the state of mind she's in. I wouldn't put anything past her. But what can I do? And, on top of everything, this clinic has guards armed with Colt Pythons. I'm really worried about her."

"They have snakes at this clinic?" Donna asked, wide-eyed.

"Huh? No, not snakes. A Colt Python is a revolver capable of stopping a black rhino."

"I can give you some advice," Donna said. "If you're really worried about what Marissa might do, you should hire a private investigator for a few days. He could keep her out of trouble if she is really inclined in that direction. And I happen to know someone who is very good. I used him to follow my former husband. The bum was having an affair with two women at the same time."

"What's this investigator's name?" Robert asked. The idea of having Marissa followed hadn't occurred to him, but it had some merit.

"Paul Abrums," Donna said. "He's the best. He even got photos of my ex in bed with both girls. Separately, of course. My husband wasn't that kind of guy. And Paul's not that expensive."

"How do I get in touch with him?" Robert asked.

"I've got the number in my address book in my purse," Donna said. "I'll get it."

Marissa peered into the otoscope to try to catch a glimpse of the eardrum of the writhing infant on the examination table. The mother was attempting to hold the baby but was doing a miserable job. Annoyed, Marissa gave up.

"I can't see anything," Marissa said. "Can't you hold the child, Mrs. Bartlett? She's only eight months. She can't be that strong."

"I'm trying," the mother said.

"Trying isn't good enough," Marissa told her. She opened the examination room door and called for one of the nurses.

"I'll send someone in as soon as I can," Muriel Samuelson, the head nurse, shouted.

"For heaven's sake," Marissa muttered to herself. She was finding work exasperating. Everything was an effort, and it was difficult to concentrate. All she could think about was the pregnancy test she'd have after the weekend.

Stepping out of the examination room to get away from the shrieking infant, Marissa massaged the back of her neck. If she was this anxious already, what would it be like on Monday when she was waiting for the result?

The other topic on her mind was what she and Wendy were going to do about the Women's Clinic. They had to get into their records. That morning she'd gone to the medical records department at the Memorial and gotten one of the women to start a search for cases of granulomatous obstruction of the fallopian tubes. There'd been no problem. If only the Women's Clinic could be so cooperative.

"Dr. Blumenthal, you have a call on line three," Muriel yelled to her over the sound of crying babies.

"What now?" Marissa muttered under her breath. She went into an empty examination cubicle and picked up the extension. "Yes?" she snapped, expecting Mindy Valdanus to be on the other end.

"Dr. Blumenthal?" a strange woman's voice questioned. It was the operator.

"Yes?" Marissa repeated.

"Go ahead," the operator said.

"You sound harried," Dubchek said.

"Cyrill!" Marissa answered. "You're a pleasant surprise in the middle of a bad day. This place is a zoo!"

"Can you talk for a sec or do you want to ring me back?" Dubchek asked.

"I can talk," Marissa said. "Actually, at the moment I'm standing and waiting for a nurse before I look at a child with an ear infection. So you got me at a good time. What's up?"

"I'm finally getting back to you on those questions you raised about TB salpingitis," Dubchek said. "Well, I have some interesting news. There have been sporadic reports of a condition that's consistent with TB salpingitis from all around the country, although mostly on the West and East coasts."

"Really!" Marissa exclaimed. She was astounded. "Has anybody been able to culture it?"

"No," Dubchek said. "But that's not unusual. Remember, it's hard to culture TB. In fact, no one has, to my knowledge, seen an actual organism in any of these cases."

"Now that's strange," Marissa said.

"Yes and no," Dubchek said. "It's frequently hard to find the TB bug in tuberculosis granuloma. At least that's what my bacteriology colleagues tell me. So don't make too much of that either. What's more important, from an epidemiologic point of view, is that there are no areas of concentration. The cases seem to be widely scattered and unrelated."

"I now have five cases in Boston," Marissa said.

"Then Boston gets the prize," Dubchek said. "San Fran is second with four. But no one has actually looked into it. There have been no studies launched, so these cases represent haphazard reporting. If somebody looked, he'd probably find more. Anyway, I've got a few people checking into it here at the Center. I'll be back to you if anything interesting turns up."

"The five cases I've come across are all at one clinic," Marissa said. "I've started to search at the Memorial just this morning. What I'd really like to do is get access to the clinic's records. Unfortunately they turned me down. Could the CDC help?"

"I don't see how," Dubchek said. "It would take a court order, and with the paucity of details and low danger level to society, I doubt seriously a judge would grant it."

"Let me know if you hear anything else," Marissa said.

"Will do."

Marissa hung up the phone and leaned against the wall. The idea that tuberculous granuloma of the fallopian tube had been reported from around the country made her more curious than ever. There had to be some interesting epidemiological explanation behind it. And by a quirk of fate, not only was she suffering from the illness herself, she was part of what was the largest concentration. She had to get into the clinic's records. She had to find more cases if there were more to find.

"Dr. Blumenthal," Muriel said, stepping into the room, "I don't have anybody to help you at the moment, but I can myself."

"Wonderful," Marissa said. "Let's go to it."

The sliding glass door opened automatically as Marissa strode into the lobby level of the Massachusetts Eye and Ear Infirmary. Despite the cool late-afternoon temperature she had on only her thin doctor's white jacket. After a quick inquiry at the information booth, she veered right into the emergency area. She asked for Dr. Wilson at the emergency desk.

"She's in the back," the secretary said. She

pointed through a pair of swinging doors that were propped open.

Marissa continued her search. Beyond the propped-open swinging doors were several ophthalmologic examining rooms, each with its barberlike chair and attached slit lamp. A lone patient sat in the first room Marissa went by. In the second, the room light was out and two figures were bent over a reclining patient. Allowing her eyes to adjust, Marissa recognized one of them as Wendy.

"Now press down gently and look where you are pressing," Wendy said, guiding a junior resident through a specialized exam. "You should see the tear at the periphery of the retina."

"I see it!" the resident cried.

"Good," Wendy said. She caught sight of Marissa and waved. Turning back to the resident, she said, "Write it up and call the senior resident."

Wendy came out of the darkened room, blinking in the raw fluorescent light of the main part of the emergency room. "This is a surprise," she said. "What's up?"

"I got a very interesting call from the CDC," Marissa said. Then she lowered her voice. "Where can we talk?"

Wendy thought for a minute, then took Marissa around the back of the emergency area into an empty laser room. She shut the heavy door behind them. "You look positively mischievous. What's going on?"

"You're not going to believe this," Marissa began. She then told Wendy the gist of Dubchek's call indicating that they were dealing with a problem that had national scope.

"My word! We're on the brink of some major discovery," Wendy said, catching Marissa's enthusiasm.

"I don't think there is any doubt," Marissa said. "And there is only one minor barrier to the whole denouement."

"Wingate," Wendy said.

"Exactly!" Marissa said. "We have to see if there are more cases. I'm sure there are. There have to be. Once we have them all, we can begin to look for areas of commonality in all the subjects in terms of life-style, work, health history, all that. I'm sure if we do that with enough cases we'll come up with a theory as to the source of the TB and how it is being transmitted. Usually TB is airborne. But if no one has any lung lesions, maybe it's traveling by some other means."

"So what do you propose?" Wendy asked.

"It's Friday night. I think we should go over to the Women's Clinic and act as if we own the place. I wore my white coat over here just to try it. No one questioned me. I walked right in as if I were on the staff."

"How soon do you want to do this?" Wendy asked.

"When are you off?" Marissa asked.

"I can leave anytime now," Wendy answered.

"Get a white coat and pens and a stethoscope," Marissa said. "The more medical paraphernalia, the better."

Half an hour later, Marissa and Wendy slowly drove beneath the overhead walkway and past the opening into the courtyard of the Women's Clinic. They had started out the drive with excited chatter, but now, within sight of the clinic, they had fallen silent. Both felt nervous, tense, and a little fearful. Although Marissa tried not to think about it, Robert's comments concerning the felonious nature of what they were about to attempt were preying on her mind.

"The place is still hopping," Wendy said.

"You're right," Marissa agreed. People were entering and exiting. The windows were ablaze with lights.

"I suggest we go someplace and cool our heels for a couple of hours," Wendy said. "How about a bar?"

"I wish we could drink," Marissa said. "A glass of wine might calm me down. That reminds me, when do you have your blood test?"

"Tomorrow," Wendy said.

"You must be nervous about that too," Marissa said.

"I'm a wreck," Wendy agreed.

Paul Abrums rummaged in his right front pocket for a dime. It was still one of the bargains of Boston that if you could find an ATT phone, a local call was still only ten cents.

He let the coin drop into the slot and dialed Robert's office. It was before eight, and he was confident Robert would be there. Robert had told

132

him earlier in the day that he'd be in his office until nine. Then he'd be at home after that. He'd given Paul both numbers.

As the phone rang, Paul turned to keep his eye on the Viceroy Indian Restaurant in Central Square. Marissa had entered with her companion over an hour ago. If she happened to come out, Paul wanted to know.

"Hello," Robert answered. He was the only one in the office.

"Paul Abrums here," Paul said.

"Is there a problem?" Robert asked, somewhat alarmed.

"Not a big problem," Paul said. He spoke slowly and deliberately. "Your wife is with a short blonde woman who must also be a doctor."

"That's Wendy Wilson," Robert said.

"They're eating at an Indian restaurant as we speak," Paul said. "They drove past the Women's Clinic. I thought they were about to stop but they didn't."

"That's odd," Robert said.

"But there is something else," Paul added. "Can you think of any reason why an Asian guy in a gray suit would be following your wife?"

"Heavens no!" Robert said. "Are you sure?"

"About ninety percent sure," Paul said. "He's been on her tail too long for it to be coincidence. I noticed him when your wife left her pediatric clinic. He's a young guy, I think. Sometimes I can't tell with Asians. He's dressed in a good suit."

"That's very odd," Robert said, already glad

133

he'd taken Donna's suggestion about hiring Abrums.

"I won't take any more of your time," Paul said. "But it was curious enough for me to ask."

"Find out who that guy is," Robert said. "And why he's following my wife. God, I'm glad you are there."

"I don't mean to upset you," Paul said. "Everything is under control. You relax, I'll find out . . . Uh oh! Your wife is just coming out of the restaurant. I gotta go."

Paul hung up the phone and hurried across the street to get into his car. He had positioned it so that he could see the car that the women were in as well as the one the Asian man was driving. As soon as Marissa and Wendy pulled away from the curb, so did the Asian.

"That confirms it!" Paul muttered, pulling out. As he drove he jotted down the Asian's license number. Monday he'd call his friend at the motor vehicles bureau and find out who owned the car.

"You'd think we were about to rob a bank," Wendy said. "My pulse is racing." She and Marissa got out of the car. It was a dark, windy night.

"So is mine," Marissa admitted as they slammed the car doors. "It's Robert's fault with all his talk about felonies."

They had parked in the deserted clinic employee lot at the end of the street. Clutching their collars closed and leaning into the wind, they walked back to the clinic's courtyard. There they paused. The place was significantly quieter. Except for the lobby lights, most of the windows were dark. No one was entering or exiting. There wasn't a soul in sight.

"Are you ready?" Marissa asked.

"I'm not sure," Wendy said. "What's our plan?" Besides feeling nervous, Wendy was now shivering with cold. The temperature had dropped into the forties with a biting March wind. The thin white doctor jackets they were wearing afforded no warmth whatsoever.

"We have to find a computer terminal," Marissa said, shouting over the wind. "Doesn't matter where, just as long as we are left alone for a while. Come on, Wendy. We're going to freeze if we stay here."

"All right," Wendy said, taking a deep breath. "Let's go."

Without further delay, they crossed the courtyard and mounted the steps. On their way, both women nervously glanced at the rhododendron planter with its flattened bushes, an all-too-vivid reminder of Rebecca Ziegler's awful fate.

Marissa tried the door only to discover it was locked. She cupped her hands and peered through the glass. Inside, a cleaning crew was busy polishing the marble floor with electric polishers. She rapped on the glass several times, but the janitorial people didn't respond.

"Damn," Marissa said. She scanned the courtyard for another door, but there wasn't one.

"Who would have guessed they would have locked up already?" Marissa said.

"I'm freezing," said Wendy. "Let's get back to the car and regroup."

They turned and hurried back down the steps. Crossing the courtyard, bent over against the swirling debris, they approached a man coming into the clinic.

"The door's locked," Wendy told him as they passed. But the man just kept walking. Then, at the mouth of the courtyard another man appeared, also heading for the clinic entrance. "Door's locked," Wendy said again.

The women turned right and hurried toward the parking lot. Suddenly Marissa stopped and faced back toward the courtyard opening.

"Come on," Wendy urged.

One man, then the other, appeared. Catching sight of the women watching them, they quickly walked off in separate directions.

"What's the matter?" Wendy demanded.

"Did you see that first man?" Marissa asked.

"Sort of," Wendy said.

Marissa shivered, but this time not from the cold. "He gave me the creeps," she offered, starting to walk again. "He reminded me of a bad trip I once had with ketamine. Weird!"

In the parking lot, Wendy fumbled with her keys. Her fingers were numb; she had trouble manipulating them. Once in the car, she reached over and opened the passenger side for Marissa.

She then started the car, turning on the heater full blast.

"That was the strangest sensation I got from seeing that man," Marissa said. "It was almost like déjà vu. How can you have déjà vu from a hallucination?"

"I had a bad experience with pot once," Wendy admitted. "It was in California. Anytime I tried it after, it was the same. That was the end of pot for me."

"I had a sort of flashback recently. Robert and I were at a Chinese restaurant. It was the oddest thing."

"Well, maybe that was it," Wendy said. "I think the first guy was Chinese. At least he was Asian."

"Now you are going to make me sound like some kind of subconscious bigot," Marissa said with a nervous laugh. Any mental phenomena outside of her control made her feel uneasy.

"What should we do now?" Wendy asked.

"I suppose we don't have a lot of choice if the doors are locked," Marissa said.

"What about going in the overnight ward on the other side of the street and crossing in the connecting walkway?" Wendy suggested.

"Great idea!" Marissa said. "I guess it takes a genius to see the obvious. Let's do it!"

Wendy smiled, proud she had come up with a possible solution.

Marissa and Wendy again alighted from the car and ran to the overnight and emergency entrance opposite the main clinic building. Above them loomed the darkened walkway spanning the street.

The door was not locked; Marissa and Wendy entered with ease. Once inside they made their way down a short corridor which opened to a waiting area. A few men were looking at magazines. On the right wall was a glass-fronted security office. Directly ahead was a receptionist's desk where a nurse sat reading a paperback book.

"Uh oh!" Wendy whispered.

"Don't panic," Marissa whispered back. "Just keep walking as if we belong here."

The two women approached the desk and started to turn right into the main corridor when the woman lowered her book.

"Can I help . . ." she began, but then she stopped herself, saying only, "Sorry, doctors."

Marissa and Wendy didn't answer. They merely smiled at the woman and continued down the corridor to the stairwell. After the door to the stairwell closed behind them, they nervously giggled.

"Maybe this is going to be easy after all," Wendy said.

"Let's not get cocky," Marissa warned. "This ruse won't work if we run into anybody who recognizes us, like our own doctors."

"Thanks," Wendy said. "As if I didn't have enough to worry about."

They started up the stairs.

"Hell!" Paul Abrums muttered as he watched the Asian enter the overnight ward of the Women's

Clinic. What had started out as a simple job was rapidly becoming complicated. His first orders had been merely to tail Marissa, find out what she was up to, and, if she happened to go into the Women's Clinic, keep her from doing anything illegal. But that was before the mysterious Asian appeared. Now Robert had told him to find out who this guy was. What was more important? Paul didn't know. And now his indecision had forced his hand. Having let the women go into the clinic by themselves, he was forced to follow the Chinese fellow.

Stubbing out his cigarette, Paul jogged across the street and yanked open the clinic door just in time to see the Asian make a right down a corridor.

Paul hurried ahead, taking in his surroundings. First he saw the receptionist's desk with a night nurse reading a novel. Next he spotted the waiting area with a few men sitting reading magazines. Catching sight of some movement through a glass panel to his right, Paul slowed his steps. He found himself looking into a security office. Inside, he saw the Asian man he'd been following talking to a uniformed guard.

"Can I help you?" the woman at the desk asked. She'd lowered her book and was looking at Paul over the top of her glasses.

Paul walked over to the desk. He absently fingered a small metal tin of paper clips, trying to think of the best ruse to adopt. "Has Mrs. Abrums come in yet?" he asked.

"I don't believe so," the woman said. She

scanned the sheet on the clipboard before her. "No, she hasn't."

"Guess I'll have to wait then," Paul said. He glanced back toward the glass-fronted security office. The Asian and the uniformed guard were facing forward and seemed to be conferring over something below the window.

Trying not to be too obvious, Paul took a stroll around the waiting area, feigning impatience by alternately looking out the front window and then at his watch.

After the woman had gone back to reading her book, Paul wandered into the same corridor the Asian had entered. About ten feet down was the entrance to the security office. The door was ajar. Spotting a drinking fountain at the end of the corridor, Paul walked briskly to it. After a drink, he sauntered back toward the waiting area, pausing at the security office's open door on his way.

The two men had not moved from the window. Paul could see that they were watching a bank of TV monitors mounted below the sill. Paul tried to overhear what they were saying, but it was impossible; they were speaking another language. He assumed it was Chinese, but he was no expert. The other detail that caught his eye was that the guard was armed with a .357 Magnum, an unusual piece for hospital security. As a retired police officer, it all seemed odd to Paul, very odd indeed.

"Cripes! They're locked!" Wendy said after trying the fire doors barring the way to the clinic's main building. They had crossed over the street in the glass-enclosed walkway, thinking they were home free until they encountered this final barrier.

"This place is shut up like Fort Knox," Marissa said. "Damn!"

"I don't have any other ideas," Wendy said. "What about you?"

"I think we've given it our best shot," Marissa said. "I guess we'll just have to try our ruse in the daytime when the clinic is open."

Turning back, the two women hurried over the walkway. They didn't want to be seen from the street. But before they got to the overnight clinic side, Wendy stopped.

"Wait a sec," she said. "This seems to be the only connection between the two buildings."

"So what?" Marissa said.

"Where are the pipes for water and heat and electricity?" Wendy asked. "They can't have built separate power sources for both buildings. It would be too impractical."

"You're right!" Marissa said. "Let's try the stairwell again."

Returning to the stairs, the women descended to the basement level and cracked the door. The corridor beyond was poorly illuminated, and as far as they could tell, deserted. They listened for a few moments but heard no noises. Entering cautiously, they began to explore.

Most of the doors off the main corridor on the side facing the main building were locked. The open ones turned out to be storage areas. Eventu-

141

ally, to their encouragement, the corridor itself turned in the direction of the main building.

Advancing to the corner, they cautiously peered around, then abruptly pulled back. Someone was coming toward them. Almost at the same moment they began to hear the sound of approaching footsteps as they echoed in the narrow hallway.

Panicking, Marissa and Wendy ran back toward the elevators. There wasn't much time. The footfalls were getting louder. Frantically, they began trying the doors along the way, hoping to find one that wasn't locked.

"Here!" Wendy whispered. She had discovered a cleaning closet filled with a slop sink and mops. Marissa slid inside and Wendy followed, pulling the door closed behind her.

The two women held their breath as the footsteps bore down on them. They had no idea if they had been seen or not. When the footsteps passed their door without hesitation, Marissa and Wendy breathed a sigh of relief. They heard the elevator doors open, then close. Then silence.

"Whew," Wendy whispered. "I don't think my nerves can take much more of this slinking around."

"It's a good thing whoever that was didn't see us," Marissa said. "I doubt if our doctor's coats would help us down here."

"Let's get out before I have a heart attack," Wendy said.

Marissa gingerly opened the door. The corridor was clear. Venturing out, they returned to where the corridor took a bend toward the main building. No one was in sight.

"Okay," Marissa said. "Let's go." The corridor dipped down and then up again. Thick exposed pipes ran along the left wall and along the ceiling.

At the end of that corridor, they came to another fire door. This one wasn't locked. Pushing through, they entered the basement of the main clinic building.

A red Exit light marked the door to the stairwell. Feeling progressively more and more nervous, Wendy and Marissa entered and hurried up two flights, passing the ground floor where the janitorial staff had been working on the marble.

At the door to the second floor, they paused and listened for sounds of activity. Thankfully the place was as quiet as a mausoleum.

"Ready?" Wendy asked, putting her shoulder to the door.

"As ready as I'll ever be," Marissa said.

Wendy cracked the door against its automatic closer. The hall beyond was dark and the fluorescent light from the stairwell spilled out onto the vinyl flooring in a bright, shiny puddle. After listening again for a moment, they quickly stepped from the stairwell and let the door close quietly behind them.

The light was extinguished with the closing of the door. They waited for their eyes to adjust; there was still a bit of light coming from the streetlights outside. Once they could see again, it didn't take them long to get their bearings. They were just beyond the main elevators, near the waiting room of the in-vitro unit. This was an area of the clinic the women knew only too well.

Edging slowly down the corridor, they advanced to the waiting room itself. There the illumination was somewhat better.

Marissa and Wendy skirted the receptionist's desk, making a beeline for the doorway to the main corridor. This gave access to the doctors' offices, examining rooms, procedure rooms, and the in-vitro laboratory.

The first door they opened was to an examination room. In the dim light spilling in from the hall, the room took on a particularly sinister aspect. The stainless-steel table gleamed in the darkness, and with its stirrups, it appeared more like a medieval torture device than a piece of medical equipment.

"This place gives me the creeps in the dark," Wendy said as they circled the room.

"My thoughts exactly," Marissa said. "Besides, there's no terminal in here."

"Let's check the doctors' offices," Wendy suggested. "We know there will be a terminal in each of those."

Farther down the corridor there were a few dim lights from glazed laboratory doors; otherwise the whole clinic was dark. They moved quickly but carefully, Marissa trying the doctors' offices on the left while Wendy tried those on the right. All were locked.

"They certainly are careful," Marissa said. "I

swear this place seems more like a bank than a clinic."

"I don't think any of the offices will be open," Wendy said, stopping halfway down the hall. "Let's go back and try ultrasound. I think each of the units has terminals."

"I'll try the rest of the offices," Marissa said. "You go to ultrasound."

"Oh no!" Wendy said. "I'm not going anyplace by myself. I don't know about you, but I'm really spooked in here."

"Me too," Marissa said. "The idea of coming in here sounded a whole lot better before we got in."

"Maybe we should go," Wendy said. "We're not handling this well."

"Let's try ultrasound first," Marissa said. "At least it's on the way out."

The women retraced their steps toward the waiting area. The sharp cry of a siren made them both jump. The siren got louder, then faded. They realized with relief that it was only a passing police car.

"God!" Wendy exclaimed. "We really are in bad shape."

Passing by the receptionist's desk a second time, they tried the door leading to the ultrasound area. It was unlocked. Making their way down this narrower corridor, they began trying the doors to the three ultrasound rooms. They were able to open the very first door they tried.

"A promising sign," Marissa said. Since there

145

were no windows from which they'd be seen, they turned on the light switch. Marissa went back and closed the door to the waiting area and then the door to the ultrasound room.

The room was about twenty feet square and had two entrances: the one they'd just entered and another that connected to the lab. The ultrasound unit dominated the back of the room along with the examination table. All the complicated electronic components were built into a console that included a computer terminal.

"Eureka!" Wendy said as she stepped over to the terminal. She sat herself down on a stool with casters and pulled herself close. "You don't mind, do you?" Wendy asked. "Computers was my minor in college."

"Please," Marissa said. "I was hoping you'd take over here."

"Keep your fingers crossed," Wendy said as she turned the terminal's power switch on. The screen blinked to life as it emitted an eerie greenish glow.

"So far so good," Wendy said.

"Ahhee!" Alan Fong, the uniformed security guard, exclaimed. "You were right. The women have entered!" He spoke excitedly in Chinese, a Cantonese dialect to be exact. He pointed to a pinpoint of light in the middle of a board below the TV monitors. The board was a schematic of the computer layout of the clinic.

"Where are they?" David Pao asked in the same

dialect. He was considerably calmer than his co-hort.

"They have entered the computer in one of the ultrasound rooms," Alan said. He punched up the ultrasound room monitors from his own computer terminal.

"Not that room," Alan said. He made another entry into the computer. The monitor screen remained blank.

"Trouble?" David Pao asked.

"Not that room either," Alan said. He entered the code for the third ultrasound room.

The monitor screen blinked. Then an image emerged. Wendy could be plainly seen seated in front of the computer terminal built into the ultrasound console. Marissa was standing next to her.

"Want me to record it?" Alan asked.

"Please," David said.

Alan slipped a tape into a VCR and electronically connected it to the appropriate monitor. He then pushed the Record button.

"How long?" Alan asked.

"It doesn't matter," David said. "That's probably enough already."

Alan stopped the tape, ejected it, and then carefully labeled it.

"It is time to deal with them now," David said, taking some black leather gloves from his pocket and pulling them on.

Alan extracted his long-barreled revolver from his holster and checked the cylinder. It was loaded with soft-nosed bullets.

David's calm face showed the barest hint of a sarcastic smile. "I hope they do not resist."

"Do not worry," Alan said with a broader smile. "We can always make them resist."

"No trouble figuring this filing system," Wendy said. "It's pretty straightforward. Here comes my record." Having typed up the appropriate commands, Wendy entered her social security number via the terminal's keyboard. As soon as she pressed the Execute button, the information-page of her Women's Clinic file filled the screen.

"What did I tell you!" Wendy said, obviously pleased. As she was about to advance to the next page, Marissa restrained her and pointed to the category of occupation. "What's this 'health care worker'?" Marissa asked.

"A mild deception," Wendy explained. "I didn't want them to know I was a physician. I was afraid it would get back to the General and my private life wouldn't be so private anymore."

Marissa laughed. "I did the same sort of thing for the same reason."

"It's uncanny how we think alike," Wendy said.

"Now that we can call up individual records, what do you think is the best way to proceed?" Marissa asked.

"It's simple in theory," Wendy said. "What we need is that diagnostic code the woman up in medical records said they had for granulomatous blockage of the fallopian tubes. We just have to find it. I'm hoping we'll come across it in my chart or yours. It will appear as some kind of alphanumeric designator."

"We can use Rebecca Ziegler's record as well," Marissa said. She got out the dead woman's social security number.

They scanned Wendy's entire record, paying particular attention to the page containing the pathology of her fallopian tube biopsy. By the time they'd reached the final page, they'd come across a number of possible candidates for the code designator. Marissa jotted them down.

"Content-wise, there's nothing in here that I didn't already know," Wendy said. "At least nothing that would tempt me to jump out the window. Let's go on to yours."

"Try Rebecca's first," Marissa suggested. She handed Wendy the social security number.

Wendy entered the number and executed. Instantly the computer responded by flashing "no file found."

"I was afraid of that," Marissa said. "All right, go to mine." She recited her social security number and Wendy entered it. Soon Marissa's record was on the screen.

Wendy scrolled directly to the pathology page. Reading carefully, they spotted several notations they had also taken from Wendy's records.

"That's curious," Wendy said. "Check out the microscopic."

Marissa began to read it again.

"Do you notice anything strange?"

"I don't think so," Marissa said. "What caught your eye?"

"Let's see if you see it," Wendy said. Quickly she went back into her own record and called up her pathology page. "Read the microscopic!"

Marissa did as she was told. "Okay," she said when she'd finished. "What's on your mind?"

"Still don't see it?" Wendy questioned. "Just a second." She cleared her record and went back to Marissa's pathology page. "Read again," she suggested.

When Marissa was finished, she looked at her friend. "I get it now," she said. "They're exactly the same. Word for word, verbatim."

"Exactly," Wendy said. "Do you think that's weird?"

Marissa thought for a moment "No, I guess I don't," she said. "These reports were undoubtedly dictated. Doctors frequently dictate from rote when they are dictating similar cases. I'm sure you've heard surgeons dictating. Unless there's a complication, their dictations come out verbatim all the time. I did it myself when I was on surgery. All it suggests to me is that there are more cases here at the Women's Clinic: something we've suspected all along."

Wendy shrugged. "Maybe you're right," she said. "It just seemed odd at first. Anyway, let's get back to what we were doing. I'll try running a search using some of these possible code designators that we've found in both our charts."

Going back to a system utility menu, Wendy

began trying the various letter and number combinations Marissa had written down. The third one resulted in a list of eighteen numbers that appeared to be social security numbers.

"This looks very promising," Wendy said as she prepared to print out the list.

The only sound in the ultrasound room had been the barely audible click of the keyboard keys, but just as Wendy was about to push the Print key, Marissa heard the sound of a door opening not too far away.

"Wendy!" she whispered. "Did you hear that?"

Wendy responded by turning off both the computer terminal and the light. They were plunged into utter darkness.

For several minutes both terrifed women strained their ears to pick up the slightest sound. All their previous fears had congealed into one moment. They held their breath. In the far distance they heard the muffled sound of a refrigerant compressor switching on in a lab. As intently as they were listening, they even heard a bus go by on Mt. Auburn Street, almost a block away.

Groping soundlessly, they found each other's hands for a modicum of comfort and held on. Five minutes crawled by.

Finally Wendy spoke in a barely audible whisper: "Are you sure you heard a door?"

"I think so," Marissa answered.

"Then I think we'd better get out of here," Wendy said. "All of a sudden I have a terrible feeling."

"All right," Marissa agreed. "Try to stay calm." She didn't feel too calm herself. "Let's head over to the door."

Still holding on to each other and fearful of turning on the light, they blindly inched across the room with their free hands out in front of them. They moved a half step at a time until they touched the wall. Advancing along the wall, they came to the door to the narrow hall.

As quietly as she could manage, Marissa opened the door, first a crack, then wider. At the end of the short hallway they could see weak light coming from the waiting room windows.

"My God!" Marissa said. "The door to the waiting room is open. I know I closed it."

"What should we do?" Wendy pleaded.

"I don't know," Marissa said.

"We have to get to the stairwell," Wendy said.

For the next few moments, the two were paralyzed with indecision. They let another few minutes go by. Neither heard another sound.

"I want out of here," Wendy said at last.

"Okay," Marissa answered. She was equally as eager. Together they edged down the corridor to the lip of the waiting room. Slowly they leaned out and scanned the shadows. Beyond the waiting area and down another short hall they could see the red glowing Exit sign indicating the stairwell.

"Ready?" Marissa asked.

"Let's go," Wendy said.

The two women hurried across the waiting area, moving toward the hall that would lead to the stairwell. But they didn't make it. They stopped dead in their tracks as Marissa let out a stifled cry of surprise. Directly in front of them, a figure had stepped out from the recess of one of the elevators. His face was obscured by shadows.

Wendy and Marissa spun around in hopes of making it back to the ultrasound room. But they stopped again. In front of them the door to the ultrasound area swung shut with a slam. To their horror another dark figure stepped from behind the door.

The two threatening figures began to advance. Cornered from ahead and behind, they were trapped.

"What is going on here?" Marissa asked. She tried vainly to make her tone sound authoritative. "I'm Dr. Blumenthal and this is Dr.—"

But she didn't finish her sentence. A blow flashed out of the darkness and caught her on the side of the head, hurling her to the floor with her ears ringing.

"Don't hit her!" Wendy shouted. She tried to go to Marissa's aid, but was met by a similar blow. The next thing she knew, she was sprawled on the carpet.

Then the lights went on.

Marissa blinked in the sudden glare. Her head was throbbing from the blow. She pushed herself up to a sitting position. She rubbed the spot where she'd been hit just over her left ear. Then she looked at her palm, half expecting to see blood. But her hand was clean. She glanced up at the man standing over her. He was a security guard dressed in a well-pressed, dark-green uniform with epaulets. Marissa saw that he was an Asian. He smiled down at her, his black eyes shining like onyx.

"Why did you hit me?" Marissa demanded. She had never expected such violence.

"Thieves!" the guard snarled in heavily accented English. His hand shot out again and slapped Marissa in the same spot he'd hit her the first time.

A burning pain went through Marissa's face as she again fell to the carpet.

"Stop!" Wendy called as she tried to get to her feet. But the man in the gray suit kicked her feet out from under her. She fell back to the floor, knocking the wind from her lungs. Helplessly, she struggled to get a breath.

"Why are you doing this?" Marissa wailed. She pushed herself up to her hands and knees, then struggled to her feet. She was beginning to think she was dealing with two lunatics. She tried to speak again, but before she could say a word, her ketamine-inspired nightmare came back as vividly as it had at the restaurant, adding to her panic.

"Thieves!" the guard repeated. Mercilessly he stepped up to Marissa and slapped her a third time, knocking her back against the receptionist's desk.

The desk broke Marissa's fall. She sent a few dispensers and a metal stapler crashing to the floor.

Survival instinct told her to make a run for it,

154

but she could hardly leave Wendy. Marissa glared at her assailant. "We're not thieves!" she shouted. "Are you crazy?"

The guard's smile broadened into a hideous grin, exposing decaying teeth. The next second, his expression was stern. "You call me crazy?" he snarled. He reached for his revolver.

Wide-eyed with terror, Marissa watched as the man raised the gun and aimed its barrel directly at her. She heard the horrifying mechanical click as the guard cocked the gun's hammer back. He was going to shoot her.

"No!" Wendy shouted. She'd regained her breath and was sitting up.

Marissa couldn't speak. She thought of uttering some plea, but the words wouldn't come. She was paralyzed with fear. She couldn't take her eyes away from the blank hole of the barrel as she braced for the shattering blast.

"Hold it!" a voice cried out.

Marissa winced, then opened her eyes. The gun hadn't fired. She sucked in a lungful of air as the gun in front of her face lowered. She hadn't even been aware she'd been holding her breath.

Marissa allowed her eyes to leave the gun and rise to the guard's face. He was staring in disbelief toward the short hallway to the elevators and stairwell. Marissa's eyes followed his line of sight. Standing there, holding a gun of his own in both hands, was a rumpled figure. The gun was trained steadily on the guard.

"Aren't you guys overreacting?" the stranger

155

asked. "Now I want you to put that gun on the desk and move over to the wall. No fast moves. I've shot a lot of people in my day. One more wouldn't make much difference."

For a moment no one moved or spoke. The security guard's gaze shifted from the newly arrived intruder to the Chinese man in the gray suit. He seemed to be contemplating whether or not to comply.

"The gun on the desk!" the stranger repeated. Turning to the man in the gray suit, he added: "Don't you move!" The man had started to circle the room.

"Who are you?" the guard asked.

"Paul Abrums," the man said. "Just a workaday, retired cop trying to earn a few dollars to supplement my pension. Certainly is lucky I was in the neighborhood to keep things from getting out of hand here. Now, I'm not going to tell you again: put the gun on the desk!"

Marissa stepped aside as the guard moved to the receptionist's desk and laid his revolver down. Wendy got up from the floor and joined Marissa.

"Now," Paul said. "If you two gentlemen would kindly step over to that wall and put your hands on it, I'd feel a lot better."

The two Asians looked at each other, then complied. Paul went to the desk and picked up the revolver. He stuffed it into his trouser pocket. Turning his attention back to the men, he went up behind the guard and frisked him for additional weapons. Satisfied, he turned to the man in the gray suit.

In a flash, the man in the gray suit spun around with a guttural yell, kicking the gun from Paul's hand and sending it flying across the room. It clattered to the floor near the windows.

Without missing a beat, the man assumed a crouched posture. With another yell, he aimed a second kick at Paul's head.

Having been caught off-guard by the first kick, Paul was prepared for the second. An experienced street fighter, he ducked the kick and grabbed a chair and slammed it into his attacker's midsection. The chair and the man ended up in a tangle on the floor.

Next, the security guard assumed a crouched position suggesting martial arts training. He came at Paul from the side as Paul vainly tried to extract the long-barreled Colt from his trouser pocket. Abandoning the gun for the moment, Paul grabbed a lamp from an end table and used it to parry the guard's lightning thrusts.

As more chairs began to fly, Marissa and Wendy dashed back through the door to the ultrasound area. They had one goal in mind: to get back to the safety of the overnight ward.

Tearing open the door to the ultrasound room they had been in only minutes before, they hastily turned on the light and ran through to the door to the lab. Once in the lab, Wendy found the light switch and flipped it on. Marissa closed the door. Noticing it had a lock, she locked it behind her.

Continuing on, they sprinted between lab benches and incubators to the door that led to the main corridor. Before they made it, they heard the ultrasound room's door being rattled behind them, then its glass panel being shattered with a smash.

Arriving in a panic at the door to the main corridor, Wendy tried to open it, but it was locked. As she struggled with the bolt, Marissa turned into the room to see the security guard coming after them. Picking up some laboratory glassware, she began throwing it at the approaching figure. The smashing glass slowed the guard but didn't stop him.

At last, Wendy managed to yank the door open. The two women dashed out into the darkened main corridor. Hoping to avoid the waiting area, they turned right. In a full panic, they ran headlong down the hall, hoping to wind up at another stairwell.

Sliding to a partial stop and almost falling in their haste, the women had to negotiate a ninety-degree right-hand turn in the darkened corridor. As they ran now they could see a window at the end with lights from the city diffusing in. Unfortunately there were no red Exit signs. Behind them they heard the laboratory door bang open. The guard was not far behind.

Skidding to an abrupt stop as the hall terminated at the window, Marissa and Wendy frantically tried the doors on either side. Both were locked. Glancing up the corridor, they could see the guard had reached the bend. He started down toward them, slowing his steps. He had them cornered.

On the right wall, Marissa noticed a glass cabinet. She yanked it open and grabbed the heavy brass nozzle of a canvas fire hose. Its coils fell out onto the floor in a serpentine mass.

"Turn on the faucet," Marissa yelled to Wendy.

Wendy reached into the cabinet and tried to turn the knob. It wouldn't budge. She put both hands on it. With all her strength, she pushed. Suddenly, the valve began to move. Wendy spun it wide open.

Marissa held the heavy nozzle with both hands. She pointed it down the corridor at the approaching guard. Although she had braced herself, Marissa was not prepared for the force of the jet that finally burst forth. The power was enough to knock her backward, tearing the hose from her grip. The nozzle flailed wildly under the force of the uncontrolled jet.

Marissa scrambled out of the way of the hose as it sent a pressurized stream of water in every direction. Spotting a fire alarm next to the cabinet, Wendy pulled down the lever, activating both an alarm and the sprinkler system. With the same stroke, an alarm in the Cambridge fire station was set off, interrupting a highly contested game of poker.

Both Marissa and Wendy had been sobbing for some time. As embarrassed as they were about their emotions, they couldn't help it. Their feelings had run the gamut from terror to relief to humiliation. Then the weeping had taken over. It had been an experience neither would forget. Both agreed it had been the worst of their life.

Marissa and Wendy were sitting on scarred wooden chairs whose varnish was coming off in flakes like a peel after a bad sunburn. The chairs were in the center of a blank, dingy room that was mildly littered with trash and smelled of alcohol and dried vomit. The only picture on the wall was the humorless face of Michael Dukakis.

Robert and Gustave were sitting across from them. George Freeborn, Robert's personal attorney, was in a chair by the window balancing an alligator briefcase on his lap. It was 2:33 in the morning. They were at the district courthouse.

Just as she finally began to gain control of herself, Marissa's eyes welled.

"Try to pull yourself together," Robert told her.

Marissa glanced at Wendy, who had her head down, her face pressed into a tissue. Every so often her shoulders would shake. Gustave, who was sitting next to her, put a hand on his wife's shoulder.

At the conference table in the center of the room sat a no-nonsense woman of about forty-five years of age. She wasn't happy to be there, as she'd let everyone know. She'd been pulled from her bed in the middle of the night. On the table in front of her was one of the many forms that had been filled out that night. She was completing it with exaggerated strokes of her pen.

Glancing at her watch, the woman raised her head. "So where's the bail bondsman?" she asked.

"He has been called, Madam Magistrate," Mr. Freeborn assured her. "I'm certain he will be here momentarily."

"If not, these ladies are going back into the lockup," the magistrate threatened. "Just because they can afford a high-priced lawyer doesn't mean they should be treated any differently by the law."

"Absolutely," Mr. Freeborn agreed. "I spoke with the bail bondsman myself. He will be here immediately, I assure you."

Marissa shuddered. She'd never been in jail before, and she didn't want to go back. The experience that evening had been overwhelming. She'd even been handcuffed and strip-searched.

When the fire department had arrived at the Women's Clinic, she and Wendy had been ecstatic. The flailing hose had kept the security guard at bay. But along with the firefighters had come the police, and the police had listened to the guard. In the end, Marissa and Wendy had been arrested and led away in handcuffs.

First they'd been taken to the Cambridge police station where they had been read their rights a second time, booked, fingerprinted, and photographed. After they'd been allowed to call their husbands, they were put into the police station lockup. They'd even had to endure the indignities of using exposed toilets.

161

Later on, Marissa and Wendy had been taken from the police station cells, re-handcuffed, and driven to the Middlesex County Courthouse, where they had been reincarcerated in a more serious-appearing jail. There they'd been given dry prison garb to replace the wet clothes they'd had on.

The magistrate was kept waiting another ten minutes before the bail bondsman arrived. He was an overweight, balding man. He entered carrying a vinyl briefcase.

The bondsman strode directly to the conference table, placing his briefcase on it with a resounding thud. "Hello, Gertrude," he said, addressing the magistrate. He released the latch on his case.

"Did you walk here, Harold?" asked the magistrate.

"What are you talking about?" said the bondsman. "I live out near Somerville Hospital. How could I walk here?"

"I was being sarcastic," the magistrate said with a disgusted expression. "Forget it. Here are the bail and bond orders for these two ladies. They are for ten thousand each."

The bondsman took the papers. He was impressed and pleased. "Wow, ten thousand!" he said. "What did they do, hit the Bay Bank in Harvard Square?"

"Just about," said the magistrate. "They're to be arraigned by Judge Burano on Monday morning for breaking and entering, trespass, malicious destruction of property, larceny through unauthorized computer entry and theft of private files, and . . ." The magistrate consulted the form in front of her. "Oh, yes! Assault and battery. Apparently they beat up on a security guard."

"That's not true," Marissa yelled, unable to contain herself. Her sudden outburst brought fresh tears. She blurted out that it had been the other way around: the guards had attacked them. "And Paul Abrums, a retired policeman, will testify to it," she added.

"Marissa, shut up!" Robert said. He still couldn't believe his wife's escapade.

The magistrate glared at Marissa. "You are perhaps forgetting that Mr. Abrums is also a defendant in this action and will be facing the same charges when he gets out of the hospital."

"Mrs. Buchanan is very upset," Mr. Freeborn said.

"That's obvious," the magistrate said.

"Which one's Buchanan and which is Anderson?" the bondsman asked, coming over to the men.

"I'll take care of this," Mr. Freeborn said. "Mr. Buchanan's banker is waiting for your call to arrange collateral for both suspects. Here is the number."

The bondsman took the number.

"You can use this phone," the magistrate said, pointing to the phone on the conference table with her pen.

As soon as the bondsman made his call, the rest of the paperwork went swiftly.

"That's that," the magistrate announced.

Marissa stood up. "Thank you," she said.

"Sorry you didn't like our accommodations here at the courthouse," the magistrate told her, still miffed at what she thought was the special attention Marissa and Wendy had been able to arrange through Mr. Freeborn.

Mr. Freeborn accompanied both couples as they left the deserted courthouse. Their heels echoed loudly against the marble floor.

Marissa and Wendy were chilled by the time they got to their respective cars. They climbed in in silence. No one had spoken since leaving the conference room.

"Thanks for coming out, George," Robert called to the lawyer.

"Yes, thanks," Gustave called.

"See you all Monday morning," George called back. He waved as he climbed into his sleek black Mercedes.

Robert and Gustave exchanged glances. They shook their heads in mutual sympathy.

Robert got into his car and slammed the door. He glanced at Marissa, but she was staring straight ahead, her jaw set. Robert started the car and pulled out into the street.

"I'm not going to say I told you so," he said finally as they crossed over the old Charles River Dam.

"Good. Don't say anything." After her ordeal, Marissa felt she needed comforting, not a lecture.

"I think you owe me an explanation," Robert said.

"And I don't think I owe you anything," Marissa said, glaring at Robert. "And let me tell you something: those guards were crazy back in the clinic. I was almost shot in the face at point-blank range. The man you hired told you so. They even beat us!"

"It all sounds a little hard to believe," Robert said.

"Are you suggesting we're lying to you?" Marissa asked, incredulous.

"I believe that's what you believe happened," Robert said evasively.

Marissa faced forward. Once again her emotions were caroming around like a squash ball. She didn't know whether to cry more or pound the dashboard. Undecided, she just clenched her fists and gritted her teeth.

They drove in hostile silence along Storrow Drive. After they got on the Mass Pike, Marissa turned to him. "Why did you have me followed?" she demanded.

"Apparently it was a damn good thing I did."

"That's not the point," Marissa said. "Why did you have me followed?" she repeated. "I don't like it."

"I had you followed to try to keep you out of trouble," Robert said. "Obviously it didn't work."

"Someone has to try to follow up on these TB

cases," Marissa said. "Occasionally risks have to be taken."

"Not to the point of doing something plainly illegal," Robert said. "You are obsessed with this thing, and irrational. It's become a crusade, and it's driving me crazy. I can't believe you. You're still trying to justify unjustifiable behavior."

"What if I told you we discovered eighteen cases of TB salpingitis in the Women's Clinic alone?" Marissa asked. "Do you think that might bear out my suspicions? And that eighteen probably isn't even counting Rebecca Ziegler. Her record was already erased from the computer. What do you think about that?"

Robert shrugged irritably.

"I'll tell you what I think. I think they have something to hide," Marissa said. "I think there was something in Rebecca's record that they didn't want anyone to see."

"Come on, Marissa!" Robert snapped. "Now you're getting melodramatic and paranoid. This is all conjecture. In the meantime, we'll be footing some all-too-palpable legal fees to try to keep you out of jail."

"So it all comes down to money," Marissa shot back. "That's your biggest concern, isn't it?"

Marissa closed her eyes. Sometimes she wondered what had ever possessed her to marry this man. And now she had the threat of a jail sentence looming in her immediate future. Things seemed to be going from bad to worse to worse still, like the unraveling of a Greek tragedy.

166

Marissa opened her eyes and stared at the on-rushing road. Her mind jumped from one anxiety to another. She wondered what effect the guard's blows might have had on her embryo transfer. Monday was to be her day of reckoning in more ways than one. Not only was she to be arraigned on an array of criminal charges, she was scheduled for her pregnancy blood test.

Fresh tears welled in her eyes. The way things were going, it wasn't hard to predict how that blood test would turn out. All of a sudden it wasn't so surprising that Rebecca Ziegler had jumped to her death. Maybe she'd been under similar stress. But, then again, maybe she hadn't jumped. Maybe she'd been pushed. . . .

8

APRIL 2, 1990
9:35 A.M.

ALTHOUGH MARISSA and Wendy had spoken on the phone early Saturday morning, Marissa did not see her friend until Monday morning at the courthouse. As she and Robert entered the courtroom, they saw Wendy, Gustave, and their lawyer sitting in the pewlike benches on the left. Robert tried to steer Marissa to an empty row on the right, but she resisted and went over to her friend.

Wendy looked awful. She stared ahead as if in

167

a trance. Her eyes were red, rimmed, and sunken. It was obvious she'd been crying, probably a lot. Marissa touched her on the shoulder and whispered her name. Seeing Marissa, fresh tears began to streak down her cheeks.

"What's the matter?" Marissa asked. Wendy seemed more distraught than expected.

Wendy tried to speak but couldn't. All she could do was shake her head. Marissa grabbed her arm and pulled her out of her seat. Together they walked back through the milling crowd and out of the courtroom.

Spotting a ladies' room, Marissa steered her friend into the lavatory.

"What is it?" Marissa asked. "Is it something between you and Gustave?"

Wendy shook her head again and sobbed. Marissa hugged her tight. "Is it this legal stuff?" she asked.

Wendy shook her head. "It's my blood test," she said at last. "I had it drawn on Saturday. I'm not pregnant."

"But that was only the first test," Marissa said. "They'll have to do another to see how much the hormone goes up." She was trying to be optimistic, but she knew that if Wendy thought she wasn't pregnant, then she probably wasn't. The news sent an icicle through Marissa's heart. Just that morning before coming to the courthouse, Marissa had stopped at the Memorial for her blood to be drawn for the same test.

"The hormone level was so low," Wendy sobbed, "I can't be pregnant. I just know it."

"I'm so sorry," Marissa said.

"Do you think what happened at the clinic Friday night could have had an effect on the transfer?" Wendy asked.

"Oh, no!" Marissa said, even though the same awful thought was in her mind.

"Excuse me," said a gum-chewing woman in a tight mini-skirt. "Either of you Dr. Blumenthal?"

"I am," Marissa said with surprise.

The woman hooked a thumb over her shoulder. "Your husband is waiting. Says he wants you out there immediately."

"They must be starting the arraignments," Marissa said to Wendy. "We have to be there."

"I know," Wendy said, still crying. She took tissue from Marissa and wiped her eyes. "I look terrible," she said. "I'm afraid to look in the mirror."

"You look fine," Marissa lied.

The two women left the ladies' room together. Robert was standing right outside the door with his hands on his hips.

"What's the matter now?" he asked with exasperation after taking one look at Wendy. "You do understand that you have to be in the courtroom when your cases are called, don't you?"

Marissa addressed him in a low, barely civil tone. "Look, I know it's hard for you to appreciate, but Wendy is grief-stricken because her latest embryo transfer didn't take. To us, it's as bad and as real as a miscarriage."

Robert rolled his eyes. "Come on," he said. "She can save it for her therapist. I'm not about to let you jeopardize yourselves by missing your arraignment."

Despite Robert's concern, Marissa and Wendy weren't called for another thirty minutes. As they nervously waited, Mr. Freeborn explained that the cases were taken in the order that the involved arresting authority completed the appropriate paperwork. So they had to wait while a parade of characters were arraigned on a variety of charges such as manslaughter, robbery, attempted rape, drug trafficking, driving under the influence, receiving stolen goods, and assault and battery.

Finally, at ten-twenty, the clerk of the court called out: "Cases 90-45CR-987 and 988, the Commonwealth versus Blumenthal-Buchanan and Wilson-Anderson."

"Okay, that's us," Mr. Freeborn said, standing and motioning for Marissa to do the same.

Across the aisle, Marissa could see Wendy stand with her lawyer. He was a tall, thin man whose jacket sleeves were too short, making his arms and bony hands seem unnaturally long.

Together the foursome moved from the gallery section to a spot before the bench.

Judge Burano appeared disinterested. He continued to peruse the array of papers laid out in front of him. He was a heavyset man in his sixties, with wrinkled features that gave him an uncanny resemblance to a bulldog. Reading glasses pinched the end of his broad nose.

The clerk cleared his throat, then read in a loud voice for all to hear. "Marissa Blumenthal-Buchanan, you are hereby charged by the Commonwealth of Massachusetts with breaking and entering. How do you so plead?"

"Mrs. Marissa Blumenthal-Buchanan pleads not guilty," Mr. Freeborn said with his commanding voice.

"Marissa Blumenthal-Buchanan, you are hereby charged by the Commonwealth of Massachusetts with trespass," the clerk of the court droned on. He went through the entire list of charges, and each time Mr. Freeborn entered the same not-guilty plea.

When Marissa's charges had been read and recorded and her pleas entered, the clerk of the court repeated the same process with Wendy.

At that point a woman Marissa guessed to be an assistant district attorney stood up. With several sheets in her hand for reference, she addressed the court: "Your honor, the Commonwealth requests the reimposition of the bail previously set by the magistrate in these two cases. These are serious charges, and it is our understanding that there was significant property damage at the involved clinic."

"Your Honor, if I may," Mr. Freeborn said. "My client, Dr. Blumenthal-Buchanan, is an esteemed physician in our state who has received national recognition for her work. I believe strongly that she should be released on her own recognizance. I would like to make a motion that the bail set by the magistrate be dropped."

"Your Honor," Wendy's lawyer said, "I would like to echo my esteemed colleague's motion. My client, Dr. Wendy Wilson-Anderson, is on the staff at the renowned Massachusetts Eye and Ear Infirmary as an ophthalmologist. She is also a property owner in the Commonwealth."

For the first time since Marissa and Wendy had come forth, the judge glanced up from his paperwork. He regarded the group before him with a cold eye.

"I will reduce bail to five thousand for each defendant," he said.

Just then, a well-dressed man in a handsome business suit approached the prosecution's table. He tapped the woman ADA on the shoulder and spoke to her at length. Once he had finished, the woman began conferring with her two colleagues.

"We will set a pre-trial conference date for May 8, 1990," the clerk of the court said.

"If it please the court, Your Honor," the assistant district attorney said, once again approaching the bench, "there has been a development in this case. Mr. Brian Pearson would like to address the court."

"And who is Mr. Brian Pearson?" Judge Burano demanded.

"I am counsel for the Women's Clinic, Your Honor," Mr. Pearson said. "It was within the premises of the Women's Clinic that the alleged crimes were committed by the defendants. Dr. Wingate, the director of the clinic, has instructed me to petition the court with respect to this matter. Although the defendants' behavior is not condoned in any way, the clinic does not wish to press charges, provided the women acknowledge their liability and give their word that they will respect the property of the clinic in future and pay reasonable compensation for the repair of damages their acts caused."

"This is unusual, to say the least," Judge Burano said. He cleared his throat. Turning to the assistant district attorney, he asked: "What is the Commonwealth's opinion of this development?"

"We do not object, Your Honor," the assistant district attorney said. "If the clinic doesn't want to press charges, then the Commonwealth won't insist."

"Well, isn't this curious," the judge said, turning his attention back to Marrisa and Wendy. "Nolle prosequi! This certainly is a first in my court. But if no one wants to prosecute, then it behooves me to lessen the judicial burden of the Commonwealth by dropping the case. But before doing so, I intend to voice an opinion."

Judge Burano leaned forward, studying the women. "From the material I've gone over, it suggests to me that you two adults have been acting mighty irresponsibly, especially in your capacity as physicians. I don't countenance such obvious disrespect for the law and for private property. The case is dismissed, but you two wom-

173

en should feel indebted to the Women's Clinic for its generosity."

Marissa felt a tug on her arm. She looked at Mr. Freeborn, who motioned for her to go. The clerk of the court was already calling out the case number for the next arraignment.

Confused but happy to be escorted out of the courtroom, Marissa waited until they'd reached the cigarette-smoke-filled hallway before speaking. Robert was directly behind her with Wendy and Gustave in tow.

"What happened?" Marissa demanded.

"Simple," Mr. Freeborn said. "Like the judge said, the clinic decided to be magnanimous and not press charges. The ADA went along with it. Of course we'll have to negotiate the 'reasonable' compensation."

"But other than that, it's over?" Marissa asked. It seemed like the first good news she'd gotten in months.

"That's right," Mr. Freeborn said.

"What kind of compensation do you think it might involve?" Robert asked.

"Not a clue," Mr. Freeborn said.

Wendy put her arms around Marissa and gave her a big hug. Marissa patted her back. "I'll call you," Marissa whispered in her ear. Even with the charges dropped, Marissa knew Wendy would still be depressed.

Wendy nodded, then left with Gustave and their lawyer.

Robert conferred with Mr. Freeborn for a few

more minutes. Then the two shook hands and Robert escorted Marissa to their car.

"You girls were mighty lucky," Robert told Marissa as they pulled into traffic on the Monsignor O'Brien Highway. "George had never heard of such a thing. I have to hand it to the clinic, that was pretty big of them, asking for the charges to be dropped."

"It's all a clever cover-up," Marissa said.

Robert looked at her as if he'd not heard. "What?"

"You heard me," Marissa said. "It was a clever trick to keep the public from finding out what kinds of beasts they employ for guards. It was also a good way to get us to drop our inquiries into this TB issue and maybe Rebecca Ziegler's death."

"Oh, Marissa!" Robert moaned.

"The judge doesn't know any of the other details," Marissa said. "He doesn't have any idea of the dimensions of this case."

Robert beat the steering wheel with his fist. "I don't know if I can take this anymore."

"Stop the car!" Marissa said.

"What?"

"I want you to pull over."

"Are you getting sick?" Robert asked.

"Just do it."

Robert glanced over his shoulder and pulled into the roundabout in front of the Science Museum.

Marissa opened her door, got out, and slammed the door behind her. She started walking. Confused, Robert lowered his window and called after her. "What the hell is going on?" he demanded.

"I'm walking," Marissa said. "I need to be by myself. You're driving me crazy."

"I'm driving you crazy?" Robert called after her in disbelief. For a moment he was indecisive. Then he muttered, "Jesus Christ!" Rolling up his window, he drove off without looking back.

With her hands shoved deep into her raincoat pockets, Marissa walked along the Esplanade that bordered the Charles River. It was another overcast day. The color of the river was gunmetal gray. Puddles dotted the walkway.

Marissa walked as far as the Arthur Fiedler shell, then crossed over to Arlington Street. At the corner of Arlington and Boylston she took the T out Huntington Avenue to her pediatric clinic.

Marissa entered the building through a back door. She wasn't interested in talking to anyone. With effort she climbed the fire stairs, then snaked through several exam rooms, making her way to her office. Closing her door, she didn't bother to turn on her light. She was confident no one knew she was there, and as depressed as she was, she wanted to keep it that way.

She didn't bother to check her messages for fear the results from her pregnancy test had already been called in. Instead, she sat and brooded at her desk. Never had she felt so isolated and alone. Except for Wendy, she couldn't think of anyone to talk with.

After an hour, she began to entertain the idea

of seeing some walk-in patients to take her mind off things, but then she quickly realized she was still too distraught to concentrate.

All she could think about was the Women's Clinic.

When the telephone rang, she lifted the receiver off the hook before the first ring had completed. It had startled her.

"Hello?" she said.

"Dr. Blumenthal?" a woman's voice asked.

"Yes," Marissa said.

"This is the lab over at the Memorial," the woman said. "We have your beta human chorionic gonadotropin level. It was only two mg/ml. We can do another in twenty-four or thirty-six hours if you'd like, but it doesn't look good."

"Thank you," Marissa said, her voice completely flat. She wrote down the value, then hung up the phone. It was exactly as she feared: a result just like Wendy's. She wasn't pregnant!

For a moment Marissa merely stared at the figure she had written on her scratch pad. Then her vision blurred with tears of grief. She was so tired of it all. She began to think of Rebecca Ziegler again and the troubles that drove the poor woman to suicide—if it was suicide.

Suddenly the phone rang again. Marissa grabbed the receiver with the ridiculous hope that it was the lab at the Memorial calling to say they had made a mistake. Could she be pregnant after all?

"Hello?" Marissa said.

"The operator told me you were in," the receptionist explained. "You have a visitor down here in the main reception. Should I . . ."

"I can't see anyone," Marissa said. She hung up the phone. Almost immediately it rang again. This time she ignored it. After nine rings, it stopped.

A few minutes later there was a knock on her door. Marissa didn't move. There was a second knock, but she continued to ignore it, hoping whoever it was would go away. Instead, she saw the knob turn. Marissa faced the opening door, ready to snap at whoever dared disturb her. But when she saw Dr. Frederick Houser's portly figure at the threshold, she softened.

"Is there something wrong, Marissa?" Dr. Houser said. He was holding his wire-rimmed glasses in his hand.

"A few personal problems," Marissa said. "I'll be all right. Thank you for your concern."

Undeterred, Dr. Houser stepped into the room. Marissa could see that someone was with him. With some surprise, she immediately recognized Cyrill Dubchek.

"I hope I'm not intruding," Cyrill said.

Flustered, Marissa stood up, straightening her hair.

"Dr. Dubchek told me you and he worked together at the CDC," Dr. Houser said. "When the receptionist called me to say that you weren't seeing visitors, I thought it was time for me to intervene. I hope I've done the right thing."

"Oh, of course!" Marissa said. "I had no idea it was Dr. Dubchek. Cyrill, I'm so sorry. Come in, sit down." Marissa gestured toward an empty chair. She hadn't seen Cyrill for several years, but he'd not changed one iota. As usual he was impeccably dressed and was still as handsome as ever.

Thinking of her own appearance, Marissa became acutely self-conscious. She knew she looked as terrible as she felt, especially with all her recent bouts of tears.

"I think I'll let you two have some privacy," Dr. Houser said tactfully. With that, he quickly left and closed the door.

"He told me you've been having quite a time with this infertility treatment," Cyrill told her.

"It has been a strain," Marissa admitted. She collapsed into her desk chair. "Only moments ago I learned that the last embryo transfer was not successful. So I'm afraid I've been crying—again. I've been doing more than my share of crying over the last few months."

"I'm so sorry," Cyrill said. "I wish there was some way I could help. But you look fine."

"Please!" Marissa said. "Don't look at me. I can't bear to imagine what I look like."

"It's a bit hard to have a conversation without looking at you," Cyrill said with a sympathetic smile. "Although it is true you look as if you've been crying, you still look as pretty as ever to me."

"Let's change the subject," Marissa said.

"Then I'll tell you why I stopped by," Cyrill

said. "I had to fly up here on other business, but early this morning one of the people over in bacteriology came to my office with the news that there has been one other concentrated area of TB salpingitis cases like the ones you are interested in."

"Oh?"

"The location surprised me," Cyrill said. "Would you care to guess?"

"I don't think I have the mental strength," Marissa said.

"Brisbane," Cyrill said.

"Australia?"

"Yup, Brisbane, Australia. It's part of what they call over there the Gold Coast."

"I'm not even sure where on the Australian continent Brisbane is," Marissa confessed.

"It's in Queensland, on the east coast," Cyrill said. "I've been there once. Charming city. Great climate. Lots of new high-rises along the beach south of the city. It's an attractive area."

"Anybody have any thoughts as to why there would be a concentration there?" Marissa asked. As far as she was concerned it might have been Timbuktu.

"Not really," Cyrill admitted. "There has been some increase in TB in general, especially in those countries allowing significant immigration from Southeast Asia. Whether the Brisbane area has gotten more than its share of boat people, I haven't the foggiest. There has been some increase in TB here in the U.S. above and beyond what could be expected with immigration from endemic areas, but I believe that's secondary to drugs and AIDS rather than any change in the pathogenicity of the bacteria. At any rate, here's a paper on the cases in Australia."

Cyrill handed Marissa a reprint of an article that appeared in the *Australian Journal of Infectious Diseases*.

"Apparently the author is a pathologist who found twenty-three cases similar to those you've described. It's quite a good paper."

Marissa began to flip through the article. It was hard for her to get excited. Australia was halfway around the world.

"The fellow from bacteriology told me something else," Cyrill continued. "He said that there was a case of disseminated TB at the Memorial. I mention it only because the patient is a twenty-nine-year-old woman from a well-to-do Boston family. Her name is Evelyn Welles. The demographics of the case jumped out at me. I thought it might interest you as well. So there you have it."

"Thank you, Cyrill," Marissa said. She tried to smile. She was afraid she was about to start crying again. Seeing an old friend was reanimating her fragile emotions.

Cyrill stayed for another fifteen minutes before he insisted he had to leave. He had to be back in Atlanta that evening.

After Cyrill had departed, Marissa's depression returned. She sat at her desk for a long time without doing much of anything. At least she didn't cry. She just stared out the window at the deteriorating day. But eventually she began to think of the information Cyrill had brought her. She glanced down at the journal article. She'd read it later. Meanwhile there were things she had to do. Picking herself up, she pulled her coat back on and forced herself to drive to the Memorial.

The patient, Evelyn Welles, was in isolation in intensive care, with a chart that reflected the difficulties of her case; it weighed five pounds. Marissa had little difficulty finding her. Nor did she have trouble finding the resident attending to her care. He was a slight fellow from New York City with intense eyes and nervous twitches. His name was Ben Goldman.

"She's in bad shape," Ben admitted upon Marissa's inquiry. "Really bad. Moribund. I don't expect her to last much more than another day. We've got her on maximum chemo but it doesn't seem to be doing anything."

"It's definitely TB?" Marissa asked as she peered through the glass of the woman's intensive-care cubicle. She'd been intubated and was on assisted respiration. A fully gowned and masked nurse was in the cubicle giving moment-to-moment care. Multiple IV lines snaked down from clusters of bottles above her head.

"No question," Ben said. "We've gotten acid-fast bacilli from everyplace we've tried: stomach washings, blood, even a bronchial biopsy. It's TB all right."

"Any idea of the epidemiology of the case?" Marissa asked.

"Oh, yeah," Ben said. "Some interesting facts have turned up. Apparently she visited Thailand about a year ago and stayed there for several weeks. That might be a factor. But more important, we've picked up a heretofore unrecognized immunodeficiency condition. The blood boys are working on it. So far it's thought to be secondary to an undefined collagen disease. A combination of the travel and her depressed immune response could be the explanation."

"Have you been able to talk to her at all?" Marissa asked.

"Nope," Ben said. "She was comatose when she was brought in. Probably got some brain abscesses. We haven't felt it worth the risk to take her to the NMR or the CAT scan."

Marissa absently flipped through the thick chart. Despite these reasonable explanations of the patient's condition, she had a feeling that Evelyn Welles' TB could be related to the TB salpingitis cases. As Dubchek had suggested, maybe it was her age and social status.

"Has much of a GYN history been obtained?" Marissa asked.

"Not much," Ben admitted. "In view of her overwhelming infection, parts of the work-up have been left superficial. What we got on systems review, we got from the husband."

"Do you know if she's ever been seen at the Women's Clinic in Cambridge?" Marissa asked.

"Sure don't," Ben said. "But I'll be happy to ask the husband when he returns. he comes in every night around ten."

"If she has been seen at the clinic, it would be great if you could ask the husband to get a copy of her record," Marissa said. "And one other thing. Could you manage to do a smear of her vaginal secretions to see if there are any TB organisms there as well?"

"Sure," Ben said with a shrug of his narrow shoulders.

Marissa paid the taxi driver while sitting in the backseat, shoving the money through the Plexiglas divider. It was dark and raining harder now than it had been earlier so that when she emerged from the cab, she ran in an effort to keep from getting soaked.

Inside her house she took off her damp coat and hung it in the laundry room. Avoiding the kitchen, she went directly to her study. Although she hadn't eaten all day, she wasn't the least bit hungry. And though she was exhausted, she wasn't about to sleep. The visit to the hospital and the plight of Evelyn Welles had renewed her terror as much as it had reawakened her curiosity.

"It's almost nine," Robert said, surprising Marissa by his presence. She had not heard him. He was standing in the doorway, comfortably dressed, arms crossed. His tone and expression reflected his usual irritation of late.

184

"I'm perfectly aware of the time," Marissa said as she sat down and turned on her reading lamp.

"You could have called," Robert said. "The last I saw of you was when you jumped out of the car in front of the Science Museum. I was about to call the police."

"Your concern is touching," Marissa said. She knew she was being confrontational, but she couldn't help it. "In case you are interested, I'm not pregnant."

"I guess I didn't expect you'd be," Robert said, his voice softening. He shrugged his shoulders. "Well, no one can fault us for not trying. Unfortunately it's another ten thousand dollars down the drain."

"Give me strength!" Marissa whispered to herself.

"Are you hungry?" Robert asked. "I'm famished. What about going out for some dinner? Maybe it will do us some good. After all, we should celebrate your legal victory. I know it doesn't make up for your not being pregnant, but at least it's something."

"Why don't you go by yourself," Marissa said. She was in no mood to celebrate. Besides, she was certain her "legal victory," as he put it, was nothing but a clever cover-up. She also wanted to lash back at his reference to the ten thousand dollars. But she didn't have the strength to quarrel.

"Suit yourself," Robert said. He disappeared from the doorway. Marissa got up and closed the door to her study. A few minutes later she heard the muted sounds of Robert in the kitchen making himself something to eat.

Marissa had half a mind to go after him. Maybe she should try to communicate with him. Then she shook her head. She knew she could never make him understand, let alone share in her concern for the incidence of TB salpingitis. With a sigh, Marissa sat down on the love seat and began reading the article that Cyrill had given her. He was right; it was a good article.

The twenty-three cases of TB salpingitis had been seen at a Brisbane clinic that sounded similar to the Women's Clinic. The name of the clinic was Female Care Australia, FCA for short. Similar to the five cases Marissa knew in Boston, all the patients in the Australian series were in their twenties and early thirties. They were middle class and married. All except one was Caucasian. The exception was a Chinese woman of thirty-one who'd recently emigrated from Hong Kong.

The ring of the phone startled her, but she kept reading, deciding it was probably for Robert anyway.

Reading on in the article, Marissa noted that the diagnosis had been made by the histology of fallopian tube biopsy alone since no organisms had been seen or cultured. Chest X-rays and blood work had ruled out fungi and sarcoid.

In the discussion portion of the paper the author hypothesized that the problem was arising from the influx of immigrants from Southeast Asia, but he didn't elaborate on any possible mechanism.

"Marissa!" Robert shouted. "The phone is for you! Cyrill Dubchek!"

Marissa grabbed the phone.

"Sorry to bother you so late," Cyrill said, "But when I returned to the CDC I got some additional information you might find interesting."

"Oh?" Marissa said.

"These TB salpingitis cases aren't confined to the U.S. or Australia," Cyrill said. "They have been showing up in Western Europe as well, with the same wide distribution pattern. There have been no clusters like the one in Brisbane. Apparently there have been no reported cases as yet in South America or in Africa. I don't know what to make of this, but there you have it. If I hear any more, I'll call ASAP. But now you've got my interest. Let me know if you begin to develop any theories."

Marissa thanked him again for calling and they said their goodbyes. This new bit of information was extremely significant. It meant that the incidence of TB salpingitis could no longer be dismissed as a statistical fluke. It was occurring on an international scale. Even Cyrill's curiosity was now piqued. For the moment Marissa forgot her grief, anger, and exhaustion.

Marissa considered the possibilities. Could TB have somehow mutated to become a venereal disease? Could it have become a silent infection in the male like some cases of chlamydia or mycoplasma? Should she insist that Robert be checked? Could Robert have picked it up somehow on one of his many business trips? Marissa didn't like this line of thinking, but she had to remain scientific.

Reaching for the telephone, Marissa called Wendy. Gustave answered.

"Unfortunately she's not taking calls," Gustave said.

"I understand," Marissa said. "Whenever it is appropriate, tell her I've called and ask her to call me back as soon as she feels up to it."

"I'm worried about her," Gustave confided. "I've never seen her this depressed. I don't know what to do."

"Do you think she would see me if I came over?" Marissa asked.

"I think there is a chance," Gustave said. His tone was encouraging.

"I'll be right over," Marissa said.

"Thanks, I really appreciate it. I know Wendy will too."

Marissa got her coat from the laundry room and went out to her car in the garage. As she was about to get in, Robert appeared.

"Where do you think you are going at this hour?" he demanded.

"Wendy's," Marissa said, pushing the automatic garage-door opener. "At least her husband is concerned about her."

"What's that supposed to mean?" Robert demanded.

"If you don't know," Marissa said, getting into her car, "I doubt if anybody could tell you."

Marissa backed out of the garage and lowered

the door. She shook her head in dismay at how far her relationship with Robert had fallen.

It only took fifteen minutes to drive to Wendy's Victorian house. Gustave had clearly been waiting for her. He opened the door before she had a chance to ring the bell.

"I'm truly grateful for your coming out at this hour," Gustave said. He took her coat.

"Glad to," Marissa said. "Where's Wendy?"

"She's upstairs in the bedroom. Top of the stairs, second door on the right. Can I get you anything? Coffee, tea?"

Marissa shook her head and climbed the stairs.

At the bedroom door, Marissa paused to listen. There were no sounds coming from within. She knocked lightly. When there was no answer, she called out Wendy's name.

The door opened almost immediately.

"Marissa!" Wendy said with true surprise. "What are you doing here?" She was dressed in a white terrycloth robe and bedroom slippers. Her eyes were still sunken and red, but otherwise she appeared better than she had in the courthouse that morning.

"Gustave said you weren't taking any calls. He also said that he was worried about you. Really worried. He encouraged me to come over."

"Oh, for goodness' sake," Wendy said. "I'm not that bad off. Sure I'm depressed, but part of it is I'm mad at him. He wants me to be thankful for what he calls the Women's Clinic's magnanimity."

189

"Robert feels the same way," Marissa said.

"I think it was a cover-up maneuver," Wendy said.

"I agree!"

"What about your pregnancy test?" Wendy asked.

"Don't ask," Marissa said. She shook her head.

"How about something to drink?" Wendy offered. "Coffee or tea? Or hell, since we're not pregnant, how about a glass of wine?"

"That sounds wonderful," Marissa admitted.

The two women descended to the kitchen. Gustave appeared but Wendy sent him away.

"He was really concerned," Marissa said.

"Oh, let him suffer a bit," Wendy said. "This afternoon I was mad enough to have a go at him with one of those foot-long egg-retrieval needles. It would be good for him to get an idea of what I've been going through these last months."

Wendy opened a bottle of expensive Chardonnay and led Marissa into the parlor.

"I wasn't sure you'd be up for this," Marissa said once they were settled, "but I brought over a journal article for you to read."

"Just what I was hoping for," Wendy said with sarcasm. She put her wineglass down on the coffee table, then took the reprint from Marissa. She glanced at the abstract.

While Wendy scanned the article, Marissa told her everything Dubchek had related.

"This is incredible," Wendy admitted as she looked up from the paper. "Brisbane, Australia!

Do you know one of the things that makes Brisbane so interesting?"

Marissa shook her head.

"It's the main gateway to one of the greatest natural wonders of the world."

"Which is?"

"The Great Barrier Reef! A diver's paradise."

"No kidding?" Marissa said. Then she admitted, "It's not something I know much about."

"Well, it is one place in the world I've always wanted to visit," Wendy said. "Diving has been one of my passions. I started in California during my residency. I used to take all my vacations in Hawaii in order to dive. In fact, it's how I met Gustave. Have you ever done any diving, Marissa?"

"A little. I took a scuba course in college and I've gone a few times to the Caribbean."

"I love it," Wendy said. "Unfortunately I haven't done it for sometime."

"What do you think of the paper?" Marissa asked, bringing the conversation back to the issue at hand.

Wendy looked down at it. "it's a good article. But it doesn't say anything about transmission. The author mentions the possibility of an increase in TB due to immigration, but how is it communicated, especially to such a defined population?"

"That was my question as well," Marissa said. "And how does it get into the fallopian tubes? It certainly doesn't sound like blood or lymphatic spread, which is the usual way TB gets around. I wonder if it's venereal."

"What about contaminated tampons?"

"That's an idea," Marissa said, recalling that tampons turned out to be the basis of the toxic shock syndrome. "I certainly use tampons exclusively."

"Me too," Wendy said. "Trouble is, there's no mention of tampon use in the article."

"I have an idea," Marissa said. "Why don't we call Brisbane and talk to the author of the paper. We can quiz him about tampon use. It would also be interesting to know if there's been any follow-up on the twenty-three cases and if there are any new ones at the Female Care Australia Clinic. After all, this paper was written almost two years ago."

"What's the time difference between here and Australia?" Wendy asked.

"You're asking the wrong person."

Wendy picked up the phone. Calling an overseas operator, she asked about the time. Then she hung up. "They're fourteen hours ahead," she said.

"So that makes it . . ."

"About noon tomorrow," Wendy said. "Let's try."

They got the number of Female Care Australia in Brisbane from overseas information and placed the call.

Wendy put the phone on its speaker mode. They could hear the phone ring, then someone at the other end picked up. A cheerful voice with a crisp Australian accent came over the line.

"This is Dr. Wilson calling from Boston in the U.S.," Wendy said. "I'd like to speak with Dr. Tristan Williams."

"I don't believe we have a Tristan Williams here," said the operator. "Just a moment, please."

Music came out of the speaker while they were put on hold. The clinic's operator came back. "They tell me that there was a Dr. Williams at the clinic but I'm afraid he is no longer here."

"Would you tell us where we can reach him?" Wendy asked.

"I'm afraid I have no idea," the operator said.

"Do you have a personnel office?" Wendy asked.

"Indeed we do," the operator said. "Shall I connect you?"

"Please," Wendy said.

"Personnel here," a man's voice said.

Wendy repeated her request to get in touch with Tristan Williams. Again they were put on hold, this time for a longer period.

"Sorry," the man apologized when he came back on the line. "I've just learned that Dr. Williams' whereabouts are unknown. He was dismissed from the staff about two years ago."

"I see," Wendy said. "Could you transfer me to pathology?"

"Surely," the man said.

It took a full ten minutes to get one of the

pathologists on the line. Wendy said her name and what she wanted.

"I've never met the man," the pathologist said. "He left before I arrived."

"He wrote a paper while at the clinic," Wendy explained. "It concerned a series of patients at your clinic. We are interested in knowing if there has been any follow-up on any of the cases. We'd also like to know if there have been any additional cases."

"We've had no new cases," the doctor said. "As for follow-up, there hasn't been any."

"Would it be possible to get some of the names of the original cases?" Wendy asked. "I'd like to contact them directly to discuss their medical histories. We have five similar cases here in Boston."

"That would be completely out of the question," the doctor said. "We have strict confidentiality rules. I'm sorry." The next thing they heard was a click.

"He hung up!" Wendy said indignantly. "The nerve!"

"The old confidentiality obstacle," Marissa said, shaking her head in frustration. "What a pity! Twenty-three cases is probably enough to draw some reasonable inferences."

"What about talking in greater detail with the two women we found at the Resolve meeting?" Wendy asked.

"I suppose," Marissa said, losing some of her enthusiasm. It seemed impossible to get information. "What I'd like to do more is get at those eighteen cases the computer suggested there were at the Women's Clinic."

"Obviously that's out of the question," Wendy said. "But I wonder how these people at the Female Care Australia would treat us if we showed up on their doorstep?"

"Oh, sure!" Marissa said. "Why don't we wander over there in the morning and ask?"

"It doesn't sound so preposterous to me," Wendy said, her eyes alight. "I'm curious as to what they would do if we visited the clinic. I think they'd be flattered that we'd come halfway around the world to see their facility."

"Are you serious?" Marissa asked in disbelief.

"Why not?" Wendy said. "The more I think about the idea, the better it sounds. God knows we both could use a vacation. We'd have a better shot at tracking down this Tristan Williams. Someone in the clinic's pathology department is bound to know where he went. You have to admit, it would be a lot easier than trying to do it by telephone."

"Wendy," Marissa said with a tired voice, "I'm not up to traveling eighteen zillion miles to look for a pathologist."

"But it will be fun for us." Her eyes seemed to brighten. "If nothing else, we could fit in a visit to the Great Barrier Reef."

"Oh, now I'm beginning to understand your motive. Visiting the FCA clinic is the excuse for a diving expedition."

"No law against having a little fun when the work is done," Wendy said with a smile. "You look as bad as I do."

"Thanks, good friend," Marissa said wryly.

"I'm serious," Wendy said. "The two of us have had PMS for six months. We've been crying like babies. We've both put on weight. When was the last time you did any jogging? I remember you used to jog every day."

"You're really hitting below the belt."

"The point is we both could use a vacation," Wendy said. "And we're both fascinated by this string of TB salpingitis cases but we're stymied here. The way I see it, we're killing two birds with one stone."

"We might hear about some cases from the Memorial and the General," Marissa said. "We haven't exhausted our possibilities here."

"Are you going to tell me you couldn't use a vacation?" Wendy insisted.

"A little time away does have some appeal," Marissa admitted.

"Thank you for your admission," Wendy said. "You can be pretty stubborn."

"But I don't know how Robert will take it. We've been having enough trouble lately. I can just imagine his response if I suggest I want to go to Australia alone."

"I'm sure Gustave will go for the idea," Wendy said. "I know he could use the break."

"You mean our husbands would go too?" Marissa asked, puzzled.

"Hell, no," Wendy said. "Gustave needs a break from me! Let's see if I'm right."

Wendy shocked Marissa by shouting for Gustave. Her voice echoed through the high-ceilinged house. "I usually can't get away with this kind of behavior," she admitted to Marissa. She took another drink from her wineglass.

Gustave came at a run. "Something the matter?" he asked nervously.

"Everything is fine, dear," Wendy said. "Marissa and I were thinking it might be good for the two of us to take a little holiday. What do you think of that?"

"I think it's a great idea," Gustave said. He clearly seemed relieved at the change in Wendy's mood.

"Marissa's afraid Robert might not be so agreeable," Wendy said. "What's your opinion?"

"Obviously I don't know him well," Gustave said. "But I do know he is fed up with the in-vitro protocol. I think he'd like a break. Where were you girls thinking of going?"

"Australia," Wendy said.

Gustave visibly swallowed. "Why not the Caribbean?" he asked.

Later, when Marissa drove home, her mind was in disarray. It had been a strange day with roller-coaster emotions and unexpected happenings. Within minutes of leaving an excited Wendy, she began to question the reasonableness of going to Australia at the present time. Although the concept of getting away had a lot of appeal, the idea of considering such a journey was a fitting end to a mad day. Besides, she wasn't sure she could manage Robert as handily as Wendy managed Gustave.

Marissa pulled into the garage, not sure how to proceed. For a few moments she sat behind the steering wheel and tried to think. Without a specific plan, she finally got out of the car and entered the house. She took off her coat and hung it in the hall closet.

The house was still. Robert was up in his study; she could just barely hear the click of his computer keys as he typed. She paused again in the darkness of the dining room.

"This is ridiculous!" Marissa said finally. She'd never had so much trouble making up her mind. With a new but fragile sense of resolve, she mounted the stairs and walked into Robert's study.

"Robert, I'd like to talk to you about something."

Robert turned to face her.

"Wendy and I have been thinking," she continued.

"Oh?"

"It may sound a little crazy . . ."

"These days, I'd expect as much."

"We thought that perhaps it would do us good to get away for a short time," Marissa said. "Like a vacation."

"I can't take time off now," Robert said.

"No, not you and I," Marissa said, "Wendy and I. Just us girls."

Robert thought for a moment. The idea had some merit. It would give him and Marissa time to cool down. "That doesn't sound so crazy. Where were you thinking of going?"

"Australia," Marissa said. She winced as the word came out of her mouth.

"Australia!" Robert exclaimed. He snatched off his reading glasses and tossed them on top of his correspondence. "Australia!" he repeated as if he'd not heard correctly.

"There is an explanation," Marissa said. "We didn't just pull Australia out of a hat. I found out today that the only concentration of cases of TB of the fallopian tubes like Wendy and I have is in Brisbane, Australia. So we could do a little research as well as have some fun. It was Wendy's idea. She's a diving enthusiast and the Great Barrier Reef—"

"You were right!" Robert said, interrupting her. "This sounds very crazy. This is the most ridiculous thing I've ever heard. Your practice is in a shambles and you want to fly halfway around the world to continue a crusade that came close to landing you in jail. I thought you meant a little vacation, like a weekend in Bermuda. Something reasonable."

"You don't have to overreact," Marissa said. "I thought we could talk about this."

"How can I not overreact?" Robert demanded.

"It's not that unreasonable," Marissa said. "I also learned today that this odd form of TB has been showing up on an international scale. Not only in Australia, but in Europe as well. Someone should be looking into it."

"And you are that someone?" Robert asked. "In your state, you think you are appropriate?"

"I think I am very qualified."

"Well, I think you're wrong," Robert said. "There's no way you could be objective. You're one of the cases yourself. And if you care about my opinion, I think your going to Australia is preposterous. That's all I have to say."

Robert reached for his reading glasses and slipped them on. Looking away from Marissa, he turned his attention back to his computer screen.

Seeing that he really didn't intend to discuss it any further, Marissa turned and walked out the door.

The problem with going to Australia was that for the most part Marissa thought Robert was right. It seemed an extravagant idea, in time as well as expense, not that finances were her top consideration. Still, she couldn't shake the feeling: it seemed unreasonable to suddenly fly halfway around the world.

Reaching for the phone, she called Wendy. Wendy answered on the first ring, as if she were waiting by the phone.

"Well?" Wendy asked.

"It doesn't look good," Marissa said. "Robert is very much against the idea, at least of going to Australia. He likes the vacation part."

"Damn!" Wendy said. "I'm disappointed. I

was practically packing my bag. I could just feel that hot Australian summer sun."

"Another time," Marissa said. "Sorry to be such a drag."

"Sleep on it," Wendy said. "Maybe tomorrow you and Robert will feel differently. I'm sure we'd have a ball."

Marissa hung up the phone. Suddenly sleep sounded good to her. She climbed the stairs, wishing that Robert would surprise her and join her for a change.

Marissa opened her eyes and immediately knew she'd overslept. The light in the bedroom was brighter than it should have been. Rolling to the side, she glanced at the clock. She was right, it was almost eight-thirty, an hour later than usual. She wasn't surprised. Having awakened at four A.M. and unable to fall back asleep, she'd taken a piece of one of Robert's Valiums.

Pulling on her robe, she went down to the guest room and peered inside. The bed was empty and unmade. Going to the top of the stairs, she called down for Robert. If he was there, he didn't reply.

Descending the stairs, Marissa made a quick tour of the kitchen, eventually checking the garage. Robert's car was gone. Going back inside, she looked on the planning desk for a message. There was none. Robert had just left for work without so much as a note. Every time she'd thought their relationship had reached its nadir, it sank a little lower.

"Thanks for nothing," Marissa said aloud as she fought back tears. Then she shook herself. "God, I've only been awake for ten minutes and already I'm crying." She made a cup of instant coffee and carried it upstairs to drink while she got dressed.

"A note wouldn't have been asking too much," she said as she stepped into the bathroom to shower.

While she was dressing and applying her make-up, Marissa decided she had to try to get her life back to some semblance of normality. For one thing, she conceded that Robert was right: her practice was in a shambles. Maybe she should start going to work on a more regular basis. Maybe then her relationship with Robert would improve. With that idea in mind, Marissa decided to head straight for her clinic.

Checking herself in the full-length hall mirror before going to her car, Marissa muttered, "I'll even start exercising again. It would be great to get back to my old weight."

With a new sense of resolve, Marissa strode down the main corridor on her floor and turned into her office. In contrast to the other waiting rooms, hers was empty. She found Mindy Valdanus at the reception desk, opening the mail.

"Dr. Blumenthal!" Mindy exclaimed.

"Don't act so surprised," Marissa said. "Bring the scheduling book in. We have some planning to do."

"You just had a call from the intensive care

unit at the Memorial," Wendy said. She handed Marissa a phone message slip. "Dr. Ben Goldman asked you to return his call."

There was a stab in Marissa's heart. Her first thought was that Evelyn Welles had died. "Hold up on the scheduling book," Marissa said. She opened the door to her office and went inside.

After hanging up her coat, Marissa rang Dr. Goldman. One of the intensive care unit nurses answered and put her on hold while she went to get the man. Marissa played with a paper clip while she waited.

A minute later, Dr. Goldman came on the line. "I called about Evelyn Welles," he said, wasting no time.

"How is she doing?" Marissa asked, afraid to hear the answer.

"Clinically, not much change," Dr. Goldman said. "But we did some smears of her vaginal secretions like you suggested, and they were loaded with acid-fast bacilli. I mean, loaded with TB. My chief was impressed, but I didn't take credit for it. I have to admit I was tempted. How did you guess they'd be there?"

"It would take me an hour to explain," Marissa said. "What about the Women's Clinic? Did you remember to ask the husband?"

"Sure did," Dr. Goldman said. "The answer was yes. She'd been a patient there for several years."

"What about the record?" Marissa asked.

"That I don't know," Dr. Goldman admitted.

"But I asked the husband to try to get us a copy. I'll let you know if anything turns up."

"The record could be key," Marissa said. "I'd be very interested to have a look at it. Please call me back if you get it."

"Sure will," Dr. Goldman said. "And thanks for the tip about looking for TB in the vagina. I've got a GYN consult coming in sometime today."

It was getting to the point where Marissa wasn't surprised to see her suspicions borne out. It was almost gratifying to have the pieces of the puzzle begin to fall so neatly into place. If Goldman didn't come through with that record, she resolved to contact Evelyn Welles' husband herself.

There was a knock on her door, then her secretary appeared. She had Marissa's scheduling book in hand. "Do you want to go over the scheduling book now?" she asked.

"No, not now," Marissa said. "I've had a slight change of plans. I've got to go out for a little while. We'll do it as soon as I come back."

Marissa got her coat. She'd made a snap decision. The salpingitis problem was too important to ignore. She had to follow up on it. Robert had to understand. What she needed to do was have a real talk with him. No more of these halfhearted attempts. She decided to go to his office. Now that they'd both had a good night's sleep, maybe they would be in better shape to discuss their problems.

Getting into her car, and pulling out of the clinic's garage, Marissa already felt better than she had for months. She was doing something she

204

should have done long ago. She had to explain to Robert what her feelings were and listen to his. They had to stop the downward spiral.

Parking was at a premium in downtown Boston. Marissa left her car with the doorman at the Omni Parker House Hotel, slipping him a five-dollar bill. When his expression didn't change, she gave him another five. She wasn't in a position to bargain.

Crossing School Street, she entered the elegant, refurbished old City Hall building that housed Robert's office. She took the elevator to the fourth floor, making her way to a door with HEALTH RESOURCE CORPORATION etched on the glass. Taking a deep breath, she opened the door and walked in.

The reception area of the office was handsomely decorated with rich mahogany paneled walls, leather seating, and Oriental rugs. The main receptionist recognized Marissa and smiled. She was on the phone.

Marissa passed the receptionist's desk. Familiar with the office, she walked straight back to Robert's corner office. His secretary, Donna, wasn't at her desk but the steaming cup of coffee in the middle of the blotter indicated she couldn't be far away.

Marissa went to Robert's door. She glanced back at Donna's telephone to see if any of the extension lines were lit. She didn't want to interrupt Robert if he was in the middle of a call. Seeing that no one was on the phone, Marissa knocked softly and entered.

Marissa was first aware of a flurry of activity with Donna straightening up and Robert coming half out of his chair. Robert quickly sat back down. Donna self-consciously smoothed her short skirt toward her knees and adjusted a string of pearls around her neck. Her hair, which she usually wore in a chignon, had partially come undone on the side.

Stunned, Marissa stared at her husband. His tie was loosened and the top two buttons of his shirt were undone. His sandy hair, usually so neatly combed, was mussed. On the carpet by Robert's desk, Marissa spotted two high-heeled shoes.

The scene was so trite, Marissa didn't know whether to laugh or cry. "Maybe I should wait outside for a few minutes," she said at last. "It'll give you two time to finish your dictation." With that, she started to back out of the office.

"Marissa!" Robert said. "Wait! This is not what you are thinking. Donna was merely rubbing my shoulders. Tell her, Donna!"

"Yes!" Donna said. "I was just rubbing his shoulders. He's been so tense."

"Whatever," Marissa said with a false smile. "I think I'll be leaving. In fact, I've just reconsidered that idea I mentioned last night. I think I'll be going to Australia for a few days after all."

"No!" Robert said. "I forbid you to go to Australia!"

"Oh, really?" Marissa said.

With that, Marissa spun on her heels and walked out of Robert's office. She heard him call after her, insisting she come back immediately, but she ignored him. The receptionist looked up at her with a quizzical expression, having heard her boss's cry, but Marissa merely smiled and kept moving. She went directly to the elevators and punched the Down button, refusing to so much as glance back at Robert's office door.

Inside the elevator, Marissa was glad to be alone. In spite of her rage, she felt a few hot tears slide down her face. "Bastard!" she muttered.

Crossing School Street, Marissa ducked into the Omni Parker House and used a pay phone to call the airlines. Then, after picking up her keys from the doorman, she made a loop through downtown Boston and headed out Cambridge Street. She parked in the parking lot of the Massachusetts Eye and Ear Infirmary and went into the emergency area.

After checking both eye emergency rooms, she found Wendy helping a junior resident with a procedure in one of the minor surgical rooms.

When Wendy was through, Marissa took her out by the emergency room desk.

"Are you still up for the Australian trip?" Marissa asked.

"Sure!" Wendy said. "You look kind of tense. Everything okay?"

Marissa ignored her question. "How soon could you leave?"

"Pretty much anytime," Wendy answered. "When do you want to go?"

"How about today," Marissa said. "There's a

United flight that leaves at five-fifteen that can get us to Sydney with connections to Brisbane. I think we may need visas, too. I'll call the Australian consulate to check."

"Wow!" Wendy said. "I'll see what I can do. Why the rush?"

"So I don't change my mind," Marissa said. "I'll explain once we're on our way."

9

APRIL 5, 1990
8:23 A.M.

"MY GOD!" Wendy said as she and Marissa waited for their baggage in the Brisbane airport. "I never had any idea the Pacific was so immense."

"I feel like we've been traveling for a week," Marissa agreed.

They had flown from Boston to L.A. Then from L.A. they had taken a nonstop to Sydney. It was the longest flight either had ever been on: almost fifteen hours. Then, as soon as they'd passed through formalities at Sydney, they boarded an Australian Airlines plane for the final leg to Brisbane.

"I knew Australia was far away," Wendy continued, "but I didn't know it was this far."

When their luggage appeared, they cheered. Having traveled on so many flights, they were afraid they'd never see it again. They loaded the bags onto an airport pushcart and headed for the taxi stand.

"Certainly a modern-looking airport," Wendy commented.

Getting a cab was a breeze. The driver helped them with their bags and even opened and closed the cab doors for them. Once they were all settled, he turned to them and said: "Where to, luvs?"

"Mayfair Crest International Hotel, please," Marissa told him. Marissa had gotten the name of the hotel from an agent at Beacon Hill Travel. The agent had been an enormous help, essentially accomplishing the impossible: getting documents and reservations to leave the same afternoon.

"Do up your seat belts, ladies," the taxi driver said as he eyed them in the rearview mirror. "Forty dollars if the coppers catch you without them."

Marissa and Wendy did as they were told. They were too tired to question.

"Is the Mayfair a good hotel?" Marissa asked.

"It's a bit dear," the driver said, "but it's orright."

Marissa smiled at Wendy. "I like the Australian accent," she whispered. "It's like an English accent, but with a down-home coziness."

"You ladies Yanks?" the driver asked them.

Marissa said that they were. "We're from Boston, Massachusetts."

"Welcome to the Lucky Country," the driver said. "Been here before?"

"First time," Marissa admitted.

With that, the cabdriver launched into a colorful history of Brisbane, including mention of its origins as a penal colony for the worst convicts of Sydney.

Both Marissa and Wendy were surprised by the lush greenness of the land. Luxuriant tropical vegetation lined the roads, engulfing entire buildings in a riot of colors. Purple jacaranda trees competed with pink oleander and blood-red bougainvillaea.

When the undistinguished, glass-faced high-rises of the downtown area came into view, Marissa and Wendy were less impressed. "Looks like a city anywhere," Wendy said. "You'd think they could have taken a hint from the local natural beauty and done something original."

"You wonder with all this land why they have to build so high," Marissa said.

Entering the city itself, their impressions improved. Although it was past rush hour, there were people everywhere. Everyone looked tanned and healthy. Almost all the men were in shorts. "I think I'm going to like Australia," Wendy quipped.

As they waited at a light, Marissa looked at the parade of sunburnt faces. Many of the men had sandy blond hair and angular jaws. "They remind me of Robert," Marissa said.

"Forget Robert!" Wendy said. "At least for now."

During the flight, Marissa had told Wendy about her experience at Robert's office. Wendy had been horrified and sympathetic. "No wonder you'd been so eager to leave," Wendy had said.

"I don't know what I'll do when I get back," Marissa had said. "If Robert and Donna are truly having an affair, then our marriage is over."

The taxi entered a large square lined with palm trees. "That's your hotel over there," the driver said, pointing with his free hand. Then, hooking a thumb over his shoulder, he said, "On the other side, that sandstone building with the clock tower, that's Brisbane City Hall. Built in the twenties. It's got a great marble staircase. There's good view of the whole city from the top."

Checking into the hotel was effortless. Soon the women found themselves in a plainly decorated, air-conditioned room with a city view that included a portion of the Brisbane River.

After hanging up some of their clothes, they spread out on their respective beds.

"Are you as tired as I am?" Wendy asked.

"I sure am," Marissa said. "But it's a good exhaustion: like a catharsis. I'm glad we came and I'm eager to see some of the city."

"All I need is a shower and a nap," Wendy said. "Who's the tour director?"

"Sounds good to me," Marissa said. "But I don't think we should sleep too long. Otherwise we won't be able to adjust to the time difference. I think we should call the desk and have someone wake us up in a couple of hours. Then we could do some sightseeing. We'll save the clinic for tomorrow when we're fresh."

"I want to find out about getting out to the Great Barrier Reef," Wendy said. "I can't wait. I've heard it's the best diving in the world."

"Why don't you hop in the shower first?" Marissa said. "I want to look up Female Care Australia in the phone book and figure out where it is on the city map."

Wendy didn't argue. She scooted off the bed and disappeared into the bathroom while Marissa flipped through the phone book on the night-table between the beds. The clinic was located in a nearby suburb called Herston. Checking the map provided by the hotel, she noted that Herston was just north of Brisbane. She grabbed a scratch pad bearing the hotel's name to write down the address.

Marissa was about to replace the phone book when she thought about Tristan Williams. Opening the directory to the Ws, she ran her finger down the column.

Just then, the door to the bathroom opened. Steam billowed out. "Your turn," Wendy called. She had one towel wrapped around her head, another around her body. "I can't believe how good it felt, especially washing my hair."

"Our pathologist friend's not in the phone book," Marissa said.

Wendy smiled, "That would have been too easy."

Marissa put the phone book away, then stepped into the bathroom for her shower.

When the phone rang, Marissa had trouble rousing herself. Groggily she groped for the receiver. A cheerful voice at the other end of the line told her it was noon. Marissa hardly knew what to make of it. It wasn't until she saw Wendy soundly sleeping in the bed next to her that she recalled where she was.

Lying back down again, Marissa almost fell back to sleep. But remembering her own advice, she forced herself to get up. For the moment she was so exhausted that she was nauseated, yet she knew she had to adapt to the time difference.

Wendy hadn't budged. Getting unsteadily to her feet, Marissa gently shook her friend's shoulder.

"Wendy!" Marissa called softly. Then louder: "Wendy, time to wake up."

"Already?" Wendy asked groggily. She pushed herself up to a sitting position. Then she groaned. "Oh, my word! I feel awful."

Marissa nodded. "I know it's hard; I'm still exhausted. It feels like midnight but it's only noon. We'd better get used to it."

Wendy threw herself back on the bed. "Tell the tour director I died," she said.

An hour later, Marissa and Wendy descended in the elevator to the lobby, feeling much improved. A second shower and room service "tucker," as the bellboy had called the food, had revived them more than they'd expected.

Once they were in the lobby, Wendy went to a nearby travel agency to make inquiries about the

Great Barrier Reef while Marissa waited in line to speak with the concierge concerning Brisbane sightseeing. The two rendezvoused half an hour later.

"I got it all figured out," Wendy reported. "Take a look at this." She smoothed out a map of the entire Queensland coastline including all the offshore islands.

"Holy Toledo," Marissa exclaimed. "How long is this reef? It looks like it goes all the way to New Guinea."

"Practically," Wendy said. "It's well over a thousand miles long and in area it's larger than Britain. But we're going here, to Hamilton Island." Wendy poked her finger halfway up the peninsula. "It's part of the Whitsunday Island group."

"Are you sure I'm going to like this?" Marissa said. She wasn't as big on diving as her friend.

"You're going to love it!" Wendy said. "Hamilton Island is a good choice because it's got an airport that takes regular jets. We can fly directly from Brisbane with Ansett Airlines. Usually they're pretty well booked, but it turns out that April is off-season."

"Even that doesn't sound so good to me," Marissa said. "If it's off-season, there's usually a good reason, like it's not a good time to go."

"I was told that we may have a thunderstorm or two, but that's the only negative," Wendy said.

"Is diving on this reef dangerous?" Marissa asked.

"Don't worry! We'll have a dive master with us," Wendy assured her. "We'll charter a boat and head out to the outer reef. That's where there are the most fish and the clearest water."

"What about sharks?" Marissa asked.

"They didn't say anything about sharks," Wendy said. "But sharks stay out in deep water. We'll be diving on the reef itself. I'm telling you, you'll love it. Trust me."

"Well, I have some tamer information," Marissa said. "The concierge recommended we take a city bus tour. At first she said to walk around, but when I told her we'd just flown in, she told me about the buses. She said we should be sure to visit the Lone Pine Koala Sanctuary."

"Wonderful!" Wendy said with glee. "I love koalas."

The bus tour was their first order of business. They were driven around in air-conditioned comfort and viewed such sights as the French Renaissance-style Parliament House and the Italian Renaissance-style Treasury building. The streets were loaded with sidewalk cafés. Marissa couldn't get over how relaxed and casual everyone looked.

Fatigue eventually took over again. During the second hour both Marissa and Wendy nodded off as the bus slowed for a viewing of the new Queensland Cultural Center. They roused a bit for the visit to the Lone Pine Koala Sanctuary. Not only were there more koala bears than they could have imagined, there were dingos, kookaburras, kangaroos, and even a platypus. They were able to walk among the kangaroos and feed them by hand. The strength of the animals' curled front paws came as a surprise.

The most appealing creatures by far were the koala bears. Wendy was ecstatic when she learned she could hold one, but when she did, her enthusiasm waned. They had a peculiar odor that she found unpleasant.

"It's because of their eucalyptus diet," one of the keepers explained.

After they'd watched a koala bear show and learned all sorts of koala bear trivia, they'd had enough. Boarding a city bus, they returned to the hotel.

"No, you don't!" Marissa said as she restrained Wendy from collapsing on the bed.

"Please!" Wendy begged. "Tell the tour director I have a touch of the bubonic plague."

After their third shower of the day, they followed a suggestion from the concierge and took a short walk across the Victoria Bridge to the Queensland Cultural Center. In a rather modern restaurant called the Fountain Room, they relaxed for their first dinner in Australia. The view of the city across the muddy river was superb.

"I want to try something Australian," Wendy said, hiding behind a huge menu. They ended up ordering barramundi, a type of Australian perch. To complement the food, they selected a chilled Australian Chablis. Once it came and was opened for them, the two women toasted their Australian adventure.

After tasting the wine, Marissa smiled content-edly. Its crisp finish was a delight to her palate. For the moment she was blithely confident the trip would mean just the right combination of re-laxation and research.

"Ahhhh," Wendy murmured, peering into her long-stemmed glass. "Just what the doctor or-dered."

"Amen," Marissa agreed.

The next morning, after a hearty English break-fast, Marissa and Wendy hailed a cab. "Do you know this address?" Marissa asked. She'd given the driver the piece of paper with the FCA clinic's address on it.

"Sure, luv!" he said. "That's the women's clin-ic, it is. Buckle up and I can have you there straightaway."

The ride to Herston was pleasant. As they en-tered the green and hilly suburbs, they noticed a number of quaint, wide-perched, tin-roofed homes built on stilts.

"Those are called Queenslanders," the driver explained. "Built in the air to keep 'em away from water. The verandas are to keep 'em cool. Gets mighty hot here in the summer-time."

In minutes, the cab pulled up to a strikingly modern four-story building surfaced entirely with bronzed mirrored glass. The grounds were land-scaped with gorgeous flowering trees and bushes.

Getting out of the cab, Marissa and Wendy were struck by the sounds of the birds. They seemed to be everywhere: brightly colored and chirping and squawking. On the sidewalk leading to the entrance of the clinic they ran into a flock of mynah birds quarreling over a piece of bread.

As soon as the entrance doors closed behind them, the women stopped, awed by the building's interior. The FCA wasn't like any clinic they'd ever visited. The floors were gleaming onyx. The walls were a dark tropical wood polished to a high gloss.

"This place looks like a law firm," Wendy said uneasily. "You sure you got the right address?"

There was a lush garden area in the center of the building featuring the same mix of flowering trees as outside. There was even a small pond with a waterfall constructed of red granite blocks.

At one end of the spacious lobby was an information area that looked more like the front desk of a luxury hotel.

"Can we be of assistance?" asked one of the two perky receptionists. Instead of the white that was standard in American clinics, these women were dressed in brightly colored floral prints.

"We're doctors from the United States," Marissa said. "We are interested in your facility. We were wondering if—"

"From America!" the woman said with delight. "I've just returned from California. How nice of you to visit. I'll ring up Mr. Carstans. One moment, please."

The receptionist dialed a phone in front of her and spoke briefly. Hanging up, she said, "Mr.

Carstans will be out directly. Perhaps you would care to sit in our waiting area beyond those planters." She pointed with her pen.

"Who's Mr. Carstans?" Wendy asked.

"He's our public relations man," the receptionist explained. Marissa and Wendy walked over to the sitting area.

"Public relations man?" Wendy questioned. "How many clinics do you know have public relations men?"

"My thought exactly," Marissa said. "This clinic must do a healthy amount of business to justify that kind of expense."

After a few minutes' wait, a man approached them. "G'day, ladies," he said.

Carstans was a tall, corpulent fellow with ruddy cheeks. He was wearing shorts along with a jacket and tie. "Welcome to FCA. My name is Bruce Carstans. What can we do for you?"

"I'm Dr. Blumenthal and this is Dr. Wilson," Marissa said.

"Gynecologists?" Mr. Carstans asked.

"I'm a pediatrician," Marissa said.

"I'm an ophthalmologist," Wendy said.

"Our fame must be spreading far and wide," Mr. Carstans said with a smile. "Usually we only have overseas gynecologists for visitors. Are you ladies game for a tour of our establishment?"

The women exchanged glances, then shrugged. "Why not?" Wendy said.

"It would be interesting," Marissa agreed.

For the next hour Marissa and Wendy were

treated to a look at the most up-to-date medical facility either had ever seen. The clinic offered a full battery of women's medical services. There were X-ray rooms, a CAT scanner, and even an NMR machine. There were examination rooms, waiting rooms, minor surgery rooms, as well as delivery and birthing rooms. There was also an overnight ward.

By far the most impressive part of the clinic was the infertility section, boasting its own surgical wing capable of major surgical procedures. There were also six fully computerized ultrasound rooms. Filled with the absolute latest equipment, they had a Star Wars appearance. The clinical infertility lab was a huge room with large incubators, centrifuges, and modern cryogenic units.

Marissa and Wendy thought they'd seen it all when Mr. Carstans opened a heavy door and stepped aside for them to enter. The women found themselves in a glass enclosure that served as the dust-free entry to a fairyland of high-tech instrumentation. On the other side of the glass, a number of hooded technicians were at work. The laboratory looked like a space station in the twenty-first century.

"This is the heart of FCA," Mr. Carstans explained. "This is the basic research section. It is from here that many of the breakthroughs in in-vitro fertilization techniques have come. Right now we are concentrating on cryopreservation techniques for both embryos and gametes. But we are also working on fetal tissue research, particularly for Parkinson's Disease, diabetes, and even immunodeficiency problems."

"I've never seen such a research setup," Wendy said.

"It's a tribute to capitalism," Mr. Carstans said with a smile. "Private initiative and private investment. It's the only way to get things done in the modern world. The public benefits both in the availability of new techniques as well as superior clinical care."

"What are the FCA success rates with in-vitro fertilization?" Marissa asked.

"We are approaching a pregnancy rate of eighty percent," Mr. Carstans said with obvious pride. "No other program can match it."

Mr. Carstans walked the women back to the front entrance. He could tell they were impressed. "We are pleased you came to visit," he said, stopping near the waiting area where they'd begun the tour. "I think you've seen most everything. Hope you enjoyed it. Are there any questions you'd like to ask?"

"I do have a question," Marissa said. Opening her shoulder bag, she pulled out the journal article that Cyrill had given her. She handed it to Mr. Carstans. "I assume you're familiar with this article. It's about a series of cases here at FCA."

Mr. Carstans hesitated, then took the paper. He glanced at it, then handed it back. "No, I've never seen it," he said.

"How long have you been associated with FCA?" Wendy asked.

"Just shy of five years," Mr. Carstans said.

"This paper is only two years old," Wendy said. "How could the public relations department have been unaware of it? I would have thought that such a paper would have been a significant issue for you. It's about relatively young women coming down with TB in their fallopian tubes."

"As a rule, I don't read technical journals," Mr. Carstans said. "What journal was it published in?"

"The *Australian Journal of Infectious Disease*," Marissa said. "What about the author, Dr. Tristan Williams? Apparently he was on the staff here in pathology. Were you acquainted with him?"

"Afraid not," Mr. Carstans said. "But then again, I don't know all the staff. For questions like these, I'll have to refer you to Charles Lester, the director of the clinic."

"Do you think he'd be willing to speak with us?" Marissa asked.

"Under the circumstances," Mr. Carstans said, "I believe he would be happy to speak to you. In fact, if you'll be patient for a moment, I'll trot upstairs and see if he's free this very moment."

Marissa and Wendy watched Mr. Carstans disappear through a stairwell door. Then they looked at each other. "What do you think?" Wendy asked.

"Beats me," Marissa said. "I couldn't tell if he was on the level or not."

"I'm beginning to get a weird feeling," Wendy said. "This place seems too good to be true. Have you ever seen such opulence at a clinic?"

"I'm amazed that there is a chance we can meet the director," Marissa said. "I wouldn't have thought that possible without some formal introduction."

Just then Mr. Carstans reappeared. "You're in luck," he said. "The director says he'll be delighted to say hello to some esteemed colleagues from Boston, provided you have the time to spare."

"Absolutely," Marissa said.

They followed Mr. Carstans up a flight of stairs. The furnishing in the director's suite of offices was even more lavish than what they had already seen. It was as if they were visiting the office of the CEO of a major Fortune 500 company.

"Do come in!" the director said as he stood up from his desk to greet Marissa and Wendy. He shook hands with both, then indicated seats for them to make themselves comfortable. He then dismissed Mr. Carstans who discreetly left, closing the door behind him. Coming back to the women, the director said, "What about a fresh cup of coffee? I know you Yanks drink lots of coffee."

Charles Lester was a large, heavyset man, but not as beefy as Carstans. He looked like a gracefully aging athlete still up to a good game of tennis. His face was tanned like everyone else's in the city, and his eyes were set deep. He sported a thick mustache.

"Coffee would be fine with me," Wendy said. Marissa nodded, indicating that she'd like the same.

Lester buzzed his secretary and asked her to

bring coffee for three. While they waited, he engaged the two women in small talk, asking them what hospitals they were associated with and where they'd done their specialty training. Lester admitted that he'd done some fellowship work in Boston.

"You're a physician?" Wendy asked.

"Very much so," Lester said. "Some of us prefer the English system of address. As a gynecological surgeon during my training in London, I became accustomed to the title 'mister.' But as a doctor I haven't been doing much clinical work of late. Unfortunately, I've been caught at this desk doing more administrative work than I would like."

A steward brought in the coffee and served it. Lester added a touch of cream to his and sat back. He studied the women over the top of his cup.

"Mr. Carstans mentioned to me that you were inquiring about an old journal article," Lester said. "Can I ask what the article was about?"

Marissa pulled the reprint from her shoulder bag and handed it to Mr. Lester. Like Mr. Carstans, he only glanced at it before handing it back.

"What is your interest in this?" he asked.

"It's kind of a long story," Marissa said.

"I have the time," Lester answered.

"Well," Marissa began, "both Dr. Wilson and I have the same infertility problem as the women described in the article: blocked fallopian tubes from tuberculosis." She then went on to explain her background with the CDC and her training in

224

epidemiology. "When we found out the problem was occuring on an international scale, we decided to investigate. The article was sent to me by the CDC. We called the clinic here but were unable to reach the author."

"What would you have asked him if you'd been successful in reaching him?" Lester asked.

"Two things in particular," Marissa said. "We wanted to know if he'd done any epidemiologic follow-up on the cases that were reported. We also wanted to know if he'd seen any new cases. Back in Boston we know of three other cases besides ourselves."

"You do know that infertility in general is on the rise?" Lester said. "Infertility from all causes, not just from blocked tubes."

"We're aware of that," Marissa said. "But even the increase in blocked tubes is usually a nonspecific inflammatory process or endometriosis, it's not a specific infection, especially not something as relatively rare as TB. These cases raise a lot of epidemiological questions that should be answered. They might even represent some new, serious clinical entity."

"I'm sorry that you've come such a long way to learn more about that article. I'm afraid the author had entirely contrived his data. It was an utter fabrication. Not a whit of truth to it. Those were not real patients. Well, maybe one or two were real cases. The rest were fictitious. If you had reached me by phone I could have told you as much."

"Oh, no," Marissa groaned. The thought that the article could have been a hoax had never occurred to her.

"Where is the author now?" Wendy asked.

"I couldn't tell you," Lester said. "Obviously we dropped him from the staff immediately. Since then I understand he's been indicted on drug charges. What eventually happened, I don't know. I also don't know where he currently is, but I do know one thing: he is not practicing pathology."

"How would you suggest we find him?" Marissa asked. "I'd still like to talk to him, especially since I have the condition he described. Of all the data he could have dreamed up, why did he pick something so unusual? What could he have hoped to gain? It doesn't make sense."

"People do strange things for strange motives," Lester said. He got to his feet. "I hope this paper wasn't the only reason you've come all the way to Australia."

"We also thought we'd go out on the Great Barrier Reef," Wendy said. "A little work and a little play."

"I trust your play will be more rewarding than your work," Lester said. "Now if you'll excuse me, I've got to get back to my own work."

A few minutes later Marissa and Wendy found themselves standing by the front information desk again. The receptionist was calling them a taxi.

"That was rather abrupt," Wendy said. "One minute he was telling us he had the time, the next he was shooing us out of his office."

"I don't know what to make of all this," Marissa agreed. "But there is one thing I do know. I'd like to find that Tristan Williams just to wring his neck. Imagine the nerve of making up patients just to publish an article!"

"That old publish-or-perish mentality," Wendy said.

"A taxi will be along directly," the receptionist said as she hung up the receiver. "I suggest you wait outside. The taxi queue is just up the street."

The women left the FCA clinic, stepping into the glorious morning sunshine. "So what does the tour director suggest we do now?" Wendy asked.

"I'm not sure," Marissa said. "Maybe we should go out to the University of Queensland and use the medical library."

"Oh, boy!" Wendy said with obvious sarcasm. "Now that sounds titillating!"

Charles Lester had not gone back to his work. Marissa and Wendy's visit had disturbed him. It had been over a year since the last inquiry about that irritating paper by Williams. At the time he'd hoped it would be the last.

"Damn," he said aloud, smacking a fist on his desk top. He had the uncomfortable premonition that there was trouble ahead. The fact that these meddlesome women had come all the way from Boston was upsetting to say the least. Most distressing of all was the possibility that their search for Williams might persist. That could spell disaster.

He decided it was time to confer with some of his associates. After figuring the time difference, he picked up the phone and called Norman Wingate at home.

"Charles!" Dr. Wingate exclaimed with delight. "Good to hear your voice. How's everything Down Under?"

"It's been better," Lester said. "I have to talk to you about something important."

"Okay!" Dr. Wingate said. "Let me get the extension."

Lester could hear Dr. Wingate say something to his wife. In a few minutes he heard another phone being picked up. "I've got it, luv," Dr. Wingate said. Lester heard the other extension disconnect.

"What's the problem?" Dr. Wingate said into the phone.

"Does the name Dr. Marissa Blumenthal mean anything to you?"

"Good Lord, yes," Wingate said. "Why do you ask?"

"She and a companion named Wendy Wilson just left my office. They came in here with that article about TB salpingitis."

"My God!" Wingate said. "I can't believe they're in Australia. And we were so generous to them." He related the details of the pair's attempt to break into the Women's Clinic's computer record system.

"Did they get anything out of your computer?" Lester asked.

"We don't believe so," Wingate said. "But those women are troublemakers. Something will have to be done."

"I'm coming to the same conclusion," Lester said. "Thanks."

Hanging up his phone, Lester pressed his intercom. "Penny," he said, "ring up Ned Kelly in security. Tell him to get his arse up here on the spot."

Ned Kelly's name wasn't really Ned Kelly, it was Edmund Stewart. But at a young age Edmund had taken such a liking to the stories of the renowned bushranger Ned Kelly that his friends had started calling him Ned.

Although most Australian men liked to think of themselves as some reflection of the famous outlaw, Ned took to imitating him, even to the point of sending a pair of bullock testicles to the wife of a man he was feuding with. A life of contempt for authority and petty crime led people to call him Ned Kelly, and the name stuck.

Lester pushed away from the desk and walked over to the window. It seemed that just when things were running smoothly, some irritating problem had to crop up.

Lester had come a long way from his humble origins in the outback of New South Wales. At age nine he'd arrived in Australia from England with his family. His father, a sheet-metal worker, had taken advantage of liberal immigration policies in the immediate post-World War II period.

The Australian government had even paid passage for the whole family.

Early on, Lester had gravitated toward learning. He saw it as his ticket out of the sapping dullness of the vast Australian interior. In contrast to his brothers, he thirsted for knowledge, taking correspondence courses to supplement the meager schooling available in his tiny hometown. His studies had led him to medical school. From then on he'd never looked back. Nor did he tolerate hindrances. When people got in his way, he stepped on them.

"Watchagot?" Ned asked as he came through the door. Behind him was Willy Tong, a slightly built but muscular Chinese man. Ned kicked the door shut with a resounding thump, then sat on the arm of the couch. He was not a big man, but he exuded toughness. Like Carstans, he wore shorts along with a shirt and tie. On his sleeve was sewn the logo of the security department of the clinic. His face was tanned to a lined, leathery texture. He looked as if he'd spent his entire thirty-eight years in the desert sun. Above his left eye was a scar from a knife fight in a pub. The argument had been over a pitcher of beer.

Lester was chagrined to have to resort to such men. It was a bore to have to deal with the likes of Ned Kelly. Yet occasionally it was necessary, as it was at present. Lester had met Ned purely by accident when he was in his last year of medical school. Ned had come into the university hospital with one of his many gunshot wounds. During the course of his recuperation, they'd become acquaintances. Over the years Lester had used Ned for various projects, culminating in his being hired as head of the clinic's security department.

"We have a couple of women interested in that article by Williams," Lester said. "It was the same article that brought that gynecologist from L.A. here. Do you remember? It was about a year ago."

"How could I forget," Ned said with a sinister smile curling his lips. "He was the poor man who had that awful auto accident. Remember him, Willy?"

Willy's eyes narrowed as he smiled broadly.

"These women were talking about finding Williams," Lester said. "I don't want that to happen."

"You should have let me take care of Williams way back when," Ned said. "It would have saved a lot of trouble."

"He was too much in the spotlight at the time," Lester said. "But let's not worry about that now. Now we have to worry about these women. I want something done, and I want it done before they dredge up any more information on TB salpingitis."

"You want it to look like some kind of accident?" Ned asked.

"That would be best," Lester said. "Otherwise, there will be an investigation, which I'd prefer to avoid. But can you manage an accident when there are two people involved?"

"It's more difficult," Ned admitted. "But cer-

231

tainly not impossible. Be easy if they rent a car. Yanks are lousy left-hand drivers." He laughed. "Reminds me of that gynecologist. He almost killed himself without our help."

"The women's names are Marissa Blumenthal and Wendy Wilson," Lester said. He wrote them down and handed the paper to Ned.

"Where are they staying?" Ned asked.

"I don't know," Lester said. "The only thing I do know is that they are planning to go out on the Reef."

"Really!" Ned said with interest. "Now that bit of info could come in handy. Do you know when they plan to go?"

"No," Lester said. "But don't wait too long. I want something done soon. Understand?"

"We'll start calling hotels as soon as we get downstairs," Ned said. "This should be fun. Like going out in the bush and shooting 'roos."

"Excuse me," Marissa whispered. "I'm Dr. Blumenthal and this is Dr. Wilson." Wendy nodded hello. They were standing at the main circulation desk of the University of Queensland Medical School Library.

They had driven halfway to St. Lucia, where the university was located, when they'd asked the taxi driver if he knew where the medical school library was. To their surprise, he'd responded by "throwing a u-ey" and heading directly back to Herston. The medical school, they'd learned, was a short distance from the FCA.

"We're from the States," Marissa said to the man behind the medical school library circulation desk. "And we were wondering if it might be possible for us to use the library facilities."

"I don't see why not," the man replied. "But it would be best if you inquired in the office down the hall. Ask for Mrs. Pierce, the librarian."

Marissa and Wendy walked down the corridor and into the administration office.

"Absolutely," Mrs. Pierce answered in reply to their request. "You're more than welcome to use material here at the library. Of course, we will not be able to allow any of it to circulate."

"I understand," Marissa said.

"Is there anything I could help you with?" Mrs. Pierce offered. "It's not every day we have visitors from Boston."

"Perhaps there is," Marissa said. "We were lucky enough to have been given a tour of the FCA clinic building this morning. I must say, we were truly impressed."

"We're quite proud of the clinic here in Brisbane," Mrs. Pierce said.

"For good reason," Marissa said. "What we'd like to do is to read some of their current papers. I imagine they publish quite a bit of material there."

"Indeed they do," Mrs. Pierce said. "They have been our leaders in reproductive technologies here in Australia. They are also generous contributors to the medical school; we have a lot of their material."

"We're also interested in a certain Australian

pathologist," Wendy said. "His name is Tristan Williams. We have a reprint of one of his papers that appeared in an Australian journal. We'd like to see if he's done any subsequent articles."

"We'd especially like to locate him," Marissa interjected. "Perhaps you may have some suggestions as to how we might do that."

"It didn't mention where he practiced in the article?" Mrs. Pierce asked.

"He'd been at the FCA when he published the paper," Wendy said, "but that was two years ago and he's since left the FCA staff. We asked over there at the clinic, but no one seemed to have a forwarding address."

"We have an annual publication by the Royal College of Pathology," Mrs. Pierce said. "It contains the hospital and university affiliations of all Australian pathologists. I think that would be the most fruitful place to start. Why don't you come with me? I'll acquaint you with our reference and periodical rooms."

Marissa and Wendy followed Mrs. Pierce. The woman was quite striking: she had flaming red hair and was quite tall, particularly in contrast to Marissa and Wendy. Together the three women descended a curved stairway leading to the lower floor. Mrs. Pierce's pace was brisk. Marissa and Wendy had to hurry to keep up with her.

Mrs. Pierce stopped at a group of computer monitors. She put her hand on the top of the first screen. "Here are the terminals for literature searches. This would be the easiest way to search for Dr. Williams' latest articles.''

Leaving the computer area, Mrs. Pierce walked to a series of low bookshelves. She pulled a dark-covered volume from the shelf and handed it to Wendy. "Here's the Royal College of Pathology's publication. That's the best way to locate a pathologist, at least in terms of his professional associations.''

Leaving the shelves, Mrs. Pierce strode off at a determined pace. Marissa and Wendy hurried after her.

"She must do triathlons on the weekends,'' Wendy muttered under her breath to Marissa.

Mrs. Pierce led them to another corner of the periodical room. "This section here,'' she said, making a sweeping gesture with her hand, "is devoted to FCA-related articles. So that should keep you busy for a while. If you have any further questions, please feel free to come see me back in the office.''

After Marissa and Wendy thanked Mrs. Pierce, she left them on their own.

"Okay, what first?'' Wendy asked.

"Look Williams up in the book you're holding,'' Wendy said. "If it says he's gone to Perth I'll scream. Did you know that's about three thousand miles away from here?''

Wendy set the book on top of one of the periodical shelves and turned to the Ws. There was no Tristan Williams.

"At least he's not in Perth,'' Wendy said.

"I guess Mr. Charles Lester was telling us the truth," Marissa said.

"Did you doubt him?" Wendy asked.

"Not really," Marissa answered. "It would have been too easy for us to check." She scanned the surrounding shelves. "Let's take a look at some of this FCA material."

For the next hour Marissa and Wendy pored over articles on a wide range of topics related to reproductive technology. The scope and breadth of FCA research was as impressive as the clinic itself. It soon became clear that FCA had played a pioneering role in fetal/fertility research, especially in regard to the use of fetal tissue for treatment of metabolic and degenerative diseases.

Most of the articles they merely skimmed. Those dealing with in-vitro fertilization they put aside. Once they had finished a cursory look at all the material, they turned back to the articles on in-vitro fertilization.

"I'm impressed but confused," Wendy said after half an hour. "I must be missing something."

"I have the same feeling," Marissa said. "When you read these articles in sequence, it shows that their percent success per cycle in terms of achieving pregnancy was going up every year. Like for five cycles the success rate went from twenty percent in 1983 to almost sixty percent in 1987."

"Exactly," Wendy said. "But what happened in 1988? Maybe it's a misprint."

"Can't be a misprint," Marissa said. "Look at the data for 1989." She tossed a paper onto Wendy's lap. Wendy studied the figures. "Curious that they didn't even calculate the per-cycle pregnancy rate after they'd made such a big deal out of doing it in every other year."

"It's a simple calculation," Marissa said. "Do it yourself for five cycles."

Wendy pulled a piece of paper from her purse and did the division. "You're right," she said when she'd finished. "It's the same as 1988, and when compared to 1987, it's much worse. Less than ten percent. Something was going wrong."

"Yet look at the pregnancy rate per patient," Marissa said. "They changed the basis of their reporting. They didn't talk about achieving pregnancy per *cycle* anymore, they switched to pregnancy per *patient*. And that still went up in both 1988 and 1989."

"Wait a second," Wendy said. "I don't think that's possible. I want to graph this stuff. Let me see if I can find some paper." Wendy walked over to the reference desk.

Meanwhile, Marissa went back to the figures. As Wendy suggested, it didn't seem possible for rates per cycle to go down while rates per patient went up. And not only that, the pregnancy rate per patient in 1988 approached eighty percent!

"Ta da!" Wendy said as she came back, triumphantly waving several sheets of graph paper. She set to work, swiftly sketching two graphs.

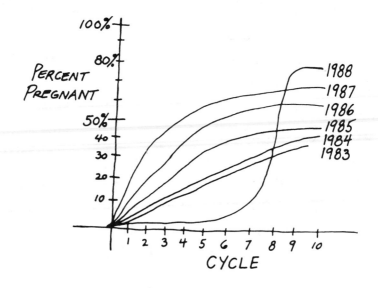

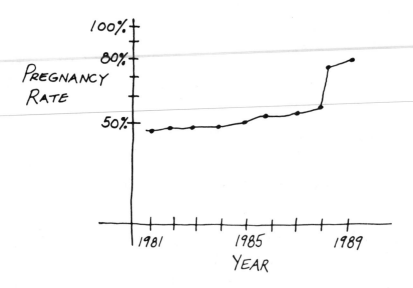

After briefly studying her efforts, she pushed the paper across the table to Marissa. "There has to be something we're missing," she said. "This still doesn't make sense to me."

Marissa examined the graphs Wendy had drawn. It didn't make sense to her either. Seeing the supposedly related curves going in different directions seemed contradictory.

"The crazy part is that they can't be bogus statistics," Wendy said. "If they were making them up, they certainly wouldn't have had the per-cycle success rate go down. They wouldn't be that stupid."

"I don't know what to make of it," Marissa said. She handed the graphs back to Wendy, who folded them and put them in her purse.

"Let's sleep on it," Wendy suggested.

"Maybe we should go back to FCA and ask Mr. Lester," Marissa said. "But first let's check to see if our Tristan Williams has been writing any more papers."

After returning all the FCA journal articles to their proper shelves, Marissa and Wendy returned to the computer terminals that Mrs. Pierce had pointed out to them. Wendy sat down while Marissa leaned over her shoulder. Without much difficulty, Wendy set the computer to run a search for all articles written by Tristan Williams. After she pushed the Execute button, it took the computer only a few seconds to flash the result. Tristan Williams had written only one published article, and that was the one they already had.

"Not what I'd call a prolific bloke," Wendy said.

"That's an understatement," Marissa said.

"I'm starting to get a bit discouraged. You have any suggestions now?"

"Sure do," Wendy said. "Let's have lunch."

After inquiring at the circulation desk, Marissa and Wendy walked over to a cafeteria-style lunchroom and bought sandwiches. Taking them outside, they sat on a bench beneath a beautiful flowering tree of a species neither one recognized.

"Do you think it's really worth the effort to try to find this Williams character?" Wendy asked between bites. "After all, he might not even appreciate our seeking him out. Sounds like this episode with his one and only paper was his undoing."

"I suppose my interest is mere curiosity at this point," Marissa admitted. "Maybe we should try one more thing. Let's try calling the Royal College of Pathology and ask them about him. If they don't know anything or if they tell us he's in some distant place like Perth, we'll give up. This already is beginning to feel like a wild-goose chase."

"And then we'll let ourselves have some fun!" Wendy said.

"Right," Marissa said.

Once they finished eating, they returned to the library and consulted the Royal College of Pathology's publication for the society's address and phone number. Using a public phone in the library, Marissa made her call. The phone was answered by a cheerful operator who connected Marissa to an administrator named Shirley

240

McGovern once Marissa told her why she was calling.

"I'm terribly sorry," Mrs. McGovern said after Marissa repeated her question. "It is the College's rule not to give out information on its members."

"I understand," Marissa said. "But perhaps you can tell me if he is a member of your organization."

There was a pause on the line.

"I've come all the way from America," Marissa added. "We're old friends . . ."

"Well . . ." Mrs. McGovern said, "I suppose it is all right to tell you that he is no longer a member of the College. But beyond that, I cannot tell you more."

Marissa hung up the phone and told Wendy what little she'd learned. "Although she certainly implied that he had been a member in the past," Marissa added.

"I suppose that further corroborates Mr. Lester's story," Wendy said. "Let's give up on the bastard. The more I think about him publishing a fictitious paper, the less I want to talk to him. Let's go diving."

"I'll make you a deal," Marissa said. "As long as we're on the medical school campus, let's find the alumni office and see if he happened to go to school here. If this alumni office is anything like ours, they'd be sure to have the man's latest address to hit him up for money. If they don't know of him, then we'll give up."

"You've got yourself a deal," Wendy said.

The alumni office was in the main administration building on the second floor. It was a small operation with only a three-person staff. The director, a Mr. Alex Hammersmith, was cordial and eager to help.

"The name's not familiar," he said in response to their inquiry, "but let me have a go at our master list."

He had a computer terminal on his desk and he typed in Tristan Williams' name. "How do you know this bloke?" he asked, keying the computer to start its search.

"Old friend," Marissa said evasively. "We came to Australia on the spur of the moment and decided to try to look him up to say hello."

"Bloody friendly of you," Mr. Hammersmith said as he glanced over at his screen. "Here we go. Yes, Mr. Tristan Williams was a graduate here, class of 1979."

"Do you have his current address?" Marissa asked. This was the first encouraging lead they'd had all day.

"Only his work address," Mr. Hammersmith said. "Would you care to have that?"

"Very much so," Marissa said, motioning Wendy to give her a piece of paper. Wendy handed her another sheet of graph paper from her purse.

"Mr. Williams is close by," Mr. Hammersmith said. "Only a few blocks away at the Female Care Australia clinic. It's near enough to walk."

Marissa sighed. She handed the graph paper back to Wendy along with the pen. "We've already been there," she said. "They told us he'd left two years ago."

"Oh, dear!" Mr. Hammersmith said. "Terribly sorry about that. We try to keep our files up to date, but we're not always successful."

"Thank you for your help," Marissa said, getting to her feet. "I suppose Tristan and I were destined never to meet again."

"Bloody awful," Mr. Hammersmith said. "But hold on. Let me try something else here." He went back to his computer screen and began typing on the keyboard.

"There we have it!" Mr. Hammersmith said with a smile. "I've checked the faculty roster with the 1979 year of graduation. We have three people from that year on staff. My advice is to ask them about Tristan Williams. I'm sure one of them will know where he is." He wrote down the faculty names and their respective departments and handed the sheet to Marissa.

"I'd try the bloke on top of the list first," Mr. Hammersmith said. "For a while he was acting as the class secretary for the alumni journal. He works in the Anatomy Department, which is in the building directly across from this one. If after talking with him and the others you still haven't turned old Williams up, come back. I have a few other ideas that might be worth trying. I could contact the Health Insurance Commission in Canberra for one. If he's doing any outpatient billing, they'd have to have an address for him. And of course there is the Australian Medical Association.

I think they keep a data bank on physicians whether they are members or not. Beyond that, there's the State Licensing Board. There are actually a lot of ways we might track him down."

"You've been most kind," Marissa said.

"Good luck," Mr. Hammersmith said. "We Australians love to see friends from abroad. It would be a shame if you two missed each other after you've come all this way."

After leaving the alumni office, Marissa stopped Wendy in the stairwell. "You don't mind if we follow up on this, do you?" she asked. "This is a step beyond our deal."

"We're here," Wendy said. "Let's give it a shot."

Marissa and Wendy had no trouble finding the Anatomy Department, where they went and asked for Dr. Lawrence Spenser.

"Third floor," a secretary told them. "Gross anatomy. He's usually in the lab in the afternoon."

Climbing the stairs, Wendy said, "The smell alone here is starting to awaken bad memories. How well I remember it from my med school days. Did you like gross anatomy first year?"

"It wasn't bad," Marissa said.

"I hated it," Wendy said. "That smell. I couldn't get it out of my hair for the entire three months."

The door to the gross anatomy room was ajar. The women peeked inside. There were about twenty shrouded tables. Toward the rear was a lone individual wearing an apron and rubber gloves. His back was to them.

"Excuse me!" Marissa called. "We're looking for Lawrence Spenser."

The man turned around. He had dark curly hair. Compared to the people Marissa and Wendy had been seeing, he seemed pale.

"You've found him," the man said with a smile. "What can I do for you?"

"We'd like to ask you a few questions," Marissa called.

"Well, it's a little hard to converse across the room," Spenser said. "Come on in."

Marissa and Wendy entered and weaved their way among the many shrouded tables. Both women were aware that the plastic sheets were covering corpses. Wendy tried to breathe through her mouth so as not to smell the formalin.

"Welcome to gross anatomy," Spenser said. "I'm afraid I don't get many visitors."

Wendy recoiled from the sight of what he had been working on. It was the torso of a cadaver, sawed off at the umbilicus. The eyes were half open, the mouth pulled back in a sneer with the tips of yellow teeth barely visible. The skin of the left cheek had been dissected, revealing the course of the facial nerve.

Following Wendy's line of sight, Spenser said, "Sorry about Archibald here. He's been under the weather lately."

"We've just come from the alumni office," Marissa told him.

"Excuse me," Wendy said, interrupting her. "I think I'll wait outside." She turned and started for the hall.

"Are you okay?" Marissa called after her.

"I'll be fine," Wendy said with a wave. "Take your time. I'll be outside."

Turning back to Spenser, Marissa explained, "Anatomy wasn't her favorite subject."

"Sorry about that," Spenser said. "When you do this every day, you forget its effect on others."

"Getting back to what I was saying," Marissa continued. "We were over at the alumni office and Mr. Hammersmith gave us your name. We're doctors from the States. We're looking for Tristan Williams. Mr. Hammersmith said you might know of him since you two graduated together."

"Sure, I know Tris," Spenser said. "In fact, I spoke to him about six months ago. Why are you looking for him?"

"Just old friends," Marissa said. "We happened to be in Brisbane and wanted to say hello, but he'd left the FCA."

"And not under the best of circumstances," Spenser said. "Poor Tris has been going through some hard times, but things seem better now. In fact, I think he's quite happy where he is."

"Is he still in the Brisbane area?" Marissa asked.

"Hell, no!" Spenser said. "He's out in Never Never."

"Never Never?" Marissa questioned. "Is that a town?"

Spenser laughed heartily. "Not quite," he said.

"It's an Aussie expression, like the Back of Bourke or the Back of Beyond. It refers to the outback, the Australian bush. Tris is working as a general practitioner with the Royal Flying Doctor Service out of Charleville."

"Is that far from here?" Marissa asked.

"Everything is far in Australia," Spenser said. "It's a big country and most of it is like a desert. Charleville is about four hundred miles from Brisbane, out at the edge of the channel country. From there Tris flies out to Betoota Hotel, Windorah, Cunnamulla, godforsaken places like that, to visit isolated cattle stations. As I understand it, he stays out for weeks at a time. It takes a special man for that kind of work. I admire him. I couldn't do it, not after living around here."

"Is it difficult to get out there?" Marissa asked.

"It's not hard to get to Charleville," Spenser said. "There's a bitumen road all the way. You can even fly there. But beyond Charleville, I think the road deteriorates to dirt and bulldust. I don't recommend it for a holiday."

"Thanks for taking the time to talk to me," Marissa said. "I appreciate your help." In truth, she was depressed by his information. It seemed as if the closer she got to finding out about Tristan Williams, the further he slipped away.

"Happy to be of service," Spenser said. "If I were you, I'd forget about the outback and Tris. I'd head down to the Gold Coast and beach it, Aussie-style. You don't know what desolate means until you've seen some areas of the Australian outback."

After exchanging goodbyes, Marissa left and went back outside. She found Wendy sitting on the front steps of the building.

"You okay?" Marissa asked, sitting down beside her friend.

"Oh, I'm fine now," Wendy said. "Sorry to abandon you in there. You'd think I could stomach that stuff by now."

"I'm glad you had sense enough to walk out," Marissa said. "I'm sorry to have put you through it. But we found Tristan Williams."

"Eureka!" Wendy said. "Is he close?"

"Everything is relative," Marissa said. "He's not in Perth, but he's someplace out in the Australian outback. Apparently he's abandoned pathology, or pathology has abandoned him. He's working as a GP flying around to isolated locations like cattle ranches."

"Sounds like a romantic do-gooder job for someone who falsified data for a journal article."

Marissa nodded. "His home base is a town called Charleville, which is about four hundred miles from here. But he's away for weeks at a time. I think it would be pretty tough to track him down. What do you think?"

"Sounds like a lot of effort for a questionable payoff. But let's think about it. Meanwhile, we deserve a break from all this effort. Let's go diving. After that maybe we'll have more enthusiasm."

"Okay," Marissa said, getting to her feet. "You've been patient. Let's go see how great this Barrier Reef really is!"

They caught a cab at the administration building and returned to their hotel. There they picked up their traveler's checks and walked over to the travel agent Wendy had visited the day before.

There was no problem arranging for jet transportation for the following day even though it was the weekend. They were able to reserve a room at the Hamilton Island Resort. The agent even called to be sure to get them a seaside room.

"What's the best way to arrange for a day's diving?" Wendy asked when the agent had finished the call.

"You can allow the hotel to make the arrangements," the agent said. "That certainly is the easiest. But to tell you the truth, if I were you I'd wait until I got there and find your own charter. It's a good-sized marina, there are a lot of dive and fishing boats. It's their slow time and you'll be able to bargain. You'd find a much better deal."

Wendy picked up the tickets and brochures. "That sounds terrific. We'll follow your suggestion," she said. "Thanks for your help."

"Glad to be of service," the agent said. "But there is something I should warn you about."

Marissa felt her heart skip a beat. She was already concerned about diving in exotic depths.

"What?" Wendy asked.

"The sun," the agent said. "Make sure you use a lot of block."

Marissa laughed.

"Thanks for the tip," Wendy said. She grabbed Marissa's arm and headed for the door.

"Can I help you?" the agent asked, turning to her next customer. He was a leathery Australian man. The agent guessed he was from the outback. He'd been browsing through a rack of European tour brochures to the right of the agent's desk while the American women made their plans. When they'd first arrived, the agent had thought all three were together.

"As a matter of fact, you can," the man said. "I need two return air tickets for Hamilton Island. The names are Edmund Stewart and Willy Tong."

"Will you be needing accommodations?" the agent asked.

"No, thanks," Ned said. "We'll take care of that when we get there."

10

APRIL 7, 1990
1:40 P.M.

PRESSING HER nose against the window of the Ansett jet, Marissa could see the broad expanse of ocean thousands of feet below. From the moment they'd taken off at 12:40 P.M., they'd been over water. At first the ocean had been a dark, sapphire blue. But as they traveled on, the color changed.

250

It had become a brilliant turquoise. Already they could see a patchwork of underwater coral. Their journey was taking them over a tapestry of shoals, atolls, coral cays, and true continental islands.

Wendy was beside herself with anticipation. She had bought a travel guide at the airport and was reading sections to Marissa. Marissa didn't have the heart to tell her that she couldn't concentrate. Marissa was wondering what the hell she was doing flying off the coast of Australia.

Having made no progress whatsoever in their quest for information that might help them explain the origins of their infertility, Marissa began to seriously question the rationale for the trip. Perhaps she should have stayed at home and tried to get her life back in order. She wondered what Robert was doing, and how her leaving affected his behavior. If he were having an affair with Donna, leaving like she did would only give him carte blanche to carry on. If she'd been wrong, she wondered if her abrupt departure would push him into Donna's arms.

"Australia's Great Barrier Reef has taken twenty-five million years to form," Wendy read, "and there are at least three hundred and fifty different species of coral, as well as fifteen hundred species of tropical fish."

"Wendy," Marissa said at last, "maybe it would be better for you to read to yourself. Statistics like that don't register in my mind unless I read them."

"Hold on!" Wendy said, not taking the hint. "Here's one you can relate to. The visibility of

251

water can be up to sixty meters." Wendy looked at Marissa. "That's unbelievable. That's about two hundred feet. Isn't that astounding? Can you wait?"

Marissa merely nodded.

Undaunted, Wendy read on. Marissa turned back to the window and looked out at the limitless Pacific Ocean. Again she thought of Robert, nearly half a world away.

Mercifully, Marissa's thoughts and Wendy's reading were interrupted by an announcement. The captain said they were nearing Hamilton Island and would be landing momentarily. In another few minutes their plane touched down.

The island was a tropical paradise. Although Marissa and Wendy were surprised when they saw several high-rise buildings which looked starkly out of place, the rest of the island was in keeping with their expectations. The vegetation was a lush bright green, highlighted by dazzling flowers. The beaches were a sparkling white sand, the water an inviting aqua.

The check-in at the hotel went smoothly. Their seaside room was ready for them. The resort's lagoon-shaped pool tempted Marissa, but Wendy was not to be denied. She wanted to go directly to the marina to arrange for the next day's diving. She offered to go by herself, but Marissa felt obligated to go with her.

As the travel agent had said, the marina was large. Several hundred boats of all sizes and descriptions were docked there, with room for more.

Advertisements for excursions for both fishing and diving abounded. The large bulletin board on the front wall of the ship chandler's store was filled. But Wendy wasn't satisfied with the information they contained. Instead she insisted they wander out on the commercial pier to examine the boats themselves.

Marissa followed along, enjoying the surroundings more than the boats. The day was glorious. A hot, tropical sun blazed in the middle of an azure sky. Large cumulus clouds dotted the horizon particularly over the peaks of the neighboring islands. To the north in the far distance a group of dark clouds clustered, suggesting a thunderstorm on the way.

"Here's a good one," Wendy said. She'd stopped at a boat slip where one of the larger boats was moored. The name emblazoned on the transom was "Oz." It was a cabin cruiser, painted white, with a spacious cockpit. Several swivel deep-sea fishing chairs were mounted there. Against the forward bulk-head a long row of scuba tanks was secured.

"What makes this one better than the others?" Marissa asked.

"This one has a nice dive platform right at the water's edge," Wendy said, pointing to a gratelike wooden structure that hung from the transom of the boat. "I can also tell there's a compressor on board. That means they can fill their own scuba tanks. Besides, it looks like it's about fifty feet. That means it will be nice and stable."

"I see," Marissa said. She was impressed that Wendy knew so much about it. She felt she was in good hands.

"You ladies interested in fishing or diving?" a bearded man asked.

"Possibly," Wendy said. "What's the charge for a full day's diving?"

"Come on aboard and we'll discuss it," the man told her. "Name's Rafe Murray. I'm the captain of this vessel."

With experienced steps, Wendy marched out on the two-foot-wide planks that separated the boat slips and swung herself onto the gunwale of the *Oz*. Then she stepped down onto the deck of the boat.

Marissa tried to follow with the same bravado, but hesitated with one foot on the dock and one foot on the boat. The captain lent her a hand for balance and she was able to step on board.

A handsome, muscular younger man came out of the cabin. He smiled and tipped his lived-in Australian hat to the women.

"This here's my first mate and dive master, Wynn Jones," the captain said. "Knows the reef like the back of his hand, he does."

Wendy asked if they might tour the boat, then followed the agreeable captain from bow to stern. Satisfied, she sat down in the cabin with the captain and bargained for an all-day dive rate. Marissa had never seen this tough side of her friend.

Eventually a deal was struck and Wendy and Rafe shook hands. At that point, the captain asked

254

if the women would care for a couple of "stubbies," which Marissa soon learned were small brown bottles of beer.

After the beer, Marissa and Wendy climbed up onto the gunwale and leaped to the dock. Wynn gave Marissa a hand to make sure she made it.

"Goddamn cheap son-of-a-bitch bastard Yanks," the captain said as Wynn rejoined him in the cabin. "She got me down so low it will barely pay for the petrol."

"We haven't been out for four days," Wynn reminded him. "We'll just go to the closest reef and let them look at some dead staghorn coral. It will serve'm right."

"Hello!" a voice called.

"Now what?" Rafe said. He squinted through the cabin door. "Maybe things are looking up. We got a Nip."

"I don't think he's a Nip," Wynn said. "He looks Chinese to me."

Rafe and Wynn walked out into the afternoon sunlight.

"What can I do for you, sir?" Rafe called to the man on the pier.

"Are you available for charter tomorrow?" the man said.

"What do you have in mind?" Rafe asked. He could always forget the women.

"I want to do some serious fishing on the outer wall of the reef," the man said.

"We're at your service," Rafe said. "But the

outer reef is forty nautical miles away. It'll be somewhat dear."

"I'm prepared to pay," the man said. "But I don't like crowds. You got many people scheduled tomorrow?"

Rafe raised his eyebrows at Wynn, trying to decide what to say. He didn't want to lose this Chinese man's money, but he didn't want to pass up the Yanks' money either.

Wynn shrugged.

Rafe turned back to the Chinese man. "We just signed up a couple of ladies to do some diving," he said. "But I can always cancel them."

"Two ladies won't bother my fishing," the man said. "But leave it at that. No more passengers."

"Fine by me," Rafe said, trying to hide his excitement. "Come on aboard and we'll make the necessary arrangements. For a day's charter to the outer reef, we'll need some money up front."

Nimbly, the Chinese man jumped on board. "The name's Harry Wong," he said. "I don't have a lot of time at the moment. How about two hundred dollars to reserve the boat?" he opened his wallet and took out the money.

Rafe took the bills. "This will do just fine," he said. "Any particular time you'd like to depart?"

"What time did you tell those women?" the man asked.

"I told them eight o'clock," Rafe said. "But that can change."

"Eight is fine," the man said. "But I might

want to sleep on the way out to the outer reef. Do you have a cabin I could use?"

"Absolutely," Rafe said. "You can use the main cabin."

The Chinese man smiled. "See you at eight," he said. He leaped from the boat to the pier, then walked briskly away.

Willy Tong was pleased. He knew Ned Kelly would be too. The only weak part of the whole plan had been the problem of getting the women to the outer reef. Now that seemed assured. He entered The Crab, a pub along the waterfront, and ordered an amber. He hadn't had a chance to finish his beer when Ned showed up.

"How'd it go, mate?" Ned asked as he hopped onto a barstool.

"Smooth as silk," Willy said. He told Ned the details.

"Perfect!" Ned said. "I didn't have any trouble either. I rented one of those big powerboats that have enough engine to drive a supertanker. Come on, finish your beer. We got to go buy bait. A lot of bait."

The Hamilton Island Resort had so many ethnic restaurants to choose from, Marissa and Wendy had trouble making up their minds. They eventually settled on Polynesian, thinking it was the closest thing to local. To get into the mood they had purchased bright floral-print sarongs in the hotel's gift shop.

Having concluded the arrangements for the following day's diving, Marissa and Wendy had spent the rest of the afternoon lounging around the pool, soaking up the warm tropical sun. Although it hadn't been crowded, there had been enough sunbathers poolside to make people-watching interesting. They'd even struck up a conversation with several single men who were intrigued to discover the women hailed from Boston.

Marissa was amazed at the number of Australians who had visited the States. Many had made it to Boston. Australia seemed to be a land of travelers. The six weeks' holiday they got every year had to be a boon to the adventurous.

"Let's order some champagne to celebrate being here," Wendy suggested. "I'm so excited about tomorrow, I can't stand it."

The food was "interesting," as Wendy had put it, but pork wasn't Marissa's favorite. And eating off large tropical leaves didn't strike her as appetizing.

While they were waiting for dessert, Marissa looked at Wendy. "Have you been thinking much about Gustave?" she asked.

"Of course," Wendy said. "Be hard not to, even though I'm trying. Have you been thinking about Robert?"

Marissa admitted that she had. "It started on the plane," she said. "Do you think I ought to call? I may have overreacted about Donna."

"Go ahead and give him a call," Wendy said.

"If it's on your mind, I think you should do it. Maybe I should call Gustave."

The dessert arrived. It was called Coconut Extravaganza. They both tried it. Wendy said she thought it was so-so. She put down her spoon. "I don't think it's worth the calories."

Marissa leaned forward. "Wendy," she said with a lowered voice. "There is an Asian man behind you who's been watching us."

Wendy responded by twisting in her seat. "Where?" she asked.

Marissa grabbed her arm. "Don't look," she said.

Wendy faced her companion. "What do you mean, don't look? How am I supposed to see who you mean?"

"Be subtle!" Marissa whispered. "He's three tables behind you, he's with a dark-haired man whose face I can't see. Uh oh!"

"What's the matter?" Wendy asked.

"The guy with the dark hair is looking this way now," Marissa said.

Wendy couldn't contain herself any longer. She twisted around again. Turning back to Marissa, she said, "Well, so what? They like our new sarongs."

"There's something about the Asian man that makes me feel uncomfortable," Marissa said. "It's almost a visceral reaction."

"Do you recognize him?" Wendy asked.

"No," Marissa admitted.

"Maybe he reminds you of those creeps at the Women's Clinic," Wendy suggested.

"That's a thought," Marissa agreed.

"Maybe he's from the People's Republic," Wendy said. "Everybody that I know who's gone to China has told me that they stare to beat the band."

"He's driving me crazy," Marissa said, forcing herself to look away. "If you're finished, let's get out of here."

"I'm done," Wendy said, tossing her napkin over her coconut extravaganza.

Emerging from the dining room into the outdoors, Marissa looked up in awe. She had never witnessed such stars as she did in the velvety purple of the Australian night. Gazing at their intensity, she felt instantly better. She wondered why she was so sensitive about that Asian. After all, he'd been far across the room from them.

Back in the hotel room, Marissa sat down on the edge of her bed and figured out what time it was in the States. "It's seven-fifteen in the morning in Boston," she said. "Let's call."

"You call first," Wendy said. She stretched out on the bed.

With trembling fingers, Marissa dialed her home. As the distant phone rang, she tried to think of what she would say. By the fourth ring, she knew Robert wasn't home. Just to be certain, she let it ring ten times before hanging up. She turned to Wendy.

"The bastard's not home," Marissa said. "And he never leaves for the office before eight."

"Maybe he's on a business trip," Wendy said.

"Fat chance," Marissa said. "He's probably with Donna."

"Now don't jump to conclusions," Wendy warned. "There are probably plenty of explanations. Let's see what happens to me." She sat up and dialed her number.

Marissa watched as Wendy waited. Finally Wendy dropped the receiver back into its cradle. "Gustave's not home either," she said. "Maybe they're having breakfast together." She tried to smile.

"Gustave is a surgeon," Marissa said. "What time does he usually leave for work?"

"About seven-thirty," Wendy said. "Unless he has surgery. It's true he's been doing a lot of surgery lately."

"Well, there you go," Marissa said.

"I suppose," Wendy said. She didn't sound convinced.

"Let's go for a walk," Marissa said. She stood up and stretched out a hand for her friend. Together they wandered out onto the beach. For a while neither of them said a word.

"I have a bad feeling about my marriage," Marissa said at last. "Lately Robert and I seem to see everything differently. It isn't just the mess with Donna."

Wendy nodded. "I have to say this infertility

business has put an enormous strain on Gustave and me."

Marissa sighed. "And to think of the promise our relationship started with."

The women stopped. Their eyes had adjusted to the darkness. Ahead they saw the silhouette of a couple nestled in an embrace.

"Makes me feel nostalgic," Wendy said. "And sad."

"Me too," Marissa agreed. "Maybe we'd better head in another direction."

They wandered back to the resort. There they happened to pass by a couple with a crying toddler in a stroller. Both the man and the woman were happily window-shopping, ignoring the wailing child.

"Can you believe those people, bringing such a small child out to an island like this?" Wendy said. "Poor thing is probably sunburned."

"I think it's awful for them to keep the child up this late," Marissa said with equal vehemence. "It's obvious the child is exhausted."

Marissa caught Wendy's eye. They both smiled at each other, then shook their heads.

"Envy is a terrible thing," Wendy said.

"At least we recognize it for what it is," Marissa said.

Wendy had Marissa up at the crack of dawn for a big English breakfast of coffee, eggs, bacon, and toast on their lanai. As they ate, a huge tropical sun rose into a cloudless sky. They got to the boat just before eight and the captain already had both diesels idling. After first tossing on board their shoulder bags with their bathing suits and other paraphernalia, Wendy and Marissa climbed over the gunwale.

"G'day!" Rafe said. "Ready for adventure?"

"You bet," Wendy said.

"You ladies mind lending a hand here?" Rafe asked.

"Not at all," Wendy said.

"Then cast off those stern lines when I give a yell," Rafe said. He then went into the cabin. Wynn was already out on the bow making preparations. The sun glistened off his shirtless back.

Marissa felt the boat tremble as the engines were revved up. Wynn began to release the bowlines.

"Okay, ladies," Rafe yelled. "Cast off."

Wendy took the starboard line, Marissa the port. They slipped them from their cleats and tossed them onto the dock. With a shudder, the boat moved out of the slip.

Until they got out of the marina, Marissa and Wendy stayed in the stern, watching the activity in the bustling port. Once the boat reached open water and the captain increased their speed, they went forward to the cabin.

Wynn was still on the bow deck, lounging against one of the two dinghies, smoking a cigarette. Marissa noticed he was sporting a different hat, one just as woebegone as the day before, but with a fishnet around the hatband for a decorative touch.

263

Marissa spotted something on deck that had not been there the day before: a cage made of heavy steel bars. At its top it was attached by a cable to one of the forward davits.

"What's the cage for?" Marissa yelled over the sound of the engines. She pointed through the windshield.

"That there is a shark cage," Rafe said, eyeing an upcoming buoy.

"What the hell is that for?" Marissa asked. She turned to Wendy, who shrugged. "We're not going someplace where there are sharks, are we?" Wendy asked Rafe.

"This is the ocean," Rafe yelled. "Sharks are in the ocean. There's always the chance that one might be around. But relax! The cage is just a precaution, especially on the outer reef where I'm taking you two lucky ladies. The outer reef's where all the fish are as well as the best coral. Even the visibility is the best out there."

"I don't want to see any sharks," Marissa yelled.

"Probably won't," Rafe yelled in reply. "It's Wynn who wants the cage. Just to be safe. It's like a seat belt."

Marissa led Wendy down into the saloon and closed the door behind them. The throbbing noise of the engines abruptly decreased.

"I don't like the sound of this," Marissa said urgently. "Shark cage! What are we getting ourselves into?"

"Marissa, calm down!" Wendy said. "Everything the captain said is right. Even in Hawaii I saw sharks on occasion. But they don't bother divers. I think we should be impressed that these guys even have a shark cage. It just means they're very careful."

"You're not concerned?" Marissa asked.

"Not in the slightest," Wendy said. "Come on, don't get yourself all worked up. You're going to love this, believe me."

Marissa studied her friend's face. She obviously believed what she was saying. "Okay," Marissa said. "If you can honestly tell me it will be safe, I'll try and relax. I just don't like the idea of sharks. I've always had a mild phobia for the ocean that hasn't kept me out of it, but it certainly has made me aware when I'm in it. And as I said before, I don't like slippery, slimy creatures."

"I can personally guarantee you will not have to touch one slippery, slimy creature," Wendy said.

Marissa and Wendy felt the boat shudder as it was pushed up to full throttle. "Come on," Wendy urged. "Let's go up on deck and enjoy this."

Buoyed by her friend's enthusiasm, Marissa followed her on deck.

The boat headed almost due east, directly into the rising sun. At first they were cruising through clear turquoise water, but soon they began to pass over the reef itself. Then the water became a deeper blue.

Wendy got Wynn to break out the scuba gear so she could check it out. She went over all the technical aspects with Marissa to refresh her memory.

Once all the diving gear had been checked, Marissa and Wendy sat in the sport-fishing chairs and enjoyed the spectacular view.

"I'm surprised that we're the only ones on such a large boat," Wendy said to Wynn when he joined them.

"It's our off-season," Wynn explained. "If you came back in September or October, we'd be full to the gunwales."

"Is it better then?" Wendy asked.

"You can count on the weather more," Wynn said. "Plus there never are any waves. It's always calm."

Almost the moment Wynn mentioned waves, Marissa felt the boat start to shudder against a building chop.

"Can't get much better weather than this," Wendy said.

"We've been lucky lately," Wynn agreed. "But we'll hit some surf on the outer reef. It shouldn't be too bad though."

"How much further do we have to go?" Marissa asked. The Whitsunday Islands were now mere specks on the western horizon. It seemed to her they were heading to the center of the Coral Sea. Being this far from land revived her misgivings.

"Another half hour," Wynn said in answer to her question. "The outer reef's about fifty miles from Hamilton Island."

Marissa nodded. She was beginning to think

she was about as fond of boating as Wendy was of gross anatomy lessons. She would just as soon have gone snorkeling. Then they could have stayed within sight of shore.

At just after ten o'clock the captain slowed the engines and sent Wynn forward to the bow. He told the women he was searching for a particular channel to anchor in. "Best goddamn diving in the world," he told them.

After a half hour of searching, Rafe yelled for Wynn to drop anchor. Marissa noticed they were between two enormous heads of coral. Over their tops the waves were cresting. The surf had increased to approximately three feet.

"Anchor's on the bottom," Wynn shouted.

Rafe cut the engines and the boat quickly drifted until it faced northwest, heading into the wind. From the stern Marissa could see that they were moored about thirty feet from the outer wall of the reef. The color of the water abruptly changed from emerald green over the reef to the deep sapphire of the ocean beyond.

Now that the boat was no longer moving ahead, it was more susceptible to the waves. The boat began to pitch from the waves coming into the channel at the same time it rocked back and forth from the wash of the waves cresting on the coral heads. Marissa began to feel queasy from the rough, irregular motion. Steadying herself with one hand, she turned around and made her way back to Wendy, clutching the rail with every step.

"Is this where we're diving?" Wendy asked Rafe.

"This is it," Rafe said. "You ladies have a good time. But stay with Wynn here, understand? I got some work down in the engine room, so it will be just the three of you. Don't go swimming off on your own."

"Lower that cage before you go below," Wynn called.

"Oh, yeah," Rafe said. "I almost forgot."

"Let's get our suits on," Wendy said to Marissa. She tossed Marissa's shoulder bag to her, then went below.

Marissa was impressed how at ease Wendy seemed at sea. She negotiated the deck as calmly as if they were still back at the dock.

After passing through the saloon, Wendy entered one of the cabins. Marissa went to the one opposite and tried the door. Finding it was locked, she tried another. It was open and she went in.

Within the confines of the narrow space, Marissa had some difficulty changing out of her clothes and into her bathing suit. By the time she emerged, she was feeling even more nauseated than she had before she went belowdecks. The faint smell of diesel fuel no doubt contributed. When she got back on deck she felt better but still not great. She hoped that once she got into the water, the feeling would pass.

Wendy was already pulling her tank on over her buoyancy vest when Marissa reached her. Wynn was giving her a hand. Marissa slipped on her vest.

A terrible grinding screech resulted from Rafe's efforts at deploying the shark cage. Marissa watched as the cage was lifted high above the deck, then swung out to starboard. With a high-pitched whir, it was dropped into the water.

Once Wynn had finished helping Wendy, he came over to Marissa to strap on her tank. He guided her to the stern of the boat.

Wendy was already on the dive platform, ready to go. Her mask was on, as were her heavy work gloves. As the swells hit the boat, she was alternately submerged to her knees and then dry. After pulling on her own mask and gloves, Marissa struggled over the stern and stood next to Wendy. The water felt cold at first, but Marissa soon got used to it. The water was incredibly clear. Looking directly down, she could see the sandy bottom at about thirty feet. As she looked farther out she saw that the sand abruptly dropped off to incalculable oceanic depths.

Wendy tapped Marissa on the shoulder. "Do you remember the diving sign language?" Wendy asked. Her voice sounded nasal with her mask covering her nose.

"Sort of," Marissa said.

Wendy went over all the key signals, demonstrating them with her free hand. She had to hold on firmly with the other so she wasn't knocked from the platform. Marissa held on with both hands throughout the review.

"Got them?" Wendy asked.

Marissa signaled okay.

269

"All right!" Wendy said, slapping her on the shoulder.

"You ladies ready?" Wynn asked. He had joined them at the stern of the boat, taking a seat on the gunwale.

Wendy said she was all set. Marissa merely nodded.

"Follow me!" Wynn said. He put in his mouthpiece, then somersaulted backwards into the water. Wendy followed almost immediately.

Marissa put in her mouthpiece and took her first breath of the cool, compressed air. Turning her head, she looked longingly into the boat. She caught sight of Rafe as he disappeared below. Glancing back into the water, she saw some algae stream past, then some seaweed. The current seemed swift, heading out to sea.

Unable to delay any longer, Marissa grabbed hold of her mask, let go of the boat, and plunged into the water.

The instant the bubbles disappeared, Marissa was astounded. It was as if she had leaped into another world. The clarity of the water was beyond her expectations. She was surrounded by butterfly and angel fish. Thirty feet ahead, Wendy and Wynn were waiting at the lip of the channel. She could see them as clearly as if they were suspended in the air. Below her the sand sparkled, giving her the impression she could see each and every grain. Looking to her right and left, she saw walls of coral in fantastic shapes and colors.

Behind her she could see the bottom of the boat with the shark cage suspended from its cable.

Without the slightest effort Marissa found herself carried by the current toward the other two.

After everyone had exchanged okay signs, they started to swim out of the channel, veering to the left. Marissa paused at the channel's edge and peered uneasily into the eerie abysmal depths. The sound of her breathing echoed in her ears. Fighting against a primeval terror, she shuddered to think of what creatures were lurking in the cold, black vastness.

Marissa saw that Wendy and Wynn had already left her behind. She swam hard to catch up to them, scared of being left alone.

Her fears were soon overcome by the sheer beauty of the world around her. All her phobias vanished as she found herself enveloped in a silvery cloud of cardinal fish.

As she followed the others into a coral gorge, she was thrilled by the number and variety of fish. They came in every size and shape and in colors more brilliant than anything on land. The coral was equally dramatic, with colors that rivaled the fish and in shapes that ranged from brainlike masses to antlerlike growths. Diaphanous sea fans waved sinuously in the current.

Distracted by the beauty, Marissa realized the others had disappeared. She hurried forward, rounding a large coral head. Wynn was stopped up ahead. She saw him reach into a net secured to his waist. When he pulled out his hand she saw

271

that he held some baitfish. In an instant he was surrounded by batfish and parrot fish. He clearly wasn't interested in these species because he waved them away. Instead he went close to the opening of a large underwater cave and began to wave the bait through the water.

Marissa's heart leaped into her throat, almost causing her to spit out her mouthpiece. Out of the shadows of the cave swam an enormous six-foot, six-hundred-pound potato cod. Marissa was about to panic when she noticed that Wynn was not only unperturbed but was enticing the fish to come all the way out. Then to Marissa's amazement, the huge fish took the baitfish directly from Wynn's hand.

Wendy swam up behind Wynn and signaled that she wanted to try to feed the behemoth. Wynn gave her several baitfish and showed her how to hold them out.

The cod was happy to oblige, opening its huge mouth and sucking in the bait like an enormous underwater vacuum cleaner.

Wynn motioned for Marissa to swim over, but she was happy to stay where she was and indicated as much via hand signals. She watched Wendy feed the fish, but it was not easy to stay in one place. The surge from the wave action on the reef swept her to and fro, forcing her to fend herself off the coral with her gloved hands. The motion reawakened the queasiness she'd felt on the boat.

Once the potato cod had devoured all the baitfish Wynn was willing to offer, it lazily drifted back into its lair. Wendy went to the very lip of the cave and peered in. Then she swam back to Marissa and motioned for her to follow.

Reluctantly, Marissa swam after Wendy. They passed the cave's mouth and dove close to the sandy bottom. Wendy pointed into a crevice, then backed away so Marissa could take a look.

Marissa hung on to the coral so the current didn't pull her along as she let her eyes adapt to the shadows. She was glad she was wearing the heavy gloves. Finally Marissa saw what Wendy had pointed to: a large green moray eel with its mouth open and its needlelike teeth bared.

Marissa recoiled from the sight. This was precisely the sort of creature she hoped not to see.

Wynn joined the two girls. Pulling out another baitfish, he managed to coax the moray out of its crevice, terrifying Marissa in the process. It writhed through the water, snatching the baitfish in its horrid jaws, then retreating to its hideaway.

As Wendy took a baitfish from Wynn and tried to get the eel to come out again, Marissa began to comprehend that beneath the reef's veneer of spectacular beauty lurked an entirely predatory world. The potential for danger lay everywhere. It was a violent, eat-or-be-eaten world. Even some of the exquisite coral was razor-sharp to the touch.

While Wendy and Wynn devoted themselves to the eel, Marissa heard a low-pitched vibration that made her look up toward the water's surface. The sound became progressively louder, but just as Marissa was about to become alarmed, it stopped.

Holding her breath, she listened intently. All she heard was the hiss of the waves above. When it became clear that neither Wendy nor Wynn was concerned about the sound, Marissa decided to ignore it too.

After Wendy had tired of the game with the moray eel, she and Wynn recommended swimming along the reef. After twenty more feet, they entered yet another coral gorge. Again Wendy stopped and pointed for Marissa's benefit.

Marissa joined Wendy cautiously, hoping another eel hadn't caught her eye. To her relief, Wendy had spotted some colorful clown fish ensconced in the poisonous tentacles of a bed of sea anemone. The fish were a neon orange with vivid white stripes edged in black. For several minutes both Wendy and Marissa were entertained by their antics.

After almost an hour of diving, Marissa began to tire. She still felt mildly nauseated and was fatigued from fighting the surge. It was a constant struggle to keep from being knocked against the coral. Finally Marissa decided she'd had enough.

Signaling Wendy and Wynn, Marissa indicated that she wanted to return to the boat. Wendy nodded and started to come with her, but Marissa signaled for her to stay. Marissa didn't want to drag her friend back until Wendy was good and ready.

Wynn gave Marissa the okay signal. He and Wendy waved a farewell. Marissa waved back, then turned and started swimming for the boat.

When she got to the mouth of the channel where the boat was anchored, she looked back at Wendy and Wynn. They were intently examining something on the face of the coral about sixty feet away. Marissa swam into the channel. Ahead she could see the *Oz*'s keel, the shark cage, and what looked like another smaller boat off to the left.

Reaching the dive platform, Marissa hauled herself up onto it. Exhausted, she was content to sit for a minute with her legs dangling in the water and her back against the stern of the boat. As the boat rose and fell, the platform was alternately submerged up to her navel, then dry.

Marissa removed her mouthpiece and shoved her face mask up on her forehead. After wiping her eyes, she reached up and grabbed the rail that ran around the stern. Still she didn't stand. She continued to sit on the dive platform. It seemed that the motion of the boat was worse than the surge.

"Guess I'm just a landlubber," she told herself. She was embarrassed such relatively calm seas could have such an effect on her, but then she had always been susceptible to motion. As a child, she had often gotten carsick.

While she was waiting to feel better, Marissa became aware of progressive movement around her legs. Bending over, she saw a profusion of small, eager fish darting about. Looking more closely, she saw bits and pieces of fish go by with the current, then a larger blur of what looked like blood and entrails. The building school of fish was busily feeding.

Marissa was preoccupied and baffled as she watched this growing feeding frenzy of colorful tropical fish. But then things turned serious. Out of the blue streaked a five-foot barracuda-type fish which tore through the offal before disappearing as quickly as it had appeared. The smaller fish, which had scattered upon the larger predator's arrival, soon returned in ever greater numbers.

Marissa's blood ran cold. By reflex she drew her legs up onto the dive platform. Just as she did, more coils of intestine went by in a swirl of dark color that had to be blood.

Above and beyond the sloshing of the waves against the boat's stern, Marissa heard distinct splashing noises. Standing up, she peered into the boat. Moving to port so that she could see better in the direction the noise was coming from, Marissa spotted two men. One was on the smaller boat she'd seen from below; the other was on the *Oz* itself. Both were busily emptying buckets of chum into the water. With the breeze Marissa caught a fetid whiff of decaying fish.

Rafe was nowhere to be seen. Turning back to look at the water off the stern, Marissa saw a widening patch of blood that was now staining the surface dusky red. Fish had begun leaping from the water in their frenzy for the food.

Marissa shouted at the men. "Hey!" she yelled. "There are divers in the water!"

The men's heads shot up and they glanced at

Marissa. She noticed one was Asian. Then they went back to their task, furiously dumping the rest of the offal.

"Rafe!" Marissa yelled.

The Asian man leaped from the *Oz* onto the deck of the smaller boat with the boat's bowline in hand. Then, with a roar of a powerful engine and a puff of gray exhaust, the smaller boat sped away to the west.

"Rafe!" Marissa yelled again as loud as she could.

Rafe came out of the cabin, shielding his eyes from the blazing sun. Smudges of grease were on his cheeks. He had a large wrench in his hand.

"There were two men dumping chum into the water," Marissa yelled. "They're heading away in a speedboat." Marissa pointed to the receding launch.

Rafe leaned over the gunwale and glanced at the boat. "My word, they're heading west!" he said. "They're were supposed to fish out beyond the reef."

"Fish!" Marissa cried. "Look what they dumped into the water!"

Rafe looked down. "Jesus!" he cried. He ran back to the stern and eyed the expanding patch of red. Fish were leaping from the water in even greater numbers. "Jesus!" he repeated.

"Could this mess bring sharks?" Marissa asked him.

"Good Lord, yes!" Rafe said.

"Oh, my God!"

Despite her terror, Marissa pulled her mask back over her eyes and nose. She put her mouthpiece back into her mouth, then leaped into the water.

Fish of every size and shape swarmed around her. Visibility was drastically reduced. Biting down on her mouthpiece, Marissa swam ahead, trying not to think about anything but getting Wendy back into the boat.

By the time Marissa neared the mouth of the channel, she saw her first shark; small and white-tipped, it was slowly circling the offal. The ghastly creature terrified Marissa more than anything she'd seen in her life. Keeping her eye on the shark, Marissa swam to the left, close to the wall of coral. While she was still watching, the shark suddenly darted forward into the feeding melee and snared a rope of intestine. Then another larger shark appeared out of nowhere and gave chase.

Trembling uncontrollably, Marissa rounded the edge of the mouth of the channel, scanning the distance for sight of Wendy and Wynn. More sharks appeared, progressively larger than the first two, including one Marissa recognized as a hammerhead. The big fish looked prehistoric, like a monster left over from the dinosaur age.

Up ahead Marissa finally saw Wynn. Wendy was directly below him, exploring a crevice; only her legs and flippers could be seen. Marissa swam toward them, but even before she got there, Wynn turned and looked her way.

Frantically, Marissa pointed over her shoulder

at the feeding frenzy that had developed. Wynn responded by ducking down and giving Wendy a tug. Then he swiftly swam toward Marissa with strong strokes.

Marissa began to head back to the boat. To her left she saw one shark ram another shark. A huge gash was left along the side of the one that was hit. The next thing she knew, the wounded shark was rapidly eaten alive by several others.

Wynn passed Marissa and turned into the channel. Marissa glanced back, expecting Wendy to be right behind him. Instead, all she could see were Wendy's flippers. She was still head-down in the same crevice. For a second, Marissa debated what to do. Then Wendy's head popped up, looking for Wynn. She immediately spotted the school of sharks, whose numbers seemed to be increasing by the second.

Wendy started for Marissa in a panic. As abruptly, she was forced to stop when several sharks came between them. Marissa started to swim a sort of backstroke toward the opening of the channel, keeping Wendy in sight at all times. Her terror had increased to the point that she felt she was running out of air.

All at once the sharks scattered with powerful sweeps of their tails. Marissa felt it was an answer to a prayer until she saw what had made them flee. Out of the gloomy blue depths loomed a great white shark. It was at least four times the size of the sharks Marissa had previously seen.

When Wendy spotted the leviathan, she panicked. With arms flailing and legs wildly kicking, she started forward. Marissa did the same. At the lip of the channel Marissa hazarded a look back. Wendy was still following at the same frantic pace, but Marissa could also see the colossal shark cruising behind her. The beast seemed to be taking a keen interest in Wendy.

The shark momentarily paused. Then, with a single sweep, it streaked directly at Wendy. Tilting its head to the side, the huge fish caught Wendy around her chest and gave her a horrendous shake. Wendy's mouthpiece came out of her mouth and bubbles fluttered to the surface. Then a cloud of blood billowed into the water and obscured the scene.

In total panic, Marissa turned and swam into the channel. She could hardly think, she was so utterly afraid. She caught sight of the bottom of the boat and the shark cage. Wynn was already inside; Marissa headed straight for him.

As soon as she reached the cage, Marissa grabbed the door and tried to push, but the door didn't open. Wynn was holding the door on the inside, pushing against it. Marissa couldn't imagine what he was trying to do. She tried to look into his eyes but his mask only reflected glare.

Turning, Marissa saw the monstrous shark come around the lip of the channel with blood streaking out of its mouth.

With only seconds to spare, Marissa ducked around to the other side of the cage. She pulled herself into a tight ball, desperately clutching the steel bars.

With a sudden, powerful jolt the great white rammed the cage, grabbing it with its prodigious jaws.

Marissa managed to hold on while the shark tried to bite through the steel bars. Over Wynn's shoulder Marissa could see right into its mouth, studded with rows of six-inch teeth. The titan's eye was a huge oval of impenetrable blackness.

Several of the cage's bars bent under the force of the shark's jaws. The fish shook the cage with such force that Marissa lost both her mask and her mouthpiece. Yet still she held on.

The shark then disengaged itself, leaving behind some of its teeth. Marissa grabbed for her mouthpiece with one hand, still clinging to the cage with the other. With her mask gone, her vision was blurred. But she could make out Wynn as he put in his own mouthpiece and began frantically pulling on a rope that led to the surface. She noticed a large laceration across his arm that was bleeding profusely.

Apparently giving up on biting through the cage's strong bars, the shark began circling it. Moving in the same direction, Marissa struggled to keep the cage between herself and the great white. Suddenly, the cage started to rise. Knowing she'd be doomed without its protection, she kicked furiously in an effort to stay with it, clambering up with her hands on the steel bars. Just as the cage broke the water's surface, she was able to roll onto its top.

Scrambling forward, Marissa reached for the hoisting cable. Just as she made contact, the shark hit the cage and rocked it once more. In the process, Marissa rolled partway off, her legs dangling in the water. In a panic, she lifted them and curled herself around the cable, holding on for dear life.

11

APRIL 8, 1990
11:47 A.M.

MARISSA REMAINED in a tight ball around the hoisting cable until she felt the cage settle on the deck of the boat. Only then did she open her eyes.

Rafe was already opening the cage door, swinging it out and away. Wynn struggled through the small door. He had a hand over the gash on his arm. Despite the pressure, it was bleeding profusely.

Marissa let go of the cable and, with her flippers still on, managed to climb down from the top of the cage. It took a few moments for the awful truth to sink in: Wendy wasn't on the boat with them. In her mind's eye, she saw Wendy in the shark's jaws.

"Wendy's still in the water!" she screamed. But Rafe was busy attending to Wynn's wound. The

282

two men had rushed to the spot where they kept an emergency first-aid kit.

Tripping over her flippers, Marissa tried to run after them. She struggled out of her scuba tank, letting it drop on the deck. Then she bent down and pulled off her flippers.

When she reached the men, Rafe was trying to stem the arterial blood flow with a pressure bandage.

"What about Wendy?" Marissa screamed.

Rafe didn't even look up from his dressing attempts. "Wynn says there was a hungry great white down there."

"We have to find her!" Marissa screamed. "We can't leave her there. Please!"

"That's the best I can do for now, mate," Rafe said to Wynn, who nodded. Wynn clamped his hand over the bandage.

Unable to control herself, Marissa broke into tears. "Please!" she screamed.

Rafe ignored her and went to his radio to request assistance from the shore patrol.

Marissa was beside herself. After the captain got off the radio, she pleaded with him between sobs to go into the water to find Wendy.

"What do you think I am?" Rafe shouted. "Bloody crazy? You don't go into the water when there's a great white in the neighborhood. I'm sorry about your friend, but there's nothing I can do but wait and see if she surfaces. She could have fled into the coral heads."

"I saw the shark grab her," Marissa moaned. "You have to do something," Marissa pleaded.

"If you can think of anything besides going in the water, let me know," Rafe said, going back to attend to Wynn.

Not knowing what else to do, Marissa sank to her knees, covered her face with her hands and wept.

Soon she became aware of an increasingly loud whirring noise. Sitting up against the gunwhale, she spotted a helicopter bearing down on them. When it was directly above the *Oz*, it began to hover. Marissa could see a man at an open door, clutching a hoist secured to the side of the craft.

Rafe went back to the radio and had another conversation with the shore patrol, then he contacted the helicopter pilot overhead. Rafe told him that they had been able to stop the bleeding. Between the two of them, they decided that it wasn't worth the danger of trying to get Wynn up to the helicopter now that the bleeding was under control.

"I'm still missing one diver," Rafe said into the radio.

"We'll send out a patrol boat," the chopper pilot said. After signing off, the helicopter dipped forward, then sped back toward the mainland.

Rafe hung up the radio receiver. "Guess we'd better wait for the patrol boat to get here," he said.

"I can't believe you people!" Marissa yelled.

"You really aren't going to do anything about Wendy, are you?"

Rafe ignored her while he checked Wynn's dressing. It was staying dry.

"And you," Marissa said with venom, pointing at Wynn. "You wouldn't let me in that damn cage."

"I was trying to help you," Wynn said. "The door opens out, not in. I was trying to show you, but you wouldn't let me."

Marissa's eyes went to the cage. The door was ajar; she could see that it did indeed open out.

Marissa turned to Rafe. "Who were those men who threw the chum into the water?" she demanded.

"Two blokes who had wanted to go fishing," Rafe said. "It was the Asian fellow who hired the *Oz*. He'd stayed in his cabin until the powerboat arrived. I don't know why they had it. Guess they decided against fishing after all and just dumped their bait. I wouldn't have let them do that if I'd known."

"It was the bait that brought the sharks," Marissa said.

"Undoubtedly," Rafe said.

Marissa didn't know what to think. She was still trembling. An hour passed. Still the patrol boat was nowhere to be seen. The water around the boat cleared. Even the waves calmed. Looking off the stern, Marissa could no longer see any fish.

"My arm is starting to bleed again," Wynn announced anxiously.

Rafe examined the bandage. "A little," he agreed. "It's not bad. But let's head in. To hell with that patrol boat."

"We're not going until we look for Wendy," Marissa said.

"It's no use," Rafe said. "She would have appeared by now if there was any chance."

"If you refuse to look," Marissa said, "then I'll go myself." She walked over to the bank of scuba tanks and pulled one free. Then she picked up her flippers, which were still on the bow deck.

When Marissa returned, Rafe grabbed her arm. "You're crazy if you go in that water."

Marissa indignantly pulled her arm from his grasp. "At least I'm not a coward."

"I'll go," Wynn said, standing up unsteadily.

"You're not going anywhere!" Rafe yelled. "All right! I'll go have a look."

Clearly fuming, Rafe went below, then came back wearing his swimming togs. He suited up in a buoyancy vest and tank, then grabbed a pair of flippers, a mask, and a three-foot steel rod. "I want you to lower me in the cage," he told Wynn.

All three went forward. For a moment they eyed the bent bars on the front of the cage. "I can't believe a living thing could do that," Rafe said. Then he climbed inside and put on his flippers and mask.

"Lower away," Rafe called.

Wynn went to the winch and lifted Rafe and the cage about a foot off the deck. Using only his good arm, he maneuvered the cage out over the water.

Marissa helped steady it. Then he lowered the cage until he felt a tug on a rope he had in his hand.

Peering over the side, Marissa and Wynn watched Rafe as he eventually swam out of the cage. He disappeared under the boat. In another minute or two he popped up on the dive platform.

"All's quiet down here," he said. "Now, where was Wendy when you last saw her?"

"I'll come with you," Marissa said. Despite her fears, Marissa felt she owed that much to Wendy. She swiftly suited up. Wynn helped her with her tank. In another minute she was on the platform next to Rafe.

"I'm impressed," Rafe said. "I really am. Aren't you scared to go back into the water after what happened?"

"I'm terrified," Marissa said. "Let's go before I change my mind."

Instead of jumping far from the boat, Marissa eased herself into the water, scanning in all directions. But Rafe was right: the water was as peaceful and serene as when she'd first entered it that morning. A few butterfly and angel fish swam by. She glanced back at the shark cage, determined to be ready to make a swim for it should the need arise.

Turning to Rafe, Marissa motioned toward the mouth of the channel. There was less of a current than there had been earlier. Where the channel opened into the ocean, they hesitated. Even in the distance they couldn't see anything larger than a few parrot fish nestled along the wall of the reef. The monster that had terrorized her not an hour before was nowhere to be seen.

Marissa's heart skipped a beat when she felt something touch her arm. Turning, she saw it was only Rafe. He signaled to her, asking which way they should go. Marissa pointed. Together, they headed in that direction.

After they'd gone about thirty feet, Marissa stopped Rafe with her hand. She signaled that they were now where she last saw Wendy. They began to scour the sandy floor, but they discovered nothing, not even a piece of diving gear.

Finally, Rafe motioned for them to return to the boat.

Climbing onto the dive platform, Marissa felt crushed. Wendy was truly gone. Not a trace was left of her. It seemed too incredible to be true. For the moment Marissa couldn't even cry anymore.

"Really sorry, luv," Rafe said. He slipped out of his gear. "Wynn and I feel terribly about all this, we do. Never happened on the *Oz* before, I can assure you of that. Terrible accident, it was." Then he went forward and had Wynn pull up the shark cage while he used the radio.

Rafe told the shore patrol that the patrol boat had yet to appear. He gave them their position again and told them that although a diver was still missing, they were coming in to get medical attention for the injured first mate.

Once the diesels were started, Rafe had Wynn

hoist up the anchor. Then they started back for Hamilton Island.

"You say you actually saw the shark seize the poor woman around the chest?" Mr Griffiths, the Royal Australian police inspector, asked.

Marissa and Rafe were standing in front of the chest-high desk at the police station on Hamilton Island. They had gone there directly after dropping Wynn off at the medical facility.

"Yes," Marissa answered. She could still see the gruesome tragedy, making her feel weak.

"And you saw blood?" the inspector asked.

"Yes, yes!" Marissa cried. Tears began to run down her cheeks. She felt Rafe's arm on her shoulder.

"And you went back into the water and searched the area?" Mr. Griffiths asked.

"We did, indeed," Rafe answered. "Mind you, it was over an hour later. Both myself and Miss Blumenthal here went back and searched. We found nothing. Not a trace. But my first mate tells me it was the largest shark he's ever seen, probably twenty-five, thirty feet."

"And this is the woman's passport?" Mr. Griffiths asked.

Marissa nodded. She had gotten the passport from Wendy's bag.

"Nasty buisness," Mr. Griffiths said. Then, looking at Marissa over the top of his reading glasses, he added: "Would you be willing to notify

289

the next of kin? It might be best coming from a friend."

Marissa nodded, wiping away the tears.

"We'll schedule a coroner's inquest," Mr. Griffiths said. "Anything either one of you would like to add?"

"Yes," Marissa said. She took a deep breath. "The sharks were attracted by chum that was thrown into the water deliberately."

Mr. Griffiths removed his glasses. "What are you implying, young lady?"

"I'm not sure Wendy's death was an accident," Marissa said.

"That is a serious allegation," Mr. Griffiths said.

"There was an Asian man on the boat," Marissa said. "He didn't appear until we were out at the reef and already in the water. I happened to come back to the boat by myself while we were diving. I saw him and another man throwing chum into the water."

Mr. Griffiths looked at Rafe. Rafe raised his eyebrows. "We did have a Chinese customer on board," he admitted. "Said his name was Harry Wong. He'd chartered to fish on the outer reef. He was met by a friend in a big powerboat. They had a lot of bait. The last I talked with them they were going out in the powerboat after marlin. Apparently they changed their minds about fishing, and being uninformed, they just dumped their bait."

"I see," Mr. Griffiths said.

"I'm not convinced they were uninformed," Marissa said.

"Well, that's why we have coroner's inquests," Mr. Griffiths said. "It's a chance to question all the details."

Feeling her cheeks flush, Marissa tried to control her self long enough to express her suspicions. She told Mr. Griffiths that she thought the Asian man might have been the same one who had been staring at her and Wendy the night before in the dining room of the Hamilton Island Resort.

"I see," Mr. Griffiths said. He toyed with his pen. "Well then, I can understand how upset you must be. If it is any solace, I can personally assure you that we will be making extensive inquiries into this tragedy."

Marissa was about to continue when she thought better of it. She wasn't sure about what she was saying herself. Until the moment she'd voiced the opinion about the Asian being the same one in the hotel dining room, she hadn't thought of it. Besides, it was clear to her that the police inspector was being patronizing. She had the distinct impression she was being humored.

"If there is nothing more for the moment," Mr. Griffiths said, "you two may go. But we would like to request that you remain on the island. We'll be contacting you tomorrow. I can also assure you that there will be an extensive search of the area for Mrs. Wilson-Anderson's remains."

Marissa and Rafe left the police station together. Rafe walked her back to her hotel. In the lobby, he paused before leaving her and said: "I'm really sorry for what happened. If I can help while you are here, please come down to the *Oz*."

Marissa thanked him, then went up to her room. After closing the door and seeing Wendy's belongings, she burst into fresh tears.

"I can't believe this has happened," Marissa said with a choking voice a half hour later once her sobs had tapered off. Getting up from the bed, she got Wendy's suitcase and packed away all her things. While she worked, she thought about everything that had been happening in the past few months. It seemed to her that the consequences of her infertility were beginning to spiral into horrendously tragic proportions.

After putting Wendy's packed suitcase into the corner of the closet, Marissa walked over and sat on the edge of the bed. For several minutes she eyed the phone, trying to muster her courage.

Finally, she picked up the receiver and dialed her home in Weston. The phone rang only twice before Robert's groggy voice said, "Hello?" Marissa realized that it was after two A.M. in Boston.

"Robert!" Marissa blurted out. "Something terrible has happened." Then, before she could tell him anything, she burst into hysterical tears again. It took five minutes before she could tell him about Wendy.

"My God!" Robert said.

Marissa described her suspicions; that Wendy's death might have been deliberate, not accidental.

Robert didn't reply at first. Then, like the police

292

inspector, he reminded her that she'd had a terrible shock. "After such an experience your imagination can do strange things," he told her. "You might be trying to ascribe blame where there is none. Anyway, try to relax. Try not to think too much."

"Could you come?" Marissa suddenly asked.

"To Australia?" Robert said. "I think you should come home instead."

"But the police told me to stay on the island," Marissa said.

"The formalities can't take more than a day or so," Robert said. "It would take me almost two days to get there. Besides, it would be hard for me to leave now. It's only a week before April fifteenth, and you know what that means: taxes. It's better for you to come home as soon as you can."

"Sure," Marissa said, her tone suddenly flat. "I understand."

"Should I call Gustave?" Robert asked.

"If you would," Marissa said. But then she changed her mind. "On second thought," she added, "maybe I should do it. Gustave may want to talk to me."

"All right," Robert said. "Then call me back as soon as you know when you're arriving."

Marissa put the receiver down. Calling Gustave was going to be the hardest phone call she'd ever made. She tried to think of what to say, but there was no way she could soften the news. Finally, she picked up the phone and dialed.

Gustave answered on the first ring. As a surgeon, he was no doubt accustomed to being awakened in the night. He didn't even sound as if he'd been asleep, though Marissa was sure he had been.

She got to the point quickly, telling Gustave exactly what had happened. She was even able to hold back her tears until she had finished relating the day's events.

On the other end, over the thousands of miles, there was only a heavy silence.

"Gustave—are you all right?" Marissa asked, her voice breaking.

After a pause, Gustave said, "I . . . I suppose I will be. It's . . . just so hard to believe. But Wendy always was a bit foolhardy when diving. Where are her belongings?"

"I've packed them," Marissa said, surprised and relieved that Gustave was taking the horrid news so well. She guessed he was relying on his practiced surgeon's objectivity and that the reality would hit later when he was alone.

"It must have been a terrible shock for you," Gustave said. "Are you all right?"

"I'm managing," Marissa said.

"Marissa, I appreciate your calling. If you could just ship her belongings to me I would be most grateful. I'll contact the Australian authorities. I'd better go. Goodbye."

The line clicked dead and Marissa slowly replaced the receiver in its cradle. Her heart ached with the same pain she knew Gustave was feeling.

Flopping back on the bed, Marissa covered her

face with her hands and sobbed until she could no longer cry. Then, with her hands still covering her face, her sadness began to transform to irritation, then even to anger.

Instead of being pleased with how much in control Gustave had been, it began to bother her. When she replayed the conversation in her mind, she hated that Gustave had sounded so cold and detached, as if she had been giving him a report on one of his patients and not on his wife. It made her suddenly wonder if the problems spawned by the infertility treatments were such that Gustave was relieved to some extent by Wendy's untimely death.

Rethinking Gustave's conversation made Marissa do the same with Robert's and with a similar result. The idea that Robert wouldn't volunteer to come instantly to Australia, knowing what kind of trauma she'd experienced, was unforgivable. Taxes! What an absurd excuse. After all that had happened, she would have hoped that he would make their marriage a priority.

Marissa got up from the bed and walked to the window. The ocean glistened in the late afternoon sunlight. It was hard to believe that Wendy had met such a brutal fate in so serene a milieu. She wondered what her own fate would have been had nausea and fatigue not forced her back to the boat. Maybe she'd be dead as well. Maybe that had been the idea: to get rid of them both.

Marissa's throat went dry. She swallowed hard. She was thinking dangerous thoughts, maybe even crazy ones. Her mind went back to the vicious Chinese security guards at the Women's Clinic. Could they possibly be related to the sinister Chinese aboard the *Oz?* Marissa wondered if there was any connection between the Women's Clinic in the States and the FCA in Australia.

Marissa went out onto her balcony. She sank into the chaise lounge. That Wendy died for nothing hit her hard. How could she just let it go and return to Boston? Her thoughts drifted to the elusive Tristan Williams. Why would a trained pathologist make up the ridiculous data that could easily be proven false, all for the questionable benefit of publishing an article? It just didn't fit.

Marissa tapped her fingers nervously against the arm of her chair. She thought again of those men tossing chum over the side. If they were so innocent, why did they flee the instant she called out to them? She could assume Tristan Williams had committed professional hara-kiri on a whim. She could talk herself into believing that those two on the *Oz* had not realized what they were doing. But the whole weird thing was beginning to remind her of the way she felt in the early days of the Ebola outbreaks when she'd been with the CDC. Back then, Marissa had begun to suspect a sinister force at work long before her colleagues did. Despite setbacks, she clung to her beliefs, ultimately proving the existence of a cabal even more diabolic than she had ever imagined. Now, as then, she was beginning to think it was time to go with her instincts.

Even if she didn't have much more than a hunch that there was more to these events than met the eye, she had to dig deeper. Impulsively she went back inside and called Robert back. She woke him a second time.

"I need you here, Robert," Marissa said. "The more I think about Wendy's death, the more I think it was caused deliberately."

"Please, Marissa. You're overreacting. You've had a tremendous shock. Shouldn't you just get on a plane and come home?"

"But I think I should stay."

"I cannot come to Australia," Robert said. "I told you business is—"

Even though she realized she was being unreasonable, Marissa hung up on him before he could finish his sentence. Then she realized there was something he could do. Snatching up the phone, she dialed Robert yet again.

"I'm glad you called back," Robert said. "I was hoping you'd come to your senses."

"I want you to find out something for me," Marissa said, ignoring Robert's comments. "I want to know if there is any business connection between the Women's Clinic in the States and Female Care Australia."

"I can check in the morning," Robert said.

"I want you to do it now," Marissa said. She knew Robert's computer was hooked up to several business data banks.

"If I do this," Robert said, "will you come home and stop asking me to come to Australia?"

"I'll stop asking you to come to Australia," Marissa said.

"Give me your number and I'll call you back."

Five minutes later Marissa's phone rang. Robert had been faster than she'd expected.

"You were right if you guessed they were associated," Robert said. "Both the Women's Clinic, Inc., and Female Care Australia Limited are controlled by an Australian holding company by the name of Fertility, Limited. I found it out by reading the back page on a prospectus on the Women's Clinic."

"What are you doing with a prospectus on the Women's Clinic?" Marissa asked. "I thought it was a private company."

"They floated a big stock offering a few years ago to finance their nationwide expansion," Robert explained. "It's been a good stock. I've been very pleased with it."

"You own stock in Women's Clinic?" Marissa asked.

"Yes," Robert said. "I have a significant position with both the Women's Clinic and FCA."

"You own stock in FCA as well?"

"Sure do," Robert said. "I bought it on the Sydney Exchange."

"Sell it!" Marissa shouted.

Robert laughed. "Now let's not confuse emotions with business," he said. "I see both stocks splitting in the near future."

"I think there is something seriously wrong with these companies," Marissa said with vehemence. "I don't know what it is they're up to, but I think it may be linked to these cases of TB salpingitis."

"Don't tell me you're back on that crusade," Robert whined.

"Just sell the stock," Marissa said.

"I'll take your recommendation under advisement," Robert said evasively.

Marissa slammed the phone down, cutting off Robert before he could say more.

Anger had now overcome to a large degree her sadness about Wendy. Although she thought that her hormone-induced hyperemotional state might have had something to do with her change in mood, she didn't care. Instead of giving in to depression, she opted for action. Picking up the phone, she called the Royal Flying Doctor Service in Charleville.

"Yes," the woman at the other end of the line told her, "Dr. Tristan Williams is with us, but he's out at isolated cattle stations at the moment. He won't be back for several days."

"Does he have a specific schedule?" Marissa asked.

"Indeed he does," the woman said. "Unless there is an emergency. Our doctors have a regular route whenever they leave for a loop of the outback."

"Could you tell me where he will be two days from now?" Marissa asked. She thought that should give her enough time to get there no matter how far away it was.

"Hold the line," the woman said. She was gone for several minutes. When she came back on the line she said, "He'll be near a town called Windorah. He's to make a call at the Wilmington Station."

"Does Windorah have a commercial airport?" Marissa asked.

The woman laughed. "No, not quite," she said. "In fact it doesn't even have a bitumen road."

Marissa next called the airport to see about connections to Charleville. With reservations made on an airline called Flight West, she quickly packed her bags and went down to the lobby. After making arrangements for Wendy's bag to be brought to the hotel's storage room, she checked out.

During the short ride to the airport, she began to wonder about defying the police inspector's request to remain on Hamilton Island. She wondered if security people at the airport might try to stop her. But there was no problem and she boarded the plane for Brisbane without any incident.

In Brisbane she had a short wait before she boarded a commuter plane with only twelve seats. At a little after nine in the evening, the plane lifted off the tarmac and headed due west toward Charleville, a town situated on the edge of the broad expanse of the Australian outback.

While Marissa was flying over the Great Dividing Range, a series of mountains separating the narrow, lush coastline from the rest of Australia, Ned Kelly and Willy Tong climbed the stairs in the mostly darkened FCA clinic and headed for the deserted administration area. The door to Charles Lester's office was ajar. The two men walked in unannounced.

Charles looked up from a puddle of light emanating from his brass desk lamp. The shadows made his deep eyesockets appear blank like a man with no eyes. His mouth beneath his heavy mustache was clamped shut with the corners downturned. Charles was not happy.

"Sit down!" he ordered.

Ned flopped casually into one of the chairs facing the desk while Willy leaned up against a bookcase.

"I just heard what happened on the evening news," Lester said. "You've managed to make things worse. First, you only got rid of one of the women. The one you let get away is talking about her friend's death being deliberate because she saw you two blokes. The police, it seems, are investigating."

"How were we to know one of them would come out of the water while we were throwing in the chum?" Ned said. "It was a bit of bad luck. Otherwise it would have worked. We tossed in enough bait to summon every shark from the entire Coral Sea."

"But eliminating one and raising suspicions is not what you were supposed to do," Lester snapped. "Now it is imperative rather than merely advisable that this second woman be eliminated.

301

It said on the news that her name was Dr. Marissa Blumenthal-Buchanan."

"I know which one it is," Ned said. "The sheila with the brown hair."

"You want us to go back to Hamilton Island and hit her?" Willy asked.

"I want you to do whatever it takes," Lester said.

"What if she's already left the island?" Ned asked.

"I doubt she's left with an investigation underway," Lester said. "But let's call the hotel. You said she was staying at the Hamilton Island Resort?"

"That's the one," Ned said.

Lester picked up his phone and, after obtaining the number, called the hotel. To his dismay he learned that Mrs. Buchanan had already checked out.

Lester stood up and leaned over his desk. "I want you mates to clean this affair up. Ned, you start looking for this woman in the usual hotels, here and in Sydney. Use our government connections to find out if she's left the country. Willy, I want you to visit Tristan Williams and hang around. This Mrs. Buchanan had originally talked about finding the man. If she were to have a conversation with him, a bad situation could conceivably get far worse."

"What if she's already left the country?" Ned asked.

"I want her disposed of," Lester said. "I don't

care where she goes, the States or even Europe. Is that clear?"

Ned stood up. "Perfectly clear," he said. "It'll be a challenge. But then, I like challenges."

12

APRIL 9, 1990
7:11 A.M.

MARISSA WOKE up feeling exhausted. She had not had a good night's sleep. She had checked into a tidy motel in Charleville and, though her bed was comfortable, she'd hardly done more than doze. Every time she closed her eyes, she'd see that great white shark. The few times she managed to fall asleep, she'd be shocked awake by a nightmare vision of Wendy in the shark's jaws. Finally, in the wee hours of the morning, she did sleep fitfully for almost three hours.

Although she wasn't hungry, Marissa forced herself to eat some breakfast before setting out for the car rental office.

As she walked down the street in Charleville, Marissa had the feeling she was in a time warp and was back in a Midwestern town in the United States fifty years previously. The quaint Victorian character that she'd expected to see in Brisbane was evident in some of the homes and office buildings. The air was clear and bright, and the streets were free of litter. And the early-morning sun was hot enough to suggest what its noontime power would be.

At the car rental office in the Shell station, Marissa rented a Ford Falcon. She asked for a map, but the attendant didn't have one to offer.

"Where are you planning to go?" he asked in a slow Queenslander drawl.

"Windorah," Marissa said.

The man looked at her as if she were crazy. "What on earth for?" he asked. "Do you know how far it is to Windorah?"

"Not exactly," Marissa admitted.

"It's over two hundred miles," the agent said. "Two hundred miles of nothing but wallabies, koos, and lizards. Probably take you eight to ten hours. Better fill up that reserve tank in the trunk. There's also one for water. Fill that up just to be sure."

"What's the road like?" Marissa asked.

"Calling it a road is being generous," the agent said. "There's a sealed strip, but there'll be a lot of bulldust. Not much rain this season. Why don't you give me a ring tomorrow from Windorah? If I don't hear from you I'll let the police know. There's not much traffic out there."

"Thank you," Marissa said. "I'll do that."

Marissa drove the car back to her room. She found it awkward driving on the left. Once she was there she had the proprietor ring up the Royal Flying Doctor Service for her. She made sure there hadn't been any emergencies to interrupt Tristan Williams' schedule.

After filling her reserve gas and water tanks, Marissa drove straight through Charleville and picked up the road to Windorah. As the agent had said, near the outskirts of town the paved road suddenly narrowed to a single lane.

At first Marissa somewhat enjoyed herself. The sun was behind her and not in her eyes, although she knew that would change as the day wore on. The solitude of the land was a good balm for her raw emotions.

The road was a sandy orange color and it sliced across the channel country, an arid, desertlike expanse of space cut by curious, narrow-ribbed valleys or arroyos that carried away the meager rainwater in the rainy season. Birds were everywhere, taking flight as she bore down on them. She even began to see the fauna that the agent had mentioned. Occasionally she passed a water hole ablaze with the color of hibiscus.

Despite the dramatic scenery, monotony soon set in. As the miles passed, Marissa began to be relieved that the car rental agent had agreed she would call when she got to Windorah. Marissa had never traveled through a more desolate area in her life; the idea of the car breaking down was truly frightening.

The driving wasn't easy, either. The rough road meant she had to struggle with the steering wheel. The dust billowing in her wake eventually started to work its way into the car, covering everything with a fine layer.

By noon she was sure the temperature had climbed well over a hundred degrees. The heat created the illusion of rolling undulations. There were other natural distractions as well; later in the afternoon she had to slam on the brakes, coming to a sliding stop to allow a pack of wild boar to continue to cross the road.

At a little past eight in the evening, after eleven hours of driving, Marissa began to see meager signs of civilization. Twenty minutes later she pulled into Windorah. She was glad to be there, although the town was hardly a scenic oasis.

At the center of town stood a one-story green, clapboard pub-cum-hotel with a wooden veranda. A sign proclaimed it as the Western Star Hotel. Across the road from the Western Star was a general store. A little farther down the way was a gas station that looked like it was circa 1930.

Marissa entered the pub and endured the stares of its five male customers. They had paused in their dart game and were looking at her as if she were an apparition. The pub owner came over and asked if he could help her.

"I'd like a room for two nights," Marissa said.

"Do you have a reservation?" the man asked.

Marissa studied the man's broad face. She thought he had to be joking, but he didn't crack a smile. She admitted that she didn't have a reservation.

"There's a boxing troupe in town tonight," the man said. "We're pretty busy, but let me check."

He went over to his cash register and checked a notebook. Marissa glanced around the room. All the men were still staring at her. None of them moved or said a word. They didn't touch their bottles of beer.

The man came back. "I'll give you number four," he said. "It was reserved, but they were supposed to check in by six."

Marissa paid for a night's lodging, took the key, and asked about food.

"We'll fix you up something here in the pub," the man said. "As soon as you freshen up, come on back."

"One other question," Marissa asked. "Is the Wilmington Station close to town?"

" 'Tis," the man said. "Quite close. Less than three hours' drive due west."

Marissa wondered how many hours it would take to get to a distant station if it took three to get to a close one. Before she went to her room, Marissa used a public phone to ring the car rental agent to say that she had made it.

She was pleased to discover that her room was reasonably clean. She was surprised to see mosquito netting draped over the bed. Only later would she learn how important it was.

The rest of the evening passed quickly. She wasn't very hungry and barely touched her food. She did enjoy the ice cold beer. Eventually she found herself in friendly conversation with the men in the bar.

She was even persuaded to join them at the boxing show, which turned out to be an opportunity for the locals to box with professionals. The ranchers would win twenty dollars if they were able to last three one-minute rounds, but none of them ever did. Marissa left before it was over, appalled by the violence the drunken men subjected themselves to.

The night was terrible. Marissa was again bothered by horrid dreams of sharks and Wendy being eaten. On top of that, she was tormented by drunken shouts and fights outside her door. She also had to do battle with all manner of insects that somehow managed to penetrate the netting around her bed.

By morning, Marissa was even more tired than she'd been the day before. But after a shower and some strong coffee, she thought she could face the day. Armed with directions from the hotel owner, she drove out of Windorah and headed to the Wilmington Station on a dusty dirt road.

The cattle ranch looked just as she imagined it would, consisting of a series of low-slung wooden sheds, white clapboard houses with sheet-metal roofs, and lots of fencing. Many dogs, horses, and cowboys were in evidence. Over the scene hung the unpleasant but not unbearable ripe, musty odor of cow dung.

In contrast to the staring disbelief her arrival caused in the pub in Windorah, Marissa was shown every possible hospitality at the cattle station. The cowboys, referred to as stockmen, literally fell over each other trying to help her, getting her a beer and offering to take her to the makeshift airstrip for the doctor's scheduled noon arrival. One of the stockmen explained their behavior by telling her that an attractive unaccompanied female showed up at a cattle station about once every hundred years.

By eleven-thirty Marissa was out at the airstrip, sitting in her Ford Falcon under a lone gum tree. Out in the sunlight closer to the strip was the Wilmington Station Land-Rover. Just before twelve, she got out of the car and left the tree's shade. Shielding her eyes from the sun, she searched the pale blue sky for a plane. The day was just as hot as the previous one and just as cloudless. Nowhere could she see a plane. She listened hard but the only thing she heard was the breeze throught the acacia.

After ten minutes Marissa was about to get back into the car when she heard the faint drone of an airplane engine. Raising her eyes to the sky again, she searched for the source of the sound. She didn't spot it until it was almost on top of her.

The plane banked around the airstrip. The pilot seemed to be deciding whether or not he wished to land. At last, after a second pass, he brought the plane down.

The Beechcraft KingAir taxied toward the Land-Rover, then pulled around into the wind.

The pilot feathered the engines and prepared to deplane.

Marissa walked briskly toward the plane as the pilot was opening the cabin door. The man who had been sitting in the Land-Rover stepped out into the sunlight, flicking a cigarette butt into the dust.

"Dr. Williams!" Marissa called.

The pilot stopped just beside his plane. He looked in Marissa's direction. He was carrying an old-fashioned doctor's bag with brass trim.

"Dr. Williams!" Marissa repeated.

"Yes?" Tristan said warily. He eyed Marissa from head to toe.

"I'm Dr. Marissa Blumenthal," Marissa said. She stuck her hand out. Tristan shook it hesitantly.

"Glad to know you," he said. He didn't sound as if he was sure.

Marissa was mildly surprised at the man's appearance. He didn't look like a pathologist, at least not like any of the pathologists she knew. His face was heavily tanned and he was sporting about a three-day growth of beard. He was wearing a beat-up, classic, wide-brimmed Australian outback hat tacked up on the side.

Instead of a doctor, Tristan Williams looked more an outdoorsman, a stockman perhaps. He had rugged good looks and sandy-colored hair a shade lighter than Robert's. He had an angular jaw like Robert's, but that's where the similarities ended. Tristan's eyes were deeper set, though Marissa could not tell their color since he was squinting in the glare. And his lips weren't narrow like Robert's. They were full and expressive.

"Would it be possible to talk to you for a moment?" Marissa asked. "I've been waiting for you to come. I've driven all the way from Charleville."

"My word!" Tristan said. "It's not very often I get met out here by a good-looking sheila. I'm sure the folks at Wilmington Station can wait for a few minutes. Let me tell the driver."

Tristan walked over to the Land-Rover, storing the doctor's bag in the back seat of the vehicle. Marissa noticed that he was slightly taller than Robert, well over six feet.

When he returned, Marissa suggested they sit in her car in the shade. Tristan agreed.

"I've come all the way from Boston to talk with you," she said once they were in the car. "You've not been easy to find."

"All of a sudden I'm not sure I'm going to like this," Tristan said, eyeing Marissa. "Being found hasn't been something I've been interested in."

"I want to talk to you about a paper you wrote," Marissa said. "It was about tuberculous salpingitis."

"Now I know I'm not going to like this," Tristan said. "If you'll excuse me, I have patients to see." He put his hand on the door handle.

Marissa reached out and grabbed his arm. "Please," she said. "I have to talk to you."

"I knew you were too good to be true," he said. He pulled away from her grip and got out of the car. Without looking back, he walked over to the Land-Rover, got in, and drove away.

Marissa was stunned. She didn't know whether to be hurt or angry. After all the effort she'd gone through to find him, she couldn't believe he wouldn't give her more time than that. For a moment, Marissa sat in her car watching the dust from the Land-Rover billow in the air. Then, hastily, she started the Ford Falcon, put it in gear, and gave chase.

By the time Marissa arrived at the Wilmington Station, she was covered with dust. The entire drive she'd been enveloped in the wake of the Land-Rover. Even her mouth felt gritty.

Tristan had already gotten out of the Land-Rover. He was heading up the long walkway toward a small house, medical bag in hand. Marissa ran to catch up to him. Falling in step alongside him, she tried to catch his eye. She had to take five steps to keep up with his every three.

"You have to talk with me," she said when it became clear he intended to ignore her. "It's very important."

Tristan stopped short. "I'm not interested in talking with you," he said. "Besides, I'm busy. I've got patients to see, including a very sick little girl, and I hate pediatrics."

Marissa brushed her dusty hair from her forehead and squinted up at Tristan. Even though his eyes were deeply set, she could now see they were blue. "I'm a pediatrician," she said. "Maybe I could help."

Tristan studied her face as he chewed on the inside of his cheek. "A pediatrician, eh?" he said. "That's mighty convenient." His eyes strayed to the front door of the house. When he looked back at Marissa, he said: "I can't turn that down, not with what I know about pediatrics."

The patient turned out to be an eight-month-old baby girl who was acutely ill. She had a high fever, a cough, and a runny nose. The child was crying when Marissa and Tristan entered her room.

Marissa examined the infant while Tristan and the anxious mother watched. After a few minutes, Marissa straightened up and said: "It's measles, without doubt."

"How can you tell?" Tristan asked.

Marissa showed him the small white spots inside the infant's mouth, the reddened eyes, and the faint rash just beginning to appear on the forehead.

"What should we do?" he asked.

"Just get the fever down," Marissa said. "But if complications occur, the child should be hospitalized. Is that possible?"

"Certainly," Tristan said. "We can airlift her to Charleville, or even Brisbane if necessary."

For the next few minutes Marissa discussed the situation with the mother, describing the telltale signs of trouble. Then they discussed where the child could have picked up the virus. It turned out that two weeks previously, the family had visited relatives in Longreach, where there had been a sick child.

After discussing prophylaxis for the other children at the station, Marissa and Tristan left the mother and walked toward the next house on Tristan's list.

"Thank you for helping," Tristan said as they mounted the stairs to the second porch.

"I think you could have handled it without me," Marissa said. She was tempted to say more, but her intuition told her to wait.

Marissa stayed with Tristan and helped see the rest of the patients at the station. All were routine except for an old woman of ninety-three who was dying of cancer but refused to be taken to a hospital. Tristan respected her wishes and simply provided for her pain.

Walking out of the last house, it was Tristan who brought up the paper. "I guess my curiosity has gotten the best of me," he said. "What possibly could have motivated you to come all the way out here to ask me about a journal article that was discredited?"

"Because I'm suffering from the syndrome you described," Marissa said, keeping pace with him. They were heading toward the communal food-service area. "And because the syndrome has been appearing around the United States and even in Europe." She wanted to ask straight off why he'd made up cases, but she was afraid such a question would end the conversation.

314

Tristan stopped and studied Marissa. "You had tuberculous salpingitis yourself?" he asked.

"Confirmed by biopsy," Marissa said. "I never knew I'd had it. If I hadn't tried to get pregnant, I probably never would have known."

Tristan seemed deep in thought.

"I've been trying to learn something about it," Marissa continued, "but it's been difficult. In fact, it's been a disaster. I've just lost a friend. I'm even wondering if she was killed."

Tristan stared at her. "What are you talking about?"

"I came to Australia with a friend," Marissa explained. "A woman suffering from the TB salpingitis just like me. We came because of your article, and inquired about you at FCA in Brisbane. They were less than helpful there."

Marissa went on to describe what had happened out on the reef, saying that she felt that Wendy's death might not have been accidental. "And I'm beginning to think that my own life may be in jeopardy," she added. "But I really can't say I have any evidence of that."

Tristan sighed. "This all brings back bad memories," he said with a shake of his head. He tilted his hat back and scratched his forehead. "But maybe I'd better tell you my story so that you have some idea what you are up against. Maybe then you'll go home and live your life. But the telling will take a while. And it's for your ears only. Agreed?"

"Agreed," Marissa said.

315

"All right," Tristan said. "Let's go inside and get a couple of stubbies."

Tristan went into the canteen and walked directly into the kitchen. The crew were busy cleaning up from the noonday meal. From the fridge he got two ice cold beers and carried them into the empty dining room. Motioning toward one of the picniclike tables, he popped the tops of the beers and handed one to Marissa. She sat down facing him.

"I was employed by FCA directly from my specialty training in pathology," he said after a long pull on his beer. "I was impressed by the organization. It was expanding. Right after I was hired, the chief of the department, that's what he called himself, came down with hepatitis and had to take an extended leave. Since there were only two of us in the department back then, I found myself the chief." Tristan chuckled.

"Almost immediately," he continued, "I started seeing these cases of granulomatous salpingitis, one after another. I knew it was unique, and having just come from training, the possibility of making some kind of academic discovery held great appeal. I have to admit I also liked the idea of getting a paper in one of the journals. So entirely on my own, I decided to write the cases up.

"My first suspicion was tuberculosis, despite TB being rare here in Australia. But since we'd been having a recent increase in immigration from Southeast Asia, where TB is still endemic, I thought it was possible.

316

"But I had to be sure it was TB. I ruled out fungi through elaborate stains. It definitely wasn't fungi. I looked exhaustively for organisms, but could never find any. But still I was sure it was TB."

"What about sarcoid?" Marissa questioned.

Tristan shook his head. "It wasn't sarcoid," he said. "The chest X-rays were all normal and none of the patients had swollen glands or eye problems.

"So I was confident that it was TB although I had no idea how it was spread. But then I made an association with something else that was going on at the clinic. About a year before I began seeing these cases, the clinic had started having Chinese technicians and security people rotate through some sort of fellowship program. I thought that the clinic was training the technicians in in-vitro fertilization to go back to Hong Kong where they'd come from. But I wasn't sure. They always came in pairs and didn't stay long. Only for a few months. Many didn't even speak English. But the fact that they were coming from Hong Kong, where there had been a significant influx of Southeast Asian boat people, made me think they might have had something to do with the rash of TB salpingitis."

"Where did they go after their fellowships?" Marissa asked, recalling the pair of Chinese at the Women's Clinic.

"I had no idea," Tristan admitted. "I assumed back to Hong Kong. I had never been interested, at least not until I started looking into the TB cases. Then I became curious. So I scheduled a meeting with Charles Lester, the director of the clinic, and I asked him about the Chinese. But he told me it was classified information. All he would say was that it had something to do with the government!"

Tristan shrugged. "What could I do? I asked a few other people, but no one seemed to want to talk about it. But then a pair of Chinese got in a bad car accident. Bad enough to kill one and hospitalize the other. They hospitalized him in the FCA facility. He was the only male patient they'd ever had.

"I made it a point to visit the bloke, just about every day. He was tight-lipped but could speak English. Not a lot, but enough. His name was Chan Ho. I tested him for TB without anyone else knowing, but was disappointed when he tested negative because it blew holes in my theory. Still in the process of stopping by every day I got to know the fellow a bit. I learned he was some kind of Buddhist monk. He'd learned Chinese martial arts as part of his studies. Now, that caught my attention; martial arts have been my sport since I've been knee-high to a wallaby. When the bloke got out of the hospital, I invited him to come to my gym. He turned out to be unbelievable at kung fu."

Marissa remembered how the Chinese man in the gray suit had disarmed Paul Abrums with a deft kick.

"Then I learned something else: Chan loved

beer. He'd never had any until he'd come to Australia, or so he said. I discovered that after a few good Australian beers he loosened up. That's when he really surprised me. I found out he wasn't from Hong Kong at all, he came from a town near Guangzhou in the People's Republic of China."

"He was from Communist China?" Marissa asked.

"That's what he told me," Tristan said. "I was surprised too. Apparently he'd just passed through Hong Kong—illegally, I might add. One night I managed to get him really pissed—"

"You got him angry?" Marissa was confused.

"No! Drunk," Tristan said. "Then he really opened up. He told me that in the PRC he'd been a member of a secret society, a martial arts organization called the White Lotus. He said that it was because of his martial arts ability that he'd been brought out of China by one of the Hong Kong triads called the Wing Sin. Apparently the FCA footed the bill. He led me to believe that they paid big bucks for him and his companion to be smuggled here to Australia."

"But why?" Marissa asked. Tristan's story was going in directions she'd never anticipated. They seemed far afield from the issue of TB.

"I had no idea," Tristan admitted. "But it all intrigued me. Seemed like a weird kind of program, especially since it was supposed to involve the government. I started thinking all sorts of things, like maybe it had something to do with

319

Hong Kong being turned over to the PRC in 1997."

"The last thing Communist China needs is in-vitro fertilization," Marissa said.

"Don't I know it," Tristan said. "Nothing made sense to me. So I tried quietly asking around the clinic again, but still I couldn't find anyone who would say anything about these visitors, especially anyone in administration. I talked to the director again, but he warned me to leave it alone. I should have taken his advice."

Tristan tipped his head back and finished his beer. Standing, he asked Marissa if she was ready for another. She shook her head. She hadn't finished the one she had. While Tristan went back into the kitchen, she reviewed in her mind what he'd told her. It was certainly curious, but hardly what she'd come thousands of miles to hear.

Tristan came back with a new beer and reclaimed his seat. "I know this all sounds weird," he admitted. "But I was convinced that if I could figure out why the Chinese were there, then I'd be able to explain the salpingitis cases. That might sound strange, but they were happening at the same time, and I was convinced it couldn't have been by chance. And whether the PRC needed it or not, I thought that these Chinese technicians were being trained in in-vitro techniques. When they were at the clinic, they were always in the in-vitro lab."

"Do you think it could have been the other way around?" Marissa asked. "Maybe the Chinese were providing information rather than getting it."

"I doubt that," Tristan said. "Modern technical medicine is not one of China's strong suits."

"Yet around the time you're talking about," Marissa said, "the FCA did start to show a rather sudden increase in overall efficiency with their in-vitro. I read about it in the medical school library."

"From having talked with Chan Ho for many hours, there's no way he'd be able to add to our technical knowledge."

"What about his companion?" Marissa asked. "The one who died."

"Chan refused to talk about him," Tristan said. "I asked him on many occasions. All I learned was that he was not a martial arts expert like Chan."

"Maybe he was an acupuncturist," Marissa suggested. "Or an herbalist."

"Possibly," Tristan said. "But I can assure you that FCA did not start doing acupuncture as part of the in-vitro protocol. But Chan did lead me to believe that he had felt responsible for his companion since he was afraid he would be sent back to the PRC after the bloke died."

"Sounds like the companion was the more important of the two," Marissa said. "Maybe he did provide some knowledge or skill."

"It would be tough to get me to believe that," Tristan said. "They were all quite primitive fellows. What I started to think about was drugs."

"How so?" Marissa asked.

"Heroin smuggling," Tristan said. "I know that Hong Kong has become the heroin capital for moving heroin from the Golden Triangle to the rest of the world. I came to think that the explanation for all this weird activity was the movement of heroin, especially since TB is endemic in the Golden Triangle."

"So these Chinese duos were couriers?" Marissa asked.

"That's what I was thinking," Tristan said. "Maybe the one who didn't know martial arts. But I wasn't sure. Yet it was the only thing that seemed to justify the money that had to be involved."

"That means the FCA has to be in the drug business," Marissa said. In her mind's eye she remembered the surprising opulence of the clinic. That lent a certain credence to what Tristan was saying. But if that were the case, how did TB salpingitis fit in?

"I was planning on investigating it," Tristan said. "I intended to use my next vacation to go to Hong Kong and trace the trail back to Guangzhou if necessary."

"What made you change your mind?" Marissa asked.

"Two things happened," Tristan said. "First, the chief of pathology came back, and second, my paper came out in the *Australian Journal of Infectious Diseases*. I thought I was about to become professionally famous for describing a new clinical syndrome. Instead it turned out to be a king hit on me. As I said, I'd never cleared the paper with the administration. Well, they went crazy. They wanted me to recant the paper, but I wouldn't. I got on my academic high horse and bucked the system."

"The cases in your paper were real patients?" Marissa finally asked. "You didn't make them up?"

"Of course I didn't make them up," Tristan said indignantly. "I'm not a complete alf. That's the story they put out. But it wasn't true."

"Charles Lester told us you'd made them up."

"That lying bastard!" Tristan hissed. "All twenty-three cases in that paper were real patients. I guarantee it. But I'm not surprised he told you differently. They tried to force me to say the same. But I refused. There were even threats. Unfortunately, I ignored the threats, even when they were extended to my wife and my two-year-old son.

"Then Chan Ho disappeared and things got ugly. My pathology chief wrote to the journal and said I'd manufactured the data, so the paper was officially discredited. Then someone planted heroin in my car which the police found following an anonymous tip. My life became a living hell. I was indicted on drug charges. My family was intimidated and tormented. But like an idiot, I stood up to it all, challenging the clinic to deny the existence of the patients whose names I had saved. Drunk on idealism, I wasn't going to give up. At least not until my wife died."

Marissa's face went ashen. "What happened?" she asked, afraid to hear the rest.

Tristan looked down at his beer for a moment, then took a swig. When he looked back at Marissa his eyes were filled with tears. "It was supposedly a mugging," he said in a halting voice. "Something that doesn't happen too often here in Australia. She was knocked down and her purse was taken. In the process, she broke her neck."

"Oh, no!" cried Marissa.

"Officially she broke her neck hitting the pavement," Tristan said. "But I thought the fracture resulted from a kung fu kick although I couldn't prove it. But it made me terrified for my son's safety. Since I had a trial to face, I stayed, but I sent Chauncey to live with my in-laws in California. I knew I couldn't protect him."

"Your wife was American?" Marissa asked.

Tristan nodded. "We met when I was doing a fellowship in San Francisco."

"What happened at the trial?" Marissa asked.

"I was acquitted of most of the criminal charges," Tristan said. "But not all. I served a short time in jail and had to do some community service. I got fired from FCA, obviously. I lost my specialty certification but managed to hold on to my medical license. And I fled out here to the outback."

"Your son is still in the States?" Marissa asked.

Tristan nodded. "I wasn't about to bring him here until I was certain it was over."

"What an ordeal."

324

"I hope you will take it to heart," Tristan said. "You are probably right about your friend's death not being accidental. You're probably also right about your own life being in danger. I think you'd better leave Australia."

"I don't know if I can at this point," Marissa said.

"Please don't be as foolish as I was," Tristan said. "You've already lost a friend. Don't persist. Forget your idealism. All this represents something very big and very sinister. It probably involves organized Chinese crime and heroin, a deadly combination. People always think of the Mafia when they think of organized crime, but the Mafia is a Girl-Scout operation compared to the Chinese syndicate. Whatever is at the bottom of it all, I realized I couldn't investigate it on my own. Nor should you."

"How could organized Chinese crime be associated with TB salpingitis?" Marissa asked.

"I haven't the slightest idea," Tristan said. "I doubt there is a direct causal link. It has to be some unexpected side effect."

"Did you know that FCA is controlled by a holding company that also controls all the Women's Clinics in the States?"

"I do," Tristan said. "That was part of the reason I went to work for FCA. I knew that they were planning to expand around the globe primarily because of their in-vitro fertilization technology."

Marissa touched Tristan's arm. Even though

her loss was different, she felt the kinship of shared tragedy. "Thank you for talking with me," she said softly. "Thank you for being so open and trusting."

"I hope it has the desired effect of sending you home at once," Tristan said. "You must give up this crusade you are on."

"I don't think I can," Marissa said. "Not after Wendy's death, and not after all the suffering that the TB salpingitis has caused me and so many others. I've come this far and risked this much. I have to find out what's going on."

"All I can tell you is that a similar compulsion ruined my life and killed my wife," Tristan said. He sounded almost angry. He wanted to talk her out of her foolishness, but seeing the glint of determination in her eyes, he knew it would be in vain. He sighed. "I'm getting the idea that you are a hopeless cause.

"If you have to proceed, then I suggest that you contact the Wing Sin Triad in Hong Kong. Maybe they will be willing to help—for a price. That was what I was planning to do. But I have to warn you that it will be dangerous since the Hong Kong triads are notorious for violence, especially when heroin is involved; the amounts of money are astronomical. The heroin alone coming from the Golden Triangle is worth over a hundred billion dollars a year."

"Why don't you come with me?" Marissa said. "Your son is safe in America. Why not follow up on what you had planned to do years ago? We can do it together."

Tristan laughed aloud. "Absolutely not," he said. "Don't even try to tempt me. I ran out of idealism two years ago."

"Why would FCA and the Women's Clinic be involved with drugs?" she asked. "Just for the money? Wouldn't they be risking too much?"

"That's a good question," Tristan said. "I've asked it myself. My guess is that they might be part of a money-laundering scheme. The clinic needs lots of capital for continued global expansion."

"So the Chinese coming from the PRC are couriers for money or drugs or both," Marissa said.

"That's my guess," Tristan said.

"But that brings me back to the tuberculosis," Marissa said. "How does that fit in?"

Tristan shrugged. "As I said, I don't have all the answers. I suppose it has to be an inadvertent effect. I don't have a clue as to how the women pick it up. TB is usually an airborne infection. How it gets to the fallopian tubes is beyond me."

"That's not how you make a diagnosis in medicine," Marissa said. "All the symptoms and signs have to be related directly to the main diagnosis. Almost always it is one disease. I think TB has to be considered central to the problem."

"Then you're on your own," Tristan said. "There's no way I can explain what's happened with that caveat."

"So come with me," Marissa begged. "You certainly have as much at stake as I do in learning the truth."

"No!" Tristan said. "I'm not getting involved. Not again. Recently I've been thinking that enough time has passed and I've saved a lot of money, enough to take my son back and move someplace far away, maybe even the States."

"Okay," Marissa said. "I guess I can understand." Her tone said she didn't understand at all. "Thank you again for talking with me." The two stood up. Marissa stuck her hand out and Tristan shook it.

"Good luck," Tristan said.

Marissa squinted as she stepped outside into the blazing hot sun. She walked to her car and looked in at the dust. She was not relishing her ride back to Windorah, nor the odyssey back to Charleville the next day.

She got into the car as carefully as possible to avoid raising a dust cloud. After starting the engine, she drove out of the Wilmington Station, waving to a few of the stockmen working on a run of fence. She hung a left and started back toward Windorah.

As she drove through the forbidding countryside, she reviewed everything Tristan had told her. Although she hadn't found out anything new about the TB salpingitis, she'd learned much she'd never expected, all of it disturbing. Perhaps the most disturbing was the suggestion of foul play in Tristan's wife's death. If Tristan was right, Marissa felt that lent greater plausibility to the idea that

328

the sharks had been deliberately attracted by the two men tossing the chum. And if that were the case, her own life was in jeopardy.

Marissa drove the car by reflex as she wondered what she could do to protect herself. Unfortunately she didn't have any particularly startling ideas. If people she didn't know wanted to kill her, how would she know who they were? It was hard to protect herself from the unexpected. Danger could come at any moment.

Just then, as if to prove her fears, she became aware of an odd vibration. At first she thought her car had been tampered with. She glanced at the gauges and dials on the dashboard. All registered normal. Yet the vibration soon crescendoed to a roar.

In a panic, Marissa gripped the steering wheel. She knew she had to do something fast. In desperation she slammed on the brakes and threw the steering wheel hard to the left. The car skidded sideways. For an instant, Marissa felt it was about to roll over.

The instant Marissa came to a jolting halt, a plane thundered overhead, missing the top of her car by barely ten feet.

Marissa knew then that the people who had killed Wendy had somehow found her. Now they would concoct an accident to dispense with her.

Her car had stalled. Frantically, she tried to restart it. Through the windshield she could see that the plane had looped up, banked, and was now coming back toward her. In the distance it looked no bigger than an insect, but already its sound was rattling the car.

With the engine going at last, Marissa put the car in gear. The plane was almost on her. Ahead was a lone acacia tree. For some crazy reason, Marissa thought that if she could get to the tree, it would provide a modicum of protection. She threw the wheel to the right to straighten the car, then gunned the engine. The car shot forward.

The plane was headed right for her. It had dropped to less than ten feet from the ground. It was roaring along the road directly at her. Behind the plane, the dust billowed hundreds of feet into the air.

Realizing she wasn't going to make it to the tree, Marissa slammed on the brakes again and raised her arms protectively in front of her eyes. With a thundering growl the plane came at her, then pulled up at the last second. The car shuddered as the plane screamed overhead.

Opening her eyes, Marissa floored the gas pedal again. Within seconds she had the car off the road and under the tree. Behind her she could hear the plane returning.

Twisting in her seat, she faced around, fully expecting to see the craft coming at her. But instead, it was paralleling the road. As it passed by her, its wheels touched down. The high-pitched drone of its twin engines dropped to a deeper roar. That was when Marissa recognized the plane. Inside was Tristan Williams.

Relief quickly changed to irritation as Marissa

watched the plane slow to a near stop, turn, then taxi back. When it was alongside her car, it turned again, facing down the road. The engine was cut and Tristan jumped from the cabin.

He walked up to Marissa with his hat jauntily pushed back on his forehead. "Marissa Blumenthal!" he quipped. "Imagine meeting you out here!"

"You scared me to death," Marissa said hotly.

"And you deserved it," Tristan said with equal vehemence. Then he smiled. "Maybe I'm a little crazy, too. But I had to let you know that I've changed my mind. Maybe I owe it to my wife's memory. Maybe I owe it to myself. Whatever. I've got some holiday time and a lot of cash, so I'll go with you to Hongkers and we'll see if we can figure this thing out."

"Really?" Marissa asked. "Are you sure?"

"Don't make me reexamine my decision," Tristan warned. "But I couldn't let you wing off to Hong Kong by yourself under these circumstances. I'd feel guilty, and I've already experienced enough guilt for a lifetime."

"I'm so pleased," Marissa said. "You have no idea."

"Don't be too pleased," Tristan said. "Because it's not going to be any proper holiday, I can assure you of that. It's not going to be easy and it'll definitely be dangerous. Are you sure you want to go through with it?"

"No question," Marissa said. "Especially now!"

"Where are you headed at the moment?" Tristan asked.

"I'm staying at the Western Star Hotel," Marissa said. "I was planning on driving to Charleville in the morning."

"Here's my suggestion," he said. "Go back to the Western Star and wait for me. I'll meet you there. I've got another station to visit. I can arrange to have this rental car driven back to Charleville if you have the fortitude to fly with me in my KingAir."

"I'd do anything to avoid that drive from Windorah to Charleville," Marissa said.

Tristan tipped his hat. "See you at the Western Star." He turned and started back toward his plane.

"Tris!" Marissa called.

He turned.

Marissa blushed. "Can I call you Tris?" she asked.

"You can call me anything you want," Tristan said. "Here in the land of Oz, even Bastard is a term of endearment."

"I just wanted to thank you for volunteering to go with me to Hong Kong," Marissa said.

"Like I said, better hold back on your thanks until you see what we're getting ourselves into," Tristan said. "Have you ever been to Hong Kong?"

"No," Marissa said.

"Well, hang on to your kookaburra. The outback of Australia is the absolute opposite of Hong-

332

kers. It's a city out of control, especially now that it's scheduled to be handed over to the PRC in '97. The place is a bit desperate, and it's always operated on money and money alone. Everything is for sale in Hong Kong, even life itself. And, in Hong Kong life is cheap. I mean it. There it's not just a cliché."

"I'm sure I wouldn't have been able to handle it on my own," Marissa said.

Tristan eyed her. "I'm not so sure of that," he said. "You've given me the impression that you've got more than your share of pluck and determination." With a final smile, Tristan turned back to his plane.

Soon the engines were roaring again and the props were sending a torrent of dust into the air. With a final wave, Tristan released his brake and the KingAir leaped forward, soaring off into the searing sun.

13

APRIL 10, 1990
7:15 A.M.

"TIME TO get up!" a voice called, stirring Marissa from what felt like a drugged sleep. "The Williams' Oriental tour is about to begin and it starts with a stockman-style breakfast."

Marissa's eyes blinked open. Tristan was at the

333

window, pulling back the curtain. Weak early morning sunlight streamed into the room.

"Let's go!" Tristan said. He came over to the bed and gave the covers a tug. Marissa grabbed them in panic. Tristan laughed, then spun on his heels. "I'll expect you in half an hour in the morning room," he said before pulling the door closed behind him.

Marissa glanced at the room. It was the guest room in Tristan's small house on the outskirts of Charleville. The room was a dormered space, quaintly decorated with a flower print wallpaper. The bed was wrought-iron with an eyelet comforter.

They'd moved swiftly once Tristan told Marissa he would accompany her to Hong Kong. They'd gotten back to Charleville before dark after an uneventful flight. From the air Marissa began to realize just how vast and arid a country she was in. She had once read that Australia was the oldest continent on earth. From above, it looked it.

She had spent the night at Tristan's house only after a mild argument. At first she'd been reluctant, but Tristan had been insistent.

"If you can't trust me to spend the night in my guest room, then how are you going to trust me in Hongkers?"

Marissa had relented in the end.

The evening had passed quickly. Tristan spent most of the time making arrangements to go on holiday. He called his colleague, Bob Marlowe, to arrange for him to cover Tristan's professional responsibilities.

Marissa had slept better than she had on the two previous nights.

Reluctantly, she slipped her legs from under the blanket and got out of bed.

After a hearty breakfast of porridge, eggs, and sausage, Tristan made a few more final arrangements, including a visit to his bank. Then together they went out to the Charleville airport and boarded a Flight West commuter to Brisbane.

In Brisbane they transferred airports to catch the 11:15 Qantas flight to Hong Kong. Before going through passport control, Marissa took Tristan aside to tell him that the police inspector had asked her to stay on Hamilton Island.

"What if they detain me?" she asked. "What if they arrest me?"

"Come on!" Tristan responded with a laugh. "You don't really think Royal Australian police are that efficient, do you?"

The uniformed man in the passport control booth barely looked at her.

The flight was peacefully uneventful. Once again Marissa was amazed by the expansive Pacific. Until this trip, she'd had no idea what a big ocean it was. In silent testimony to how much better she was feeling now that she had Tristan to count on, Marissa soon drifted off to sleep.

Right on schedule, the Qantas jet's wheels touched down with a thump at Kai Tac Airport at 5:43 P.M., giving Marissa her first sight of Hong

Kong. Despite the purpose of their trip, she couldn't help feeling a shiver of excitement.

From the air, the colony had looked like a peaceful collection of rocky, forested islands set in an emerald-green sea. But from the airport runway it already looked quite different. Across the impossibly congested harbor of bobbing vessels, it looked starkly urban, like a futuristic city crowded with skyscrapers of concrete, steel, and mirrored glass. Even through the plane's porthole she could sense the exotic, mysterious nature of the busiest and richest of all Chinese cities.

Formalities at the airport were swift. As they waited at the luggage carousel for their "swag," as Tristan called it, they were approached by a representative from the Peninsula Hotel, where Tristan had booked adjoining rooms. To Marissa's surprise, they were escorted out of the terminal building to a waiting Rolls-Royce.

"Isn't this a bit extravagant?" Marissa asked as they pulled out of the airport. "This must be one fancy hotel."

"And why not!" Tristan said. "Don't you Yanks have the expression 'you only go around once'? I'm on holiday and I haven't been on holiday for years. I intend to try to enjoy myself, even if we are here on serious business."

Marissa wondered what Robert would say when he saw the charges.

The hotel car quickly got bogged down in rush hour traffic, the likes of which Marissa had never seen. She was shocked when the driver said traffic was better than usual.

Even in the hushed interior of the Rolls-Royce limousine, Marissa was overwhelmed by the clamor and clutter of the city. As Tristan had implied, it was different enough from the Australian outback to make her think she'd traveled to another planet.

They were snared in a crush of double-decker buses, trams, cars, bicycles, motorbikes, and people, lots of people. By the time they arrived at the hotel, Marissa felt drained, as if she'd had to walk the entire route.

But once the hotel doors closed behind them, the world changed again. The huge lobby with its gilded ceiling was decorated in a restrained yet luxuriant fashion with only a hint of Oriental flavor. The most disturbing sounds were those caused by high-heeled shoes clicking against the polished marble floor. The melodious sound of a grand piano added to the elegant atmosphere.

The check-in procedure was accomplished with minimum confusion. They left their passports with the receptionist. A manager accompanied them up to their connecting rooms on the sixth floor. At Tristan's insistence, he unlocked the connecting doors. Tristan said that there'd be no taking chances; he wanted ready access in case of any trouble.

Marissa joined Tristan at the window. They had a sweeping view of Hong Kong Harbor, which was filled with boats of every description and size.

Tristan pointed out the green and white ferries that were passing each other in their runs to and from Hong Kong Island across the way. There were junks and sampans with graceful butterfly sails. Lighters were moored against the freighters anchored in the middle of the channel. Highly varnished launches sped through the choppy waters. Even a huge cruise ship was slowly edging its way into its berth at the ocean terminal.

The luggage quickly followed. Tristan tipped the bellman, who silently bowed and exited, closing the door behind him.

"Well!" Tristan said, rubbing his hands together. "Here we are in Hong Kong. How do you like it so far?"

"I can see what you meant when you described it," Marissa said. "It's a bit overwhelming."

"How about a little refreshment before dinner?" Tristan suggested. Without waiting for an answer, he picked up the phone and called room service. He ordered beer.

"None for me," Marissa called before Tristan had hung up. She'd had enough beer in Australia to last her for some time.

"Change that to champagne," Tristan said into the phone. "Two glasses."

Marissa was about to object, but Tristan had already hung up.

"I'm not in much of a festive mood," she said.

"Come on now, Marissa," Tristan said, stretching out on the bed. He tossed his hat like a saucer into an easy chair. "You have to lighten up a touch. You should enjoy yourself as well. There's no harm in it."

With Wendy's horrid death still on her mind, Marissa hardly felt she should be expected to enjoy herself. "I want to get down to business," she said. "How are we going to contact the Wing Sin Triad? What's our first step?"

There was a soft knock on the door before Tristan could reply. He leaped from the bed and threw the door wide open. A waiter with white gloves bowed and entered. He was carrying a tray with a champagne cooler and two long-stemmed glasses.

"Now this is service," Tristan said with admiration. "That's the fastest response time I've ever seen." He pointed to the desk. "Right here, mate, if you would."

The waiter silently put down the tray, then backed out of the room with a bow.

Tristan had the wire cage off in the blink of an eye, then popped the cork. To his delight it caromed off the ceiling. He filled the glasses and carried them over to Marissa, handing her one.

Reluctantly Marissa took the glass he offered her.

Tristan raised his glass up to eye level. "To our Hong Kong sleuthing," he said.

Marissa clinked his glass with hers. They both drank.

"Now that's what I call bubbly," Tristan said. Then, turning to the window, he pointed out. "You haven't said anything about the view. What do you think?"

"It's astonishingly beautiful," Marissa said, eyeing the mountains of Hong Kong Island. White villas dotted the dark green foliage. Below, at the water's edge and beginning to creep up the hills, were the modern high-rises, opulent testimony to Hong Kong's power as a major economic center.

"It's more beautiful than I thought it would be," Tristan said.

Marissa agreed. She hadn't imagined it would be so modern. But then Tristan's comment sank in. Turning to him she asked, "Haven't you been here before?"

"First time," Tristan said, still enjoying the view.

"But the way you talked about it," Marissa said, "I was sure you'd been here."

"A lot of my friends have been here," Tristan said. "But not me. I've heard a lot about the place and have always wanted to come. Just never had the chance."

Looking back over at Hong Kong Island, Marissa felt a twinge of disappointment. She had counted on Tristan's knowledge of Hong Kong to speed their inquiries.

"So anyway," Marissa said, "back to my question. What's our first step in contacting the Wing Sin Triad?"

"I don't know," Tristan said. "Let's try to come up with some suggestions."

"Wait a minute," Marissa said, putting her glass down. "You're telling me you don't have any plan for contacting this Wing Sin Triad?"

"Not yet," Tristan admitted. "But it's a big organization. I don't think we will have any trouble making contact."

"Oh, give me a break!" Marissa said. "This is a fine time to let me know you've never been here before and that you don't have any ideas about contacting these triad people. What are we going to do, go out on the street and start asking passers-by?"

"We'll do what we have to," Tristan said.

Marissa stared at him in disbelief. She was beginning to wonder what kind of ally she'd come up with.

"But first things first," Tristan said. "Let's go to dinner. I'll call downstairs and get a proper suggestion for an authentic Chinese restaurant from the concierge."

"You do that!" Marissa said.

She took a shower and changed her clothes. By the time she was ready, she'd recovered her composure to a great degree, but she was still irritated with him. She felt deceived. At the same time she was thankful he'd come and that she wasn't on her own.

For dinner the concierge sent them to a "typical" Chinese restaurant. It was a four-story affair with a colorful façade painted bright gold and crimson. There were myriad dining rooms within, each lit by extravagant crystal chandeliers. Like Hong Kong itself, the place was bustling.

Both Marissa and Tristan were a bit unsettled by the apparent confusion. People were everywhere. Large tables of noisy diners dominated each room. Everybody seemed to be shouting. The scene reminded Marissa more of a stadium event than a restaurant. Despite the hour, crying babies could be heard in every direction. And over the tumult floated strident Chinese music coming from hidden speakers.

Eventually Marissa and Tristan found a table. They were handed large menus bound in gold and crimson. Unfortunately for them the menus were written in Chinese characters with no translation. They tried to hail a waiter, but were roundly ignored. Finally one waiter approached. At first he pretended not to speak English. Then he seemed to change his mind. He spoke to them in English, but he was distracted and less than helpful in translating the menu. Despite these obstacles, Marissa and Tristan ordered dinner.

"Do you have any idea what we'll be getting?" Marissa yelled over the din after the waiter disappeared.

"I haven't the slightest," Tristan answered.

The noise in the restaurant precluded normal conversation. Marissa and Tristan were content merely to observe.

In short order, their dinner arrived. It included a sizzling wok filled with unidentifiable wriggly vegetables. There was a basket of dumplings, something from the sea in a dark, salty sauce, several bowls of rice, and some haunches of greasy bird. There was also a pot of green tea.

Perhaps most surprising of all was that the food

was delicious. Even if in the end they weren't quite sure what it was, they heartily enjoyed it.

Leaving the boisterous restaurant, they stepped out into the street, whose traffic had scarcely lessened from rush hour time. They were on the Kowloon side of Hong Kong in the Tsim Sha Tsui section. Rather than hail a cab, they decided to walk back to the hotel.

The city was ablaze with color and light. Huge neon signs stretched two stories high. Every shop was open, their windows filled with Panasonic radios, Sony Walkmans, cameras, VCRs, and TVs. Every third doorway was an entrance to an underground bar or nightclub. Music blared. Attractive, saucer-faced Chinese women in tight, Chinese-style dresses beckoned with coy smiles. In addition to the noise and visual panoply, Marissa was bombarded with an array of smells: a potent combination of food, cooking oil, incense, and diesel exhaust.

Despite a press of people, Marissa and Tristan were able to talk as they walked, provided they stayed close enough.

"I've got an idea about contacting the Wing Sin Triad," Tristan said as they waited for a traffic light.

"Wonderful," Marissa said. "What is it?"

"The concierge!" Tristan said. "Those blokes are supposed to know everything in the city. If he knows where to eat, he probably knows the triads." Tristan flashed a knowing smile.

Marissa rolled her eyes. As far as she was concerned, it wasn't a masterful suggestion.

"I have an idea, but not about contacting the triads," Marissa said. "It might be helpful to visit one of the big hospitals in town. We can find out if TB is currently a problem here in the colony. We can even ask if they've seen any TB salpingitis."

"Good thinking," Tristan said.

Once they reached their hotel, Tristan insisted they go directly to the concierge's desk. While they waited to speak with him, Marissa began to have second thoughts about questioning the concierge about the triads. She thought it would be like going to New York and asking to get in touch with the Mafia. Excusing herself, she stopped by the front desk for their passports, then went across the lobby to wait in a sitting area.

"Can I help you?" the concierge asked Tristan in impeccable English.

"I think so, mate," Tristan said. He looked over his shoulder to make sure no one was listening, then he bent forward. "I need some confidential information."

The Chinese man leaned away from Tristan, eyeing him uneasily.

"I want to talk to somebody in the Wing Sin Triad," Tristan said.

"I've never heard of it, sir," the concierge said.

"Come on now," Tristan said. He took twenty dollars from his pocket and put it on the desk. "I've come a long way."

"Triads are illegal in Hong Kong," the concierge said. He pushed the money back to Tristan.

"I don't really care about their legal status," Tristan said. "I just want to talk to somebody in the Wing Sin. I need some information. I'm willing to pay."

"I beg your pardon," the concierge said, "but I don't know anything about triads." He seemed nervous, even edgy.

Tristan studied the concierge's face for a moment, then nodded. "Okay, but why don't I leave this twenty here in case you remember. We'll be here for a few days."

The concierge looked down at the twenty-dollar bill with disgust. It was hardly enough to justify the risk. As far as tips and squeeze were concerned, the Australians were the worst. They truly were barbarians.

The concierge raised his eyes and watched the man cross the lobby and meet with a dark-haired Caucasian woman, then head up to the bar. As soon as they were out of sight, he reached down and picked up the receiver on one of his many telephones. He'd had a lot of strange requests since he'd worked at the Peninsula, but this was one of the strangest.

Marissa swirled the ice cubes in her glass of mineral water and listened to Tristan reminisce about his childhood in a suburb of Melbourne. It sounded idyllic. He'd commuted each day to an English-style public school in the city via a green tram and

345

a red train. He'd had a stamp collection and went to church on Sunday. His father was a school-teacher.

"It was a sheltered life," he admitted. "But very pleasant. To this day, I have a definite nostalgia for its simplicity.

"Unfortunately my father died," Tristan said. "He'd never been the picture of health. All the sudden he wilted and died. Wasn't even sick that long. After that, we moved from Melbourne to Brisbane where my mother's family was involved in the restaurant business on the Gold Coast. That's how I happened to go to the University of Queensland."

Marissa was exhausted. The traveling was taking its toll. She enjoyed listening to Tristan, but was eager to turn in. She was also thinking about phoning Robert. "Maybe we should call it a day," she said when there was a lull in the conversation. "I think I'd better give my husband a ring to let him know I'm here."

Marissa had told Tristan about her childhood in Virginia and about her surgeon father and how she'd ended up in medical school. She'd also been careful to tell him about Robert, purposefully avoiding mention of their current marital problems.

"Yes, of course, call him!" Tristan said, standing up for Marissa. "Why don't you go on up? I'll be along soon. I thought perhaps I might quiz some of the taxi drivers about the Wing Sin."

Marissa took the elevator to the sixth floor. She

had her key in hand, but the moment the elevator door parted, the hall porter appeared from nowhere and opened her door for her. She tried to thank the man but he bowed and wouldn't even look her in the eye.

She called Robert as soon as she got in. She decided to make it a collect call, not sure how her finances would hold out.

"You just caught me on the way to the office," he told her after accepting the charges.

"Have you sold the stock?" Marissa asked. She thought of it as the call was going through.

"No, I haven't sold the stock," Robert admitted. "When are you coming home? And where are you? I tried calling your hotel. I was told you'd checked out."

"I'm not in Australia anymore," Marissa said. "I'm calling to let you know I'm in Hong Kong."

"Hong Kong!" Robert yelled. "What the hell are you doing in Hong Kong?"

"Just a little investigative work."

"Marissa, this is too much!" Robert fumed. "I want you home. Do you understand?"

"I'll take it under advisement," Marissa said, echoing Robert's reply to her request to sell his stock. Marissa hung up. There was no point trying to talk to him. He didn't even inquire about how she was feeling.

Marissa went to the window and gazed out at the scene. Even in the dark of night, Hong Kong boiled with activity. It could just as well have been the middle of the day. The lights of multitudinous

347

vessels moved like fireflies over the surface of the water. Across the harbor in Central on Hong Kong Island, the windows in the office high-rises were all ablaze, as if the businessmen could not dare to take an hour off. In Hong Kong the seductiveness of capitalism was complemented by the sheer power of human endeavor on a twenty-four-hour basis.

Just then Marissa heard a door close. She assumed it was Tristan. Within seconds there was a knock on the connecting door. Marissa told him to come in.

"Good news, luv," Tristan said excitedly. "One of the Caucasian doormen gave me a tip. He said there is a place not far from here where the triads reign supreme."

"Where?" Marissa asked.

"In an area called the Walled City," Tristan said. "It isn't really walled, but it was way back when. It was built as a fort in the twelfth century by the Sung dynasty. The Japanese occupying forces in World War II had the walls torn down to extend the runway at Kai Tac Airport. But the salient feature is that the British and the Chinese could never decide who had jurisdiction. So this little area has existed over the years in a kind of political limbo. Yet it's right here on the outskirts of Kowloon."

"You sound like a tour operator," Marissa commented.

"Apparently it's rather infamous," Tristan said. "The doorman said that if we wanted to contact the triads, he thought the Walled City would be a good place to start. What do you say about heading over there and giving it a go?"

"Now?" Marissa questioned.

"You're the one who's so eager," Tristan said.

Marissa nodded; it was true. It was also true that her unsatisfying phone conversation with Robert had filled her with nervous energy.

"Okay!" she said. "Let's give it a try."

"Good show," Tristan said. He got his hat. Together they headed for the door.

The Chinese taxi driver wasn't enthusiastic about their intended destination. "I don't think you want to go to the Walled City," he said. Marissa and Tristan were already in the backseat of his Toyota. "It's not a place for tourists."

"But we're not going as tourists," Tristan said.

"The Walled City is a pocket of crime," the driver warned. "The police don't go in there."

"We're not looking for the police," Tristan said. "We're looking for the Wing Sin."

Reluctantly the driver put the car in gear. "It's your heads," he said.

They pulled away from the hotel and turned up Nathan Road into the gaudy glow of Tsim Sha Tsui nightlife. Just like the harbor, the city was as busy as it had been during the day. Their cab inched through swarms of pedestrians, cars, and buses. Above, garish neon lights lit the night sky. Across the road hung banners emblazoned with huge Chinese characters.

Feeling overwhelmed by the sights, Marissa

turned inward into the taxi. With all the talk about triads, she asked Tristan what they were.

"They're secret societies," Tristan explained, "with all the usual secret oaths and rituals. The term triad comes from the relationship among heaven, earth, and man. They started hundreds of years ago as subversive political organizations, but soon found crime more rewarding. Especially the ones that either came to Hong Kong or were founded here. There are supposed to be about fifty gangs in Hong Kong alone, with thousands upon thousands of members."

"That's comforting," Marissa said with a short laugh.

"The Chinese have the dubious distinction of being the inventors of organized crime," Tristan continued. "That's one of the reasons they're so good at it. Centuries of experience. These days the bigger triads have branches in Europe, the U.S., Canada, even Australia. Anywhere there is a Chinese community there are likely to be triad members."

"And maybe also TB salpingitis," Marissa added.

Tristan shrugged. "Possibly. But Chinese crime is nothing new."

"I have to admit," Marissa said, "until I met you, I'd never heard of triads."

"I'm not surprised," Tristan said. "Most people haven't. The Mafia gets all the attention and the triads like it that way. But the triads are worse than the Mafia. At least the Mafia has a family-oriented morality, no matter how twisted it may be. Not so with the triads. The triads only concern themselves with money. Profit is the only ethic they know."

"I don't like the sound of all this," Marissa said uneasily.

"I warned you," Tristan said.

The taxi driver stopped on Tung Tau Tsen Road.

"Where's the Walled City?" Tristan questioned, leaning between the seats to see ahead.

"This is as far as I go," the driver said. He pointed through the windshield. "See those tunnel openings across the street? That's how you get in. The Walled City is this mess here to our right. If you want my advice, don't go in. It's dangerous. Let me take you to a nice nightclub, real sexy."

Tristan opened the taxi door, got out, and held it for Marissa. "Thanks for your advice, mate," he said. "Unfortunately, we've got business with the Wing Sin."

As soon as the door closed, the taxi made a quick U-turn. The driver hit the gas and was off.

"Are you sure about this?" Marissa asked. The taxi driver's warning and Tristan's rundown on triads made her wonder how dangerous it was.

"Looks rather formidable, doesn't it?" Tristan said.

They were standing before a honeycomb of tenements, ten to eleven stories high. The buildings were jammed together and had fallen into utter disrepair. What more recent construction there

351

was appeared to have been completely haphazard. Clothes were strung on lines that stretched from building to building. No roads led into this corner of town. There were only the dark tunnels the taxi driver had pointed out.

"Let's give it a go," Tristan said with a shrug. "We can always leave."

Reluctantly Marissa followed Tristan along Tung Tau Tsen Road, heading for one of the tunnels. On one side loomed the dark mass of the concrete slum. On the other side, in sharp contrast, were brightly lit windows of a row of dentists' offices containing jars of pickled teeth, parts of jawbones, and sets of smiling dentures. Above the dental offices were more normal-appearing apartment blocks with balconies, potted plants, and TV aerials.

There were plenty of people on the dental side of the road, with the usual sounds of blaring radios, TVs, and conversation. But the other side of the road was ominously quiet and dark, with only infrequent lights.

Leaving the area of normal life and activity, Marissa and Tristan approached one of the tunnels that led into the Walled City.

Together they peered down the lonely corridor. The view was hardly inviting. The narrow, dark passage ran for about fifty feet before angling off to the side. The floor was loose dirt littered with broken pieces of concrete. The walls were covered with graffiti. The ceiling was a tangle of electric wires and cables with infrequent bare light bulbs. Water dripped into slick puddles in several spots.

Suddenly a horrid screaming noise occurred that made Marissa involuntarily grab Tristan. Both leaped from fright as a 747 thundered overhead heading for a landing at Kai Tac, barely missing the tops of the buildings.

"I'd say we're a bit high-strung," Tristan remarked with a nervous laugh.

"Maybe we'd better skip this Walled City," Marissa suggested.

"I don't know," Tristan said. "If we want to contact the Wing Sin, this place looks promising to me."

"It looks terrible to me," Marissa said.

"Come on," Tristan urged. "As I said before, we'll leave if it doesn't work out."

"You first," Marissa said reluctantly.

Tristan stepped within the opening; Marissa followed close behind. They walked down the narrow passageway that soon began to smell like a sewer. Just after turning the first corner even Marissa had to bend to keep her head from touching the tangle of electric cables that ran along the ceiling. The farther they trekked, the more the sounds of the city died away.

After several more turns the passageway led to a confluence of tunnels heading in several directions. There were also darkened stairways that led both above and below ground level. Everywhere there was trash and debris.

Choosing at random, they walked down another

passage. Rounding a corner, they saw the first signs of life. In a series of ill-lit alcoves sweating men and women labored over antiquated sewing machines. They seemed to be making men's shirts. Marissa and Tristan nodded greetings but the people just stared at them as if they were ghosts.

"Anybody speak English?" Tristan asked brightly. If anyone did, they didn't volunteer. "Thanks anyway," he said. He motioned for Marissa to move on.

They delved deeper into the maze. Marissa began to wonder if they would be able to find their way back. She wavered between disgust and fear. She had never been in a more revolting place in her life. Such standards of living were beyond her imagination.

Rounding another corner that smelled particularly rank, Marissa saw a pile of rotting garbage with a pack of feeding rats. "Oh, God!" she cried. She hated rats.

The passageway opened up again with another series of narrow alcoves. In some, open-pit fires burned, adding to the oppressive smell and heat and transforming the place into a kind of medieval vision of hell. They passed a bakery where loaves of bread were stacked on its dirty floor. Next door was a snake vendor with some of his wares hung up by wire. Others were housed in wicker baskets.

"Are you looking for heroin?" someone asked.

Marissa and Tristan turned. A young Chinese

boy of about twelve years of age was standing in the shadows behind them.

"Ah!" Tristan said. "Just what we need. Someone who speaks English. We're not interested in drugs, mate. We're looking for someone in the Wing Sin Triad. Can you help?"

The boy shook his head. "This is 14K territory," he said proudly.

"Is it now?" Tristan said. "Now where would we be apt to find Wing Sin territory?"

The boy pointed to his left down a corridor as a number of fierce-looking teenage boys stepped out of doorways.

"Thanks, mate," Tristan said. He touched the brim of his hat. Then he pulled Marissa away.

"I don't like this at all," Marissa said as they groped in a particularly dark passage, half bent over. She stepped in a puddle of water and wondered what kind of foul fluid it was.

"At least we're getting close," Tristan said. "That boy was the first person to acknowledge he'd heard of the Wing Sin."

The corridor opened up again on a small, rubbish-strewn courtyard. A young girl was sitting on a stairway.

"Would you care for some honey?" she asked timidly. "Only two dollars."

"Honey!" Tristan repeated. "That's an old term."

"What does it mean?" Marissa asked, staring at the girl. She was dressed in a ragged, Chinese-style dress with a high collar and a traditional slit.

"We Australians prefer to use the 'f' word," Tristan said.

Marissa was appalled. "But she's only about ten!"

Tristan shrugged. "The Chinese like their whores young."

Marissa couldn't take her eyes off the girl. The child stared back at her blankly. Marissa shuddered. Never had she realized just how sheltered she'd been, growing up in Virginia.

"Uh oh!" Tristan said. "Looks like a welcoming party."

Marissa followed his gaze. A group of young toughs dressed in leather outfits decorated with stainless-steel chains was approaching. Their ages ranged from about fifteen to twenty.

A particularly muscular member of the group held up his hand, effectively stopping the others. "What are you doing here?" he demanded in fluent English. "Don't you know that *gweilos* are not allowed in the Walled City?"

Tristan told him that they were trying to contact the Wing Sin Triad.

"What for?" the young man asked. "Are you after drugs or sex?"

"Neither," Tristan said. "We're looking for information. We're willing to pay."

"Let's see your money," the man said.

Tristan wasn't sure what to do. He would have liked to defuse the situation, but he didn't know how. He scanned the intent faces watching him. No one made a move, but Tristan knew they were prepared to. Slowly, he reached into his pocket and drew out his wallet. Taking a few bills out, he held them up.

"One of them has a knife!" Marissa whispered, spotting a glint of steel.

"Run!" commanded Tristan, tossing the money into the air and giving Marissa a push back the way they'd come. Needing no more encouragement than that, Marissa turned and fled down the dark passageway. She stumbled over debris and bumped into a wall. Behind her she heard Tristan following. She soon reached the confluence of passageways they had passed moments before. She couldn't remember which way they'd come from. Tristan collided with her, then grabbed her hand. Together they ran down the widest corridor.

Behind them echoed unintelligible shouts from the youths who'd confronted them. Having seized the money, they were now in hot pursuit.

Marissa and Tristan realized they were lost. They arrived at a courtyard they had not yet seen. A small, shuttered house stood at its center. Above was the first patch of sky they'd seen since they'd entered the Walled City.

Skirting the house, they entered another tunnel. From the shouts and catcalls they could tell that the thugs were gaining on them. The Chinese youths had an unfair advantage: they knew the place.

Rounding a corner, Marissa and Tristan came across another spate of alcoves. One of the rooms was a restaurant with a large cauldron of boiling crab-claw soup. A half dozen simple wooden tables surrounded the pot. A few old men were playing Mah-Jongg at one of them.

Skidding to a stop, Tristan pulled Marissa into the tiny restaurant. Several of the tables overturned. Mah-Jongg tiles scattered on the rough wooden floor.

The pursuers were on them in a flash, as out of breath as Marissa and Tristan. Several were brandishing knives. Their faces were tight with determination.

Pushing Marissa into a corner behind him, Tristan assumed a kung fu stance, expecting one of the young Chinese to make a lunge at him.

Instead everyone froze again, including the elderly patrons, who'd moved against a far wall, as far from the frenzy as possible. The Chinese youths seemed to respect, perhaps even fear, Tristan's threatening posture. The muscled fellow stepped forward.

Tristan eyed him warily. "You're not being very friendly," he said, trying to make light of the situation. "If you tell us how, we'll be happy to leave. Just say the word."

"For a little squeeze we'll show you out," the youth said.

"Squeeze?" Tristan questioned.

"Money," the youth said. "The rest of your money. And your watches as well."

"Then you will let us go?" Tristan asked. "You'll show us out of here?"

"Yes," the Chinese youth said. "We will accept that your debt has been paid."

The youths with the knives lowered their weapons slightly, as if to display their sincerity.

Tristan reached for his wallet again. Pulling it out, he withdrew what money he had in it and put it on the nearest table. He then pulled off his watch and put that on top of the bills.

"And the woman's," the muscular man said.

"That's not very chivalrous," Tristan said.

The man sneered. "On the table," he said.

"Sorry, luv," Tristan said. He stuck out his hand. Marissa slipped off the watch that Robert had given her and handed it to Tristan. He added it to the small pile on the table.

"There you go, mate," Tristan said. "Now let's have you live up to your side of the bargain."

The man came forward and picked up the money and the watches. He hastily divided the money among the others. The watches he pocketed.

"As long as we're now on good terms," Tristan said, "what about the Wing Sin? Are you fellows part of that illustrious organization?"

"No," the leader growled. "We're the Wo Sing Wo. The Wing Sin are pigs." He spat on the ground.

"Any idea where these pigs could be located?" Tristan asked.

The man turned to confer with one of his companions. At length he said: "Tse Mau will show you out of the Walled City. Don't come back."

One of the toughs stepped forward, glaring menacingly at Tristan.

"After this type of welcome," Tristan said, "I can assure you that we will not be back."

The Chinese youths parted, allowing Tristan and Marissa to pass. Tristan reached behind for Marissa's hand and led the way.

"Ah!" Marissa yelled when one of the youths reached out and squeezed one of her breasts. Tristan whirled, but Marissa pushed him forward.

They walked quickly through the maze, the young Chinese staying five or six paces ahead. They didn't talk. After taking a half dozen turns, Marissa began to fear that they were not being led out, but only farther within. But after another turn the passageway suddenly opened out into the cool night air. Across the street the well-lit dentist's office appeared like a beacon. Even the strident Chinese music coming from the radios sounded better to Marissa now that they were out.

Tse started back into the corridor, but Tristan called him by name. The man turned.

"Do you speak English?" Tristan asked.

"Yes," he said haughtily. Marissa estimated that he was about twenty; he seemed to be one of the older members of the group.

"That makes things easier," Tristan said. "I wanted to ask a favor. You see, we're low on cash at the moment. I know you were given some money back in that rat hole. Could you spot us a bit to get back to the hotel?"

Tse responded by pulling out his knife. It was

about eight inches long, with an upward curve at the tip like a miniature scimitar.

Marissa winced. She couldn't believe that Tristan had risked the youth's wrath with such a request.

But Tristan's move was calculated. He'd hoped the thug would brandish the knife again under these different circumstances. As soon as the knife appeared, Tristan struck with lightning speed. In an instant, the knife clattered to the ground. With a yell, Tristan treated Tse to a series of punches, followed by a spinning kick that knocked him down.

Tse cowered against the wall as Tristan kicked the knife into a street sewer. Then he went over to the Chinese youth and yanked him to his feet by the front of his leather vest.

"Now about that money you were so kindly offering . . ."

Tse hastily withdrew the bills he had in his pocket and handed them over. Tristan checked the man's wrist. "Too bad," he said. "No watch."

"Tristan!" Marissa called. "Let's get out of here!"

"Ta," Tristan said to Tse, then he calmly followed Marissa.

"Did you have to do that?" Marissa demanded angrily when Tristan caught up with her. "Was that stunt some kind of masculine ego trip? We'd just gotten out of one mess and you were trying to get us into another."

"That's not the way I see it." Tristan said. "Besides, we needed cab fare.

"Hold it!" Tristan said, stopping abruptly.

"What now?" Marissa cried.

"We have to go back," Tristan said. "I lost my favorite hat."

Marissa yanked her arm from Tristan's grasp and strode off. She didn't find his antics the least bit entertaining. She was beginning to tremble. The confrontation in the Walled City had unnerved her, and the initial shock was wearing off. It had been a mistake to go in there. She was angry at Tristan for having jeopardized them in the first place; she was even angrier with him for taking the risk of the final confrontation with Tse.

Tristan again caught up with Marissa and fell in step without another word. Only a block away from the dark entrance to the Walled City, the normal hectic confusion of Kowloon began. They easily found a cab that carried them back toward the Peninsula Hotel.

During the ride, Marissa brooded. She began to realize that she would have to come up with some idea of how to contact the Wing Sin Triad if that's what they hoped to do. If the venture to the Walled City was the best thing Tristan could come up with, she'd better not rely on him.

Some years back she'd read a thriller where the hero needed information in a strange town. He got it by hiring a limousine. The idea was that a good limo driver knew his city inside and out, the legitimate side and the illegitimate.

Turning to Tristan she said, "I've got an idea."
"Wonderful," Tristan said. "Let's hear it."

Robert paced his study, swearing under his breath, occasionally punctuating his string of curses by stopping to pound a fist on his desk. Marissa had indeed caught him as he was about to leave for work. But the call had so irritated and disturbed him, he'd put down his briefcase to fume until he got some composure back.

"What the hell is she doing in Hong Kong?" he said aloud. "She's carrying this nonsense to ridiculous extremes, chasing around the world on a whim."

Robert sat down in front of his computer. He wondered if he should call their doctor. What if Marissa was having a nervous breakdown? Shouldn't he intercede?

Robert sprang out of his chair and began pacing again. He just couldn't stay still. What should he do? Up until that moment, he'd thought the best thing was to let Marissa wear herself out with this wild-goose chase. Australia was one thing, but Hong Kong!

"Why did I ever marry?" Robert asked himself, reverting back to a verbal dialogue with himself. "Oh, for those good old bachelor days when my worst worries were getting my shirts from the laundry." He stopped his pacing. "Hell," he snapped. "I still have to get my shirts from the laundry." He tried to think of what marriage had brought him, and at that moment he couldn't think of anything.

"What am I going to do?" he wondered. "What should I do? What can I do?" he said aloud. Deep down, more than anything, Robert simply wanted his wife back. If she wouldn't come willingly, maybe it was time to go get her.

Robert stopped his pacing and stared out the window. He had another thought. What if she wasn't in Hong Kong? What if she'd been lying or was being sarcastic? Then he remembered the call had been collect. Sitting down in his desk chair, Robert dialed the phone company. After a minor hassle, he got the calling number. It was a Hong Kong number. He dialed it, hoping to find out the name of the hotel or wherever it was she was staying. When the phone was picked up he had his answer: the Peninsula Hotel, the same hotel that he'd stayed in the two times he'd been to Hong Kong on business.

Robert disconnected but kept the receiver in his hand. One thing was clear: he could not sit idly by forever and allow Marissa to chase around the world as she pleased. He had to put his foot down and stop this craziness, especially thinking how much it was undoubtedly costing.

On an impulse Robert called the airlines to find out about direct service from Boston to Hong Kong.

When he was finished with the airlines he called his office and had his call put through to Donna.

"Donna, I might not come in today," Robert said.

"All right," Donna said. "Anything special you want me to do?"

"Just be sure to get those letters out that I dictated last night," Robert said. "And one other thing. I don't think I'll be able to make dinner tonight after all."

"Now that's too bad. Why not?"

Willy Tong knocked on the door of the two-story house on the corner of Eucalyptus and Jacaranda streets in Charleville. A dog barked inside the house, but Willy wasn't worried. He could tell it was one of those little lapdogs, probably a Yorkie. From inside, someone flipped on a porch light. It was one of those big bowl fixtures like an opaque goldfish bowl. Finally the hardware clicked and the door swung inward.

Instinctively Willy positioned himself for the worst-case posibilities. But the man he was facing was hardly a threat. He was built like a broomstick, with thick glasses.

"Are you Dr. Marlowe?" Willy asked.

"Righto," Dr. Marlowe said.

"The Royal Flying Doctor Service gave me your name," Willy said. "I called to talk with Dr. Williams, but they said he was on holiday and you were available for his patients."

"I am indeed," Dr. Marlowe said. "Is there some kind of problem?"

"It's my wife," Willy said. "When will Dr. Williams be back?"

"In about a week," Dr. Marlowe said. "He left this morning. His departure was unexpected so I'm afraid he was unable to inform his patients. What's the problem with your wife?"

"She's been ill for years," Willy said. "It took me a long time to convince her to allow Dr. Williams to attend her. I know she won't see anyone else. She's not sure about Western medicine."

"I understand completely," Dr. Marlowe said. "If it's not an emergency, you can wait for Dr. Williams to return."

"Perhaps a phone call would do," Willy said. "Maybe if he just adjusted her medications. Would it be possible to ring him?"

"If you don't mind ringing Hong Kong," Dr. Marlowe said. "He left word that he could be reached at the Peninsula Hotel. If you'll wait a moment, I have the phone number." Dr. Marlowe ducked back inside his house.

Willy glanced through the screen door. A small, dark-brown-and-tan long-haired dog snarled at him. He tried to think of a way to find out about the woman, but nothing came to mind.

"Here you go," Dr. Marlowe said, coming back to the door and handing out a slip of paper. "Good luck. If you need me, just ring."

Willy stalled for a moment, hoping to think of something. But his mind couldn't come up with anything that didn't sound suspicious. Instead, he

366

merely thanked the doctor and walked back to his rented car.

Once in the car, Willy sped back to the Charleville airport. While he waited for his charter flight to be fueled, he called Charles Lester.

"I found out something interesting," Willy said as soon as Lester had picked up the phone. "Tristan Williams left suddenly for Hong Kong this morning."

"That doesn't sound good at all," Lester growled. "Was the Blumenthal woman with him?"

"I don't know," Willy said. "If I stayed here I might be able to find out."

"I want you in Hong Kong immediately," Lester said. "For the moment we'll assume she's with him. Fly through Sydney; there are more connections. Ned is checking with emigration about the woman; by tomorrow we'll probably know for sure. Any idea where he's staying in Hong Kong?"

"The Peninsula Hotel," Willy said.

"Good show," Lester said. "If she's there, kill her. And while you're at it, kill Williams too. With him out of the country his death will cause fewer questions."

"You want it to appear like an accident?" Willy asked. Such an assignment would be difficult.

"Whatever," Lester said. "Just get the job done. The Wing Sin will supply you with a weapon. And even if the woman's not around, kill Williams anyway. He's been a thorn in our sides ever since he wrote that damned paper."

Willy rang off, pleased with his assignment. Knowing Hong Kong as well as he did, it would be an easy one.

Walking over to the charter desk, Willy leaned over. "There's been a change," he said to the agent. "I'm going to Sydney, not Brisbane."

14

APRIL 14, 1990
8:00 A.M.

A FAINT knock on her door roused Marissa. She decided to ignore it. She rolled over and stuck her head under the pillow. Despite the pillow, she heard a second knock.

Propping herself up on one elbow, she asked who was at the door. She heard a muffled voice. Throwing back the covers, she slipped into a hotel bathrobe and went to the door. She repeated her question.

"Room service," a voice said.

"I didn't order room service," Marissa said.

"Room 604," the voice said through the door. "Breakfast for eight o'clock."

Marissa unlocked the door and opened it. She barely had it open before the person waiting barreled in.

"Surprise!" Tristan said, jumping ahead of the room service cart. He handed Marissa a bouquet of flowers. "You didn't order breakfast, but I did. Breakfast for two." Tristan directed the porter to set up the table by the window overlooking the harbor.

Marissa shook her head. She never knew whether to be pleased or irritated by Tristan's pranks.

"I've been out and about since sunrise," Tristan said. "It's a glorious day." He came back and snatched the flowers from Marissa's hand. She hadn't moved from the door. Returning to the table, he stuck the blossoms into a vase he had ready for them.

"What are you standing around for?" Tristan asked, seeing that Marissa had not budged. "We've got a busy day. Get a move on!"

Marissa headed for the bathroom. As she closed the door behind her she saw the porter back out of the door to the hall.

Marissa looked at herself in the mirror over the sink. What she saw frightened her. Her skin was sallow. There were dark circles under her eyes. Her hair hung down limply with none of its usual luster. Then she glanced in the full-length mirror behind the door. That made her feel a bit better; at least she was losing some of the weight she'd gained on the hormones.

"I'll be anxiously waiting in my room," Tristan called through the door. "Give a yell when you're ready for the tucker."

Marissa smiled in spite of herself. Tristan's playful behavior, his good humor, and his Australian dialect were a balm for her troubled soul.

Moment to moment she couldn't anticipate which bad thoughts would plague her: Wendy's violent death, her deteriorating relationship with Robert, her life that was generally in ruins, or her inability to conceive.

Marissa's smile faded as she thought about her life. There didn't seem to be much more that could go wrong. On top of everything else she still didn't feel physically or mentally normal, even though she'd been off the hormones for a week. She wondered when her old equilibrium would return.

A shower, some makeup, and clean clothes helped improve Marissa's spirits. When she was ready, she rapped on the connecting door. Tristan instantly appeared. They breakfasted in front of the window with a view of Hong Kong Island in the distance. As they ate, the green mountains slowly emerged from their enveloping morning mist.

"I already ordered a limo as you suggested," Tristan said as they sat back to enjoy their coffee. "I told the concierge we wanted an experienced driver. He said that all their drivers were experienced."

"What's our schedule?" Marissa asked.

"First we should go to the bank where I wired the money," Tristan said. "After the experience last night, I have a feeling that we'll be needing a lot of squeeze. Then I thought we'd follow through with your other suggestions and visit one of the hospitals. We can ask about Wing Sin there, as well as TB. If we still don't have any leads for the triad, we'll ask the limo driver. What do you say?"

"Sounds good to me," Marissa answered.

When they got downstairs and walked outside the hotel, they found that the limo was already waiting. It was a black Mercedes sedan. The driver introduced himself as Freddie Lam.

"To the Hong King National Bank, Freddie," Tristan said as he settled comfortably in the back of the Mercedes.

It took almost half an hour to cover the quarter-mile of congested city traffic to the bank.

"We could have walked here quicker," Marissa commented.

The bank was an impressive marbled affair, and was extremely efficient. The impeccably dressed banking officer's expression did not alter when Tristan made his withdrawal.

"That seems like a lot of money," Marissa said as they climbed back into their limo.

"A lot of squeeze," Tristan corrected. Then, leaning over the seat, he told Freddie to take them to the New World shopping center.

"Don't you think we should go directly to the hospital?" Marissa said. She couldn't believe Tristan had any interest in shopping.

"Patience, luv!" Tristan said.

In a vast hall of waterfalls, escalators, and shops of every kind, Tristan pushed Marissa into one of the jewelry stores. There he insisted she pick out a watch to replace the one she'd lost the night before.

"Come on, Marissa," Tristan said when she tried to object. "I feel flush today." He patted the side pocket of his trousers, where he'd stuck the money from the bank. "Besides, I feel responsible for last night."

Eventually they both bought watches. Tristan paid cash after bargaining the price considerably lower. Proudly they wore their new watches out of the shop.

Climbing back into the car, Tristan again leaned over the seat. "Back to the hotel, Freddie," he said.

Freddie smiled and touched the shiny black brim of his cap.

"That reminds me," Tristan said as he settled back. "I have to replace that Aussie hat of mine. Too bad, it was just getting broken in."

"That hat looked as if you'd run over it several times with your plane," Marissa said.

"I did," Tristan replied. "That's what it takes."

At the hotel they waited in line at the cashier's desk. When it was their turn, Tristan filled out a card for a safe deposit box. They both signed it. Then Tristan deposited most of the cash he'd withdrawn from the bank.

With that accomplished, they went out to the limo and climbed back inside. Tristan leaned forward. "Freddie, what's the biggest hospital here in Kowloon?" he asked.

"Queen Elizabeth Hospital," Freddie said.

"Then that's where we want to go," Tristan said.

As their limo lurched forward, the concierge stepped out of the hotel accompanied by three young Chinese men dressed in dark blue suits. The concierge pointed at the departing sedan as it made a left on Salisbury Road.

"That's their car," he said in Cantonese. "Did you get a look at them?"

The three Chinese nodded. "You've done well, Pui-Ying," one of the men said. "The Wing Sin remembers its friends."

The three men climbed into their own waiting black Mercedes, instructing the driver to follow the sedan.

The man behind the Mercedes' wheel was an aggressive driver. He was accustomed to Hong Kong traffic. Pedestrians gave way instantly upon seeing the license plate. It was 426. Without much difficulty, the sedan slipped in behind Marissa and Tristan as they proceeded north on Nathan Road.

"How should we do this?" one of the men asked.

"We won't know until we see where they are going," another said. "It shouldn't be difficult."

The man who was riding in the front seat with the driver took a snub-nosed .38 caliber pistol from his shoulder holster. Holding the gun on his lap, he snapped out the cylinder to check all the chambers. Satisfied, he returned it to the holster.

They followed in silence as the sedan turned right on Jordan Road and merged into Cascoigne. They were surprised when the next turn put them on Princess and were even more surprised when

373

the car they were following turned into the grounds of Queen Elizabeth Hospital.

"Maybe one of them is sick," one of the men said.

"We'd better be more careful here," another said. "Occasionally there are police."

The driver slowed as Marissa and Tristan's car did. When Marissa and Tristan pulled to the side of the road and parked directly in front of the hospital's main entrance, the driver pulled up directly behind.

The men watched as Marissa and Tristan got out and walked into the hospital. They glanced around for any police. Seeing none, they got out of their car. Standing in the sunlight, they searched again for signs of the police, but there were none to be found.

"I suggest we use their car," one of the men said.

The others nodded.

All three lit cigarettes, then walked ahead.

Freddie had rolled his window down and had picked up the morning's *South China Morning Post*. He loved the gossip columns. As he was reading he suddenly felt a cold piece of metal pressed against the base of his skull, just behind his right ear.

Afraid to move quickly, he turned only his eyes to the right. He had an idea what had been pressed to his head. He saw that he was right: it was a gun.

Looking up, Freddie found himself looking into

the face of a youthful Chinese man with a cigarette clenched between his teeth. Behind him were two others.

"Please get out of the car," the man with the gun said. "Slowly and quietly. No one will be hurt."

Freddie swallowed with difficulty. He knew that these men were triad foot soldiers. Knowing how easily this type of man killed, Freddie was terrified. At first he couldn't move, but a nudge with the barrel of the gun helped. Slowly, he climbed from the car.

"Please walk back to the other car," the man with the gun told him. Freddie walked. When he reached the other car, the man told him to get inside. Freddie did as he was told. The man with the gun got in beside him. Ahead, Freddie saw the other two get into his sedan.

Arriving at Kai Tac Airport always filled Willy with happiness. Although he felt himself to be Australian to the core, having been born in Sydney, his father and mother had come from Hong Kong. Willy had always had a great affinity for the colony. Besides, he still had family there.

The first thing he did was rent a car. Although parking in Hong Kong was a nightmare, he wasn't concerned. The car was to serve as a base of operations and could be abandoned at any time. To rent it he used false documents. He had brought several sets.

His first destination was a restaurant in the

Mong Kok section of Kowloon, one of the most densely populated areas of the world. The restaurant was located on Canton Street, which was narrow and grossly congested. But with an appropriate amount of squeeze to the local policeman, he left the car between two canvas-covered stalls filled with pots, pans, and dishes.

The restaurant was nearly deserted at that time of the morning. Willy went directly into the kitchen, where sweating cooks were preparing the food for lunch. The floor was covered with an inch layer of grease and packed debris.

Beyond the kitchen were several rooms that served as offices. In the first an elderly woman dressed in a black high-collared silk dress was sitting at a desk. Before her was an abacus. The wooden balls clicked as she went over some figures.

Willy bowed with respect, then told the woman who he was. She didn't speak. She opened one of the desk drawers and extracted a package of brown paper tied with string. She handed it to Willy, who bowed again.

Back in his car, Willy pulled off the cord and peeled back the paper. The gun was a Heckler and Koch 9-millimeter. It was brand new. He hefted the weapon. It fit nicely in his hand.

Pulling out the magazine, Willy made sure it was loaded. He saw that there was a handful of additional shells in the brown paper. These Willy put into his trouser pocket, although he knew he wouldn't be needing them. In fact, he'd feel just as confident with just two bullets. The magazine held eight.

Sliding the gun into his breast pocket, Willy glanced at himself in the rearview mirror. The gun was bulky. He buttoned the jacket. He was wearing his best suit, knowing that he'd have to go into the Peninsula Hotel. He checked the mirror again. With the button done, it looked much better.

After starting the car, Willy drove to Nathan Road and headed south. As he approached the Peninsula Hotel, he began to feel a tingle of anticipation. Of all the various things he did for Female Care Australia, this was the kind of action he liked the best. Originally he'd been hired only because he spoke fluent Cantonese. But gradually he'd been given other responsibilities, and he'd proven himself over the years. In the "security" department, he was second only to Ned Kelly.

Pulling up directly in front of the hotel, Willy parked in an empty slot despite a sign forbidding it. He got out of the car and approached the doorman. He palmed two hundred dollars in Hong Kong currency and gave it to the man. "I trust my car will be all right where it is?" he asked in Cantonese.

The doorman bowed, slipping the money into his pocket.

Willy entered the hotel with a sense of pride. He was living testament to the Hong Kong ethic of diligent individual effort yielding success. As a child growing up dirt poor in Sydney, he had never imagined that one day he would be walking into a world class hotel and would feel comfortable doing so.

At a bank of house phones, Willy asked the operator to put him through to Marissa Blumenthal. He waited, hoping that she was indeed a guest. Without much ado, he was put through to her room. At first he planned on hanging up immediately, but he hated to forgo the thrill of speaking with his mark. But no one picked up.

Willy dialed the operator again, this time asking for Tristan Williams. There was no answer in his room either. Willy guessed they were out together. That was a good sign. He needed them together. His plan was simple. He would walk up and shoot each of them once in the head. Preferably, he would make his move in a crowded area. Then he would simply drop the gun, leave, and melt into the crowd. He'd done it plenty of times before. In Hong Kong, it was easy. In Australia, it was a lot more difficult.

Leaving the phones, Willy went to the newsstand and bought himself a copy of the *Hong Kong Standard*. With newspaper in hand, he walked into the main part of the lobby and took a seat where he could keep an eye on both the front door and the front desk. What he planned to do was wait for his quarry to come to him.

"Medicine in Hong Kong is an interesting mix," Dr. Myron Pao said. "I was trained in London, so obviously I favor Western-style medicine. But

378

I don't ignore the traditional medicine either. Herbalists and acupuncturists have their places."

Marissa and Tristan had found an internist who was on the staff of the hospital and who was happy to show them around. Accustomed to private hospitals in Boston, Marissa was amazed by the conditions in the Queen Elizabeth Hospital but impressed by the productivity. The number of patients seen in the clinics and treated on the wards was astonishing. Dr. Pao explained that Chinese families handled much of the patients' personal care themselves.

"What about tuberculosis?" Marissa asked. "Is that much of a problem here in Hong Kong?"

"Everything is relative," Dr. Pao said. "We see an average of about eight thousand new cases of TB each year. But that's with a population of about five and a half million. Considering the crowded living conditions, I don't think that is alarming. I'm sure that one of the reasons we don't see more is because we vaccinate children with BCG. Contrary to your experience in North America, we find BCG quite effective."

"Has there been much of an increase in the incidence of TB over recent years?" Marissa asked.

"There was when boat people from Vietnam, Cambodia, and Laos first arrived," Dr. Pao said. "But currently that is being contained in the Lantau Island compounds."

"What about TB salpingitis?" Marissa asked.

"I haven't seen anything like that," Dr. Pao said.

"None?" Marissa asked. She wanted to be sure.

"Not that I know of," Dr. Pao said.

"What about in the People's Republic of China?" Marissa asked. "Do you know what their experience is with TB?"

"They have a bit more than here," Dr. Pao said. "Respiratory problems in general have a high incidence in the PRC. But they also use BCG extensively with equal success."

"So there's no big problem?" Marissa asked. "No recent upswing, anything like that?"

"Not that I know of," Dr. Pao said. "And I'd have heard. We have a significant amount of communication with the PRC on medical matters, particularly with Guangzhou."

Marissa was at a loss.

"Do you know anything about the Wing Sin Triad?" Tristan asked.

"That's a dangerous question in Hong Kong," Dr. Pao said. "I know they exist, but that's about all."

"Would you know how to contact them?" Tristan asked.

"Definitely not," Dr. Pao said.

"One other question," Marissa said. She was beginning to feel they were taking too much of the doctor's time. "Can you think of any reason for mainland Chinese to go to Australia to learn in-vitro fertilization techniques or, on the other hand, if they could at all contribute to in-vitro?"

Dr. Pao thought for a moment, then shook his head. "I certainly can't," he said. "The problem the Chinese medical authorities face is how to prevent conception, not promote it."

"That was my feeling as well," Marissa said. "Thanks for your time."

Together, Marissa and Tristan walked out of the bustling hospital.

Marissa shook her head dejectedly. "That was a waste of everybody's time, especially Dr. Pao's. Did you see the list of patients he's scheduled to see today?"

Tristan held one of the main entrance doors open for her to pass. "Sometimes negative results are as important as positive ones," he said, taking her arm. "Don't be so hard on yourself. Coming here was a good idea."

"What are we going to do now?" Marissa asked as they walked toward their limo. From the hospital grounds they could hear the dull roar of the city as it throbbed in the background.

"We'll ask Freddie," Tristan said. He looked at her dark brown eyes and smiled. "Then we'll know if that thriller you read in the past had the real lowdown."

When they arrived at the car, their driver jumped out of the driver's seat and opened the rear door. Marissa had one foot inside the car when Tristan pulled her back. He had realized the driver wasn't Freddie anymore. At almost the same time Marissa spotted a second Chinese stranger sitting in the backseat.

"Where is our other driver?" Tristan asked. The man holding the door was younger, lighter, and wearing a dark blue business suit, not a chauffeur's uniform.

"Please, but the other driver had another engagement," he said.

"Isn't that a bit irregular?" Tristan asked.

"Not at all," the man said. "It happens frequently when customers request particular drivers."

"There's a man in the car," Marissa said.

Tristan bent over to look.

"Please get in the car," the man holding the door said.

"Tristan!" Marissa exclaimed with a gasp. "He has a gun."

Tristan straightened up. Glancing down, he saw a snubnosed revolver in the man's hand. The man held it close to his side, pointing it at Tristan's belly.

"What is this, mate, some sort of joke?" Tristan asked, slightly shifting his feet.

"Please get in . . ." the man repeated. But he was cut short by Tristan's blow first to the side of his neck, then to his wrist. With the second blow, the man's gun clanked against the pavement. A spinning kick to the man's chest hurled him against the car, slamming the door in the process.

Tristan grabbed Marissa's hand and yanked her through low bushes that bordered a small patch of grass. On the other side of the grass was the street with its usual complement of traffic and pedestrians. Hazarding a look back, Tristan saw that another man had joined the two that had been in their limo, and now all three were coming after them.

Tristan had hoped that as soon as they got to a city street, they could merely melt into the crowd. But unfortunately this wasn't the case. They hadn't gotten enough of a head start. The men could still see them. All they could do was keep running.

They ran west into the Yaw Ma Tei section of Kowloon, desperately looking for one of the policemen they'd seen on motorbikes when they had been driving earlier. They would have settled for a traffic cop, but none were to be found.

The crowds of Chinese pedestrians parted as they ran. They seemed curious but not willing to become involved.

Tristan and Marissa came to a wide thoroughfare totally jammed with double-decker buses and stalled traffic. Even the bicycles had been forced to a standstill, making crossing the road difficult. Reaching the other side, they could see that the width of the road was all that separated them from their pursuers.

Once they were in the heart of the Yaw Ma Tei district, the congestion got worse still. Without meaning to, Marissa and Tristan turned into a market street with hundreds of canopied stalls loaded with herbs, clothes, fish, kitchenware, fruits, sweets, and other foods. In their haste, they collided with shoppers and even some of the vendors.

Despite her fear, Marissa began to falter. The hormones and her added weight made running a strain. Unintentionally she began to pull against Tristan's hand.

"Come on!" he urged when he realized she was falling behind.

"I can't!" she cried through gasps.

Tristan knew she wouldn't be able to keep up with him much longer. What they needed was a place to hide. Tristan veered between several stalls, frantically searching. There seemed no place to go. The space between the line of stalls and apartment blocks was filled with discarded produce rotting in the sun. Cats foraged in the gutter for whatever they could find. There were no open doorways. Everything was shut tight. Even the windows on the ground floor were tightly shuttered. Then Tristan noticed a small side street about half a block away.

"Come on," he urged. "Just a little further."

Reaching the street, they turned into it. It was so narrow only one car could drive down it at a time. They passed an open-air shop with a row of skinned ducks hanging by their necks. Next door to that was a shop that sold edible insects and then another that sold snakes.

Separated from the general din of the market street with its clamor of car horns, jackhammers, and spirited bargaining, the side street was comparatively quiet. The main sounds came from hidden radios and from the click of Mah-Jongg tiles. Elderly Chinese were busy playing the game on wooden tables. As Marissa and Tristan dashed by, the elders gave them a cursory glance before going back to their gambling.

"Who are these people chasing us?" Marissa managed between labored breaths. "What's going on? Why are they after us?"

"I have no clue," Tristan said, equally as winded. "But I'm quickly learning to dislike Hong Kong. Swimming in croc-infested rivers in the Northern Territories is healthier, I'm convinced. I've always had a dislike for guns." Nervously, Tristan glanced over his shoulder. He was relieved to see no one was following them down the narrow street.

"I've got to sit down for a moment," Marissa said. With all her infertility treatments and little or no exercise, she wasn't in shape for this kind of exertion. Just ahead there was a tea shop with gleaming pots hanging above a beaded doorway. She pointed. "How about something to drink?"

After another look behind them, Tristan reluctantly agreed.

The tea shop occupied a windowless room that looked more like a storeroom than a public space. The tables were worn, unfinished wood. A handful of customers were seated at several. In the usual Chinese tradition, they spoke at a level just below a shout. Combining the loud conversation with the *de rigueur* Chinese music blaring from a tiny Panasonic, the atmosphere was hardly restful.

Even so, Marissa was pleased to sit down. Her legs ached and she had a pain in her side.

The proprietor eyed them suspiciously. He walked over to them and addressed them in guttural Chinese.

"Sorry, mate," Tristan said. "Don't speak Chinese. How about a cuppa tea. Any kind. You choose."

The man looked at Tristan without comprehension. Tristan mimed tea drinking, then pointed to the other customers. Apparently understanding, the man disappeared through a back doorway covered with strings of beads matching those that hung in the entrance from the street.

"Convenient there were no police around," Marissa said sarcastically, her chest still heaving. "We've been in Hong Kong for less than twenty-four hours and we've had to run for our lives twice. Neither time have we seen a single policeman."

"I warned you that this trip wouldn't be a proper holiday," Tristan said.

"Should we go to the police now?" Marissa asked.

"I don't know what we'd tell them," Tristan said. "Besides, they certainly wouldn't be apt to help us find the Wing Sin."

"Maybe we're in over our heads," Marissa said.

"That's obvious." Tristan turned around and looked for the proprietor. "Where in blazes is our tea?"

Marissa wasn't concerned. She didn't care about the tea particularly.

Tristan stood up. "Hong Kong is a place of extremes," he said. "Orders come instantly or take forever." He walked toward the curtain the proprietor had disappeared through. Parting the beads he looked within. Then he returned to the table and sat down.

"There's a bevy of scraggly old guys in there smoking pipes," he said. "I think we've stumbled onto one of the old-fashioned opium dens the authorities tolerate for the sake of a handful of aged addicts. Opium is one of the grimiest and most despicable legacies of British colonial history, yet it provided the basis for the founding of Hong Kong."

"Should we go?" Marissa asked. At the moment she wasn't interested in history.

"Whenever you're ready."

"How are we going to get out of here?" Marissa asked.

"We'll skirt around through these back streets," Tristan said. "When we get to that large thoroughfare we ran across, we'll snag a taxi."

"Let's do it," Marissa said. "The sooner I get back to the hotel the better I'll feel."

Tristan pulled the table back for Marissa to stand. Getting to her feet, she stretched each of her aching legs, then walked stiff-legged to the door and ducked through the beads. When Tristan did the same he bumped into her. Marissa was frozen. Directly in front of the tea house was a black limousine.

The three men in dark blue suits who had been

chasing them earlier were casually lounging around the car in various states of repose. Spotting Tristan and Marissa, the man near the front of the car straightened up. Marissa recognized him as the one who'd posed as Freddie. His snub-nosed revolver wasn't in evidence. Instead, he had a more serious-looking machine pistol dangling at his side.

Tristan grabbed Marissa's wrist and turned back into the restaurant only to see its heavy wooden door slam shut in his face. He was about to try to force it open when he heard the locks on the other side slide into place.

With resignation, Tristan turned back to the street.

"Please," the man with the machine pistol said. He motioned toward the back of the car. Tristan saw a large tear at the elbow of the man's suit. He guessed it happened when he'd knocked him down.

At first neither Tristan nor Marissa moved. But the man with the gun would no longer tolerate delay. A short burst of fire from his machine pistol against the pavement was a forceful persuader. Bullets ricocheted haphazardly down the street, forcing the Mah-Jongg players to dive for cover. This was a man who could be casual about killing.

After that display, Marissa and Tristan complied with his wish. They approached the car's rear door, but the man with the gun shook his head. With his gun, he motioned toward the back of the car. One of the other men unlocked the trunk and lifted the hood.

"You want us in the boot?" Tristan asked.

"Please," the man with the gun said.

"This should be cozy," Tristan said as he climbed into the small space and curled up. Marissa hesitated, but followed suit, curling up against Tristan.

Then the hood was slammed, plunging them into complete darkness.

"First time I've ever embraced a woman in a boot," Tristan said. His right arm was draped around Marissa's body.

"Can't you be serious for once?" Marissa said.

"Kind of like a couple of kippered herrings in a tin," Tristan said. They heard the car engine start, then they lurched forward as the limo proceeded down the narrow alley.

"The expression is 'sardines in a can,'" Marissa said.

"Not where I grew up," Tristan said.

"Tris, I'm scared," Marissa said, fighting tears. "What if we suffocate in here? I've always been terrified of tight places."

"Close your eyes," Tristan suggested. "That will help a bit. Just breathe normally. Smothering's not our worry. It's where they're taking us."

To help mitigate Marissa's claustrophobia, Tristan chatted on about anything he could think of.

After innumerable turns, starts, and stops, the

car came to a final halt and the engine cut off. Marissa and Tristan could hear the car doors open and close. A few seconds later, the trunk was unlocked and the hood was raised.

The same three men were staring down at them.

"Out of the car, please," the man with the gun said.

A bedraggled Marissa climbed from the trunk, followed by Tristan. They were inside a huge warehouse piled high with seagoing containers.

"Move," the man with the gun said. He pointed to a space between two containers.

Tristan put his arm around Marissa. With shared terror, they walked together in the direction indicated, worrying what was about to happen. Beyond the containers was a closed door. They stopped, waiting for further instructions. One of their abductors opened the door and motioned them inside.

Entering through the door, Marissa and Tristan found themselves in a long hallway. Following unspoken commands, they walked to the end of the corridor before being stopped before a blank door. One of the men knocked. From within someone replied in Chinese, and the door was opened.

Marissa and Tristan were pushed inside.

The room looked like an office, complete with a desk, file cabinets, office equipment, bulletin boards, and huge calendars with photographs of oceangoing vessels. At the desk was a Chinese man somewhat older than the three who had abducted

Marissa and Tristan. He was immaculately dressed in a white silk suit with gold cuff links and tietack. His coal-black hair was brushed back from his forehead and held in place with lacquer-like hair spray. Another Chinese man in a gray business suit stood at his side.

As Marissa and Tristan were nudged before the desk, the man in the white suit leaned back, putting his hands behind his head. He studied Marissa and Tristan from head to toe. Then he rocked forward, propping his elbows on a large ledger open on his desk.

The man spoke in rapid Chinese. Immediately several of the men in the blue suits stepped forward and searched Marissa and Tristan. They removed their wallets and watches and put them on the desk. Then they stepped back.

As if he had all the time in the world, the man in the white suit lit a cigarette. He clamped it between his teeth like a cigar. Cocking his head to the side to keep the smoke from his eyes, he picked up the wallets and went through them, looking at pictures and credit cards. What money was there he removed and put on the desk. Then he looked up at Marissa and Tristan.

"We are curious as to why you have been asking about the Wing Sin," he said in perfect English with an English public school accent. "Triads are against the law in Hong Kong. It is dangerous to talk about them."

"We are doctors," Marissa said before Tristan

could respond. "All we are interested in is information. We are trying to investigate a disease."

"A disease?" the man asked with disbelief.

"Tuberculosis," Marissa said. "We're trying to follow the trail of a certain type of infection of tuberculosis that has been showing up in the United States, Europe, and Australia."

The man in the white suit laughed. "What is this?" he questioned. "Triads are now being looked to for medical knowledge? What an irony! Politicians have been calling the triads a disease for years."

"We're not after medical knowledge from the Wing Sin," Tristan said. "Just information about illegal aliens that the Wing Sin has been bringing out of the People's Republic of China for an Australian company called Female Care Australia or Fertility, Limited."

The man in the white suit eyed both foreigners. "The astonishing thing about this conversation is that I believe you," he said with another, less humorous laugh. "What you are saying is so preposterous, no one would be capable of making it up. Of course, true or not, it does not absolve you from the dangers inherent in talking about the Wing Sin in public."

"We're willing to pay for information," Tristan said.

"Oh!" the man in the white suit said. He smiled as did his henchmen. "You Australians have a commendable way of striking to the heart of a matter. And since everything in Hong Kong is for sale, perhaps we might be able to do business. In fact, if you were to offer something small like ten thousand dollars Hong Kong, I'd be willing to make a few inquiries and see what I could find out for you. No guarantees, of course."

"How about five thousand," Tristan countered.

The man in the white suit laughed again. "I admire your courage," he said. "But you are not in a bargaining position. Ten thousand."

"All right," Tristan said. "When do we get our information?"

"Meet me at the top of Victoria Peak at ten tomorrow morning," the man in the white suit said. "Be sure to take the tram."

"Fine," Tristan said. He stepped forward and reached for Marissa's and his wallets and watches.

The man at the desk deflected Tristan's hand. Then he picked up the wallets and handed them to him. "The money and the watches, unfortunately, we'll have to keep," he said. "I'm sorry, but it is a bit of booty for my men for bringing you to me. The money we can consider as down payment for the ten thousand dollars." He then shuffled through the cash and pulled out a single ten-dollar bill. He handed that to Tristan. "For travel expenses from the dropoff point."

Tristan took the bill. "Thanks, mate, kind of you. But tell me, are you a member of the Wing Sin?"

"Knowing you are unfamiliar with civilized behavior coming, as you do, from Australia, I will forgive you for asking such a question. I should also like to warn you to avoid the police between now and our meeting. You will be watched. I will see you tomorrow with the money."

With a mere wave of his hand, the three men in suits came forward and escorted Marissa and Tristan out of the room. As they excited, the man in the white suit went back to his ledger book.

"Friendly bloke," Tristan commented with obvious sarcasm as they marched down the long corridor and out into the warehouse. At the car they paused.

"Not in the boot again, mate!" Tristan said as one of the men raised the trunk hood.

In the same position as they'd arrived but with a bit less apprehension, Marissa and Tristan were motored out of the warehouse. "I could learn to like this mode of transport," Tristan said, snuggling up closer against Marissa.

"Tris!" Marissa said. "Come on. Talk to me like you did before. It took my mind off being shut in here."

"Well, for one thing," Tristan said, "it's obvious why they put us back in here. They don't want us to know where this warehouse is located."

"Tell me more about your childhood," Marissa said.

After clearing his throat, Tristan obliged her.

The second trip was much shorter than the first. In fact, when the trunk hood was raised they were surprised, not only because so little time had passed, but also because the motor of the sedan was still running.

Getting out into the harsh sunlight, Marissa and Tristan squinted as they tried to get their bearings. They were on a city street in front of the Mong Kok entrance to the Hong Kong subway. A few pedestrians stopped and gawked at them momentarily, but then moved on. It was enough to make Marissa wonder if it was common to see people climbing out of the trunk of a car in Hong Kong.

The men in the blue suits did not say a word. They calmly got back into the car and drove off.

"So much for an interesting morning," Tristan said. "How about going back to the hotel?"

"Please!" Marissa said. "I'm a nervous wreck. I don't know how you can be so calm. Feel me, I'm shaking." Marissa put her hand on Tristan's forearm.

"You are shaking!" Tristan said. "I'm sorry for putting you through all this, but at least we've now made contact. Maybe things will go better from now on. Provided, of course, that you want to go on."

"I think so," Marissa said. She didn't sound certain. "But I don't think I could handle another chase."

They descended into the MTR. They were pleased to find it clean and bright. The ride to the Tsim Sha Tsui station was rapid, comfortable, and—better still—uneventful.

From the MTR station it was only a short walk back to the hotel. Passing one of the many jewelry stores along the way, Marissa jokingly mentioned that they needed new watches again.

"If this keeps up," Tristan said, "keeping us in watches will be the dearest part of the whole trip."

Stopping at a traffic light, Tristan took Marissa's arm and leaned over to talk into her ear. "I hate to alarm you again, but I think we are being followed. There are two men behind us, dressed like the ones who chased us. They've been with us since the underground."

"Oh, no!" she said. "What should we do? I'm not running. I can't."

Tristan straightened up. "Relax!" he said. "We're not running; in fact, we're not going to do anything. The man in the white suit told us we'd be watched. These men behind us are probably his men. I suppose the only thing we shouldn't do is talk to any policemen."

Marissa's eyes roamed the busy intersection. In contrast to all their prior experience, there were now plenty of policemen. In their smart blue uniforms, they confidently patrolled the streets. "Where were these guys when we needed them?" Marissa asked.

"This is a tourist area," Tristan explained.

Reaching the hotel, they paused as the doorman graciously bowed and pulled the door open for them. "I want to stop at the front desk," Tristan said as they entered. "I've got to get more money out of the safe deposit box. I'd also like to go over and give that concierge a king hit. I have a feeling he's the one who tipped off the triad. And to think he took my twenty dollars to boot."

"Don't cause any scenes," Marissa said, taking

his arm to press her point. Knowing Tristan, she wouldn't have been surprised if he'd walked over and slugged the man.

Together they stepped up to the marble-topped counter. While Tristan vied for the attention of one of the hotel staff, Marissa's gaze roamed around the lobby. As usual, it was crowded. High tea in the elegant lobby had been a tradition at the Peninsula for over half a century. Jeweled women and men dressed to the nines were seated at cloth-covered tables. Waiters with white gloves scurried back and forth from the kitchen. Trolleys of confections and pastries were wheeled through the elegant set. Classical piano music provided the ultimate touch.

Suddenly Marissa's grip on Tristan's arm tightened enough for him to wince. "Tristan!" Marissa gasped. "There is a man coming this way. A man that I think I recognize."

Marissa's eyes had originally passed over this man as just another face in the crowd. But then her mind had forced her eyes back to look at him more closely. There was something about his face and the way he wore his coal-black hair that had jogged her memory. She'd watched him put down his paper and stand up. She'd seen him look at her and then start across the room. She'd seen his hand go inside his jacket. That had been when she'd gripped Tristan's arm.

"Who's that, luv?" Tristan asked.

"He's headed our way," Marissa whispered. "The Chinese man in the gray suit. I've seen him before. I think he's the man who threw the chum in the water when Wendy died!"

Tristan's eyes swept the lobby. There were so many people. But he quickly picked out the Chinese man elbowing his way through the milling crowd. His right hand was thrust into his jacket. He appeared to be holding something.

Tristan sensed danger was at hand. There was something volatile in the way the man was approaching them. Tristan felt he had to do something. There was no time to flee, especially with the crowds pressing in on them. Behind him he could hear the assistant hotel manager calling his name. The Chinese man was only ten feet away. He was almost on them. He seemed to be smiling. The hand in his jacket started to move. Tristan saw a glint of metal.

With a high-pitched yell, Tristan pushed off the hotel desk and tackled the man. In the last instant before he made contact, Tristan saw the gun coming from beneath the man's lapel, but Tristan collided with the man before he had pulled the gun free. The force of Tristan's momentum carried them both backward to slam into a large round marble-topped table. The table tipped over, sending china and cakes flying in every direction. The eight people who'd been seated at the table were hurled to the floor.

In an instant, panic spread. What had moments ago been a scene of utter decorum now gave way to pandemonium. People scattered, some screaming, others simply running for cover.

Tristan was only interested in the gun. As he and the Chinese man rolled off the upended table, Tristan managed to grab the man's wrist. The gun fired, sending a shot into the gilded ceiling.

Attempting to use a kung fu move, Tristan was shocked to find himself thwarted, his opponent as fast and as practiced as he. Giving up on martial arts, Tristan bit the man's arm. Only then did the gun clatter to the floor.

But biting the man caused Tristan to lose his position. The stranger took full advantage, flipping Tristan over his shoulder. Tristan cushioned himself as best he could as he crashed to the floor with a thud. As soon as he hit, he rolled to avoid being kicked. Then he bounced to his feet, assuming a crouched position. But before he could move he felt himself seized from behind by several other men.

In front of him, Tristan saw the Chinese man back away. Another man tried to restrain him, but the Chinese executed a perfect kung fu move, sending the interloper to the floor with a crushing kick to the chest. The Chinese man made a run for the front door, darting through panicked hotel guests. Once outside, he melted instantly into the large crowd that had formed in front of the hotel.

Tristan did not struggle against the men holding him. Having noticed the small radio transmitters on their belts and earpieces in their ears, he was confident they were hotel security people.

Marissa ran over and demanded that Tristan be released. She even started to tug on the house detectives' arms when they ignored her. But the assistant manager had an immediate effect. Having witnessed the whole episode, he had Tristan immediately released.

Marissa threw her arms around Tristan's neck, and pressed herself against him. "Are you all right? Are you hurt?"

"Just my pride," Tristan said. "The bloke was better at kung fu than I was."

"Should we have you see the house doctor?" the assistant manager asked.

"Don't bother," Tristan said, motioning toward Marissa. "This is all the treatment I need." Marissa was still holding him tight with her head buried against his chest.

"How did you know the man was armed?" the assistant manager asked.

"Just an Aussie's sixth sense," Tristan said.

"The hotel owes you something for your bravery," the assistant manager said. "Undoubtedly that man was planning on a robbery of some sort."

"A liquid reward wouldn't be refused," Tristan said. "Do you people have any Foster's?" He put his arms around Marissa and squeezed her back.

Once he got out of the hotel, Willy turned right and slowed his pace to a rapid walk. He didn't want to draw attention to himself by running. His desired destination was the crowded Star Ferry terminal. When he reached it, he was relieved to lose himself in the throng. Hundreds of people

400

were milling about waiting for the next ferry, which was just then nosing into the pier.

After the Kowloon-bound passengers were allowed to disembark, those waiting were allowed to board. Willy let himself be swept along by the human tide.

He remained on the lower deck with the majority of the people. He stayed close to a large family, as if he were a member. No one seemed to think twice about his presence. After the short ten-minute trip, Willy disembarked and walked up toward the Mandarin Hotel.

The Mandarin was in the same category as the Peninsula. He knew he'd have no difficulty making an overseas call from there. The problem wasn't making the call, but rather that it would be so unpleasant. It was Willy's first major failure, and he wasn't pleased.

Before he entered the Mandarin Hotel, he took advantage of his reflection in a store window to straighten his clothes and comb his hair. Once he felt he looked presentable, he went into the lobby. Downstairs, in a room just outside the men's room, he found a bank of telephones affording some privacy. Taking a deep breath, he rang Charles Lester.

"The Blumenthal woman is here," Willy said as soon as he had Lester on the phone.

"I know," Lester said. "Ned found out through emigration. She took a flight from Brisbane."

"I tried to have a conference with the interested parties a few minutes ago," Willy said, using their

401

established patois in case they were overheard. "But things went badly. I failed. The Williams fellow was uncooperative and actively canceled the meeting before I could use my material."

Willy held the phone away from his ear as a string of Australian expletives sizzled over the line. Once he heard Lester revert to a more normal pitch, he put the phone back to his ear.

"The situation keeps getting worse and worse," Lester complained.

"It will be much harder to have a conference now," Willy admitted. "Everyone will expect us. But if you would like, I'll do my best to arrange another meeting."

"No!" Lester said. "I'll have Ned come and have the meeting. He has more practice. All I want you to do is make sure that these customers don't get away. Watch the hotel. If they change hotels, follow them. It would only exacerbate the problem if we lose contact with the Blumenthal woman in Hong Kong."

"I also lost the material I was going to show them," Willy said. "It was left at the conference site."

"Then you'll have to get some more," Lester said. "Was what you had adequate?"

"It was perfect," Willy said. "Absolutely perfect."

The Royal Hong Kong police inspector was what Tristan called a "bloody pom" when he described him to Marissa later on. He even looked British

402

with his gray skin tones and his baggy English suit, complete with a vest and fob. He and Tristan were sitting in the manager's office of the Peninsula Hotel.

"Let us go over this again," the inspector said in his clipped English accent. "You'd just handed over your safe deposit key when you became aware of this gentleman of Oriental appearance approaching you."

"That's right, mate," Tristan said. He knew his jocular Australian phraseology would grate on the inspector's nerves. It was purposeful torture. The police inspector had been grating on him for almost two hours.

Tristan tried to be patient. He knew that the reason the inspector was making a fuss over the incident was because the police didn't like to have trouble in an area so crucial to tourism, particularly tourism in a place as posh as the Peninsula Hotel.

". . . At that point you turned around and saw the man coming at you," the inspector continued.

"That's right," Tristan said. It was the twentieth time they'd gone over this.

"How did you know he was approaching you rather than someone else?" the inspector asked.

"He was looking directly at me," Tristan said. "Giving me the evil eye." Tristan glowered at the inspector in mock imitation.

"Yes, of course," the inspector said. "But you had never seen this man before?"

"Never!" Tristan said with emphasis. He knew

this was the point of particular interest to the police. But Tristan had not been willing to divulge that it had been Marissa who had recognized the man. As long as the police failed to question Marissa, they'd never find out. Tristan didn't want to admit to everything he knew, fearing that if he did so, the meeting with the Wing Sin the following morning would be compromised.

Finally, after two hours, the inspector gave up, but he concluded by saying that he might want to question Tristan further and that Tristan should stay in Hong Kong until further notice. Immediately upon his release Tristan went to the house phone and called Marissa.

"I'm free at last," he said. "Let's celebrate by going out and replacing our watches!"

They went back to the same jewelry store where they'd gotten the first replacements. The second time around, Tristan insisted on an even better deal than before. After a brief protest, the clerk obliged.

Returning to their rooms, they locked themselves in. They decided to stay in for the remainder of the day. Not having eaten since breakfast, the first thing they did was order food.

While they waited for room service they sat by the window in front of the spectacular view.

"Hong Kong's beauty reminds me of the Great Barrier Reef," Marissa said, gazing out the window. "Its splendor masks its violent eat-or-be-eaten core."

Tristan nodded. "As the man in the white suit said, everything is for sale. Everything!"

"Do you think he'll still show?" Marissa asked. "I wonder if the Wing Sin will learn of your two hours with the police?"

"I don't know," Tristan said. "But you can bet that episode in the lobby will make the newspapers. So he'll read about it and at least we'll have an excuse."

Marissa sighed. "What an experience Hong Kong has been. I know you warned me, but I could never have imagined what we've had to go through. I'm a nervous wreck. I'm afraid to leave the hotel. Heck, I'm afraid to go down to the lobby. Just getting these new watches was an ordeal. I kept expecting something dreadful to happen."

"I know how you feel," Tristan said. "Remember, we can always just leave. We don't have to see this through."

"I suppose we could," Marissa said halfheartedly.

For a few minutes Marissa and Tristan watched the harbor in silence.

"I think I want to keep going," Marissa said at last. She straightened up in her seat. "As much as all this terrifies me, I can't give up, not now. I'd never be able to live with myself. I can't help but feel we're close to figuring it all out. Besides, every time I close my eyes, I see Wendy."

"And I see my wife," Tristan said. "I know I'm not supposed to say this, but being with you reminds me of her. Please don't take offense; I'm not making conscious comparisons. It's not that you look like her or even act like her. It's something else, something about the way you make me feel." Tristan surprised himself. It wasn't like him to be so up front about how he was feeling.

Marissa gazed into Tristan's blue eyes. She could only imagine the anguish the man must have suffered when his wife died. "I won't take offense," she said. "In fact, I'll take it as a compliment."

"It was meant as one," Tristan said. Then he smiled self-consciously and looked away toward the door. "Where the devil is that food? I'm famished."

During their meal, they remembered Freddie, the limo driver. They wondered what had happened to him. They hoped he was all right. They couldn't believe that he was complicit in their kidnapping, but then again, in Hong Kong everything had its price.

"Talking about Freddie reminds me," Tristan said. "If we're going to persist in this, I think we should hire another car and get a driver who could double as a bodyguard."

"And who speaks Cantonese," Marissa added. "There've already been several times when that would have been helpful."

"Maybe if we're lucky he'll let us ride in the trunk," Tristan teased.

Marissa smiled. How Tristan could keep his sense of humor through all this was beyond her.

After they finished their meal, they pushed the table aside and returned to the chairs by the window. Marissa sipped the remains of her wine while Tristan enjoyed another can of Foster's Lager the hotel had managed to find for him.

Marissa's thoughts had drifted back to the incident in the lobby. "If that Chinese man downstairs was the same one who threw the chum in the water back in Australia, then he must be in the employ of Female Care Australia."

"That's what I assumed," Tristan said.

"They must really want us out of the way. They must be desperate, especially to try to shoot us in public like that. With Wendy they went to great pains to make it look like an accident."

"The irony is they must think we know more than we do," Tristan said. "If I were they and I knew how little we know, I wouldn't bother with us."

"Maybe they're not as afraid of what we know as what we could find out," Marissa sighed. "I wonder how he tracked us down."

"That's another good question," Tristan said.

"Maybe we should change hotels."

"I don't think it would make much difference," Tristan said. "This city seems to have an information underground. Take the proprietor of that tea shop, for instance; obviously he let the Wing Sin know we were there. I bet that if we change hotels, it wouldn't remain a secret, not for long. At least here the security people are on the alert and will recognize the fellow who tried to attack us if he tries to come back."

"And we'll have to be very careful," Marissa said, "especially tomorrow morning when we rendezvous with the man in the white suit."

"My thoughts exactly," Tristan said. "I think we can assume that his loyalty will lie with whoever pays him the most squeeze. We might have to take more than the agreed-upon ten thousand Hong Kong."

"Can you afford this, Tris?" Marissa asked.

Tristan laughed. "It's only money," he said.

15

APRIL 19, 1990
8:47 AM

DRESSED IN his Sunday best and carrying a bouquet of flowers, Ned Kelly walked along Salisbury Road taking in the sights. He'd been to Hong Kong on a number of occasions. As always, he enjoyed the colorful scenery. He'd gotten in late the night before and had stayed at the Regent Hotel, thanks to Charles Lester. Ned had never stayed in such luxurious accommodations. His only regret was that he'd arrived so late, he'd not been able to take advantage of any of the sizzling nightlife the Tsim Sha Tsui had to offer.

As he approached the Peninsula Hotel, he began

to look in the parked cars for Willy Tong. That had been the instructions. He found him sitting in a green Nissan Stanza parked in front of the Space Museum directly across from the hotel. Ned opened the passenger door and slid in on the front seat.

"You look smashing, mate," Willy said. "The flowers for me?"

"I do look good, don't I?" Ned said, pleased with his Harris tweed jacket, gabardine slacks, and brown loafers. He laid the flowers on the back-seat. "What's the lay of the land?"

"It's been quiet since the uproar I caused," Willy said. "I don't know what could have happened. It was a perfect setup. The lobby was crowded just the way you told me was best. I was no more than two or three paces away from Williams when he whirled and attacked me!"

"Bad luck!" Ned said. "Was the woman there?"

"Of course," Willy said. "She was standing right next to him. In another ten seconds I'd have shot both of them."

"Maybe she recognized you from the boat," Ned said. "Anyway, it doesn't matter. They still in the hotel?"

"Yes," Willy said. "I've been here most of the night. I tried calling again and was immediately put through. They haven't moved."

"That's nice," Ned said. "What about the gun?"

"I got it," Willy said. He leaned in front of Ned

and snapped open the glove compartment. He took a handgun out and handed it buttfirst to Ned.

Ned whistled. "A Heckler and Koch!" he said. "My, my, this is first class. What about the silencer?"

Willy reached back into the glove compartment and handed Ned a small rectangular box. Ned opened the box and unwrapped the silencer.

"There's something nice about using new equipment," Ned said. "One thing about FCA. They go first class on everything." Ned screwed the silencer into the pistol. It lengthened the barrel by a third. Then he snapped out the magazine and checked the shells. After making sure the chamber was empty, Ned cocked the gun and pulled the trigger. It had a nice, full-bodied click. "Perfect," he said.

Replacing the clip and ramming it home, Ned cocked the pistol. It was ready for action.

Twisting in his seat, he eyed Willy. "This is not going to take long. I want you to pull the car over there in front of the hotel and have the engine running. Give me about five minutes before you come over, understand?"

"Righto," Willy said eagerly.

"I'm off," Ned said. He moved forward on the seat and slipped the gun into his belt at the small of his back. Reaching into the backseat, he lifted the bouquet. Then he got out of the car. Hesitating before he crossed the road, he leaned into the car through the open window.

"I haven't seen this Williams fellow for several years," Ned said. "Will I recognize him?"

"I think so," Willy said. "He's about your height, sandy blond hair, angular features. Looks more like a stockman than an MD."

"Got it," Ned said. He was about to leave when Willy caught his attention.

"You won't have any trouble recognizing the woman, will you?" Willy asked.

"Especially not if she's in her bathers," Ned said with a wink.

Ned dodged the traffic on Salisbury Road, mindful of the gun tucked in his belt. He didn't want to dislodge it.

At the Peninsula, the doorman opened the door for him, and he entered the lobby.

At that time of the morning, the lobby was relatively busy with international travelers checking in or checking out. Luggage was piled in heaps near the bellman's desk, where the bell captain was struggling to keep order. It was to the bellman's desk that Ned walked.

Ned singled out one of the younger bellboys and approached him as he was piling bags onto a bellman's trolley. Kelly had learned a smattering of Cantonese through his dealings with the Chinese over the years. In Cantonese he asked the young man for a favor. The boy seemed surprised to be addressed by a *gweilo* in his native tongue.

Ned slipped the boy a thousand dollars Hong Kong, more than many months' wages. The boy's eyes widened.

"Some friends are staying here," Ned said. "I want to know their room so that I can surprise them. But I don't want them to know. Understand?"

The boy nodded, then flashed a broad smile.

"The names are Williams and Blumenthal. I don't know if they have separate rooms or a single."

The bellboy nodded again and dashed over to the bell captain's desk. Peering past the captain, who was busy on the phone, the bellboy perused the master guest list. In a flash he returned. Ned had lighted up a cigarette in the interim.

"Pleased to say that it is 604 and 606," the bellboy said with another smile and multiple bows. Ned reached out and stopped him from making a scene. Ned thanked him and walked over to the newsstand. While he leafed through the latest *Time* magazine with the flowers tucked under his arm, he kept his eye on the bell desk to make sure his dealings with the bellboy didn't arouse any suspicions. But they hadn't. The ecstatic bellboy had gone back to loading his cart as if nothing had happened.

Ned replaced the magazine. He switched the flowers to his right hand. With an expert eye, he picked out the hotel security people in the lobby. There were two, but neither one had particularly noticed him.

Walking directly to the elevators, Ned pushed the Up button. Things were going smoothly. So far he was pleased. He anticipated giving Lester a call in about fifteen minutes. He was looking forward to the substantial bonus Lester had promised him for a job well done.

By the time the elevator doors opened on the sixth floor, Ned's pulse was racing. Despite his conscious attempts to keep himself calm, when he got this close to action, he got tense.

Familiar with the customs of Hong Kong luxury hotels, Ned waited by the elevator once he was on the sixth floor. He gave the hall porter a chance to approach from his cubicle. Ned smiled broadly. "Hello, friend," he said in Cantonese.

The hall porter was an elderly Chinese. He smiled weakly, confused as to who this man could be. He wasn't expecting any new guests that morning.

"I have a present for you," Ned said. He handed the man a thousand dollars Hong Kong.

The man's toothless jaw dropped.

Ned smiled again. "I need you to help me for a moment," he said. "I want you to open my sister's door. 604. It's her birthday."

Slipping the bills into his pocket, the hall porter led Ned down the corridor to 604 with a shuffling gait. He was about to knock, but Ned grabbed his arm before his fist hit the door.

"No," Ned said. "It's a surprise."

The porter nodded, then fished in his pocket for his keys. Selecting the proper one, he slipped it into the lock.

As the porter pushed in the key, Ned glanced

up and down the corridor. Then he reached behind his back and extracted the long-barreled gun.

The door opened a crack. The porter started to step aside, but Ned put his hands on the man's back and shoved him forward with as much force as he could muster. The porter's body collided with the partially open door, pushing it open with a bang. The porter sprawled head first on the carpet inside the room.

Instantly, Ned leaped into the room. He dropped the flowers and held the Heckler and Koch in both hands, elbows locked. His quarry was sitting on the bed with light from the window backlighting his sandy blond hair.

From Ned's position, looking down the sights of his automatic pistol, Tristan Williams looked confused as he sprang to his feet. Ned shot him twice in the forehead, just above the eyes. The gun made only a spitting noise. Tristan went backward over the bed. It was easy as pie.

Wheeling around, Ned looked for the Blumenthal woman. She wasn't in the room. Then he noticed the open connecting door. From within, he could hear the sound of water running.

Ned turned and silently closed the door to the hall. Then he pointed the gun at the hall porter, who was frozen with fear on the middle of the carpet. Ned motioned with the gun for the man to move toward the closet.

Ned opened the closet door, then roughly shoved the porter inside. He softly closed the door behind him, then locked it.

414

Moving back to the connecting door, Ned listened. The water was still running. Slowly, he leaned into the room. It was empty, and the bed was stripped of its linens. But the bathroom door was ajar about four inches. Now he could hear the running water more clearly. The Blumenthal woman was filling the tub.

Without a sound, Ned moved across the room to the bathroom door. Sucking in a deep breath, he raised a foot and kicked it open. In an instant, he was inside.

The Blumenthal woman was kneeling by the tub. Her back was to the door. He had surprised her completely. She was beginning to rise to her feet when Ned pumped two bullets into the back of her head. She pitched forward into the tub, overturning a bucketful of soapy water in the process.

Ned looked at the bucket with confusion. Stepping over the soapy water, he grasped the woman by the hair and yanked her head back.

"Damn!" he muttered. It wasn't the Blumenthal woman at all. It was a Chinese cleaning lady.

Ned let go of the woman's hair. She slumped lifelessly back into the tub. He went back to the first room. Going around the bed, he bent down for a closer look at Williams' body. It was tough to get a good look at him, since the body was jammed between the bed and the wall. With some difficulty Ned managed to straighten Williams out. Then he sifted through his pockets and pulled out the man's wallet. Flipping it open, Ned swore aloud. It wasn't Williams! It was a Robert Buchanan! Who the hell was Robert Buchanan?

Ned straightened up. What had happened? Had the bellboy given him the wrong room? he wondered. He gave the room a quick search. In a suitcase at the foot of the bed he found a packet of American Express travelers checks. The name on them was Marissa Blumenthal.

Going to the door to the hallway, Ned put his ear to it and listened. Not hearing anything, he opened the door. The hall was empty. Taking the "Do Not Disturb" sign from its hook, he draped it over the outer doorknob. Then he left, closing the door behind him.

Descending to the ground floor, Ned casually strolled around the lobby. He wandered through the breakfast room and several of the function rooms. Nowhere did he see anyone resembling Williams or Blumenthal. Finally, he gave up and headed for the door.

Just outside the hotel's entrance, Ned found Willy sitting in the Nissan with the motor running. Ned opened the door and got in.

Willy could tell that something was wrong.

"Williams and the woman weren't there," Ned said with irritation. "Are you sure you didn't see them leave the hotel?"

"No way!" Willy said. "And I've been here almost all night. They didn't leave."

Ned stared ahead through the windshield. He shook his head. "Well, they weren't in their rooms. And now I've succeeded in messing things up even worse than you did. I killed the wrong people!"

"Hell!" Willy said. "What are we going to do now?"

Ned shook his head. "One thing that we aren't going to do is collect that bonus. That's the sad part. I suppose we'll have to turn it over to the Wing Sin. Let's go."

"I hate to say this," Marissa said, "but I think I like this watch better than the last one. It's more feminine." Marissa was admiring her Seiko tank-style watch.

"Quite attractive," Tristan agreed. He looked at his own. "Maybe I should have tried a different style. Well, maybe I'll get my chance. We're still in Hong Kong. So far it's been a watch a day."

They inched ahead a few more feet.

"How long is this tunnel?" Marissa asked. She was starting to feel the way she did when they'd been locked in the trunk.

"Beats me," Tristan said. He scooted forward and lowered the glass separating the back compartment from the driver. "Hey, Bentley, how long is this tunnel?"

"A little less than a mile, Mr. Williams," Bentley said.

Tristan settled back. "Did you hear?" he said.

"Unfortunately," Marissa said. "At this rate, it will take an hour just to get over to Hong Kong Island. I've never seen traffic like this."

Marissa and Tristan were in the depths of the

Cross Harbor Tunnel. They'd met up with their new driver that morning after leaving the hotel through the employee entrance. Tristan had thought it wise to leave as surreptitiously as possible.

Bentley had turned out to be just what they'd hoped. Bentley Chang, their new driver, was all muscle and the size of a Sumo wrestler. In the language department, he could have qualified for work at the UN. He spoke the Queen's English in addition to Japanese, Cantonese, Mandarin, and some Hakka and Tanka. He also convinced Tristan that he was knowledgeable in kung fu. He inspired Marissa's confidence with the pistol he carried in a shoulder holster.

His car was equally impressive. It turned out to be an armored Mercedes normally reserved for visiting dignitaries. When Marissa asked Tristan what it cost, he told her not to ask. He'd made the arrangements the night before, calling the limousine company himself instead of using the concierge.

By the time they got to the lower tram station for the run up Victoria Peak, it was nine-thirty.

"And I was hoping we'd be early," Tristan said.

Before they got out of the car, Tristan went over the instructions he'd given Bentley earlier, namely that Bentley was to drive to the peak and watch from a distance. If anything went amiss, Tristan would signal by running his hand through his hair twice. If Bentley saw that, he was to intervene as he saw fit. If everything went off without a hitch,

Bentley would drive down to the dropoff point and wait for Marissa and Tristan to come down in the tram.

"Any questions?" Tristan asked the muscular Bentley.

"Just one," Bentley said. "If you are involved with narcotics, please let me know."

Tristan laughed. "No, we're not involved with drugs of any kind."

"I will be angry if you are not truthful," Bentley said.

"I wouldn't want you to get angry," Tristan assured him.

The ride up in the red tram, which was really a funicular railway, turned out to be a delight. Quickly they left behind the concrete of Central and rose up into wooded slopes filled with bowers of jasmine, wild indigo, daphne, and rhododendrons. Even from the confines of the tram, they could hear magpies singing.

The peak itself turned out to be a disappointment. The morning mist still shrouded the mountaintop, and Marrisa and Tristan could see nothing of the reputed view. The foliage, however, was quite beautiful, particularly the exotic trees still beaded with dew.

Trying to make their presence apparent, Marissa and Tristan circled the Peak Tower a number of times. The tower was a three-story shopping mall with restaurants, an ice cream stand, a drugstore, and even a supermarket. Marissa was intrigued by the stalls that sold Chinese handicrafts.

As they wandered, they kept an eye out for three men who'd abducted them the day before. But they saw no one they recognized except Bentley. He'd arrived as directed. As agreed, he remained unobtrusively in the background. Neither he nor Tristan and Marissa exchanged so much as a nod.

By quarter after eleven, Tristan and Marissa were ready to give up.

"I suppose word of the to-do at the Peninsula got to them," Marissa said.

"Damn," Tristan said. "Now I don't know what to do. We're back to the beginning."

Slowly they ambled back toward the upper tram station, feeling depressed. After such high anticipation, this was quite a letdown.

"Excuse me," an elderly woman said, approaching them. She was wearing a broad-brimmed straw hat with black fringe. She'd been sitting on a bench near the tram entrance. "Are you Mr. Williams?" she asked.

"I am," Tristan said.

"I am to extend apologies from Mr. Yip," she said. "He was unable to make your morning meeting. But if you would please go to the old Stanley Restaurant, he will be happy to see you."

"When?" Tristan asked.

"That is all I know," the woman said. She bowed and hurried off with a shuffling gait.

Tristan looked at Marissa. "What does that mean?"

"I guess the man in the white suit is Mr. Yip."

"But when are we to go to the Stanley Restaurant?" Tristan asked. "And where is it?"

"I would assume we should go directly," Marissa said. "As for where, let's ask Bentley."

They descended in the Peak tram. Bentley was waiting in the armored Mercedes by the time they got down. Marissa and Tristan piled into the backseat. Tristan asked Bentley if he'd ever heard of a restaurant called Stanley's.

"I have indeed, sir," Bentley said.

"Where is it?" Tristan asked.

"Why, it's in Stanley, sir," Bentley said.

Tristan slid back in the seat. "Okay, Bentley," Tristan said. "Let's go to Stanley."

To Marissa's chagrin, the first leg of the trip was through another tunnel that was over two miles long. Until the experience of riding in the trunk of the car, she'd never known she'd disliked tunnels.

Thankfully the traffic moved relatively swiftly; although this Aberdeen Tunnel was longer than the Cross Harbor, the car went through it significantly quicker. When they emerged, the landscape had transformed from the urban sprawl of Kowloon and Central to an almost rural beauty. The beaches were rimmed with bright sand and the water was the emerald green Marissa had seen from the jet on their arrival from Brisbane.

As they motored along the attractive coastline toward Stanley, Tristan slid forward again. "Bentley," he asked, "have you ever heard of a man by the name of Mr. Yip?"

"That is a common Chinese name," Bentley said.

"When we met this Mr. Yip he was wearing a rather distinctive suit," Tristan said. "It was white silk."

Bentley turned to look at Tristan. The car did a little fishtail as he quickly redirected his attention to the road.

"You met a Mr. Yip in a white suit?" Bentley asked.

"Yes," Tristan said. "Is that surprising?"

"There is only one Mr. Yip that I know who wears white suits," Bentley said, "and he is an enforcer."

"You'll have to explain," Tristan said.

"He is a 426," Bentley said. "That means he's a red poll, which is an executioner for a triad. The executioner carries out all the triad's dirty work, no matter the activity: loan-sharking, prostitution, gambling, smuggling, anything like that."

Tristan looked back at Marissa to see if she'd heard what Bentley had to say. She rolled her eyes. She'd heard.

"We are going to the Stanley Restaurant to meet this Mr. Yip," Tristan said.

Bentley braked and pulled over to the side of the road. He put the car in Park and turned off the ignition. Then he turned around to look directly at Tristan. "We have to talk," he said.

For the next fifteen minutes, Tristan and Bentley renegotiated Bentley's hourly rate. Going to a meeting with Mr. Yip was not something covered by his basic fee. Once the deal was settled, Bentley started the car, and they again pulled out into the road.

"Do you know which triad Mr. Yip is with?" Tristan asked.

"I'm not supposed to talk specifically about the triads," Bentley said.

"Okay," Tristan said agreeably. "I'll name the triad I think he's with and you nod. How's that?"

Bentley considered for a moment, then agreed.

"Wing Sin," Tristan said.

Bentley nodded.

Tristan sat back. "Well," he said. "That confirms our suspicions. Obviously Mr. Yip knows what we want to know. The question is whether he plans to tell us or not."

"This whole business has an unnerving way of escalating," Marissa said. "Mr. Yip scared me the first time we met him. Now that I know who he is, I'm even more frightened."

"There's still time to change our minds," Tristan said.

Marissa shook her head. "We've come this far," she said. "I'm not giving up now."

Stanley turned out to be an attractive, modern suburban town built on a peninsula with broad sandy beaches on either side. The vista out over the emerald sea was magnificent. The buildings themselves were less impressive, most being four-story, unimaginative, white concrete affairs.

Bentley pulled into a parking area along the shore line, then nosed the car around so that it was pointing out into the street. He turned off the engine and nodded toward the building to the right. "That's Stanley Restaurant," he said.

Marissa and Tristan inspected the restaurant. From the outside it was as nondescript as the other buildings in the town.

"You ready?" Tristan said.

Marissa nodded. "As ready as I'll ever be."

Bentley got out of the car and opened the rear door. Marissa and Tristan stepped out into the bright sunlight. Before they could take a step, doors opened on a number of other nearby cars, and a half dozen Chinese men got out. They were all dressed in business suits. Marissa and Tristan recognized three of them. They were the men who'd kidnapped them the day before.

At first, Bentley reached for his gun, but he quickly reconsidered. Several of the men had machine pistols in plain sight.

Thinking that her worst fears had materialized, Marissa froze in her tracks. She was amazed at the cool nonchalance the men exhibited in brandishing such firearms in public.

"Please remain where you are," one man said as he strode forward. He reached into Bentley's jacket and withdrew his pistol. Then he spoke to Bentley in Cantonese. Bentley turned and got back into the Mercedes.

Turning his attention to Marissa and Tristan, he frisked them for weapons. Not finding any, he nodded toward the restaurant. Marissa and Tristan started walking.

"Certainly helpful we brought Bentley," Tristan said "Nice to know my money was so well spent."

"They always seem to be a step ahead of us," Marissa said.

The interior of the restaurant was simple but elegant, with antique-style wooden tables and peach-colored walls. Since it was still before twelve, there were no customers. Waiters were arranging the flatware and polishing the crystal.

A French maître d' in a tuxedo welcomed them and was about to ask them if they had a reservation when he recognized their escorts. Immediately he bowed and showed them to a small separate dining room one flight up.

Mr. Yip was sitting at a table. In front of him was his large ledger book as well as a cup of tea. He was dressed as before in a spotless white silk suit.

Their escort spoke to Mr. Yip in Cantonese. Mr. Yip listened while he studied Marissa's and Tristan's faces. When his henchman had finished, he closed his ledger book and leaned forward on it with his elbows. "You have insulted me by bringing an armed guard," he said.

"No insult was intended," Tristan said with an uneasy smile. "We had an unfortunate incident yesterday. Someone tried to kill us."

"Where?" Mr. Yip asked.

"At the Peninsula Hotel," Tristan answered.

Mr. Yip gazed up at the man who'd brought Marissa and Tristan in to see him. The man nodded, apparently confirming the story. Mr. Yip looked back at Marissa and Tristan and shrugged. "Attempted assassinations are not so uncommon," he said. "It's the price of doing certain business in Hong Kong. There have been any number of attempts on my life."

"It is not something we are accustomed to," Marissa said.

"Regardless," Mr. Yip said, "it was a mistake to bring a guard to a meeting with me. Besides, he could not have protected you."

"We are foreigners," Marissa said. "We don't know the rules."

"I will forgive you this time," Mr. Yip said. "Did you bring the money?"

"Too right, mate," Tristan said. "But how about our information first?"

Mr. Yip smiled and shook his head in amazement. "Please, Mr. Williams," he said. "Do not trouble or irritate me any more than you already have. And don't call me 'mate.'"

"Righto," Tristan said. "I suppose our bargaining position is a bit weak." He dug into his pocket and pulled out a hotel envelope in which he'd put ten thousand Hong Kong dollars. He handed it to Mr. Yip. "For your entertainment expenses." He smiled.

Mr. Yip took the envelope. "You are learning our Hong Kong business practices quickly," he said. He tore open the envelope and flipped through the money. Then he slipped the money into his jacket pocket.

"I have learned that the Wing Sin are doing business with an Australian company called Fertility, Limited," Mr. Yip said. "They have been bringing out pairs of Chinese men from the People's Republic for several years, about every two months. The Wing Sin have been arranging transportation from a pickup on the Pearl River north of Zhuhai to Aberdeen. From there they take them to Kai Tac and put them on planes for Brisbane. It has been a comfortable, profitable business relationship: not overwhelmingly so, but it is adequate."

"Who are these men?" Tristan asked.

Mr. Yip shrugged. "I don't know and I don't care. It was the same with the students from Tiananmen Square. We didn't care who they were. We just wanted to be paid for their transport."

"Why are they being smuggled out of the PRC?" Tristan asked.

"No idea," Mr. Yip said. "It is not important for the Wing Sin."

Tristan threw up his hands in frustration. "You haven't told us anything that we didn't know before," he complained.

Marissa shifted uneasily. She was afraid Tristan would irritate the man.

"I agreed to make inquiries," Mr. Yip said. "And indeed I did. Perhaps to mitigate your chagrin I can offer one additional service. Perhaps you would find it beneficial to visit the captain of the junk who does the actual pickup."

Marissa could tell Tristan was livid. She was

terrified he might do something to jeopardize their safety. She hoped he would be interested in Mr. Yip's offer. She knew she was. Maybe the captain could provide the information they were looking for.

Tristan caught her eye. "What do you think?" he asked. "You interested?"

Marissa nodded.

"Okay," Tristan told Mr. Yip. "We'll give it a go. How do we find this captain?"

"He's in Aberdeen," Mr. Yip said. "I'll have one of my business associates show you the way." Mr. Yip then gave their escort instructions in rapid Cantonese.

"I was so afraid you were about to do something silly in there," Marissa said.

"That ratbag cheated us," Tristan said indignantly. "That hoon poofter took our money and gave us a bunch of claptrap."

"Sometimes I wonder if you speak English," Marissa said.

They were back in the armored Mercedes with Bentley at the wheel. They were following a comparably armored Mercedes that was leading them to the captain Mr. Yip had mentioned.

Bentley was quiet, humiliated by the episode in the Stanley Restaurant parking lot.

"This junk captain better have something interesting to say," Tristan warned.

"Or you'll do what?" Marissa questioned. "Get the Wing Sin after us as well as our friend from

Female Care Australia? Please, Tristan, try to remember who we're dealing with."

"I suppose you're right," he said morosely.

As they drove into Aberdeen, both Marissa and Tristan forgot their concerns for the moment. The town was extraordinary. The enormous harbor was choked with thousands of sampans and junks of all sizes lashed together to create an enormous floating slum. In the middle of the squalor were several huge floating restaurants gaudily decorated in crimson and gold.

"How many people live out there on those boats?" Marissa questioned.

"About twenty thousand," Bentley said. "And some of them rarely step onshore. But they are being relocated by the government."

"And no plumbing," Tristan said with disgust. "Probably not a proper dunny in the lot. Can you imagine the E. coli count in the water?"

When they got into the town proper, they saw a number of jewelry stores and banks. Aberdeen, it was clear, was a city of haves and have-nots.

"It's from smuggling," Bentley said in response to a question from Tristan. "Aberdeen was the center of smuggling and piracy long before Hong Kong existed. Of course it wasn't called Aberdeen then."

Near the Ap Lei Chou Bridge, the lead Mercedes pulled over to a sampan dockage. Mr. Yip's henchmen got out. Bentley pulled into a parking area. By the time Marissa, Tristan, and Bentley got to the quay, the man had secured a motorized sampan. The small diesel engine was chugging and sending off puffs of black smoke from its exhaust.

Everyone climbed on board. The sampan operator pushed off and they motored out into the turbid water.

"Hope this boat doesn't capsize," Tristan said. "One dunk in this water and we'd all die."

At that very moment they saw a group of young children dive off a nearby junk. Frolicking in the water, they squealed with delight.

"My word," Tristan said. "Those kids must have impressive immune systems!"

"Who are these people?" Marissa asked, even more amazed at the floating city from close up. Entire families were in evidence, with clothes hung in rigging to dry.

"Mostly the Tanka," Bentley said with a touch of derision in his voice. "They and their ancestors have been living on the sea for centuries."

"I take it you are not a Tanka?" Tristan said.

Bentley laughed as if Tristan were comparing him to some subhuman race. "I'm Cantonese," he said proudly.

"A little prejudice in the Heavenly Kingdom?" Tristan quipped.

Mr. Yip's associate directed the sampan operator up a row of junks then alongside one of the larger ones. When the sampan stopped they were abreast of an opening at about chest height. A powerfully built Chinese man suddenly appeared and glared down at them. He had a scraggly goatee and wore his black hair in an old-fashioned braid. He was wearing a quilted vest. His pants were loose but short, coming only as far as his calves. On his feet were leather thongs.

Standing with his legs spread apart and his hands on his hips, he cut an imposing figure. With a deep, gravelly voice, he spoke in animated Chinese. Bentley said he was speaking Tanka.

Mr. Yip's henchman launched into an animated discussion with the man. Both sides seemed angry. Marissa and Tristan began to feel nervous. In the middle of the debate, a doll-faced, wide-eyed child of about three suddenly appeared, staring down at the strangers from between her father's solid legs.

"They are having some disagreement about money," Bentley explained. "It doesn't involve us."

Marissa and Tristan felt relieved. They took the opportunity to examine the captain's boat. It was about forty feet long with a beam of approximately eighteen feet. The wood was an oiled tropical hardwood, giving the craft a honey color. The deck was in three levels with a poop at the stern. Just forward of midships was a mast that rose up about twenty feet.

Suddenly the captain turned to Marissa and Tristan. Pointing at them, he spoke in angry, guttural tones.

"Okay," Bentley said. "We can go aboard."

"You can go aboard," Marissa said. She looked

up into the captain's fierce eyes. They were staring at her unblinkingly.

"Please," Bentley said. "If you do not go abroad now he will be offended. He has invited you."

Marissa looked uncertainly at Tristan. Tristan laughed in spite of himself. "Well, luv," he said, "are you or aren't you?"

"Give me a boost," Marissa said.

As soon as Marissa, Tristan, and Bentley were on board, the sampan chugged away. Marissa was alarmed by its unexpected departure.

"How are we to get back?" she questioned.

"Don't worry," Bentley said. "The sampan will be back for us. The other fellow is going to get some money that was supposed to be given to the captain."

They followed the captain through a room filled with ship's stores as well as family furnishings. In one corner, a pressure stove was lit; on top of it was a simmering cauldron.

The captain led them forward out onto the forward deck. From there they climbed a ladder to the main deck.

"The captain would like to introduce himself," Bentley said as they all sat down on bamboo mats. "His name is Zur Fa-Huang."

Marissa and Tristan smiled and bowed as did the captain. Then they had Bentley introduce them. After more bowing and smiling Tristan asked Bentley if the captain was aware of what they wanted to know.

While Bentley was speaking to Zur, Marissa

noticed that two women had appeared from below, both dressed in black. The younger woman was carrying a small infant. The little girl they'd seen earlier was clinging to her mother's leg.

Bentley turned back to Marissa and Tristan. "Mr. Yip's man told the captain that it was permitted for you to ask him about people he has been smuggling out of the Middle Kingdom. I trust you understand what that is about?"

"We do indeed," Tristan said.

"Then the first order of business," Bentley said, "is to determine how much this will cost you."

"You mean I have to pay this bloke as well?" Tristan asked with dismay.

"If you want any information," Bentley said.

"Bloody hell," Tristan said. "Find out what he wants."

Bentley negotiated. In the middle of the conversation, the captain appeared to get angry and leaped to his feet. He proceeded to parade around the deck, gesturing wildly.

"What's happening?" Tristan asked Bentley.

"He's talking about inflation," Bentley said.

"Inflation?" Marissa questioned with disbelief.

"Well, he didn't use that term," Bentley admitted. "But what he's irritated about amounts to the same thing."

Marissa watched the man, trying to remember that they were dealing with a swaggering, modern-day pirate who happened to be living in one of the unabashed capitals of capitalism.

Finally a price was established at a thousand

Hong Kong dollars. After Tristan gave the man the money, he sat back down and tried to be helpful.

With Bentley as translator, Tristan asked about the men that Zur had been smuggling into Hong Kong for the Wing Sin and ultimately for Female Care Australia: who were they and where did they come from? Unfortunately, the answers were short. Zur had no idea.

Tristan couldn't believe it. "I paid a thousand Hong Kong dollars to hear that he doesn't know?" he asked with aggravation. Tristan got to his feet and paced like the captain had. "Ask him if he knows anything at all about these people. Anything!"

Bentley asked.

Once the captain had replied, Bentley turned back to Tristan. "He says that some of the men were monks. Or at least he thinks they were."

"Now that's helpful," Tristan said irritably. "Tell me something I don't know."

The captain talked to Bentley at length while Tristan fumed about all the money he'd paid for nothing.

Bentley turned back to Tristan. "The captain is upset you are not happy. He has made another offer. It seems that he is leaving this afternoon at six P.M. to make another one of these pickups. That was what he was arguing about with Mr. Yip's man. He was supposed to have more upfront money. He says that for two thousand Hong Kong dollars each, you and your wife can go with him. It only takes about three or four hours to cross the Pearl River. Then you can talk directly to the men he picks up and get answers to all your questions."

Taken off guard by this unexpected offer, Tristan hesitated. Without conferring with Marissa, he said to Bentley, "Tell him that I will only pay three thousand dollars Hong Kong, and that's final."

While Bentley translated for Zur, Marissa stood up and went over to Tristan. "I hope we know what we're doing," she said. She was miffed he hadn't consulted her and fearful about the venture. It hardly sounded safe. "Are you sure we should go through with this?"

"It could be our best bet," said Tristan. "If we can talk to a pair of these mainlanders before they get to Australia, we would most likely get to the bottom of this whole affair."

"Possibly, but we're talking about smuggling," Marissa said. "We'll be in Communist Chinese waters. And what if it involves drugs? Smuggling drugs is a capital crime in most of Asia."

"You're right," Tristan said reluctantly. "But we can find out if it's drugs."

Tristan went over and interrupted Bentley and Zur. "Ask him if picking up these men involves drugs in any way," Tristan said.

Bentley did as he was told. Zur listened, then shook his head. After a short conversation, Bentley turned back to Tristan. "No drugs," he said. "Zur has on occasion been involved with drugs, but not lately. He says that drug running has become too dangerous."

"What about his price?" Tristan asked.

"Three thousand five hundred," Bentley said. "I can't get him down any lower."

"Fine!" Tristan said. "Tell him we'll be back at six."

"Tristan," Marissa said. "I don't know . . ."

"How do we get off this junk?" Tristan asked, interrupting Marissa. He motioned for her to be quiet.

"We are not going on that piece of 'junk,'" Marissa said the moment they climbed into the armored Mercedes. She was irritated with Tristan for committing them without her approval. "Even if Zur is not involved with the drug trade, he goes into Communist China waters. If we get picked up, we could be in prison for God knows how long. We can't take that kind of risk."

"Seems to me we've been taking more risk just being here in Hong Kong," Tristan said. "The more I think about it, the more convinced I am that going with Captain Fa-Huang will be the only way to solve this affair: trace it back to its origins. That had been my original idea."

"Where to?" Bentley said from the front seat.

Tristan motioned for Bentley to wait. "People go to the PRC all the time," he said. "I happen to know that we can get visas in a matter of hours. It just means paying a little extra. If there is any trouble, then we can just say that we'd hired the captain to take us to the PRC, which is true. We'll say we were supposed to go to Guangzhou, but that the captain cheated us."

Turning to Bentley, Tristan asked: "Aren't there a lot of people going back and forth between Hong Kong and the PRC?"

"More and more each day," Bentley answered. "The PRC encourages people from Hong Kong to come to spend their dollars. I have a permanent visa and go frequently to Shenzhen."

"Good," Tristan said. "Because I was hoping you'd come with us."

"It's possible," Bentley said slowly. "But we'll have to renegotiate my hourly wage."

"I expected as much," Tristan said. "I'm finally beginning to understand how Hong Kong works." Then, turning to Marissa, he said: "Will that make you feel a little better?"

Marissa nodded, but she still had an uneasy feeling about the proposed venture. Tristan could tell she still wasn't convinced.

"Well," he said. "If you really don't want to do this, just say the word. We can still catch a plane out of here this afternoon. I personally think it's less risky than what we've been doing here in Hong Kong. Zur's apparently been doing it for years."

Marissa wasn't sure what she wanted to do. She was anxious about the proposed trip, but she hated the thought of giving up. Finally she said, "Why don't we go ahead and get the visas. Then later we'll talk about it again."

In a private suite in the Hong Kong and Shanghai Banking Corporation building, Ned Kelly waited patiently to see Harold Pang, one of the Taipans of the city. As the chairman of the board of several corporations, he was one of the most powerful men in the colony. Befitting his station, his was one of the most sumptuous homes on Victoria Peak. Yet in addition to his far-flung legitimate business connections, he was also the Dragon Head of the Wing Sin. It was largely due to this illicit position that he'd been able to achieve so much legitimately.

Ned had met Harold on several occasions, both in Hong Kong and in Brisbane. He remembered him as a gentle, cultured man who was a master at t'ai chi chuan.

"Mr. Pang will see you now," a tall, soft-spoken receptionist said in a sultry voice. Ned saw that the slit of her skin-tight traditional Chinese dress went clear up to her hipbone. He shivered from the effect, wondering how anyone got much work done with her walking around.

Mr. Pang got up from his massive desk when Ned entered his office. Behind him, through floor-to-ceiling glass, was the entire sweep of the harbor with Kowloon and the new territories in the background.

"Welcome, Mr. Kelly," Mr. Pang said.

"G'day, Mr. Pang," Ned said. "Mr. Charles Lester sends his warmest regards."

Mr. Pang bowed, then clapped his hands. Almost immediately the receptionist reappeared with an ancient porcelain tea service.

Soon Ned was relaxing on a long leather couch, balancing one of the priceless cups on his knee. He waited until the receptionist withdrew before speaking.

"Mr. Lester wanted me to thank you for the long and profitable business relationship Fertility, Limited, has enjoyed with the Wing Sin."

"It has always been a pleasure," Mr. Pang said. "As friends, we profit together. It has been a good marriage."

"Mr. Lester has also asked me to request another favor of the Wing Sin," Ned said. "There are a man and woman in Hong Kong who are interfering in our established business relationship. They must be eliminated."

"Are these people public figures?" Mr. Pang asked.

"No," Ned said. "They are only doctors. One is Australian and one American."

"If they are not public figures," Mr. Pang said, "then it will cost only one hundred and fifty thousand Hong Kong dollars."

"Isn't that somewhat high for an old business friend?" Ned asked. He felt a twinge of hope; he knew the figure was less than the bonus he had been offered. He was hoping to pick up the difference.

"Such a price only covers expenses," Mr. Pang said.

Ned nodded. "It must be done immediately," he said.

"Then you must go to see the enforcer today," Mr. Pang said. "This afternoon Mr. Yip is at the Shanghai Shipping Company's container facility in Tai Kok Tsui. He will be expecting you."

Ned bowed. He was relieved. He was also confident. When the Wing Sin promised to do something, it always got done, no matter what.

Bentley pulled the armored Mercedes directly into the receiving dock in the back of the Peninsula Hotel. The early afternoon had passed quickly with the effort of obtaining entry visas for the People's Republic of China. Bentley had proved invaluable. He'd known exactly where to go and had taken them directly to the China Travel Service office as soon as they left Aberdeen. He'd also known where to go to get the necessary passport-style photographs.

Bentley stopped the car and turned around to face his clients. "Well," he said, "what have you decided?" He knew that Marissa still had reservations about going.

Tristan looked at Marissa. "What's it to be?"

Marissa hesitated. As the business with the visas had progressed, she began to feel better about the venture. After all, they would have the necessary documents. But she still had her doubts.

"Bentley, you'd better wait," Tristan said. "It appears that we still haven't decided."

Getting out of the car, they walked into the

440

hotel lobby. Tristan went to the front desk and used the safe deposit box to get more money for the captain if they decided to go. While he was occupied, Marissa kept an eye out for the Chinese man who'd attacked them the day before.

After obtaining the money and returning the safe deposit box, Tristan led Marissa to the elevators. Marissa didn't relax until the elevator doors closed behind them.

"This tension is driving me crazy," she admitted. "I'm not sure I can take too much more of it."

"Which is another reason to go on the junk," Tristan said. "As soon as we find out what this is all about, the better. Then we can get out of this place and let them give it back to China."

The elevator arrived on the sixth floor and they stepped out. They walked slowly to their doors, weighing the pros and cons of going with the Tanka captain.

"Where's the hall porter?" Marissa asked as they neared their doors. She'd grown accustomed to the man's miraculous appearance every time they arrived on the floor.

"That is strange," Tristan said. He looked up and down the hall for signs of the man. Then he spotted the sign hanging from the knob of his door. "What the hell? Why is there a Do Not Disturb sign on my door?"

"Something's wrong," she said.

Tristan backed away from his door. "You're right," he said. Turning, he walked back toward the elevator. Marissa followed him, looking nervously over her shoulder.

They went inside the hall porter's empty cubicle. In the corner they saw a hot plate with a teakettle on it. The kettle was red hot, the water having long since boiled away.

"Something is definitely wrong," Tristan said. Going back to the elevator, he picked up the house phone and asked for security. Two minutes later the elevator opened and two security men stepped out. One was a muscular Chinese, the other a beefy Englishman.

The security men remembered Marissa and Tristan from the episode in the lobby the day before. With Marissa and Tristan standing to the side, they used their passkey to open Tristan's door.

The room was quiet except for the sound of water running in the bathtub. The connecting door to room 604 was ajar. The bed was stripped. A maid's cleaning cart was pushed to the side.

The Chinese man entered first, then the Englishman. Marissa and Tristan remained on the threshold. The Chinese security man headed for the bathroom while his partner glanced into 604.

"George!" the Chinese man called urgently. George quickly joined his partner at the bathroom door. Both their faces blanched. Then the Englishman turned to Marissa and Tristan, motioning for them to stay where they were. He explained that there had been a death.

Clearly shaken, the two security men left the

bathroom and went into 604. Marissa and Tristan exchanged an uneasy glance.

"My God!" the Englishman said.

In a moment, both security men appeared back in 606. The Englishman went to the phone at the desk. After covering the handle of the receiver with a cloth, he called the manager and told him that there had been two murders: a cleaning woman and apparently a hotel guest.

Meanwhile, the Chinese security man approached Marissa and Tristan. "I'm afraid we have two bodies in here," he said. "Please, do not touch anything. We don't recognize the man in the other room." Addressing Tristan he said, "Perhaps, sir, you might have a look and see if it is someone you know."

Tristan started forward, but Marissa stopped him by pulling at his arm. "I'm a doctor," she said to the security man. "I think I should look as well."

The security man shrugged. "As you like, madam."

With the security man in the lead, Marissa and Tristan walked into 604.

When Marissa looked down at the body, she gave out a little cry. Her hand went to her mouth in horror. The victim was lying on his back, staring open-eyed at the ceiling. There were two holes in his forehead. On the carpet behind his head was a pool of blood in the form of a dark halo.

"It's Robert!" Marissa gasped. "It's my husband—Robert!"

443

Tristan took Marissa in his arms and pulled her away from the grisly sight.

Then they heard a knocking from the closet.

The Chinese security man called to the Englishman. He bounded into the room. The Chinese man pointed at the closet. They heard the knocking again. Both men went to the door; the key was in the lock. With one standing to the side, the other unlocked the door and yanked it open. Inside they discovered the cowering hall porter.

After some encouragement, the security men managed to coax the porter out into the room. Once he understood that he was safe, he began speaking rapidly in Chinese.

When the porter finally fell silent, the Chinese security guard turned to the other. "He says the killer threatened him with a gun and made him open the door. He says the killer was a *gweilo*."

"Ask him to describe the killer," the Englishman said. "And ask whether he'd seen him before."

The Chinese security guard again addressed the hall porter. The porter responded with another long harangue. When he was done, the Chinese security guard turned to the other. "He says that he'd never seen him before, and he can't describe him because all *gweilos* look the same to him!"

The hotel manager arrived at the door to 606 and called out. Together, all five of them went through the connecting door and out into the hall.

Marissa was in shock. Tristan stayed by her side, keeping his arms around her. She hadn't said a word from the moment she'd recognized the dead man as Robert. She had no tears. At the moment, all she felt was a severe chill, as if the air conditioning had been turned up too high.

"The police are on their way," the manager said nervously. He was an Italian with a heavy accent. "Where are the bodies?"

The Chinese security man motioned for the manager to follow him and they made a brief tour. When the manager returned, he had trouble speaking.

"The hotel apologizes for this inconvenience," he said to Marissa and Tristan. "Especially after the trouble you had only yesterday."

The Englishman leaned over and whispered in the manager's ear. The manager's eyes widened as he listened. He swallowed hard before speaking again.

"I'm so sorry," he said, speaking directly to Marissa. "I didn't know that you knew the victim. My heartfelt condolences." Then to both Marissa and Tristan he said: "When I spoke to the police a few moments ago, they told me that you are not to be allowed into your rooms. You are not to touch anything. For your comfort, I've taken the liberty of preparing our Marco Polo for the interim. We will provide whatever you need in the way of toiletries and such."

Fifteen minutes later Marissa and Tristan were escorted to the lavish suite. Marissa sank into an armchair, feeling drained and immobile.

"I can't believe any of this," she finally said,

speaking for the first time since seeing Robert's body. "It's all too fantastic. Why did he come? It's the last thing I'd expected. Especially after our last phone conversation."

"What happened?" Tristan asked, hoping to get her to speak. He pulled a chair close by her. He reached out and gripped her hand.

Marissa spilled her heart out. Although she'd never made reference to Tristan about her difficulties with Robert, she now admitted that her marriage had seriously deteriorated, especially over the last few months. She told him that Robert had refused to come to Australia after Wendy died. All he wanted her to do was come home. For Robert to come to Hong Kong suddenly was entirely out of character. She buried her face in her hands. "He wouldn't have been here if it weren't for me."

Tristan shook his head. "Marissa," he said. It was hard for him to say what was on his mind, but he knew he had to be direct. "You can't blame yourself for this tragedy. You'll be tempted to, but you mustn't. You're not to blame."

"But I feel so guilty," Marissa said. "After Wendy, now Robert! If it weren't for me they would be alive today."

"And if it weren't for me, my wife would be alive today," Tristan said. "I know how you feel. I've been there. But you didn't make Robert come here. He came of his own accord. You didn't even know he would be here."

"Robert is such a good man. It's too awful.

446

Maybe it wasn't him," she said suddenly. "Maybe I was wrong."

Tristan eyed Marissa warily. He remembered how strongly he had wished news of his wife's death away. Denial was powerful in the face of such horrendous shocks.

"Call the manager," Marissa said suddenly. "We have to make sure it was Robert."

"You sure you want me to do that?" Tristan asked.

"Yes," Marissa said, tears welling in her eyes.

Tristan went to the phone by the desk. It took him a few minutes to get the manager on the line. After a brief conversation, he returned to his chair.

"The name in the wallet and on the passport was Robert Buchanan," Tristan said softly.

Marissa stared at Tristan with unseeing eyes. For a few moment, she didn't say anything.

"I can still see him clearly," she said at last. Her voice was flat and lifeless. "I can see him at his computer. Whenever he worked he always had the same expression."

"I know," Tristan murmured. Watching Marissa brought back memories of his own. He knew what she was going through.

"What time is it now on the East Coast of the United States?" Marissa asked.

Tristan studied his watch. "Between three and four A.M., I believe," he said.

"I have to make some calls," Marissa said. She stood up and walked into the bedroom to use the phone by the bed.

447

Tristan let her go. He didn't know what to do. He was concerned about Marissa's mental state. Robert's murder had to be a horrendous blow. He would have to keep a close eye on her. More than anything, he would try to get her to express her grief.

Marissa first called her parents in Virginia. Her mother offered for them to come to Hong Kong immediately, but Marissa told her not to. She would come home as soon as the authorities allowed.

Hanging up, Marissa tried to gather her courage for an even more difficult phone call. She knew she had to call her mother-in-law, and she knew how much the news would devastate her. Marissa wouldn't blame her if she held her responsible for Robert's death. But to her surprise, Mrs. Buchanan had no words of criticism for her. After an awful silence, she simply informed Marissa that she would come to Hong Kong immediately. Marissa didn't try to talk her out of it. By the time she hung up the phone, Tristan was in the doorway.

"Sorry to disturb you," he said, "but that bloody pom police inspector is here to talk with us and he wants to talk to you first."

The police inspector stayed for almost an hour, taking statements from both Marissa and Tristan. He told them that there would be a thorough investigation and that they would not have access to their belongings until it was completed. He apologized profusely for any inconvenience. He also informed them that there would be an autopsy on both victims and a formal inquest, and that they were not to leave the colony until the formalities were completed.

After the police inspector left, Marissa and Tristan sat alone. Tristan took the opportunity to try to get her to talk about her feelings.

"I just feel numb," Marissa said. "I have trouble believing it has really happened."

"Maybe we should do something," Tristan said. "Instead of just sitting here."

"I think it might help to get out of this hotel," Marissa said.

"Good idea," Tristan said, glad to hear Marissa make any kind of suggestion. "We'll move to another hotel." He got to his feet, wondering which one to choose. Only then did he remember Captain Fa-Huang. "I have a better idea," he said. "What about going on the junk? We need to do something. We need something to occupy our minds."

"I'd forgotten about the junk trip." Marissa said. "I don't think I'm up to it. Not now."

"Marissa!" Tristan said. "Too much has happened for us not to follow the trail to its conclusion." He stepped over to her and grabbed her shoulders. "Let's do it! Let's get even with these bastards."

Marissa's head was spinning. She couldn't even look at Tristan. Sometimes she thought he was crazy.

"Come on, Marissa!" Tristan urged. "Let's not let them get away with this."

Finally she looked up at him. She could feel his

determination. She didn't have the strength to argue or even resist. "All right," she said. "At this moment I feel as if I have nothing to lose."

"Good show!" Tristan cried. He gave her a forceful hug, then leaped to his feet. He looked at his watch. "We don't have a lot of time!" Rushing over to the phone, he called room service and ordered a number of boxed lunches as well as bottled water.

As soon as their order came, Marissa and Tristan descended to the lobby and exited through the service entrance as they had that morning. Bentley had moved the Mercedes to the alley. He was reading a newspaper while he waited. Tristan opened the rear door for Marissa, then ran around and jumped in the other side.

"Aberdeen!" Tristan told Bentley. "We're going smuggling."

They drove out of the alley and over to East Tsim Sha Tsui, then into the Cross Harbor Tunnel. Almost immediately they slowed to a crawl in bumper-to-bumper traffic.

Tristan eyed his watch nervously in the dim tunnel light. "Damn!" he said. "It's going to be close if Captain Fa-Huang weighs anchor at six sharp."

Marissa closed her eyes. She felt numb, as if nothing that was happening were real.

The enforcer looked over his desk at the hit man. The tension between them was natural for two experts in the same small field. They each knew that the other did similar things, just in different worlds. Mr. Yip thought that Ned was a crude barbarian. Ned thought Mr. Yip was a hoon poofter in a white suit.

They were sitting in the same office where Mr. Yip had Marissa and Tristan brought on their first meeting. Willy was outside with some of Mr. Yip's men.

"I trust that Mr. Pang rang you," Ned said.

"He did indeed," Mr. Yip said. "But he only said that we were to do business. He said that it involved dealing with a couple, for which you were to pay the Wing Sin one hundred and fifty thousand Hong Kong dollars. He did not provide further details."

"It is a man and a woman," Ned said. "One Australian, the other American. Late thirties for the man, early thirties for the woman. Their names are Tristan Williams and Marissa Blumenthal. They're staying at the Peninsula Hotel, but that may soon change."

Mr. Yip smiled to himself, realizing immediately that the Wing Sin was about to profit from both sides of a conflict. "This is a coincidence," he said. "I'm sure that the couple that you are describing have been here to see me in this very office."

"For what reason?" Ned asked.

"They paid me for information," Mr. Yip said. "They were interested in the people we have been smuggling out of the PRC for Fertility, Limited."

Ned shifted nervously in his seat. "And what were they told?"

"Very little, I can assure you," Mr. Yip said. "The Wing Sin has never bothered to interfere in Fertility, Limited, business. So," continued Mr. Yip, "how much is in this for me?"

Accustomed to doing business in Hong Kong and with the Wing Sin in particular, Ned was not surprised by this direct request for squeeze. "The usual ten percent," he said.

"The usual is fifteen," Mr. Yip said with a smile.

"Done," Ned said.

"It is a delight to do business with someone accustomed to our ways," Mr. Yip said. "And we are in luck. The couple in question is scheduled to leave this afternoon on a Tanka junk to make one of the Fertility, Limited, pickups. That will make the deed extremely easy and efficient. The bodies can be dropped into the sea. Very neat."

Ned pulled his sleeve back to look at his watch. "What time are they leaving?" he asked.

"Around six," Mr. Yip said. He got up from his chair. "I think we'd better leave immediately."

A few minutes later they found themselves stuck in traffic.

"Isn't there a faster way?" Ned asked with frustration.

"You must relax," Mr. Yip said. "Consider the job done."

Even the Aberdeen Tunnel was crowded at that

time of day. As they got out of the tunnel, the south shore proved equally congested. It was stop-and-go traffic all the way to Aberdeen.

Tristan was frantic. He could hardly sit still, looking at his watch every few minutes. In contrast, Marissa sat immobile, staring blankly ahead. Her mind was in a turmoil as her emotional numbness was beginning to wear thin. She was thinking of Robert and the better times they'd had. Not only did she feel responsible for his death, to a large degree she felt responsible for the rough months before it. Tears began to well in her eyes. She averted her head to keep Tristan from seeing. Except for a powerful apathy that overwhelmed her, she would have asked if they could turn around.

On top of her emotional pain, Marissa also began to fear going out on the open sea, worrying that she might get seasick to add to her problems. During the ride out to the junk in the motorized sampan, Marissa again considered demanding they go back. The sound of the water and the thought of the ocean not only made her queasy but also brought back the memory of Wendy's death with stark vividness.

"Good show!" Tristan exclaimed as they rounded the row of junks and saw that Captain Fa-Huang had not yet departed. The sampan pulled alongside the receiving port.

Marissa saw that the captain had company. A couple of fierce-looking Chinese men were standing at the railing on the poop deck, watching their arrival with interest.

Grabbing Tristan's arm, Marissa pointed. "Who are those men?" she asked. "They look like bandits."

"Dunno," Tristan said. "Must be the crew."

Bentley scrambled up into the opening, then turned to lend a hand. Tristan handed up the boxed lunches and the bottled water.

"Okay, luv," Tristan said taking Marissa's arm.

With a boost from Tristan and a pull from Bentley, Marissa found herself aboard the junk.

Once on the boat, they went forward and climbed the ladder to the main deck. The captain bellowed a greeting and introduced them to Liu and Maa, the two deckhands. Everyone bowed. Then the captain yelled a command and the men fell back to work.

The junk was in the final stages of preparation. Even the two women that Marissa had seen earlier were occupied. They were busy lashing down a cage containing four live chickens.

Within fifteen minutes of their arrival, the mooring lines were cast off the junk. With much straining the boat was eased out of its berth by sheer muscle power. Once in the channel, the captain fired up his twin diesels. Soon the boat was pulsating with the deep, throaty vibration of its engines, and slowly the ponderous craft chugged out of the congested harbor.

They headed due west toward the setting sun. In other circumstances, Marissa might have found the experience exhilarating. The scenery was magnificent, especially once they cleared the tip of Ap Lei Chou Island. It was then that they had a view of the wooded Lamma Island to port and the much larger mountainous island of Lantau directly ahead.

But the beauty was lost on Marissa. She sat by the railing with her eyes closed and held tight. She was glad for the strong sea breeze; it dried the tears from her cheeks before anyone could see them. And on top of everything else, she was beginning to feel a little seasick as the boat began to pitch.

Ned Kelly swore as only an Australian can swear when he found himself looking at the empty space where he'd hoped Fa-Huang's junk would be moored.

"Couldn't we have gotten here faster?" he steamed. Coming from Australia, he had trouble understanding how people could conduct their lives with so much traffic. "Ask the neighbors if Williams and Blumenthal were on the boat!"

"I am not your servant," Mr. Yip said. Ned was irritating him more than usual.

"Stone the crows!" Ned exclaimed, peering heavenward to muster some patience. He well knew Yip was a character to be reckoned with, particularly on his home turf. "Please ask them," he said. "I'm sorry if I insulted you."

Mr. Yip spoke to the family on one of the junks that had been next to Fa-Huang's. He spoke to them in Tanka, a language Ned did not understand.

Turning back to Ned, Mr. Yip said: "There were two white devils on board. That is a literal translation."

"It must be them," Ned said. "Can we go after them?"

"Of course," Mr. Yip said.

Ordering the sampan operator back to the quay, Mr. Yip had one of his henchmen bring around a sleek speedboat. Ned climbed in the front seat with Willy and the driver. Mr. Yip and two of his men got in the back. Both the men were armed with machine pistols.

With a roar, they left the quay and raced down the length of the harbor. Ned was encouraged by the boat's speed. But when they reached open water, his mood soured. The ocean was dotted with junks. They all looked alike. After cruising by a handful with no luck, they gave up.

"This American is living a charmed life," Ned complained.

He twisted in his seat and yelled to Mr. Yip over the sound of the powerful engine: "What should we do? Wait for them to come back, or what?"

"It's not necessary to wait," Mr. Yip called out. "Enjoy the boat ride. We will talk when we get to the restaurant."

"What restaurant?" Ned asked.

Mr. Yip pointed. Ahead was one of Aberdeen's enormous floating restaurants with gold dragons and crimson banners. Among the throng of dilapidated junks, it was an improbable oasis.

Fifteen minutes later Ned found himself dining in style. The sun had set and the lights of Aberdeen were blinking across the harbor. Mr. Yip took it upon himself to order a lavish feast. It was enough for Ned to forget his anger.

In the middle of the meal, one of Mr. Yip's men brought in a nautical chart. Mr. Yip spread it out on the table. "This is the Zhujiang Kou estuary," Mr. Yip exclaimed. "Most foreigners call it the Pearl River. Here is Guangzhou." He pointed with his chopstick. "And here, above Zhuhai, just north of the special economic zone that the PRC has set up above Macao, are a group of small offshore islands. It is there that Captain Fa-Huang picks up your people. If you go tonight with some of my men you can meet them. You don't have to wait for them to get back."

"How do I get there?" Ned asked, looking at the map. He could tell it wasn't that far: maybe fifty miles.

"We have a special boat coming for you." Mr. Yip said. "It is what they call a cigarette boat."

"Wonderful," Ned said. He knew that cigarette boats were capable of speed in excess of fifty miles per hour.

"There is only one problem," Mr. Yip said.

"What's that?" Ned asked.

"I'll need a bit more squeeze."

16

"MARISSA!" TRISTAN called excitedly. "We've made contact. Why don't you come on deck?"

Marissa sat up in the darkness. She had been lying on a bamboo mat in the storeroom.

It had not been a good evening. An hour and a half out of Aberdeen, after rounding the southern tip of Lantau Island, they had run into a sudden squall. Within a few minutes, the rosy sky was transformed into a black swirling mass of clouds. The slight chop gave way to five-foot swells.

The queasiness Marissa had felt at the start quickly blossomed to full-blown seasickness. Since there were no facilities on board, she could only cling to the poop deck railing and vomit off the back of the boat. When the rain came, she was forced down into the filthy hold.

Tristan had been solicitous, but there was little he could do. He'd stayed with her, but after he'd opened one of the box lunches and started to eat, the sight and smell of the food had made Marissa feel worse. She'd sent him away.

The storm had also hindered their progress. With the gusty high winds, they had been forced to reef the huge butterfly sail that they'd been

458

using up until the storm. Switching to the diesels, the captain merely kept the boat on course. Bentley explained that he wanted to conserve fuel.

Even after the storm had passed and the sail was rehoisted, the traveling had not been pleasant. The wind had all but died, and a dense mist had formed over the water creating a pea-soup fog. On several occasions, huge ships suddenly loomed out of the darkness with foghorns blasting, giving everyone on the small junk a terrible start.

But finally they had arrived, and for the last half hour they had been slowly cruising the coast back and forth between the mainland and some small offshore islands. At first Marissa had watched the shoreline with everyone else, amazed that she was looking at Communist Chinese territory. But after a time she'd retreated below to lie down for a while. By then, she was more exhausted than seasick.

"Come on!" Tristan called out. "I know you've had a bad time of it, but this is what we've come for."

Marissa struggled to her feet. She was dizzy for an instant. "Do you have any of our water?" she asked.

"Sure, luv," Tristan said. He handed her the bottle he had tucked into his back pocket.

When she'd finished drinking, she gave Tristan the bottle and wiped her mouth with the back of her hand. Then she took his arm. Together they walked out onto the foredeck. The boat was completely dark. Not a single light was lit.

The captain had started the diesels, but he had them at such a slow throttle, the only way Marissa could tell they were running was by feeling their vibration through her feet. She couldn't hear them except when the water momentarily covered their exhaust, resulting in a muted, popping sound.

Squinting her eyes, Marissa could just make out the shoreline through the mist. She could see the dim silhouette of the treetops against the sky.

It was apparent that Captain Fa-Huang was tense. So were his two crewmen. This was the most dangerous part of the whole exercise, not only because they might be discovered but also because of underwater shoals.

No one spoke. They were close enough to shore for Marissa to hear the sounds of swamp creatures. The only other sound was the lap of the waves against the side of the boat until she became aware of the whine of mosquitoes.

Suddenly, from the shadows of the trees came a distinct flash of light. It was repeated twice more in rapid succession. The captain immediately cut the engines, flashed his own light toward the trees, and gave a hand signal to his crew member in the bow. A moment later came the muted splash of an anchor being dropped into the water.

The captain and his deck mates conferred in hushed tones as the boat slowly swung around to point directly away from the shore. One of the men disappeared below briefly. When he reappeared he was wearing a bandolier and carrying an AK47 assault rifle. In the distance some exotic bird cried, casting an eerie spell over the scene.

"They are afraid of pirates," Bentley whispered to Marissa and Tristan.

"There are still pirates?" Marissa whispered.

"There have always been pirates in the Pearl River," Bentley whispered in return. "Always have been and always will be."

About five tense minutes passed with only the drone of mosquitoes and the lap of waves disturbing the silence.

Then, out of the mist appeared a small wooden boat with two figures in it. One was in the stern using a sweep oar. The other was sitting amidships, facing forward.

The captain addressed the men. The armed deckhand kept his automatic rifle pointed at them. One of the men answered timidly in a whisper. The captain listened and then motioned for them to come aboard. With that, everyone seemed to relax a little.

"It's the men they were expecting," Bentley said with relief.

The man with the sweep oar moved the small boat around the side of the junk.

Marissa leaned over the gunwale to see the two Chinese men climb aboard. They abandoned the small boat, letting it drift off into the fog.

Within seconds, the anchor chain was pulled up from the depths. The captain ordered the sail hoisted to take advantage of the light offshore breeze. Silently, the large junk sailed away from the shore. The silhouettes of the treetops soon vanished in the mist.

"We must stay very quiet for another half hour," Bentley whispered. All eyes strained into the velvety blackness; all ears listened for the slightest sound of another boat. But all they could hear was the creaking of their own rigging.

The two newly arrived Chinese men huddled together against the mast. No one spoke to them. They were dressed in simple black cotton clothing which reminded Marissa of pictures she'd seen of the Viet Cong during the Vietnam War.

"What should we do?" Tristan asked Bentley in a hushed whisper. "Can we go talk to those buggers?"

"Wait until the captain gives the word," Bentley told him. "We have to get far enough away from shore."

Even Marissa began to relax. The sea was like a sheet of black glass. Looking up, she could see the great billow of the sail against the gray mantle of the sky. Through the fog she saw a single star, a far cry from the profusion she'd seen in the Australian outback.

Lowering her eyes, Marissa was shocked to see once again the dim silhouette of treetops. They were again close to land!

"There's the shoreline again," Marissa whispered.

Tristan and Bentley looked.

"That's strange," Bentley said. "Just a moment. I'll be right back."

Bentley walked back to the poop. Marissa and Tristan could see him converse with the captain. After a lengthy conversation he came back and sat down.

"It's an uninhabited offshore island," Bentley explained. "We are entering into a lagoon where we will drop anchor."

As if on cue, the anchor plunged back into the water at the bow. At the same time the sheet holding the boom was given slack.

"Why are we stopping?" Marissa asked. She was concerned something was wrong.

"The captain said we have to wait for daybreak before starting back for Aberdeen," Bentley said.

"He never mentioned that before," Tristan said. "You mean we have to spend the whole blasted night out here?" He slapped at a mosquito that had landed on his arm.

"Apparently so," Bentley said. "The captain says that at dawn we will be able to blend with the fishing boats leaving from a village to the north. If we tried to cross the Pearl River tonight, the PRC would pick us up on their radar. Since the locals don't go out at night, we'd look pretty suspicious."

"He could have told us," Marissa complained.

"Can we talk to those blokes we picked up?" Tristan asked.

"I'll ask the captain," Bentley said. He went back to the poop.

"Sorry about this, luv," Tristan said. "I didn't know this was to be an all-night affair."

Marissa shrugged. "It could be a lot worse," she said.

Bentley came back quickly. "Captain says you can talk all you want, just not too loudly."

As the crew reefed the sail, Marissa, Tristan, and Bentley went forward and sat down across from the two PRC refugees.

"First, let's all introduce ourselves," Tristan said to Bentley.

Marissa looked more closely at the two men as Bentley began speaking. Although it was difficult to judge, Marissa guessed that they were both approximately her age. Both wore their hair cut short. Both were clearly tense and edgy. Their eyes darted from person to person in the half-light.

"This is Chiang Lam," Bentley said, pointing to the man with the slighter build. He bowed as Bentley said his name. "And this is Tse Wah."

After the introductions, Tristan told Bentley that they wanted to know where the men were from and what they did for a living. He wanted Bentley to ask them why they were being smuggled out of the PRC.

While Bentley spoke to the Chinese, Marissa and Tristan conferred to try to organize their further questions. In the background the crew was preparing for a late meal. They were also preparing to bed down for the night.

When Bentley was finished speaking with the men, he turned to Marissa and Tristan and told them that both men had come from small towns in Guangdong Province. Chiang Lam was a monk from a Buddhist order that had managed to survive the Communist era. Tse Wah was a rural doctor, a contemporary version of the "barefoot doctor" of the Cultural Revolution. Bentley went on to say that the reason they had left the PRC was because they had been promised a lot of money. Both fully intended to return. However, neither one could say why he had been offered this opportunity.

"How did they happen to be chosen?" Marissa questioned.

Bentley asked the men, then said: "Chiang says that he was chosen because of his ability in martial arts. He says that there was a competition in his monastery. Tse says he was chosen because he is a doctor. He says that there was no competition, that people just came to him and made an offer he couldn't resist. Tse has a family, a wife and a child, as well as parents and in-laws."

Marissa glanced at Tristan. "I have a feeling the key lies with the doctor," she said. Tristan nodded.

"Ask the doctor if he knows anything about infertility treatments," Tristan said. "Particularly in-vitro fertilization techniques."

"I speak some English," Tse said suddenly, surprising everyone. "Chiang doesn't, but I do. I have been studying English over the years from medical books from Guangzhou, where I was trained."

"That's encouraging," Tristan said. "It sounds as if you've been studying well."

"Thank you," Tse said. "Unfortunately, I read English better than I speak."

"Do you understand the term 'in-vitro fertilization'?" Tristan asked.

"I do," Tse said. "But I know very little. Only some mention in the books I have read."

"Are you interested in in-vitro fertilization?" Marissa asked.

In spite of nervousness, Tse laughed. "It would be of little help to me. In China we have too many people and too many babies."

"What about tuberculosis?" Marissa asked. "Is that a problem in the PRC? Have you seen much of it?"

"Not recently," Tse said. "China has a national vaccination policy with BCG vaccine. Before 1949 tuberculosis was widespread, particularly here in the south of China. But the BCG has changed that."

"What about heroin?" Tristan asked.

"We don't have any heroin," Tse said. "Drugs are not a problem in China."

"What about venereal disease?" Marissa asked.

"Very little venereal disease in the People's Republic," Tse said. "The Communists got rid of venereal disease as well as opium, and launched a program of health care that emphasized prevention over cure. There wasn't the money or the facilities for Western-style cure."

"What about your practice?" Tristan asked. "What did it involve?"

"I have a typical country practice," Tse said.

"I have a small dispensary which is responsible for health education, immunizations, and birth control for nearly four thousand rural people. We treat minor illnesses and minor accidents and refer to the district hospital when necessary."

"Do you use traditional Chinese medicine?" Marissa asked.

"We use it if the patient requests it," Tse said. "We have access to herbalists and acupuncturists. But I was trained in modern medicine in Guangzhou although I have little modern equipment to use."

Marissa looked at Tristan. "I'm running out of questions," she said.

"Me too," Tristan said. He shifted his position. They were all sitting cross-legged on the deck. Readdressing Tse, he said: "Who was it that recruited you?"

"The White Lotus Triad," Tse said.

"There are triads in the PRC?" Marissa asked.

"Very much so," Bentley interjected. "After all, it was from mainland China that they originated."

"Ask the monk why it is important that he know Chinese martial arts," Tristan said.

"I can answer," Tse said. "Chiang has been tasked to protect me."

"Why do you need protection?" Tristan asked.

"That I do not know," Tse admitted.

"Have either of you been out of the PRC before?" Tristan asked.

"Never," Tse said.

"And you have no baggage with you?"

"None."

"Are you carrying anything on your person?"

"Nothing."

"Do you have any drugs with you?"

"None."

"And you are doing this for money?"

Tse nodded. "We have been promised many years' wages. I was already given one year's wages before I left."

"How long are you supposed to be away?" Tristan asked.

"I am unsure," Tse said. "One year, maybe two at the most."

Tristan ran a hand through his hair. He shook his head and cast a dismayed look at Marissa. "I'm afraid I don't have anything else to ask. I'm baffled."

All of a sudden the group realized they weren't alone. Looking up, they saw that the captain had come forward. Once he had gotten their attention, he spoke.

Bentley translated: "The captain wants to know if we want to eat. His wife has prepared a meal for all of us."

"Why not?" Tristan said, getting to his feet. "We should get something for my bloody three thousand five hundred Hong Kong dollars."

Several hours later, Marissa and Tristan were lying together on bamboo mats on the poop deck. It was the only place they could be alone. Except

468

for an occasional mosquito and the cool, damp breeze, they were comfortable.

Marissa had not eaten anything. Instead she'd drunk most of the water they'd brought on board. Her nausea and vomiting earlier had left her dehydrated.

"I'll have to apologize again, luv," Tristan said. "I was so sure that coming here and talking to these blokes would solve everything. As it is we're no better off than before we'd come to Hong Kong. It appears as if we've risked our lives and made you bloody sick for nothing."

"I thought this would give us answers, too," Marissa said. "It's strange. I don't understand what we could be missing. There just doesn't seem to be any explanation why Female Care Australia is making this elaborate illegal effort to bring in Chinese nationals."

"I still think it has to involve drugs in some way," Tristan said. "It's got to be the heroin from the Golden Triangle."

"But these men are carrying nothing," Marissa reminded him.

"But it's the only way I can think to justify FCA's level of expense," Tristan said. "Not to mention the extent to which they are willing to go to protect whatever it is they're doing. They thought it was important enough to gun us down in public. It's gotta be drugs; don't you think?"

"I don't know what to think," Marissa said. "What you say makes some sense, but only to a point. And we still haven't figured where the TB salpingitis comes in. And if it is drugs, how does it involve a country doctor and a Buddhist monk?"

"I don't have a clue to any of those questions," Tristan said. "I'm at a loss. At one point I had an idea that this scheme might somehow involve Hong Kong being given back to the Chinese in 1997. But even that wild idea has nothing to recommend it. I'm afraid we're at a dead end."

Marissa wished he hadn't used that expression. She closed her eyes. With all that had happened, she didn't expect to sleep. But despite her physical discomfort and her emotional pain, exhaustion prevailed. Almost instantly she dozed off.

But once asleep, she started to dream. In her dream Robert was sinking into quicksand and she couldn't reach him. She was holding on to a branch, reaching for his hand. Then the branch broke and she fell . . .

An hour after falling asleep, Marissa sat bolt upright, half expecting to be in quicksand. But she was on a hard bamboo mat with Tristan sleeping next to her. Around her head was a swarm of mosquitoes and on her forehead were beads of cold perspiration.

Marissa became aware of sandaled feet moving about the deck and she opened her eyes. It was before dawn, yet the misty world had become brighter. They were enveloped in a dense morning fog that completely shrouded the nearby island. The sound of birds could be heard but nothing of the shoreline could be seen.

Sitting up, Marissa noticed that the crew was already preparing to pull up anchor. The sail was unfurled and ready to be hoisted. Below she heard a baby cry for a moment.

Getting up, Marissa stretched her cramped muscles. She was surprised that she'd slept at all, especially after waking up from the nightmare she'd had about Robert.

Once she was limber, she walked over to the railing. After making sure all those on deck were preoccupied, she swallowed what pride she had left and relieved herself over the side of the boat. When she was finished, she was comforted that no one had taken the slightest notice.

Tristan was still fast asleep. Rather than wake him, Marissa climbed down the ladder and went below. Water was boiling on the pressure stove. With the help of the wife of the captain, Marissa made herself some tea and carried it up to the poop deck. By then Tristan had awakened.

"G'day, luv," he said with his usual good humor.

Marissa shared her tea with him as the huge sail went up. Then they felt the engines start.

"Our man must be eager to get back," Tristan said. "He's going to sail and motor at the same time."

As it turned out, the captain merely used the engines to move the junk from the lagoon. Once they were clear of the land, the engines were switched off and the sheets connected to the boom were pulled in taut and cleated.

Sailing along on the light morning breeze, they began to move south, approaching a point of the mainland. As the mist rose they saw fishing boats putting out from shore. It was quite peaceful until from somewhere in the distance they began to hear the distant roar of a motorized boat.

The captain responded to the sound by barking out orders to the crew. The sail came down with a whoosh and the diesels were started. Slowly the junk came around.

Bentley walked back to Marissa and Tristan to explain that the captain was heading toward shore.

"What's happening?" Tristan questioned. He could tell the crew was agitated.

"We're heading into one of those little bays along the shore," Bentley said. "It's for protection. The captain is afraid that sound we hear might be a PRC patrol boat. He said it couldn't be a motorized sampan or junk; the engines are too big. He said if it weren't a PRC boat then it could be pirates."

"Oh, God!" Marissa said.

They were able to get within a hundred yards of shore before the source of the roar appeared. It was a cigarette boat. It seemed to be coming right toward them. Since most of the mist had evaporated, they could see the boat clearly.

The captain barked another order and both of the crewmen disappeared below. When they reappeared they were brandishing AK47 assault rifles with bandoliers looped over their forearms.

"I don't like this," Marissa said. "I don't like this at all."

The captain turned to them and yelled. Bentley translated by telling them that the captain had ordered everyone below except his deckhands.

Everyone rushed to obey. Bentley closed the wooden door that led to the foredeck, then joined Marissa and Tristan, who were standing next to the junk's entrance port. The shore was clearly visible in the early morning light.

"Is it a PRC patrol boat?" Tristan asked Bentley. From where they were standing, they could plainly hear the captain and his men conversing as the boat approached the starboard side of the junk.

"They still don't know," Bentley said nervously.

They heard the cigarette boat pull up beside the junk. Its powerful engine rumbled menacingly. Then they heard the captain shout loudly.

"He's telling them to stand clear," Bentley translated.

A shouting match developed between the captain and the people on the cigarette boat. Each sounded angry. The apparent dispute went on for some time, and as it did so, Marissa noticed that Bentley became progressively agitated.

"What are they talking about?" Marissa asked nervously.

"This is very strange," Bentley said. "The people in the powerboat say they have come for the white devils."

"What are white devils?" Marissa asked.

"I'm afraid they are talking about you and Tristan," Bentley said. "But the captain is furious that they have come out here and jeopardized him."

Marissa grabbed Tristan's arm. The argument on deck heated up. They watched Bentley's face, but couldn't read his expression.

"What's happening?" Marissa finally asked.

"It doesn't sound good," Bentley admitted. "The captain has ordered the powerboat to leave, but the boat refuses to go unless you are given to them or—"

"Or what?" Marissa demanded.

"Or you are shot!" Bentley said. "It is the Wing Sin."

"Anything you can do?" Tristan gulped.

Bentley shook his head. "Not much at this point," he said. "I can't fight the Wing Sin. Besides, the captain took my gun last night. He said he didn't allow people on his boat to be armed without his say-so."

"Oh, God!" Marissa repeated.

Tristan glanced at the shore about a hundred yards away. He wondered if they could swim for it. But just as the thought flashed through his mind, the wooden door to the foredeck was kicked open with a resounding thud. In the doorway stood one of the captain's men. He spoke rapidly, motioning with his gun.

"I'm afraid he insists you two go on deck," Bentley said. "My apologies."

Tristan turned to Bentley. "Since your bodyguard skills are a bit limited at the moment," he said, "perhaps you can still provide us with your interpreting skills. Would you mind accompanying us?"

"If the captain permits," Bentley said.

"Come on, luv," Tristan said. "This is Hong Kong, where everything is for sale. Let's see if we can't do some business with the captain."

Feeling more terrified than she had at any time in her life, Marissa let Tristan lead her past the man with the assault rifle and out into the morning light. It was turning into a pretty day now that the sun had burned off most of the haze. The water, which had been gray, had now assumed its usual emerald green. Marissa could hear the sound of songbirds coming from the nearby shore over the muffled roar of the cigarette-boat engine. The powerboat was slowly pulling up to the junk to grapple to its side.

The captain was on the poop deck. He looked down on his Caucasian passengers morosely.

Tristan spoke quickly with Bentley, who shouted up to the captain in Tanka: "The white devil offers to pay fifty thousand Hong Kong dollars for you to get him and his wife safely back to Aberdeen."

The captain's expression changed. He stroked his goatee, then glanced at the approaching cigarette boat.

Marissa recognized the two men in the front of the boat as the two who'd been throwing the chum overboard the day Wendy died.

"The white devil has just raised his offer to one hundred thousand Hong Kong dollars," Bentley yelled in Tanka.

The captain started to speak to Bentley, but then he stopped midsentence. His eyes were riveted to the cigarette boat. Finally he shook his head. "I cannot fight the Wing Sin," he said.

Bentley faced Tristan and told him what the captain had said.

"Tell him we'll double it to two hundred thousand," Tristan said.

Before Bentley could yell out this new offer, they heard a second engine's roar. All eyes were drawn to a small offshore island about a quarter mile to the east. The roar grew louder as a large, gun-metal-gray ship with a two-inch cannon mounted on its bow rounded the tip of the island.

The captain shouted to one of his crew on the main deck. The man tossed him his AK47. The captain grabbed the gun and fired a burst from the rifle over the heads of the men in the approaching cigarette boat and yelled something at the top of his lungs.

The other crewman herded Marissa and Tristan back into the hold and slammed the door on them.

"What's happening?" Tristan demanded.

"It's the PRC," Bentley said. "It's a naval patrol boat."

"What did the captain yell when he fired his weapon?" Tristan asked.

"He yelled 'Thieves,'" Bentley said.

From the hold they heard the cigarette boat take

off with a roar of its powerful engine. The junk rocked when the boat's wake hit the side.

Within seconds they heard the low-pitched concussion of the patrol boat's cannon, followed by a high-pitched whistle.

"Are they firing at us?" Marissa demanded.

"They must be firing at the cigarette boat," Tristan said. "Otherwise we'd probably already be in the drink."

The roar of the patrol boat's engine grew louder as it bore down on the junk, but then it went by with a swoosh. The junk rocked again as the departing patrol boat's wake hit the side.

"I never expected to be saved by the Chinese Communists," Tristan said.

The wooden door to the deck crashed open again. One of the crewmen stood at the door. He stepped inside and yelled something.

"What now?" Tristan asked.

"He's telling us all to get on deck on the double," Bentley said. "All of us, even the two refugees."

As Marissa reached the deck again, she could see the patrol boat heading southeast. Far in front of it the cigarette boat was speeding away.

The captain bellowed out another order. Bentley blanched. Even the refugees were upset. Chiang Lam began speaking to the captain. He seemed quite frantic.

"What's the matter now, mate?" Tristan asked.

"The captain has just ordered us to jump overboard," Bentley said.

"What!" Marissa gasped. "Why?"

"Because he knows the PRC will be back and when they do, he doesn't want to be caught with any contraband."

Chiang was still addressing the captain. He'd grown hysterical and was yelling at the top of his lungs.

"What's with the monk?" Tristan asked.

"He's telling the captain that he cannot swim," Bentley said.

The captain glared down at Chiang and pointed toward the shore. When Chiang continued his harangue, the captain pulled the AK47 off his shoulder and, without a moment's hesitation, riddled the monk with bullets. The monk's body smashed back against the railing before falling to the deck.

Marissa turned away. Tristan looked up at the captain in disbelief. Bentley climbed over the railing.

The captain yelled at one of his crew and the man rushed to the dead monk. Lifting the body from the deck, he tossed the corpse into the water.

Hastily, Tristan helped Marissa climb over the railing. Bentley went in first. Marissa and Tristan jumped together. Tse Wah was the last to leap.

As soon as Marissa was able to stop her downward plunge in the surprisingly icy water, she stroked to the surface. Turning around, she looked up at the junk. It was already moving, heading north, away from the direction of the PRC patrol boat.

"Take your shoes off," Tristan suggested. "But

478

don't let go of them. Hold them in your hands. It'll be much easier to swim."

17

APRIL 20, 1990
8:05 A.M.

BETWEEN THE weight of her wet clothes and the shoes she held in her hands, Marissa found swimming an effort. Although she had been at it for some minutes, she hardly seemed to have moved closer to the shore. Bentley and Tse had swum ahead, but Tristan stayed alongside Marissa.

"Just stay calm, luv," Tristan said. "Maybe you should give me your shoes."

Marissa gladly handed them over. Tristan had tied his laces together and had strung his shoes around his neck. Taking Marissa's, he jammed them into his pockets. Without the shoes, Marissa's swimming improved.

The shock of the shooting and the panicked jump into the water had totally occupied Marissa's consciousness, but as she swam and thought about the fact that she was in the ocean, she began to think about Wendy's death. In her mind's eye she started to see the hungry gray monsters cruising silently beneath the surface. Knowing that there was a bleeding body in the water made the fear that much more poignant.

479

"Do you think there are sharks around here?" Marissa managed to ask between strokes. She was hoping for reassurance.

"Let's worry about one problem at a time," Tristan said.

"Of course there are sharks," Bentley called back to them.

"Thanks, mate," Tristan yelled ahead. "That's just what we wanted to hear!"

Marissa tried not to dwell on it. Yet with each stroke, she half expected to be yanked from below. If Tristan had not been next to her, she knew she would have panicked.

"Just keep your eyes on the land," Tristan advised. "We'll be there soon enough."

It took a long time, but gradually the trees seemed closer. Up ahead, Marissa saw that Bentley had stopped swimming. He was standing waist-deep in water. From there he walked to shore.

By the time Marissa and Tristan arrived at the same depth, Bentley and Tse were already wringing out their clothes.

"Welcome to the PRC," Tristan said as he took Marissa's hand for the last twenty feet.

The beach was sickle shaped, extending about three hundred yards between rocky promontories. Behind the beach were lush, semitropical trees bordering a swampy marsh. Seabirds and marsh birds were everywhere. Their din was constant.

Facing back to sea, Marissa gazed out over the emerald expanse dotted with tiny offshore islands.

It was a peaceful, picture-postcard view. Sea gulls lazily circled above. There wasn't a trace of the junk, the cigarette boat, or the patrol boat.

The group relaxed on the beach, soaking up the warm sun after having been so chilled by the cold water. Tristan took their passports out of his money belt and opened them to the sun to dry. He did the same with his Hong Kong currency, weighing down the bills with seashells.

"I don't believe the captain could kill the monk like that," Marissa said with a shudder. "He didn't hesitate for a second."

"Life is cheap in this part of the world," Tristan said.

"I wonder if I'll ever recover from all this," she said. "First Wendy's death, then Robert's, now this shooting. And all for nothing!"

Tristan reached out and gripped her hand. "No one can ever say we didn't try," he said.

After the group had been resting for a half hour, they were disturbed by a distant droning noise that rapidly escalated. Having been sensitized by their recent ordeal, everyone looked at each other in puzzled consternation. The sound not only got louder, but it developed a peculiar concussive, pulsating quality.

Finally Tristan recognized it.

"It's a helicopter," Tristan cried. "Get under the trees!"

They had barely darted beneath the branches when a large military helicopter thundered over-

481

head, heading directly out to sea in the direction that the patrol boat had disappeared.

Emerging from the foliage, they stared at the aircraft, which was already a mere pinprick against the pale blue sky.

"Do you think they saw us?" Marissa asked.

"Nah!" Tristan said. "But I'm surprised they didn't see all this Hong Kong money spread out on the sand."

When everyone felt rested from the cold swim, they started across the marshlands. Assuming Tse knew where he was going, the other three fell in behind him. At first all they had to do was traverse swampy grass, but eventually they had to ford some deeper streams.

"Any crocs around this part of the world?" Tristan asked nervously when he was up to his waist, holding his partially dried money belt over his head.

"No crocodiles," Bentley said. "But we do have snakes."

"What next?" Marissa asked sarcastically.

But they didn't see any snakes. They did encounter more than a few insects. As they approached the heavily wooded higher ground, the mosquitoes came in swarms. For Marissa, this was a new fear. She asked Tse about malaria and dengue fever.

"There is always some malaria," Tse said. "But dengue fever I'm not familiar with."

"Never mind," Marissa said. There were just so many things she could worry about at once. "I suppose I should look on the bright side of things. We were lucky to get off the junk. Thank God for the Communist patrol boat."

"That's the attitude," Tristan said.

"And at least we still have our watches," Marissa added.

Tristan laughed, happy to hear that in spite of all that had happened, Marissa was capable of humor.

"Did you recognize the Caucasian man in the front of the powerboat?" Marissa asked Tristan. "He was the other man throwing chum overboard when Wendy died."

"I'd vaguely recognized him," Tristan said. "From back when I worked for FCA."

Reaching the edge of the marsh, they next climbed up through thick vegetation. Vines hung down from the branches of the trees. It was slow going. It took some effort just to go a hundred yards. Then the trees suddenly ended at the edge of a rice paddy.

"I recognize where we are," Tse said. "There is a small farming village ahead. Perhaps we should go there and get some food."

"How will we get food?" Tristan asked. "Will they take credit cards?"

"We'll use your money," Tse said.

"They'll take Hong Kong dollars?" Tristan questioned.

"Absolutely," Tse said. "There is a black market for Hong Kong dollars throughout the Guangdong Province."

"Do we have to worry about the authorities in this village?" Tristan asked.

"No," Tse said. "There will be no police. Only in Shigi will there be police."

Turning to Bentley, Tristan asked: "What do you see as our major problem being in the PRC? After all, we have visas."

"Only two things," Bentley said. "You have no entry stamp and no entry documents. Everyone must have a Baggage Declaration form. That is the form you must surrender when you leave the PRC."

"But no one will hassle us while we're here?" Tristan asked. "I thought the first walloper we came across would nab us."

Everyone looked at Tristan curiously. "What's the matter?" he asked.

"What's a walloper?" Marissa asked.

"A policeman," Tristan said. "Am I the only one who speaks English around here?"

Ignoring Tristan, Marissa addressed Bentley. "So we only have to be concerned about leaving the PRC?" she asked.

"I believe so," Bentley said. "Foreign travel has become reasonably commonplace in China, especially in Guangdong Province. So no one should bother you. But without some help, you probably will not be able to cross back into Hong Kong or Macao. Without a Baggage Declaration and also without the usual things a tourist carries, like a camera, you'll be considered smugglers and put in jail."

"At least we'll be safe," Tristan joked. "Since we don't have anything to worry about currently, let's go to that village and get some tucker."

"Food!" Marissa translated for the others.

Tse had been right. The villagers were eager to obtain the Hong Kong dollars. For what Tristan thought was a piddling amount, he treated all four to dry clothes and a hearty meal. Except for the rice, Marissa and Tristan did not recognize the food.

During the meal Marissa was reminded of Wendy's comment that people in the PRC liked to stare. While they ate, it seemed as if everyone in the entire village came to gawk at the four strangers eating in the village common room.

When they had finished their meal, Tristan turned to Tse. "Do you have any suggestions for us as to how to get out of the PRC? Maybe you know how we could get a couple of these Baggage Declaration forms?"

"I have never seen such a form," Tse said. "And if you do not have one, I'm afraid it will be a problem for you. Our government requires forms for everything, and our officials are of a suspicious nature. But I don't think you should go to the border. I think it would be best for you to go to Guangzhou. I know there is an American consulate. I've visited it in an effort to get medical books."

"That sounds like good advice to me," Marissa said.

Tristan nodded. "I wonder if there is an Aussie consulate as well."

"If not, I'm sure we can talk the American consul into helping you too," Marissa said.

"How do we go about getting to Guangzhou?" Tristan asked. "I suppose it is a long walk from here."

Tse flashed a smile. "A very long walk," he agreed. "But it is not such a long walk to the next town, which is larger than this village. Chiang and I stayed one night in the town, and I know they have a medical dispensary similar to the one where I work. I imagine they have transportation to Shigi, where the district hospital is located. From there we can go to Forshan, which is a big city."

"That sounds good to me," Tristan said. "What do you think, Marissa?"

"Sounds almost too good to be true," Marissa said. "I like the idea of having a U.S. official deal with the Communist bureaucracy. As Tse says, it's a much better idea than going to the border and trying our luck. With everything that has happened, I don't feel very lucky."

"What about you, Bentley?" Tristan asked.

"I think I will go back via Macao," Bentley said. "I have a hui shen jing, which entitles me multiple visa-free entries into the PRC. I shouldn't have much trouble. Maybe a short delay; but I'll go with you as far as Forshan."

The walk from the tiny village to the next town took only about an hour. First they passed by small plots of vegetables, then through rice paddies being worked by peasants with water buffalo. Whenever any peasants spotted them, they stopped and stared until the strange group passed from view. Marissa imagined they made for a curious sight: two *gweilos* and all four dressed in ill-fitting clothing.

Entering the town, Tse conversed briefly with a man pushing a wheelbarrow. During the entire conversation, the peasant didn't take his eyes off Marissa.

"He says the dispensary is just a little way ahead," Tse reported.

Most of the buildings in the town were either wood or brick, but the health clinic was a concrete whitewashed structure with a roof made of sun-baked tile. They entered through a low door. Both Tristan and Bentley had to duck to get in.

The first room was a waiting room. It was filled mainly with older women, a few accompanied by young children. One middle-aged man had a cast on his leg.

"Please," Tse said. "If you would wait here I will introduce myself to the doctor."

There was no space on the crude wooden benches that circled the room's periphery, so Marissa, Tristan, and Bentley stood. None of those waiting uttered a single word. They merely gawked at the trio as if they were extraterrestrial beings. The children were especially curious.

"Now I know how cinema stars feel," Tristan said.

Tse reappeared, escorted by a tall, gaunt Chi-

487

nese man dressed in a short-sleeved Western-style shirt.

"This is Dr. Chen Chi-Li," Tse said. He then introduced Chi-Li to Marissa, Tristan, and Bentley.

Chi-Li bowed. Then he smiled, revealing large, yellow teeth. He spoke quickly in guttural Cantonese.

"He welcomes you to his clinic," Tse said. "He thinks it is an honor to have an American and an Australian doctor visit. He asks if you would care to see his facility."

"What about the transportation?" Tristan asked.

"The clinic has a van," Tse said. "The van will take us to Shigi. From Shigi he said that we can take a bus to Forshan, then a train to Guangzhou."

"How much will he charge for the van?" Tristan asked.

"There will be no charge," Tse said. "We will go with several patients being sent to the district hospital."

"Fine," Tristan said. "Let's see the bugger's clinic."

With Chi-Li and Tse leading, the group toured the clinic. The rooms were essentially bare except for crude furniture here and there. The procedure room was especially stark, with a rusted steel table, a porcelain sink, and one ancient glass cabinet full of instruments.

Seeing that Marissa seemed interested in the

instrument cabinet, Chi-Li went over and opened the door for her.

Marissa winced when she looked into a tin of nondisposable needles that had become dull from overuse. It made her realize how much she took for granted in her office and at the Boston Memorial. As her eyes wandered to the upper shelf, she saw packages of vaccines, including a cholera vaccine made in the United States. Then she noticed some vials of BCG. She remembered Tse's having mentioned their use in tuberculosis inoculations. Marissa was curious about BCG, particularly since it had never been proven to be effective in the United States. She reached into the cabinet and lifted one of the vials. Reading the label, she discovered it had been made in France.

"Ask Chi-Li if he sees much tuberculosis," Marissa asked as she replaced the BCG vial. She glanced at the other contents of the cabinet while Tse spoke with the man.

"He sees about the same as I," Tse reported.

Marissa closed the cabinet door. "Ask him if he ever sees TB as a female problem," she asked. She watched Chi-Li's face as Tse translated. There was always the chance she could hit on something unexpected. But Chi-Li's expression reflected a negative response to the question. Tse translated that Chi-Li had seen nothing of the kind.

Leaving the procedure room, they walked into an examining room. A female patient was sitting on a chair in the corner. She stood and bowed as the group entered.

Marissa bowed back, sorry to have intruded. Suddenly Marissa stopped. In the center of the room was a relatively modern examining table, complete with stainless steel stirrups.

Seeing the table brought back all the unpleasant procedures she'd endured over the last year in the course of her fertility treatments. She was surprised to see such a modern piece of equipment at the clinic; nearly everything else she'd seen was quite dated and rudimentary.

Stepping over to the table, Marissa absently fingered one of the stirrups. "How did this examining table get here?" she asked.

"The same way all the other equipment got here," Tse said. "Most of the rural health clinics have such a table."

Marissa nodded as if she understood. But she didn't. Of all the pieces of modern equipment to be sent to rural clinics, it seemed strange for them to choose an examining table with stirrups. But having read of the bureaucratic mismanagement problems of Communist governments, she assumed this was just another case in point.

"We use such a table frequently," Tse said. "Birth control has been given a high priority by the government."

"I see," Marissa said. She was about to walk on when she looked back at the table. She was puzzled. "What type of birth control do you favor?" she asked. "Intrauterine devices?"

"No," Tse said.

"Diaphragms?" Marissa asked, even though

she knew they couldn't use diaphragms since they were too expensive and not effective enough. Yet why a table equipped for internal exams?

"We use sterilization," Tse said. "After one child the woman is often sterilized. Sometimes we perform sterilization even before the woman has a child if there is a request or if the woman should not have a child."

Tristan called to Marissa from the next room, but Marissa ignored him. Although she had remembered hearing that sterilization was used for birth-control in the PRC, she hated to hear a doctor speaking so coldly about it. She wondered who got to make the decision of who could bear a child and who couldn't. The issue offended her feminist sensibilities.

"How do you sterilize these women?" she asked.

"We cannulate the fallopian tubes," Tse said matter-of-factly.

"Under anesthesia?" Marissa asked.

"No need for anesthesia," Tse said.

"How can that be?" Marissa asked. She knew that to cannulate the fallopian tubes, the cervix had to be dilated, and dilating the cervix was excruciatingly painful.

"It is easy for us rural doctors," Tse explained. "We use a very small catheter with a wire guide. It is done by feel. We do not need to see. It is not painful for the patient."

"Marissa!" Tristan called. He had come back to the threshold of the examining room. "Come out here and see the garden. They grow their own medicines!"

But Marissa waved Tristan away. She stared at Tse, her mind racing. "Can Chi-Li perform this technique as well?" she asked.

"I'm sure," Tse said. "All rural doctors are taught it."

"Once you cannulate the fallopian tube," Marissa said, "what do you use to sterilize?"

"Usually a caustic herbal solution," Tse said. "It is like a kind of pepper."

Tristan left the doorway and approached Marissa. "What's the matter, luv?" he asked. "You look like you've just seen a ghost."

Without saying a word, Marissa hurried back to the procedure room and walked up to the cabinet. She studied the shelf of vaccines.

Tristan followed her, wondering what she was thinking. "Marissa," he said, as he reached out and grabbed her shoulders, swinging her around to face him. "Are you okay?"

"I'm fine," Marissa said. "Tristan, I think I just figured it all out. All of a sudden I think I understand—and if I'm right, the truth is much worse than we imagined."

The health clinic van took the four of them to Shigi and dropped them off at the Shigi bus station. Since there was frequent service to Forshan, they had only a short wait. During the trip, Marissa sat next to Tristan while Bentley sat with Tse.

"I've never seen anybody spit more than these

Chinese," Tristan said to make conversation. It was true. At any given moment someone on the bus was either preparing to spit or was in the process of spitting out the window. "What the hell is wrong with these blokes?"

"It's a national pastime," Bentley said, hearing Tristan's comment. "You see it all over China."

"It's disgusting," Tristan said. "It reminds me of that foolish American game of baseball."

Everyone on the bus seemed to be busy talking except Marissa and Tristan. Tristan had finally given up after Marissa persisted in meeting his every question with only one-word replies. She seemed to be deep in thought.

Suddenly she turned to him. "Do you know the pH indicator phenol red?"

"Vaguely," Tristan said, surprised by her sudden inquiry.

"When does it turn red?" Marissa asked. "In an acidic or an alkaline solution?"

"I think alkaline," Tristan said. "In an acid solution it's clear."

"I thought so," Marissa said. Then she lapsed back into silence.

They rode for another mile. Finally, Tristan could no longer contain his curiosity. "What's with you, Marissa?" he asked. "Why won't you tell me what you're thinking?"

"I will," Marissa said. "But not yet. We have to get out of the PRC. There are a couple of things I have to check to be sure first."

From Forshan they were able to get hard seats

on a train to Guangzhou. Bentley and Tse left them at the Forshan bus station.

By the time they got to Guangzhou it was dark. They took a taxi from the train station. On the recommendation of the driver, they went to the White Swan Hotel. During the short trip both Marissa and Tristan remarked that the city looked more Western than they'd expected, although even at night the bicycles far outnumbered the motor vehicles in the streets.

The hotel turned out to be a surprise as well. The lobby was impressive, with a waterfall. The rooms had all the modern conveniences, including TVs, refrigerators and, more importantly, direct-dial telephones. They booked a suite with two bedrooms and a view over the Pearl River.

Marissa was exhausted. She eyed the bed with longing, hoping that she would at last get a good night's rest. But even before bed, what she was interested in most was the telephone. After calculating the time on the East Coast of the United States, she decided to put off her call for a few hours. She knew it wouldn't help to wake Cyrill Dubchek from his sleep.

"They have a Western-style restaurant," Tristan said with excitement, coming into Marissa's bedroom with the hotel directory in his hand. "What do you say to a nice big steak!"

Marissa wasn't hungry, but she accompanied Tristan, who polished off a sizable slab of meat and a number of beers. Marissa ordered a chicken dish, but she hardly touched it except to move it

494

around her plate. They talked about going to the consulate in the morning with the story that they had hired a junk to take them to Guangzhou but that the captain had taken their money and forced them to jump off the boat.

"It's the best we can do," Tristan said. "And it's close enough to the truth."

Marissa said that she would try to get some State Department intervention through the CDC.

Several hours later, Marissa made her call. Knowing Cyrill's schedule, she timed the call to catch him before he left for the lab.

Although there was some static as well as a peculiar echo, Marissa could understand him easily. Marissa told Cyrill that she was calling from Guangzhou, in the People's Republic of China.

"With other people, I might be surprised to get an unexpected call from the PRC," Cyrill said. "But with you, Marissa, nothing surprises me."

"There's a rational explanation."

"I didn't doubt it for a moment."

Marissa quickly explained how she and a colleague had inadvertently entered the PRC without going through proper immigration. She told him she was afraid she would have trouble getting out. She emphasized that the colleague was the Australian doctor who'd written the paper Cyrill had given her.

"You're with the author?" Cyrill said. "I'd say that is going directly to the primary source."

"Back when I was at the CDC, you once told me that you hoped you could make it up to me

495

for what I went through in cracking the Ebola outbreaks. Well, Cyrill, you now have your chance."

"What can I do?" he asked.

"First, I'd like you to use CDC connections to pressure the State Department to get me and Dr. Williams out of the PRC. I was told that there is a U.S. consulate here. We'll go to the consulate in the morning, about ten hours from now."

"I'll be happy to see what I can do," Cyrill said. "But they may ask why the CDC is intervening."

"There is a very good reason," Marissa said. "It's extremely important that I get back to the CDC immediately. It can be considered legitimate CDC business. Tell that to the State Department and let them tell it to the PRC."

"What kind of business?" Cyrill asked.

"It concerns the TB salpingitis," Marissa said. "And that leads me to my next request. I need the CDC to get success rate statistics concerning in-vitro fertilization for all the Women's Clinics around the U.S. I want statistics about efficacy per patient as well as per cycle. And if possible, I would like data on the specific causes of infertility among the women the Women's Clinics treat with IVF."

"How many months do I have?" Cyrill asked wryly.

"We need this as soon as possible," Marissa said. "And there's more: remember that case you told me about, the young woman with the disseminated tuberculosis in Boston?"

"I do," Cyrill said.

"Find out what happened to her," Marissa said. "If she died, which I'm afraid she must have by now, get a serum sample and her autopsy report as well as a copy of her chart. Then there is a patient by the name of Rebecca Ziegler—"

"Hold on," Cyrill complained. "I'm trying to write this down."

Marissa paused for a moment. Once Cyrill gave her the okay, she continued: "Rebecca Ziegler supposedly committed suicide. She was autopsied at the Memorial. Get a serum sample from her as well."

"My God, Marissa!" Cyrill said. "What's this all about?"

"You'll know soon enough," Marissa said. "But there's still more. Is there an ELISA test for BCG bacillus?"

"Offhand, I don't know," Cyrill said. "But if there isn't, we can have it made up."

"Do it!" Marissa said. "And one last thing."

"Jesus, Marissa . . ." Cyrill sighed.

"We'll need an emergency U.S. visa for Dr. Tristan Williams."

"Why don't I just call President Bush and have him take care of all this?" Cyrill said.

"I'm counting on you," Marissa said.

She knew she was asking a lot of Cyrill, but she was convinced it was vitally important. After exchanging goodbyes, they each hung up.

"Did I hear that a trip to the States is in the

offing?" Tristan said as he peeked through the door.

"I hope so," Marissa said. "The sooner the better."

The following morning both Marissa and Tristan were pleasantly surprised by their reception at the U.S. Consulate. As soon as Marissa gave her name, they were shown into Consul David Krieger's office.

During the night, communications had been received from the State Department and from the U.S. ambassador in Beijing.

"I don't know who you people are," David told them, "but I'm certainly impressed by the behind-the-scenes flurry your being here has stirred up. It's not often I'm given instructions to issue an emergency U.S. visa. But I'm pleased to say I have one for Dr. Williams."

David Krieger himself accompanied Marissa and Tristan to the Public Security Bureau on Jeifong Bei Lu Street in front of Yuexiu Park. Although the police had been advised of the case, they still insisted on interrogating Marissa and Tristan, but did so in David Krieger's presence. They proceeded to check Marissa's and Tristan's story by dispatching several officers by helicopter to the two villages Marissa and Tristan claimed to have passed through.

During the interview, it was apparent to Marissa that the Chinese authorities associated their presence with the cigarette boat incident. Marissa was quick to say that it was at the appearance of the powerboat and the patrol boat that the captain of the junk had made them jump overboard.

When they returned to the consulate, David Krieger was optimistic that the problem would be resolved swiftly. He graciously invited Marissa and Tristan to have lunch with him. After lunch, the consul arranged for Marissa and Tristan to get some Western-style clothes. By the time they returned to the consulate, word had already arrived that Marissa and Tristan were free to leave the PRC whenever they cared to.

"If you are in a hurry," the consul said, "we can make arrangements for you to fly to Hong Kong this afternoon."

"No, not Hong Kong," Marissa said quickly. "Are there other foreign destinations available directly from Guangzhou?" She didn't like the idea of returning to Hong Kong even if only in transit. She didn't want to risk any more run-ins with the thugs from the FCA or the Wing Sin.

"There is a daily flight to Bangkok," David Krieger said.

"That would be much better," Marissa said.

"But it's out of your way if you're heading back to the States," David Krieger said.

Marissa smiled innocently. "Regardless, I think we'd both rather spend a little more time flying than going back through Hong Kong. Do you agree, Tristan?"

"Right you are, luv," Tristan said.

"Here are all the statistics we could get on such short notice," Cyrill Dubchek said, handing computer printout pages to Marissa.

Marissa, Tristan, and Cyrill were sitting in Cyrill's office at the Centers for Disease Control in Atlanta, Georgia. Marissa and Tristan had just arrived that afternoon from their grueling flight across the Pacific, flying from Bangkok to Honolulu to L.A. to Atlanta.

Even though they were exhausted, Marissa insisted on going directly to the CDC.

Marissa studied the pages carefully. Tristan looked at Cyrill and shrugged. Tristan was still in the dark as to Marissa's suspicions.

"Just as I thought," Marissa said, raising her eyes from the computer paper. "These statistics mirror those that I found in Australia with the FCA data. They show that the Women's Clinics around the country have a high rate of pregnancy per patient in their in-vitro fertilization program but a low success rate per cycle. In other words, most IVF patients at Women's Clinics get pregnant but it takes multiple cycles before they're met with success. Look how the success rate shoots up after the fifth IVF attempt."

Marissa pointed to the statistics spelled out on the computer printout she was holding in her hands.

"That's not so surprising," Tristan said. "In every clinic, most patients have to go through several attempts before they conceive. What are you getting at?"

A knock on Cyrill's door interrupted them before Marissa could reply. It was one of the technicians from the lab.

"We have the results on those ELISA tests," she said.

"That was fast," Cyrill commented.

"They were very positive," she said. "Even at high dilutions."

"All of them?" Cyrill asked incredulously.

"All of them," the technician repeated.

"That's the proof I wanted," Marissa said. When she'd first arrived at the CDC, she'd gone directly to the lab to have some blood drawn. Then she'd made arrangements for her serum to be tested with the ELISA test for BCG along with Rebecca Ziegler's and Evelyn Welles' serums.

"I don't understand," Cyrill said. "How can that be?"

"I think it is rather clear," Marissa said. "Evelyn Welles didn't have tuberculosis. She had disseminated BCG bacillus." Marissa reached for Welles' hospital chart and opened it to her autopsy page. "Look," she said, pointing to a description of the microscopic appearance of her fallopian tubes. "It says there was an intense, overwhelming infection in her oviducts. I'll tell you why that was the case: the fallopian tubes were the port of entry of the BCG. The fact that it disseminated was because of her immunological problem. And look here at the description of her cervix. It describes a recent punched-out lesion. That had to be a biopsy site." Marissa flipped through the chart until she came to the woman's last Pap smear report. "Now look at this. The Pap smear was normal four weeks before. Does that make any sense to you men?"

"I think I'm beginning to get the picture," Tristan said. "You're suggesting that the twenty-three cases of TB salpingitis that I reported were actually BCG, not TB."

"That's exactly what I'm suggesting," Marissa said. "I didn't have TB salpingitis either. I had a deliberate inoculation with BCG vaccine. I think the basis of this whole mystery is nothing but business interest. A few years ago, Female Care Australia realized that they were sitting on a potential gold mine with their IVF technology. The only trouble was that their increased success was denying them income by lowering revenue. So they decided on two courses of action to ensure increased revenues. One was to create more demand. The only absolute indication for IVF is hopelessly blocked fallopian tubes. Someone found out that the rural Chinese doctors had been clever enough to develop a way of cannulating the fallopian tubes without the need for anesthesia. So they began bringing these doctors out of China to do just what they had been doing in China: sterilizing women. The trick was to sterilize without leaving evidence of it, or leaving evidence that could be misinterpreted. Someone must have come up with the BCG vaccine. It causes an intense immunologic reaction that seals the tubes totally and destroys the organisms in the process.

That's how BCG works. On biopsy, it looks like tuberculosis. There just aren't any organisms. Obviously, they only tried this ploy on certain candidates. They chose only young, recently married, middle-class females. All they had to do was schedule these women for a minor procedure of some sort, like a cervical biopsy. I know that one ruse was to tell the patient that her Pap smear was CIN Grade #1. That's how they got me and Wendy. Neither Wendy nor I had told the clinic we were physicians. If they had known, they probably wouldn't have risked including us in the scheme. And they certainly didn't know about Evelyn Welles' immunological problem. And Rebecca Ziegler. She must have been clever enough to figure that something was wrong. I think they killed her and made it look like a suicide.

"The second part of the plan to maintain revenue was to make sure that the IVF wasn't successful too quickly. At ten thousand dollars per cycle, you can see why they'd want to run their patients through as many cycles as possible. Yet ultimately, they wanted all their patients to conceive. That meant a better reputation for them. My guess is that to make failed cycles a certainty, they just added a drop or two of acid to the culture media after fertilization took place. Before my last egg transfer, I asked to see the zygotes. I remember the solution was crystal clear. The significance of the color didn't dawn on me until just recently. The usual pH indicator in tissue culture media is phenol red, which turns clear in acid. My embryos were in acid. No wonder they didn't implant."

Cyrill cleared his throat. He looked at Marissa's flushed and angry face. He could tell she was convinced, but unfortunately he didn't share her conviction. He didn't know quite what to say. "I'm not sure . . ." he began.

"Not sure of what?" demanded Marissa. "Is it just too hard for you men to believe that women could be victimized to this extent?"

"It's not that," Cyrill said. "It's just that it is too complicated. It represents too much effort, too much conspiracy. It's just too diabolical."

"It's diabolical, all right," Marissa agreed, "but let's be clear about the motivation. This is about profit, pure and simple. I'm talking about big money. Look!" Marissa stood up and went to a small blackboard that Cyrill had in his office. Picking up a piece of chalk, she wrote down *600,000*. "This is the number of couples in the U.S. that fertility specialists estimate need IVF if they want to have a child that is genetically theirs. If we multiply that by fifty thousand dollars we get thirty billion dollars. That's billion. Not thirty million, thirty billion. And that's just in the United States. IVF could rival the world's illegal drug industry as a money-maker. Admittedly not all of the six hundred thousand are middle class, and not all could come up with the money necessary. But that is why FCA has gone to such lengths to create their own market."

"My God!" Cyrill said. "I never imagined there was that kind of money involved."

"Most people don't," Marissa said. "The whole infertility industry is totally unregulated and unsupervised. It's grown up in a no-man's land between medicine and business. And the government has just looked the other way. Anything to do with reproduction is politically dangerous."

"But such a conspiracy would require so many people," Tristan said.

"Not that many," Marissa said. "Maybe just one per clinic. At this point, I'm not about to hazard any guess as to the conspiracy's actual organizational design."

"And I was so sure drugs were at the heart of it," Tristan said.

"They still might be involved, only indirectly," Marissa said. "It will be interesting to see exactly how Fertility, Limited, came up with the staggering amount of capital they would have needed to expand as rapidly as they did across three continents. I have a suspicion that their stock offerings were only clever ruses. I wouldn't be surprised if they're tied up with the Wing Sin for ventures besides smuggling pairs of men out of the PRC. Fertility, Limited, could launder money from the Golden Triangle heroin for the Wing Sin. At least it's a possibility."

"If this is all true," Cyrill said, "then it will take a massive effort with international cooperation to break it."

"Precisely," Marissa said. "That's where the

CDC comes in. I think that the Attorney General's office and the State Department have to be alerted simultaneously. If this conspiracy is to be broken, it will take their combined power, and I think they will listen to the CDC. I can tell you it won't be easy. Any organization that is as big and as wealthy as Fertility, Limited, and its subsidiaries will have significant political clout."

"Since it is a national problem here in the United States," Cyrill said, "the FBI will have to be involved."

"Undoubtedly," Marissa agreed. "And thank God for it, because I'm certain Tristan and I are going to need some protection for a time. We may even have to hide away someplace. I'm afraid that the Wing Sin has a global reach."

Cyrill got to his feet. "I'm going to run upstairs," he said. "I want to see if I can catch the director before he leaves for the day. Would you two mind waiting here for a moment?"

After Cyrill left, Marissa faced Tristan. "What do you think?" she asked. "Honestly?"

"Honestly?" Tristan repeated. "I think you're a spunky, knackered battler."

"Please, Tristan," Marissa said. "I'm serious. Cut the Aussie babble and speak English."

"I'm being serious too," Tristan said. "I think you're beautiful. I think you're exhausted. And I think you are amazing. In fact, you're a little intimidating. And on top of all that, I think you are right. And I can't think of anyone I'd rather go into hiding with than you."

Epilogue

"WHAT'S THAT street sign over there?" Tristan asked, pointing in front of Marissa, who was sitting in the passenger seat of a Hertz rent-a-car.

"I don't know!" Marissa sighed in exasperation. "I can't see it unless you pull ahead of this tree next to us."

"Right you are, luv," Tristan said. He pulled the car ahead about a foot.

"Cherry Lane," Marissa read.

"Cherry Lane?" Tristan questioned. He bent over the map he'd drawn. "I can't figure these directions out."

"Perhaps now we could go back down the hill and ask?" Marissa said. They'd passed a service station a few minutes before.

Tristan's head shot up. "Listen," he said, "I can find the damn house, okay?"

For a moment the two glared at each other. Then they both broke into easy laughter.

"I'm sorry," Tristan said. "I suppose I'm a touch tense. Didn't mean to snap."

"I didn't mean to either," Marissa said. "I think we're both under a bit of strain."

"That's an understatement," Tristan said. "I

507

don't even know if Chauncey will recognize me. It's been over three years."

"But he's six," Marissa said. "I think he'll recognize you. I wonder what he will think of me."

"He's going to love you," Tristan said. "Mark my words."

"If we ever get there," Marissa said.

"Have faith," Tristan said. He looked back at his map. "If we could only find this Connolly Avenue."

"We just passed that," Marissa said. "I'm pretty sure that was the last street we went by."

"Then we'll just have to chuck a u-ey," Tristan said as he pulled the steering wheel all the way to the left. "It's always a bit confusing since you folks drive on the wrong side of the road."

Going back a block, they found Connolly Avenue. Connolly Avenue fed into Green Street. Within fifteen minutes they were parked in front of a white clapboard house with Victorian trim. On the front lawn was a sign that said: OLAFSONS.

"Well, here we are," Tristan said. He gazed up at the house.

"Yup," Marissa agreed. "We made it."

Neither moved to get out of the car.

Marissa was particularly nervous. The Olafsons, Tristan's in-laws, had been caring for Tristan's son, Chauncey, for the past three years. Marissa had never met them and had never seen Chauncey. While Marissa and Tristan had been hiding out under the auspices of the FBI, it had been deemed unwise for them to meet until now, Thanksgiving day.

The months since their return from the Orient had passed slowly. The government had placed them in Montana, where they shared a house in a small town. Neither of them were permitted to work as physicians.

At first it had been very difficult for Marissa. It took her a long time to adjust to Robert's death. She felt responsible for it for a long time. That he had died when they were still on such bad terms only added to her pain.

Tristan helped a lot. To a degree, he'd been through the same thing. It gave him a special empathy. He'd known when to talk with her and when to leave her alone.

On top of Robert's death, she had to contend with Wendy's. It had taken months before the nightmares of the sharks had stopped their nightly visit. She felt responsible for her friend's death as well.

Ultimately, time had been the great healer, as it was said to be. Gradually Marissa had begun to feel more like herself. She even started back to her usual exercise routine of jogging several miles a day. Losing the weight she'd gained through the fertility treatments proved a boost to her morale.

"I guess we'd better go inside," Tristan said. But no sooner had he voiced the words than the front door to the house opened, and out stepped a couple with a child.

Tristan got out of the car. Marissa did the same.

509

They slammed their doors shut. For a moment, no one said anything or moved.

Marissa looked at the child. She could see signs of Tristan in his hair and the shape of his little face. Next she looked to the couple. They were younger than Marissa had anticipated. The man was tall and slight, his features sharp. The woman was short. Her bobbed hair had a sprinkling of gray. She was clutching a tissue. Marissa realized that she was crying.

The introductions were awkward, especially with Elaine Olafson struggling through tears. "I'm sorry," she apologized. "But seeing Tristan brings back the pain of losing Eva. And we have gotten so attached to Chauncey."

For the moment, Chauncey was holding on to Elaine's leg. His eyes darted from Marissa to his father.

Marissa couldn't help but sympathize with Elaine. The woman had lost her only child and was now about to lose the grandson she had been caring for for three years.

As they entered the house, Marissa smelled the wonderful aroma of a roasting turkey. She had always loved Thanksgiving. Her memories of Thanksgiving dinners in Virginia were warm and wonderful. It had always been a comfortable, secure time.

Tristan and Eric soon retired to the den to watch football, cans of beer in hand. Marissa and Elaine went into the kitchen. After some initial shyness, Chauncey attempted to straddle both rooms, moving back and forth from the kitchen to the den every few minutes. Tristan had decided not to force anything. He wanted Chauncey to have the chance to get used to him.

"Put me to work," Marissa told Elaine. She knew for a dinner like this there would be much to do.

Elaine told Marissa to relax, but Marissa insisted. Soon she found herself rinsing the salad greens. They chatted about the journey that morning from Butte, Montana, to San Francisco. But as Elaine calmed, they moved to more personal issues.

"Tristan told Eric on the phone that you and he are planning to be married?" Elaine said.

"That's the current plan," Marissa said. It was hard for her to believe it herself. Only months previously she never would have imagined that she'd be capable of such a major step. But the transition from friendship to romance had started slowly. It had grown steadily through their months in hiding. Then, to Marissa's surprise, their budding romance had flowered with sudden and intense passion.

"And you are going to adopt Chauncey?" Elaine asked. She opened the oven and basted the turkey.

"Yes," Marissa said. She watched Elaine, waiting for the woman to look at her. "I know this is very difficult for you," Marissa said. "I can imagine how much you will miss the boy. But there is something you should know. Tristan and I plan to move here to Berkeley so that Chauncey won't have to change schools. But also so that he will be nearby. You and Eric will see him as often as you like. We know the change will be as difficult for Chauncey as it will be for you. We want to do the most we can to make it easier."

"That's wonderful," Elaine said. She smiled for the first time since they'd arrived. "I had no idea. I thought you would be moving back to Australia."

"No," Marissa said. "For now it will be better for us both here. We have a lot we'd like to put behind us. We want a fresh start."

Elaine's mood was much improved with the unexpected news about the intended move to Berkeley. "Eric and I saw you and Tristan on *Good Morning America* and on *60 Minutes*. When we heard what those clinics were doing, we were appalled. What some people will do for money!"

Marissa nodded.

"I had to laugh at what Charlie Gibson said," Elaine continued. "That comparison he made between the closing of the chain of Women's Clinics and the jailing of Al Capone."

"It does seem a bit ironic," Marissa agreed.

"Absolutely," Elaine agreed. "I know that tax evasion was the only crime they were ever able to convict Capone of. But after everything those rotten doctors did, it's hard to believe the only charges they got to stick were violations related to the hiring of illegal aliens."

"At least the clinics are closed," Marissa said. "The problem has been that it is impossible to prove that the BCG these thousands of women have been given came from the clinics in question. But they're still not in the clear. The investigations have uncovered the fact that they had been routinely scheduling cervical biopsies for normal Pap smears. And they have been finding this in both the United States and Europe."

"Aren't any of the men involved going to jail?" Elaine questioned.

"I'm hopeful that some of them eventually will," Marissa said. "The most encouraging development has been that a number of directors of branch clinics have started plea-bargaining and offering to turn state's evidence in exchange. With their testimony, we may see some convictions."

Elaine leaned closer to Marissa. "I hope they nail the bastards," she said. After a time, she asked Marissa what her plans were with respect to in-vitro. "Are you and Tristan going to try it?"

"Oh, no!" Marissa said with emphasis. "I've gone through enough cycles for my taste. I can't say it was a very positive experience. But we will have children," she added.

"Oh?" Elaine said, somewhat puzzled. She had understood that Marissa couldn't conceive.

"First, there's Chauncey. I know I'll love him as much as if he were my own. And Tristan and I plan to adopt."

"Really?" Elaine said.

Marissa nodded. "We're going to adopt a little Chinese baby from Hong Kong."

Bibliography

1. Baruch, E. L., et al, eds., *Embryos, Ethics and Women's Rights: Exploring the New Reproductive Technologies.* Harrington Park Press, 1988. This book is definitely from the feminist point of view. I recommend it since it influenced my thinking about certain issues.

2. Chase, M. E., *Waiting for Baby.* McGraw-Hill, 1990. A wonderful, moving account of what it's really like to be caught in the infertility maze. A good book for the emotional aspects of infertility.

3. Frank, D., and Vogel, M., *The Baby Makers.* Carroll & Graf, 1988. A good, easy-to-read exploration of the social aspects of the new reproductive technologies.

4. Klein, R., ed., *Infertility.* Pandora Press, 1989. A more fiery feminist viewpoint. If you were interested in #1 above, then read this.

5. Lieberman-Smith, J., *In Pursuit of Pregnancy.* Newmarket Press, 1987. Another particularly

good book about the emotional issues involving infertility and its treatment.

6. Menning, B. E., *Infertility: A Guide for the Childless Couple*, Prentice-Hall, 1988. A good general guide for the lay individual about infertility from someone who's been there!

7. Seilel, M., *Infertility: A Comprehensive Text*. Appleton & Lange, 1990. This is by far the best all-around textbook in the field of infertility. It is meant for the professional, but it can be readily understood by the interested lay person for the most part. The biggest problem is the expense.

8. Sher, G., et al, *From Infertility to In Vitro Fertilization*. McGraw-Hill, 1988. A good general guide for the lay person to infertility and in-vitro fertilization. However, it should be remembered that the main author is an MD and is associated with an infertility clinic. Therefore he has some inherent bias.

9. Spallone, P., *Beyond Conception: The New Politics of Reproduction*. Bergin & Garvey, 1989. Another book from the feminist point of view. Somewhat harder to read, but well researched on an international scope.

10. Wasserman, M. E., *Searching for the Stork*. New American Library, 1988. A wonderfully

written book that also deals with the emotional side of infertility. I have to confess that I read it twice.